LOVING SUSIE

Jenny Harper

D1610893

Published by Accent Press Ltd 2014

ISBN 9781783752638

Acknowledgements

For the information about tracing a birth parent, I am hugely indebted to the following: The National Records of Scotland staff, several of whom patiently took me through the process; the staff at Birthlink, the charity based in Edinburgh that offers a range of services to people separated by adoption with a Scottish connection; Chris Longmuir, author, whose wisdom and experience were invaluable; and to my brother-in-law, David Roulston, whose own journey through life – which brought him ultimately back into the heart of the Harper family – deserves a book in its own right.

Characters come alive when they inhabit real worlds, and I'm very grateful to Robin Stewart, then Business Development Manager at the Caledonian Hotel in Edinburgh who gave generously of his valuable time to illuminate the world of sales in the hotel business.

Likewise, most of my insights into the Scottish Parliament came from my husband, Robin Harper, who was elected to the first Parliament in 1999 – the first Green Parliamentarian in Britain – and who served there for twelve years until his retirement in 2011.

I have been blessed to have been given encouragement and advice by a number of well-known writers. Eileen Ramsay has never failed to encourage me, and without her belief in my abilities I might well have given up long ago. Brilliant crime writer Bill Daly generously gave me mentoring and editorial advice. As for my Numpties – they know who they are – thank you, friends.

Thanks are due to Elizabeth Garrett for her most generous gift of time at her beautiful cottage retreat on the east coast of Scotland.

I'd like to pay tribute to those writers who have helped me through the publishing process and patiently answered my endless technical queries. And finally, I owe a great debt to my 'support team': the very talented Caleb Rutherford, who has now designed two covers for me, with more, I hope, to come – and my friend, Jane Knights, for proofreading the manuscript.

Note: Hailesbank and the Heartlands

The small market town of Hailesbank is born of my imagination, as are the surrounding villages of Forgie and Stoneyford and the Council housing estate known as Summerfield, which together form The Heartlands. I have placed the area, in my mind, to the east of Scotland's capital city, Edinburgh.

The first mention of The Heartlands was made by Agrippa Centorius in AD77, not long after the Romans began their surge north in the hopes of conquering this savage land. 'This is a place of great beauty,' wrote Agrippus, 'and its wildness has clutched my heart.' He makes several mentions thereafter of The Heartlands. There are still signs of Roman occupation in Hailesbank, which has great transport links to the south (and England) and the north, especially to Edinburgh, and its proximity to the sea and the (real) coastal town of Musselburgh made it a great place to settle. The Georgians and Victorians began to develop the small village, its clean air and glorious views, rich farming hinterland and great transport proving highly attractive.

The River Hailes flows through the town. There is a Hailes Castle in East Lothian (it has not yet featured in my novels!), but it sits on the Tyne.

Hailesbank has a Town Hall, a High Street, from which a number of ancient small lanes, or vennels, run down to the river, which once was the lifeblood of the town.

In my novels, characters populate the shops, cafes and pubs in Hailesbank and the pretty adjoining village of Forgie, with Summerfield inhabitants providing another layer of social interaction.

You can meet more inhabitants of the town and area in *Maximum Exposure* and *Face the Wind and Fly* – with more titles to follow!

Chapter One

Susie Wallace pokes one foot reluctantly out from underneath the duvet, senses a chill in the air and pulls it back hastily. Ten seconds later she tries again. On the third attempt, she has to force herself to pivot her body through ninety degrees until she's sitting on the edge of the bed. Behind her, a rumpled form stirs as the duvet settles uneasily back into place.

'You off?' mumbles the formless shape under the covers.

Susie switches on her bedside lamp. 'Oh sorry, darling, didn't mean to disturb you.' She watches her husband Archie hunch upwards. 'I've got an early telly interview. Will I bring you tea?'

'I'll get up.'

His hair is white these days, but to Susie's biased eye, Archie's face hasn't changed in all the years she has known him. She steals a precious moment to contemplate her husband.

'What?' He pauses in the ritual scratching of the scalp, his hand hovering above the thick thatch of hair, his blue eyes paler, perhaps, than they used to be but even at this ungodly hour still swimming with tenderness and wisdom and laughter – all the things that she's always loved him for.

'Nothing. Just thinking how amazing it is that I still fancy you thirty years on.'

'Christ.'

'Did you forget?' She isn't angry, merely amused. Of course he has forgotten. Archie isn't a man for remembering birthdays, anniversaries, little landmarks of celebration. Why would he remember their thirtieth wedding anniversary when he has unrepentantly forgotten all the others?

'Just joking.' His grin breaks through, boyish as the day they met. 'I've booked The Shore for dinner.'

'Really?' Susie is astonished. 'Am I free?'

Life has changed. As an actress, she'd snogged Colin Firth, flown the wires as Tinkerbell and delivered a twenty-minute monologue naked in an off-West End theatre. Now she's no longer in theatre, she's a politician – and in the two years since she was elected to serve the people as a member of the Scottish Parliament, Archie has had to learn to negotiate diary time with her assistant.

He yawns. 'I brokered a seven o'clock slot with Karen.'

'How lovely.' She stoops and kisses him, responding involuntarily to the familiarity of his early-morning smell, then pulling herself away reluctantly as she senses his interest quicken. 'Sorry, darling, must hurry.'

Archie pulls a face and she smiles as she turns towards the shower. How close she'd come to messing everything up, in those crazy days of their early marriage – and how right she'd been to stay with him. She slips off her nightdress, but it's not just the sudden chill that makes her shiver – it's the thought of what might have happened if he'd come to hear of her folly.

Her life may have changed but Archie, thank heaven, is as important to her as ever. The thread of security and intimacy that binds them together is a precious treasure in the madness that has become her daily life.

Archie watches his wife pat her hair dry. She has never quite tamed her hazelnut curls with their glorious russet highlights and he hopes she never will. They define her. Open any newspaper in the land and Susie Wallace is likely to be there, a flame-haired beacon for her causes.

She always was passionate about some perceived injustice – it's what he loves most about her. The progression from acting into politics had been inevitable.

She reaches for the drier and he swings out of bed. 'I'll put on the kettle.'

'Will you, love? Thanks.'

Downstairs, Prince's tail thumps excitedly on the stone flagstones of the kitchen floor. He's growing old now, a little prematurely, as Labs tend to, but doggy affection is so completely undemanding that its rewards are sweet. Archie bends to pat him.

'Hello, old boy. Another morning, another day of mayhem.'

He marches to the sink to fill the kettle, then glances at the old school clock on the wall above the range. Six thirty already. Susie will have to shift – she's due at the BBC studios in Edinburgh in an hour and the drive from the cottage on the outskirts of Hailesbank can take all of that on bad days.

As the kettle begins to steam, Susie comes into the kitchen.

'That was quick.'

'I wanted to share five minutes with you before I rush off. Jon home?'

'I'll take a look.'

He pulls aside the heavy curtains that mask the door into the cobbled courtyard. Outside, a battered Volvo has been strategically abandoned, as if its owner was too tired to park it neatly into its corner. And that'll be the truth, Archie thinks, guessing that their twenty-three-year-old son arrived home in the small hours. He says, 'His car's here, so yes.'

'Good. Sorry I won't see him today, but Mannie's popping in for lunch at the Parliament. I don't suppose she'll linger.' Their daughter Margaret-Anne is a sales director for a hotel chain and lives almost as frenetic a life

3

as Susie herself.

'Give her my love. And drive safely. I'll watch you.'

'Thanks. I'll call you after.'

'And I'll see you in—' he glances at the kitchen clock, '—twelve and a half hours.'

'Hell's bells! I'm off.'

But there's frost on the car and she has to spend seven precious minutes clearing it.

An hour later, Archie makes his second cup of tea and settles in front of the television. Susie will be on in a few minutes. Prince settles himself heavily across his feet as the interviewer says, 'And in our studio we have communications specialist Brian Henderson to tell us how he believes morale could be improved at the troubled firm. Brian—'

Prince snores and his weight shifts. Archie reaches down and pats the dog affectionately. When he looks up again, a middle-aged businessman is talking. 'The key to good employee relations lies in communication—'

There is nothing remarkable about the man, yet for some reason Archie's attention is caught. He stares at the round face and receding hair.

'Culture of secrecy breeds a culture of suspicion—'

His grey suit is unremarkable, though his tie is loud. There's something about the hazel eyes that looks familiar.

'—while openness, by contrast, helps to build trust.'

Archie watches, riveted. It's more the mouth than the eyes. There's a peculiar mobility to the mouth, a certain twist to the smile, a way of moving the lips, that he has seen before.

'It takes time, naturally. It's impossible to turn a culture around in a matter of days or weeks—'

'Are you saying that—?'

He thumps the mug onto the table so hard that tea rises in a great wave and splashes onto the wood. He knows where he has seen that mouth before – or one very like it.

Jesus! Surely the secret he has kept safe for so long is not in danger of getting out now? Panic grows. Can his instincts be right about this? Is the man in the studios with Susie? Will she see him?

And then the interview is over and the presenter is introducing his wife.

The panic slowly subsides. There's no problem, he tells himself, the man must be in the Glasgow studio, Susie is in the remote in Edinburgh, there's no chance of them meeting. And anyway, he must be mistaken, it's just a coincidence.

The BBC's remote studio in Edinburgh's Tun is hardly inspiring. There's a rather tired-looking backdrop of an Edinburgh scene that has nobody fooled, and the monitor is set below the camera, so that it's all too easy to look down at the interviewer instead of engaging through the lens. Susie sets her plastic beaker of coffee down on a side table and settles onto the chair.

She isn't really nervous. She has done this dozens of times, it's no big deal – but today's different because she's going to go directly against her Party's policy. It's definitely not a good career move and she's conscious of her heart rate picking up as she waits.

'—The Government will today announce cuts in its funding for the teaching of music and drama in schools. One backbencher, however, disagrees with her own Party's policy. Good morning, Mrs Wallace.'

She's on air. 'Good morning,' Susie says brightly. 'You're right. I believe there's absolutely no case for axing funding.'

'It's easy to say that, but when there's a choice to be made between health care and—'

Susie interrupts the interviewer passionately. 'Don't you see? Sometimes I wonder if it's only politicians who

5

are unable to understand that music and drama can be powerful ways of preventing ill health from happening in the first place.' She leans towards the camera, her gaze brilliant. 'Art, music, drama, poetry all help people to make contact with places deep inside themselves where difficult emotions can fester and explode and turn these into something joyful and exhilarating. It's something they can share with others, do with others.'

'But don't you think—'

'The performing arts and literature aren't only ways of fulfilling our creativity, they also require us to work with other people. And wherever you come from, whatever your home life is like, these things can be immensely rewarding.'

'Are you saying that the arts can keep us out of the GP's surgery?'

'Yes. That's exactly what I'm saying.'

The interview continues, the journalist probing provocatively, Susie parrying with brilliance, She barely notices the time flying past, but before she has got half her points across, the interviewer says, 'Susie Wallace, thank you very much for joining us this morning.'

'It's been a pleasure.'

'And congratulations on "Home, Where My Heart Is". You must be pleased the series has finally reached our television screens again after all these years.'

'Oh. Yes. Thank you. I am. We all are – the cast, I mean.'

'That was Susie Wallace MSP, talking about arts funding in schools. We did ask for a government spokesperson on the issue, but no-one was available.'

Susie watches until the red light goes out, then takes a deep breath.

'Fabulous as ever, Susie, thanks,' comes the producer's voice.

'No problem. Thanks for inviting me on.'

She collects her handbag and briefcase and walks out of the studio. Outside she dials Archie. 'Was I all right?'

'Darling, you were magnificent. Susie Wallace in full flow is a force to be reckoned with. I was terrified.'

She laughs. It's infectious – passers-by turn their heads and smile. She nods at a sunken-cheeked man hurrying towards the newspaper offices opposite, his legs encased in tight jeans appearing stick-like and bony, like a bird's. A freelance journalist – what is his name? Justin something. Justin Thorneloe. 'Right,' she says dryly, into the phone. 'Like I could terrify you.'

'You scared me into marrying you.'

'Stop teasing, you're a wicked man.'

The sound of his chuckles keeps her smiling all the way into the nearby Parliament building.

Some people might think that Susie is the stronger one in the Wallace marriage, but she and Archie know otherwise. She is an unrepentant social being, she can work a room like a pro, though the difference between her and many others is that she genuinely loves talking to people and sorting out their problems. Where she is loud, extrovert and passionate, Archie is thoughtful, balanced and diplomatic. He's her rock, her anchor and her strength, and she very much doubts if she could scare him into anything.

Her heels click clack on the polished granite floor as she passes into the Garden Lobby, adrenalin still pumping from the interview. The sun streams through the boat-shaped windows high above her, illuminating the face of a lean terrier of a man who is striding across the great empty space of the Lobby towards her. It's Tom Coop, her chief whip. He slows and opens his mouth, his stare steely – but another colleague arrives, eager to buttonhole him.

Susie breathes again. Good. She has no doubt he'll be mad with her, but at least her wigging is deferred.

She swipes her pass to gain access to the Member Only

office area and steps into the lift. She has an hour to deal with her emails and get her papers in order, a blissful hour before the next public pressure has to be faced.

It's another normal day.

Chapter Two

'Mo will be after you,' Karen predicts when she arrives prompt at nine. She is the picture of efficiency and smartness from her tailored jacket and pencil skirt to her eminently stylish heels. She puts her large cardboard beaker of coffee down on the desk and turns to look at Susie, a hint of amusement in her intelligent grey eyes.

'I know,' Susie agrees. 'Mo and Tom both. I'm ready for it.'

Karen White, Susie's Parliamentary Assistant, is also her oldest friend. With her business degree and her guaranteed loyalty, she was the obvious choice of aide when Susie won her election battle.

The voice from the doorway, cutting in on their conversation, is rasping. 'So what did we talk about yesterday?' Maureen Armstrong, the party's chief press officer, launches herself through the door like a heat-seeking missile, red head ablaze.

'Hmm?' Susie looks up from her computer and pretends innocence. 'Weren't we going to do a release on—'

'Press matters later,' Mo cuts her off roughly. 'What did we say about talking to the media about arts funding?'

Susie is unrepentant. 'They called last night. It was too good an opportunity to miss.'

'No off-message briefings and certainly no off-message interviews,' Mo says sternly, her lips tight, her expression irate. At five foot ten and with hair that even the kindest description could not have promoted up the colour spectrum from ginger to copper, she presents a formidable front.

'Sorry,' Susie's tone barely conveys regret.

'Tom'll be after you.'

'Probably,' she agrees, her voice meek but her thoughts rebellious.

Mo appears ready to dig in, but her mobile rings in her pocket and she turns away, talking in a low, urgent voice to the caller.

Saved again, Susie thinks, the feeling of relief deeper than her unruffled exterior has conveyed. A training in acting, she finds, is the best tool a politician can have.

Karen winks meaningfully at her and says, her voice businesslike, 'Can we check diaries? And you're remembering you've got guests in half an hour?'

The Parliament's entrance lobby is a large, low-ceilinged and rather dark space. Susie considers it the least attractive space in the building, but at least visitors usually become more and more impressed as they penetrate the beating heart of the building. She usually leaves the main debating Chamber till last when she's conducting tours, for that reason. This morning, the lobby is busy already. She scans the throng for a grandmother and two small children.

'Susie? Is it you?'

Behind her, a small woman is clutching the hands of two quite young children. Nine perhaps, Susie thinks, and six?

'Mrs Proudfoot? How lovely to see you after all this time.'

'Do call me Elsie, dear. I wouldn't have recognised you, but for the hair.'

Elsie Proudfoot had been a neighbour and a close friend of Susie's mother. Susie scans the watery blue eyes, the pale, wrinkled skin, and the thin gray hair. If her own mother was still alive, she'd be ninety-five now, but Elsie is in her early eighties – either that or she's wearing extremely well.

'You're looking fantastic, Elsie.' The name jars on her lips. A lifetime of schooling in old-fashioned manners is hard to abandon. 'How lovely to see you. It's been – how long?'

'Probably your mother's funeral, dear. Ten years ago.'

'Ten years! Heavens, you haven't changed a bit,' she lies valiantly.

'You always were a charmer.'

Susie studies the children, two girls. The older is fair skinned and fair haired, the younger has black hair and a dark complexion that suggests mixed blood.

Elsie bends down to the younger child, who is staring up at Susie with wide eyes, her face serious. 'This lady is just like you, Indira,' she says chattily.

Susie waits, curious to find what point of similarity the old woman is going to draw in an attempt to pull the overawed child into the conversation.

'Why?' The little girl's question is little more than the softest of whispers.

'She's adopted too.'

The word makes no sense. Susie looks round. Someone must be standing behind her, someone else.

Indira looks relieved, as if, in this strangest of places, she can find a way of feeling at home.

There's no-one behind her. Only the ferret-faced journalist, Justin Thorneloe (who is not one of the tribe of Parliamentary news hounds in whom Susie cares to confide) hurrying to the exit.

Adopted? The word makes no sense.

Adopted?

Way off beam. A touch of dementia possibly.

'Well,' she says brightly, adopting her brightest Joyce Grenfell manner, as if she's about to address an unruly infant class. 'Well, how lovely you could make it, shall we start over here?'

She can do the tour off pat, without having to think.

11

That's just as well, because however much she tries to dismiss Elsie Proudfoot's remark, she can't put the word out of her mind.

Adopted.

The confusion of the elderly, she thinks again, though the woman actually seems rather bright and is asking good questions.

'Heavens, you can see why it was so expensive. I haven't seen a right-angle yet. You know what a right-angle is, Jemma, don't you?'

'It means, like, two corners of a square box, doesn't it Granny?'

'That's right, good. Can you imagine that, Indira?'

The small girl nods solemnly and clings to Elsie's hand. Her hair is plaited tightly and decorated at the ends with little pink ribbons. With her free hand she holds onto the end of one pigtail, her fingers playing with the bow. A kind of comfort blanket, Susie thinks.

She swipes her pass and leads them through to the interior of the building. They climb the few steps up to the Garden Lobby, Elsie exclaiming in delight at the flooding of sunlight into the top-lit space. 'Oh, how beautiful. Look, Jemma, look up there. Are those leaves?' She indicates the windows on the ceiling.

'If you like. I think the architect thought of them as boats.'

Adopted. It doesn't make any sense at all.

'Are those cameras?' Jemma asks. She's pointing at the television cameras directed at the stairway up to the chamber, a favourite place for media interviews.

'Yes indeed. They tend to leave them there, ready for a quick shot if needed.'

This lady's adopted, just like you. Susie shakes her head impatiently, trying to clear the thoughts. No. The thing's impossible. Elsie Proudfoot has got it all wrong. Her memory is clearly at fault. Maybe she has mixed her up with someone else, another neighbour perhaps?

'I think we'll be able to get into the main chamber,' she says brightly. 'Shall we go and look?'

'I've been so looking forward to this,' Elsie says as they walk. 'You see it on the telly. You've seen it, haven't you, Jemma?'

'We've done a project at school. My class might be coming to the Parliament next term.'

'That's nice,' Susie beams with forced gaiety. 'If you do come, make sure you get your Gran to let me know beforehand, won't you? Then I can come and talk to your class. Here we are.'

Somehow, she keeps talking.

'This is my desk. I put my pass in here—' she slots it into a device on the desktop, '—like this, and that allows me to vote.'

... television cameras ...

... allowed to speak for four minutes ...

... the mace presented by the Queen ...

How can she do this? How can she carry on as if everything is normal, when all the time this word is boomeranging around her mind like a crazy beast allowed free. 'Do you have any more questions?'

She longs to get rid of them. Once they are out of the building, everything will go back to normal. She can put the word out of her mind. Puff. Away. Like a dandelion head in the wind, scattered.

But dandelion seeds have a knack of planting themselves and growing, with ferocious vigour, wherever they fall and Susie has a deep sense of misgiving.

Most days in the Parliament building are filled end to end. If it isn't a debate in the Chamber, it's Committee time, or attendance is required at one of the many Cross-Party Groups in which Susie has registered an interest. She might be hosting a visiting delegation, or spending time with some of the many parties of schoolchildren who come to visit the Parliament and see how it functions. Today it's with great relief that she heads for the front desk again, this time to sign in her daughter, Margaret-Anne.

'Hi Mum!'

She spots Mannie right away, across the heads of a couple of dozen over-excited schoolchildren. She's looking radiant, her lime-green coat a breath of freshness in the dark space, her often-pale cheeks rosy from hurrying, her shoulder-length dark hair falling straight and thick to her shoulders. Not my hair, she thinks, my caramel-gold cloud trademark. Not Archie's either, brown (now grey) and wiry. As Susie crosses the entrance lobby to hug her daughter, she wonders, not for the first time, where her daughter's hazel eyes have come from; or the focus and drive that shoehorned her through school and propelled her meteoric rise through the hotel trade.

'Hello, darling.' She folds Mannie in her arms, her own cloud of curls eclipsing the dark, straight locks for a few seconds. 'So lovely you're here.'

Mannie grins. 'Saved you from a grilling, have I? I heard the interview.'

'Don't. I've been dodging behind pillars all morning.'

'Coopie after you, is he?'

'It's just a matter of time.'

'Can we get a salad in peace, do you think?'

'Oh sure, he won't tear a strip off me in public. There are too many other Members around to ogle.'

'Happy Anniversary, by the way.'

'Thank you.' Susie smiles warmly at Mannie as they weave through the throngs towards the Garden Lobby and the staff canteen. 'Okay if we slum it? I would have booked the Members' restaurant but I'm a bit pushed for time.'

'Course. I've got to get back to work myself.'

'Good. What do you fancy?'

They survey the fare on offer and plump for salad and fresh fruit.

Susie says, 'Dad's buying me dinner at The Shore later.'

'I know.'

Susie looks at Mannie suspiciously. 'Was that your doing?'

'Not at all,' Mannie says, the corners of her mouth lifting mischievously so that Susie can't read whether she's telling the truth. 'All his own idea.'

They sit near the glass wall overlooking the small garden in front of the Members' office block and settle down for a gossip amid the hum and hubbub of the canteen. Susie longs to share Elsie Proudfoot's remark with her daughter, to laugh about its absurdity with her, but some instinct makes her hold back. She needs to talk to Archie first.

'How's Cal?' Mannie has a tendency to trade in her men for a new model once every couple of years. Susie likes her current boyfriend, Callum McMaster, who works in information technology in one of the big banks. What he actually does is a mystery to Susie, but he seems dependable. Where Mannie is always building up a head of steam for a new challenge, Callum is content to work his way steadily up the rungs on the ladder he has started climbing. Anyway, he clearly adores her.

Mannie sweeps back her hair and attempts to keep it out of her way by pushing it behind her ear, where it sits, obediently, for ten seconds before slipping forwards again, the slightness of the ear defeated by the thickness of the locks. She says, 'Fine,' through a crunch of celery, dismissing the question of her boyfriend with one airy word.

'What does that mean? Fine? Fine is all right. Fine is okay so far as it goes. Fine is—'

'Cal's fine, Mum. He's off skiing with his mates next

week, to Courcheval.'

'Aren't you going with them?'

'No, no, blokey thing. It does us good to have some time apart.'

Susie longs to ask, aren't you thinking of marriage yet? Aren't you even moving in together? Her daughter shares a house with a couple of girlfriends, insisting that 'We like girly gossip' – but Callum has outlasted all her other boyfriends by eight months clear. Surely it's time for a step further in their relationship? When she was twenty-eight she'd been married for three years. Mannie was already born when she was twenty-eight.

Still, Susie hesitates at being so intrusive. Mannie is just as likely to take umbrage and choose the opposite course of action if she tries to interfere. If there's one thing Archie has taught her, it's prudence when it comes to her children – flouting your Party line is one thing, running your children's lives is quite simply unacceptable. She moves the conversation on. 'How's the job?'

'Yeah, it's all right.' Mannie looks up, laughs and elaborates. 'Our targets have been raised, again. I've got to find another four big conferences this year and increase the number of weddings by twenty percent.'

'Won't that be difficult?'

'In the current business climate, yes.' Mannie, naturally positive and cheerful, is articulate – Jonathan always ribs her that she can talk for Scotland. Now, though, she's clearly not inclined to elaborate. She changes the subject. 'Tell me how Dad is? And Jonno? Seems ages since I was home.'

'Six weeks.' As soon as she says it Susie realises it sounds petulant, so she adds hastily, 'Jon's birthday, don't you remember?'

'Yeah, sure. So how is he?'

Susie sighs. 'Still job hunting. He's got the shift at the bar, of course, but how long can he go on doing temp

16

work? He needs to get something in graphic design.'

'Nothing's come up?'

'Not yet, no. What would you advise him to do, Mannie?'

Mannie lays down her fork and knife and reaches for the small glass of fresh fruit salad. 'He's doing everything he can, Mum. It'll come good.'

'I hope so. I hate to see him down. And however nice he tries to be about it, I know he hates living at home with us. He's such an independent soul.'

They finish with a quick coffee. 'I mustn't forget to give you this.' Mannie reaches into her bag and pulls out a card. 'It's from me and Jonno.'

Susie opens the card. 'How lovely. Oh sweetheart, you shouldn't have. Really. You can't afford ... and Jon certainly can't—' The card contains a voucher for a night at one of the hotels in the chain Mannie works for, giving them a choice of four in Scotland alone.

'It's a special anniversary, Mum. Thirty years. And you're special too, you and Dad. You can't put a price on that. Besides—' she grins broadly at her mother, 'I got a good deal.'

'I'm glad.' Susie stands up. 'Your father and I really appreciate this, sweetheart. We'll book the visit as soon as his album's recorded.'

'That going well?'

'The usual.'

'Is he unbearable yet?' Mannie knows her father.

'Not yet. It might go that way.'

They chat all the way to the front desk, where Susie enfolds Mannie in a big hug. 'Sweetie, thanks so much. For the voucher, of course, but just for being here. I really appreciate it.' *More than you can guess, today*. A shard of doubt penetrates her defences. Adopted?

'Loved it. Thanks for lunch, Mum.'

And she's off, her hair swirling gloriously around her

neck, her coat bright amid a sea of dark suits. Susie watches her for a few seconds, pride rising like a wave rolling in towards the shore. *My beautiful daughter. We've done well with our children, Archie and I.*

Today, thirty years ago, she and Archie were married. She pushes thoughts of Elsie Proudfoot out of her mind.

Avoiding Tom Coop was never going to be possible for very long. When Susie gets back up to her office, there he is, like a vulture waiting to scavenge on the bones of the dead. Not a vulture, he's not nearly so magnificent a bird. A carrion crow, his black suit heightening the likeness, his nose, hooked and large in his skinny face, like a beak, poised to peck.

The similes are all Susie can do to lighten her feelings at seeing him hovering so purposefully, but they're enough to allow her to summon a smile (the rigours of a good training in dramatic expression again) and to greet him with a veneer of cheeriness. 'Tom. Hello. Are you looking for me?'

Behind him she can see Karen, pulling a sympathetic face and mouthing, 'Sorry!', her hands spread wide in a gesture of apology. There's only so much she can do to protect.

'Got a minute?' His voice is bird-like too, small and squeaky – but this man has power and can be spiteful. Susie, aware of this, schools herself to tact.

'Sure. I can give you ten, but I do have visitors due then.' The lie comes easily. 'Come on in. Karen, could you buzz me when the front desk calls please?' Code for, 'Help, don't leave me too long with him'.

'Will do.'

Susie takes the seat behind her desk. She could have taken one of the chairs at the small table, designed for one-to-one meetings, but the desk puts distance between them and gives her control – or, at least, an illusion of it. That lasts around three seconds.

'I think you know why I'm here,' Tom says, and not even the squeakiness of his voice can mask the menace of his tone.

'If you're going to talk about the interview this morning—'

'What do you think?'

Susie hasn't learnt her skills for nothing. Add media training to drama and the combination makes her a formidable interviewee. She knows it and Tom knows it. Ignoring his tone, she talks over his interruption as if he hasn't spoken, '—then I hope you'll agree I made my points clearly and pleasantly.'

'And they were completely at odds with our policy.'

'Actually Tom,' she pauses and smiles at him, keeping her voice level and polite, 'the Party doesn't have a policy on cutting arts funding.'

'It was a decision we had to take, given the current financial climate.'

'There are other things that can be cut.'

'That would hit the poor harder.'

'It's a weak argument. In my experience, the "poor" get as much from being involved in the arts as anyone else. And in any case, I was talking about schools. About education, Tom.' She leans over the desk, as if about to confide some important secret. 'And this government believes education is at the heart of our national success.'

'Meaning standards of excellence in numeracy and literacy,' he trots out the usual patter, 'as you well know.'

Susie can see that he's preparing for a long speech. Summoning her most charming tone, she says sweetly, 'And as you know, Tom, I was elected on a very specific commitment to the voters of Hailesbank – and that was a promise to defend the arts in Scotland. I can't turn round and ignore that, it would be a betrayal of trust.'

'And a raft of other policies as well. Policies most

voters would rate more highly than arts,' he says severely. 'Like health and transport. You don't have to defend all the decisions, Susie, but you don't have to speak out against them either.'

Susie says nothing. She merely allows a silence to develop. Tom grows uncomfortable. She watches it happen. Well-versed in reading body language, she notes the shift in position on the seat, the dropping of eye contact, the fiddling of the fingers. In the end, he stands abruptly, says brusquely, 'We're not pleased, Susie, not pleased at all. I would advise you to watch yourself carefully.'

Or what? Susie thinks, standing too.

'Do drop by again, Tom,' she says, moving round her desk and extending her arm towards the door in a gesture that clearly invites him to leave. 'It so good to discuss points of policy, don't you think?'

He's gone. She sinks back onto her chair, surprised to find that she's shaking slightly.

'You okay?' Karen comes in, clutching a sheaf of papers for signing. 'I was about to call through but you seemed to be surviving.'

'Oh yes. Sure. Surviving. I can handle Tom Coop.'

And, of course, she can. But will there be a price to pay later?

Chapter Three

Archie Wallace leans away from his keyboard and stretches. When he becomes lost in his music, he forgets time. This trait is a mixed blessing. On the one hand, he can go for very long periods totally absorbed in his task, but on the other, he becomes increasingly prone to knots in his neck, aches in his back, cramps in his legs and stiffness in his fingers. Most ailments he can deal with, but he'll have to watch the stiffness in the fingers. Fingers are his career.

Archie has spent a lifetime in music in one guise or another: schoolboy strummer, band member, teacher, composer. Three years ago he got together a scratch band for someone's fiftieth birthday party and they 'just rocked, Susie', as he put it when he arrived back at the cottage in the small hours, exhausted but exhilarated. The band found a common base in folk music, threaded a distinctive rock interpretation through their songs, hit on the name Celtic Rock and quickly established itself as a force for innovation and excellence in folk-rock fusion.

'You okay?' Sandie Alexander, Celtic Rock's vocalist and sometimes fiddle player, finishes a brilliantly improvised jig on a theme he has come up with and lowers her violin.

'Dying for a fag, if truth be told,' Archie grimaces wryly.

'Archie, you don't fucking smoke.' Sandie is tiny, still pretty at forty, the only woman in Celtic Rock and also – to Archie's amusement – the coarsest spoken member of the band.

He lays down his pencil and stands up. He gave up

21

smoking years ago but the lure of a coffee and a cigarette still has him in its thrall. He glances at the old school clock on the wall. One thirty already, no wonder he's hungry – he rose with Susie at six and started work immediately after her interview. 'Doesn't stop me craving the things,' he grins. Prince, roused by his movement, lurches to his feet too, his tail wagging.

'Is that the bloody time? Jesus.'

'Mmm. It's been okay though.'

'Yeah.'

'That track will play to Jake's strengths, don't you think?' Big, bearded Jake is the lead guitarist, his fingers astonishingly dextrous despite his size. Jake's opening riff in Celtic Rock's 'On the Wilder Side [Mountain Thyme 2]' – the track that established them as a chart-topping phenomenon – has become as instantly recognisable as 'Stairway to Heaven'.

'Hope the fucker appreciates the hard work we do to make him look good,' Sandie lays down her instrument and yawns. 'I'll have a fag anyway. Got to look after the old vocal chords.' She flashes a grin at Archie from behind an untidy mop of brown hair and lights up. Sandie's husky vocals have become legendary.

Archie doesn't like her smoking in the studio, but he lets it pass. 'Hungry? I can make a sandwich.'

'No ta, Archie. Got things to do.'

'You on for another session tomorrow?'

'I'll be here. But not at fucking six in the morning.'

Archie opens the door of the stables he converted into a studio many years ago, when they had so little cash he'd had to do all the work himself. Still, it feels like his. He knows every floorboard, every cable. The old oak door looks great because he spent days sanding and polishing it. The roof is watertight because he climbed up and perched there precariously for weeks on end stripping, felting, slating. Pride and familiarity blend to produce a feeling of deep inner tranquillity.

Sandie slides past him and grinds her cigarette butt into the cobbles with her heel. 'See ya, then.'

'Bye, Sandie. And well done,' he calls after her retreating figure. She sticks up two fingers without looking round. He grins. Impossible to know, with Sandie, whether she means 'fuck off, don't patronise me' or 'peace, man'. Either way, she's probably being ironic. He listens to the retreating roar of her motorbike, balances for a moment on the sill of the doorway and allows himself to luxuriate in the benevolent heat of the sun, like a lazy cat. His mind strays to Susie's thick, wild hair, the colour of liquid caramel shot through with strands of the purest dark gold. It reached her waist, back at college. He spotted her on the very first day, wasn't able to take his eyes off her – no-one could. Her ready smile and infectious laugh, and the sheer energy packed into every movement, made her a magnet for admiration.

Susie of the amber eyes.

Susie the unattainable.

God, she was beautiful then. Still is. How the heck did he finally land her? Not then, not at once, not at college at all, in fact. There, she was perpetually surrounded by a crowd of admirers, men and women, a popular girl despite her beauty. In an arena where talent and looks can be the objects of jealousy and spite, Susie MacPherson always managed to avoid it, because fundamentally she was warm-hearted.

Too warm-hearted?

Archie shakes his head to clear the unwelcome memory. Those months of suspicion and doubt were the hardest of his life. She doesn't know that he knew, he'd always believed her love was only worth having if it was willingly bestowed.

He shakes his head again. He won't allow himself to return there.

Across the yard, the front door of the cottage opens and his son Jonathan emerges, a mug in one hand, a magazine in the other. Archie waves a hand in greeting. Jon, hands full, nods and calls, 'Hi Dad!'

Jonno still lives at Cairn Cottage – for now. *It will always be home to our children, thinks Archie, whenever they need to be here.* They bought the place twenty-eight years ago for family life, able to afford the property only because it was well out of Edinburgh and in a state of almost complete disrepair. Now it looks charming, but it will be another few months before Susie can plant out her tubs in the courtyard. In summer, their lush purples and sumptuous reds added vibrant flashes of colour to the grey stone.

No matter how busy Susie is, she insists on caring for them. 'My flowers connect me to the earth,' she protests, whenever he offers to take over the task of weeding and watering.

By May, Archie thinks, it will be picture perfect – for now, he's just pleased to see sunshine. He starts across the cobbles and calls to his son, 'Morning, Jon.'

'It's afternoon, actually, or hadn't you noticed?'

Archie grins. 'Don't you be cheeky to me, my lad. I've been working since dawn.'

'Saw Sandie leaving. Get on okay?'

'Not bad at all. Another track pretty much there.'

Jonathan Wallace rearranges his long limbs to make room on the bench for his father. He's tall, like Archie, and his character is more like Archie's than Susie's, but his features more closely resemble his mother's and his amber eyes and rich reddish-brown hair are most definitely hers.

'What are you reading?'

Jon waves the magazine. '*Mac User.*'

'Riveting.'

'All right, I confess. I'm a techno geek.' He closes the

magazine and lays it on his lap. He has inherited Archie's long fingers, and their gracefulness, but the keyboard he uses is a computer one, not a piano. 'I love this stuff.'

Archie sinks down onto the bench. 'Still nothing on the job front?'

'No. Well, I suppose you could say yes. I got another thanks but no thanks this morning.'

'That's a shame. I'm sorry to hear it.'

Jon puts his hand in his pocket and pulls out some notes. 'My rent.'

Archie looks at the money, but doesn't reach for it. 'You don't need to do this, son.'

'I do.'

'Your mother and I—'

'I know. You don't need the money blah blah. But I need to give it to you, Dad.'

He so needs to be independent, thinks Archie, his heart swelling as he looks at his son. Pride at Jon's determination mixes with regret about the circumstances that are forcing him into the situation. He takes the notes, but peels one off and hands it back. 'We agreed you'd do the hens while I was so busy, remember?'

'I don't need to be paid—'

'I won't let you do them unless you take the money. Just don't tell your mother.'

The harmless conspiracy draws Jonathan close to him. Archie loves both his children, but Mannie is her mother's daughter, confident, ambitious and well established, while Jon needs more support. Archie's challenge is to find ways of helping his son that are acceptable.

On this occasion, it seems, he has judged it right. Jon takes the note and puts it back in his pocket. 'Okay, Dad. Thanks.' He's clearly aware of the game the two of them are playing. Archie can see that he has weighed the manoeuvre up in terms of its admissibility in his own strict rules of conduct and found it tolerable.

'Happy Anniversary, by the way.'

'Thanks.' Archie is amazed that Jonno has remembered.

Jon's generous mouth twists into a wry smile. 'Mannie reminded me. She was seeing Mum for lunch today. She gave her a gift from us both.'

'Jonathan.' The generosity moves him. A lump lodges in his throat and he has to fight through the swelling to speak. 'You didn't need to – but thank you.'

'Okay.' Jon is embarrassed. 'No problem. You taking her out somewhere nice?'

'The Shore.' He names a restaurant in Leith, the port district of Edinburgh.

'Cool.' He stands up. 'Better go. I've got a double shift.'

'Back late again?' Archie says sympathetically.

'Yeah.'

'See you tomorrow then. Did you do them already? The hens?'

'Yeah.' Jon pats his pocket. 'Got to earn my keep. Three eggs. I put them in the kitchen basket.'

'Great. I'll have an omelette to keep me going. Drive safely.'

'Sure. Enjoy your dinner. Hugs to Mum.'

'Bye.'

As Archie showers, he finds himself humming a new tune. It arrived, more or less fully formed in his head, after Susie's television interview and it still pleases him. He jotted the refrain down before Sandie arrived for their morning's work, but he hasn't written any words yet. They'll come later.

He dresses with unusual care, picking dark trousers instead of his usual jeans, a heavy cotton shirt in a deep hyacinth blue that Susie bought for him and that he knows she loves, and a dark gray cashmere jacket. His hair, though white now, is still thick. He uses the dryer for speed and brushes it through so that it falls in place neatly above his right eye just in the way Susie approves of.

He's feeling oddly nervous. Why be apprehensive about dinner with your wife? It isn't as if Susie has found recent fame, she's been a household name for years, ever since she was cast, age twenty-six, as a passionate lesbian in a television period drama series that really took off. What a role to achieve stardom with!

Yet he is tense – perhaps because the sight of that man on the television this morning has thrown him, or maybe because anniversaries are occasions for retrospection. Looking back disturbs memories, and there are some things he would rather forget.

Time to go.

It doesn't help that Susie is late. Archie is used to the fact that these days she perpetually fits in more engagements than are realistically feasible, but the gift of her presence is all he wants today. The pianist in the bar is playing jazz classics, but with a kind of smug swagger that irritates Archie. He's sure the guy knows he's there and is trying to show off. Any moment now he'll be asked to do a guest turn, something he only enjoys if he's in the mood, and his mood is most definitely not conducive right now.

Then there's something about Susie, when she appears, twenty-three minutes late, that he finds disconcerting. She seems distracted.

'You did well, this morning.'

'Hmmm?' She's scanning the menu, the glasses she now needs for reading perched on the end of her nose. He finds them endearing. He wants to grow old with this woman. He longs to possess her completely, but Susie is like a bird that needs to fly free and he has always known she has to fly home to her perch by her own choice. Anything less would diminish what they have.

'On the television.'

'Oh. Thanks.'

'What did Tom Coop have to say?'

She lowers the menu. 'I'll just have the sea bass.'

'No starter?'

'I'm not really hungry.'

Archie, who is ravenous, is disappointed, but he hides his feelings and says gallantly, 'Then I'll just have the fish pie. Coop?'

'As predicted.'

Goodness, she's curt. 'I was going to order champagne before the meal, but maybe you'd like to move on to wine?'

'Just a glass. I'm driving.'

'I can drive. I caught the train in.'

'It's okay. I've got to keep a clear head. There's so much on.'

Any sense of happy anticipation Archie might have had begins to evaporate. Susie is not given to moodiness, but there have been periods when her vast reserves of energy have burned out, leaving her on the verge of depression. When she was filming at Calgary Bay, for example – though of course, her strangeness then was something else entirely. Archie has to force himself to put the thought aside. Susie thinks their marriage is perfect, the children believe it, the press (thank heaven) has never probed. And it was twenty-nine years ago and has all been long forgotten.

'You all right, sweetheart?' he asks, trying to mask his concern. He doesn't have Susie's thespian skill.

'Of course. Why wouldn't I be?'

All his life Archie has been the diplomatic one. He seldom acts on impulse, preferring to gauge the situation and weigh up how to respond with care. It has worked well for him. Susie is the impulsive one, the risk taker, the maker of snap decisions. He holds his peace and moves the

28

conversation on. 'How was Mannie?'

She softens visibly. 'She was lovely. She's doing so well, Archie. They've given us a hotel voucher.'

'You're joking.'

'Isn't that sweet of them?'

'Jon can't afford it.'

She says brusquely, 'He wants to be an equal.'

'And he is. He's just not earning yet.'

'He needs to feel—'

'I know what you're saying, Susie.' Heavens, they're arguing! This isn't what he planned. His diplomatic gene kicks in again, the peacemaker in him yearning for harmony. 'It's a very generous gesture. I'll look forward to a chance of getting away. Let's order, shall we?'

'Cheers. Here's to us.' He raises his glass and chinks Susie's.

She lets him make the toast, but she doesn't offer one back.

They eat in silence.

'That was good.'

'Excellent.'

'We haven't been here in ages.'

'No. It hasn't changed.'

'The pianist is rubbish.'

Her face cracks into a small smile, the first he has seen since she arrived. 'I knew you'd say that,' she crows. 'As soon as I walked in the door and heard him, I knew he wouldn't be your taste.'

'I think he's showing off.'

'To you? Probably. People want to impress you.'

'Hmm.'

Archie likes to play down the fact that these days, in music circles, he wields a fair bit of influence. He falls silent, drawn into his own thoughts. Normally, Susie fills these small spaces with incessant chatter, regaling him with tales of her day, snippets of gossip from the

Parliament or the Party, setting forth her views on this issue or that, so that his dreaming can pass more or less unnoticed. Tonight she's silent, a fact that Archie, immersed in his own line of thought, doesn't notice for several minutes.

There's a pattern about such habits. He dreams, she talks. After a while, she pulls him out of his reverie with a 'Don't you think?' or a 'Can you believe it?' or some other hook that draws him back in. Somewhere in his subconscious, a metronome must be ticking, his innate sense of rhythm registering that something is missing. She hasn't spoken, his dream is continuing uninterrupted, there has been no pull back into the flow of conversation. He looks at her, puzzled. She's staring into the middle distance, her eyes unfocused, her face troubled. This isn't like Susie.

'What are you going to have for dessert?'

She doesn't hear him.

'Suse?'

This time she meets his gaze, and there's something in her eyes that sends a chill down his neck. 'Susie? What are you going to have for dessert?'

She tosses her serviette on the table and stands abruptly. 'Can we go?'

Astonished, he tries to make light of it. 'What, no pudding?'

To his horror, he sees tears welling in her eyes and he rises swiftly. Susie speeds towards the door. He pulls out some notes and throws them onto the table, makes an excuse to the waiter, and follows her as quickly as he can. She's at her car by the time he catches up with her, fumbling with her keys with uncharacteristic clumsiness. He catches her shoulders and turns her towards him. Something is troubling her and he has to find out what it is. He can help. As soon as she tells him what it is, he'll be able to help her sort through it. It's always been like that.

30

'Susie. Darling. Tell me what's wrong.'

For a few seconds he thinks she's going to say something, then her eyes cloud and she turns her head away. 'It's nothing. Sorry. It's been a hard day.'

'Suse—'

'I'd like to get home.'

She invests the words with such meaning that he remembers why she has won so many awards. Five words and she has conjured up a whole world, the persona of a heroine who has been to the limits of her endurance and is desperate for solace. But this time, she's playing no role, her need is real. Something has happened.

Pragmatism returns. 'Give me the keys, darling,' he says. 'I'll drive.'

Chapter Four

The remark dropped by Elsie Proudfoot being too fundamental to contemplate, Susie solves the problem by ignoring it completely. Or at least, life being so frenetically busy, she makes up her mind to shelve the issue until she has some time and space to consider it. When she wakes in the morning after their less than successful anniversary dinner, the cottage is reassuringly familiar: the bedroom with its dormer windows and cream cotton curtains, exotically lined with crimson; the convincing solidity of the chest of drawers, home to an uncatalogued assortment of lingerie, tights, tee shirts, make-up, sweaters, belts and scarves, many lurking unseen for years; the boudoir chair Archie bore home triumphantly from an auction in Edinburgh in response to her heartfelt plea for just such an item; Archie's discarded clothing from yesterday, folded neatly on his own small wooden chair; and Archie himself, curled like a cat, one hand under his cheek, innocent in slumber.

Yesterday now seems unreal. If something has shifted in her core, she doesn't know what it is – and perhaps in not knowing lies safety. If she has survived so contentedly all these years in ignorance, can this genie not be put back in its bottle?

In the kitchen, she sorts through her briefcase, grabs a quick mug of tea and puts the hotel voucher from Jonno and Mannie on the dresser with the bundle of invitations, bills, vouchers and important information that reside there. Today, at least, she will put all thought about adoption aside. Today is full of Things To Do.

First on the agenda is a meeting of the Rivo Trust, a small charity in Hailesbank aimed at helping young people who are having difficulty in coping with life to find meaning, purpose and confidence. A few years ago, the Trust was gifted an old drill hall in the town, where they now run various classes – literacy, introduction to computing, confidence-building, art and music – put on small shows, host a drop-in centre and bookstall, and run a cheerful and cheap café.

A year after her election to the Parliament in Holyrood, Susie was asked if she would like to sit on the Rivo's Board. She was well aware this was the Trust ticking boxes, but she was experienced in theatre, had a long history of volunteering with youth groups and, to cap it all, she had three initials after her name – MSP. Those initials open a lot of doors and bring a degree of kudos to any organisation with which she is associated. She accepted but, determined not to be in any way a token representative, makes it a point of honour to attend as many Board meetings as she can.

This morning she parks her car in Hailesbank High Street, feeds a couple of pound coins into the meter, and heads for the hall. Ricky Waring, the Director, receives her warmly.

'Susie! I'm so pleased you could make it. We thought you might be too busy with the battle for arts funding.' He bends his balding head and kisses her cheek enthusiastically.

It's difficult not to warm to Ricky. He has a kind of natural charm combined with gusto and a record of hard work that appear to make him the ideal man to manage the Trust. Certainly he has been there a long time – fifteen years, if Susie's memory serves her right.

'Hello, Ricky. Didn't want to let you down. How long will the meeting be today?'

He lets go of her hand and opens the door into the

meeting room. 'Couple of hours, hopefully.'

'Fine.' Susie does some quick calculations. She can be in the Parliament well before lunchtime and present in the Chamber for the afternoon debate. Excellent. She smiles at her fellow Trustees, helps herself to coffee and shuffles her papers.

The meeting seems straightforward, but try as she might, Susie finds that she can only concentrate with half of her brain. In the other half, despite her strenuous efforts to put it aside, a seven-letter word plays and replays itself.

Adopted.

You are like this lady, Indira. She's adopted too.

It simply isn't possible. How could she have reached the age of fifty-five without knowing that she is adopted? There must be a mistake. The words of the Agenda swim in front of her eyes as she struggles to concentrate.

Adopted.

'Susie? What do you think?'

Because after all, there had been no reason to conceal such a momentous fact from her. Why would her parents have done that?

'Susie?'

'Sorry, what? Forgive me, I didn't hear that.' She struggles to focus on the meeting.

'The change of auditor, what do you think?'

Change of auditor? Why are they changing the auditor? Surely this was all discussed some months ago and they voted to retain the services of the auditor they were using? 'Remind me, why are we doing this?' she asks, rather feebly.

Ricky smiles down the table, his thin, clever face radiating patience. 'I decided to tender the work again. With money tight, it seemed sensible to ensure we were getting best value and the new auditors came in with a much better quote.'

'I see. Everyone else happy?' There are general nods of

agreement, so Susie says, 'That seems fine then. About these accounts—'

She runs through a series of questions. The Trust used to have healthy reserves, now the balance in the bank seems low. What about the performance of the investments? Most of the work of the Trust depends on income from these funds.

Ricky parries her queries smoothly. 'We're awaiting the funding from the government for the Outreach Initiative, it should be in soon. And we're cutting costs – remember, we've laid off two employees.'

'Doesn't that leave you understaffed?'

'We'll be pushed, yes,' Ricky admits, 'but needs must. We'll manage and with a bit of luck, everything will stabilise when the new funding comes in. We may even be able to rehire June Mackintosh.'

Susie thinks of the warm-hearted assistant who was the backbone of Rivo for years. She has children, a girl at university, two teenagers to follow. Losing her job must be hard for her.

Adopted.

Well, what does it matter if it was true? She had loving parents, no-one could have asked for better. Adoption would change nothing.

'Any other business?' The Chair, a tubby retired church minister called Hugh Porteous, is wrapping the meeting up. 'No? Well, we'll meet again in two months' time, as usual. Thank you all for attending. The minutes will be with you as soon as I can manage to type them up. Hmm.' He smiles apologetically. 'Which won't be as speedily as Mrs M, I'm afraid, my typing skills aren't up to much.'

No-one else volunteers.

Outside, Susie slides into her car. Karen's out of the office today on a course, so she calls her mobile.

'It's me, hi. Got a minute? I really need to talk to you.'

'Sounds serious. Fallen in love with someone wickedly

unsuitable?'

'Sadly, nothing so exciting. But a little troubling.'

'Tell?'

'Are you free this evening? Archie's out at a gig. You could come for supper and stay over. I'll drag something out of the freezer.'

'No, don't do that. I'll come, but I'll stop off and raid the supermarket.'

'You're a sweetheart. I should be home by seven, any time after that.'

In the Garden Lobby at the Parliament, Susie is hurrying towards her office when Justin Thorneloe, his small, sharp nose twitching, lays a hand on her arm. She looks down at it pointedly.

'Good afternoon, Justin,' she says, calling on her professional training for the voice that registers polite attention. She looks at him inquiringly.

'Rivo Trust,' he says.

'Yes?'

'You're on the Board, aren't you?'

'Yes. That's right. It's in the Register.' All Members are required to register their interests, whether financial or memberships of organisations that might lead to partiality.

'Sure. I know. I checked.' He smiles tautly. The smile doesn't reach his eyes and the words sound more like a threat than a reassurance. 'I heard they were in trouble.'

Instantly, Susie's guard goes up. Rivo's Board minutes are posted as a matter of principle on their website, so the main points about their operation are public – but surely nothing could be up there about today's meeting already? 'They're fine,' she says carefully. 'They're just having to rein in a bit, like any other charity in the current climate.'

The man's nose quivers, as if he's scenting something. The whiff of a story, perhaps? What does he know? And if he knows something worrying, where has he learned it from? 'So Rivo is financially sound?'

'Basically, yes.'

'I see.'

He looks like a weasel, she thinks, a nasty little weasel with very sharp teeth. Most journalists are not to be trusted, but it's possible to have a reasonably good relationship with some of them and even confide in them with care. Reporters like Justin are to be avoided at all costs. Since the News of the World debacle, Susie supposes that phone hacking has become a taboo method of information gathering, but snooping takes many forms and she can envisage this particular journalist lowering himself as far down as his wiry little frame allows him.

'I must go,' she says, 'I'm late. Sorry. If you need any information, why don't you call Ricky Waring?'

'Oh I will,' he says, his eyes glinting. 'I'll do just that.'

She tries not to let him see it, but she's rattled. She thinks back to the Board meeting. Is there something amiss? More than the short-term need for cash? Ricky was his usual cheerful, capable self and the Chairman seemed relaxed and apparently untroubled.

She waves her pass at the electronic door. She has too much on her mind to worry about Rivo.

Susie gets through the day with rather less than her normal verve. Uncharacteristically, she backs out from a promise to attend a reception for a children's charity, guilt niggling her all the way back to the cottage. She feels unsettled and disorientated.

Waiting for Karen, she pulls a stack of papers from her briefcase and fiddles with them. There's always urgent work. She glances at one letter, flips it over, repeats the action with a couple more before realising that she hasn't taken in a word and turning them all back. She tries to concentrate.

Mo's handwriting catches her eye. 'We should discuss.'

She glances at the email. It's a query from Thorneloe about the Rivo Trust. He isn't letting go, is he? Susie thinks fleetingly that she must dig deeper, find out what he's getting at, and manages to turn over another dozen documents. A sheaf of lobbying letters about arts funding for schools that require a response. A briefing from the Chair of the cross-party group on literature. Some papers from the Petitions Committee.

She hears the noise of the engine first, a low purr that promises power and elegance, then comes the crunch of gravel. A car has turned onto the drive. Through the window she glimpses a streak of scarlet as Karen's small Mercedes sports car – 'my treat to myself for having had to endure the blasted menopause' – flies past the trees near the gate, the tyres no doubt spitting small stones onto the grass on either side, little hazards for the mower.

'Hi Suse!'

An arm waves wildly from the offside window and the beat of Runrig is cut off mid phrase – how that would irritate Archie. The engine falls silent and Karen emerges. She pulls out an overnight case and a small carrier bag clearly stuffed with more work.

'Sorry I've got to lumber you with this lot but you'll need it for your meeting tomorrow.' Her heels clatter on the cobbles – no compromise for the rural setting – as she crosses the small space between them. 'Bother, the food's still in the boot.'

'Let me.' Susie smiles. Karen's familiar presence is already helping to ease her anxiety.

In the kitchen Karen says, 'I don't know about you but I'm gagging for a drink.' She knows she doesn't need permission, simply pulls the cork with a practised hand.

'Remember Elsie Proudfoot?' Susie blurts out.

'The woman who came in yesterday? The old neighbour of your parents?'

'Mmm.' Susie nods.

39

'Well? What about her?'

Susie closes her eyes. Will saying the word aloud make it real? Will it make it true?

'Suse? You're alarming me.'

Surely she can tell Karen, her lifelong friend? Karen played in her father's neat garden, picked his bright dahlias. Karen practically lived in her mother's kitchen, learned there how to make a Victoria sandwich, flip a pancake, ice a chocolate cake. Karen knew her parents almost as well as she did. She draws a deep breath. 'Elsie Proudfoot says I was adopted.'

Whatever Karen is expecting, it clearly isn't this. The puzzlement in her eyes makes them grow dark. 'Adopted?'

Susie nods. The word sounds different on Karen's lips, more prosaic, less likely.

'I don't understand.'

'I don't know how I can make it any clearer, Karen. Adopted.' A voice comes back to her – her father's. *My wee giftie.*

Robert MacPherson was a bank clerk, a man of huge kindness but little imagination. Routine was his mainstay. In the Sixties, when colour was busting out everywhere and psychedelia and Carnaby Street reigned supreme, he still dressed formally in dark suits with stiff collars and tightly knotted ties in dark green or deep burgundy. He read the *Times* and played bowls. His contribution to domestic chores was the gardening and his style was neatness. Every blade of grass was trimmed to within an inch of its life, the borders of the lawn cut in sharp right angles to the flowerbeds. Weeds were anathema to him and his pride and joy were the fabulously rich colour of the many varieties of dahlia he grew each summer.

If his clothes were dull, his garden was not and despite his leaning towards orderliness, Robert MacPherson was a loving, warm-hearted man. Nothing appeared to give him more pleasure in life than getting down on his hands and knees and offering rides to his small daughter – or, later, when she was in full acting mode, submitting meekly to being draped in a curtain to be Prince Charming or donning a silly hat to become a hobgoblin. His willingness more than made up for his deficiencies as an actor.

Susie can picture him now, scooping her up in his arms, tickling and cuddling her until her indignation gives way to delighted screams. 'My wee gem', he called her. 'My wee giftie.' Did it mean something, that choice of word? *Gift. Something that has been given.* Susie senses the boundaries of her world shifting once more, feels the room turn. She clutches her glass. It's cold in her hand.

'How could—' Karen, her eyebrows furled, puzzles over the word, '—if it's true, how could you not know?'

Susie sets down her drink and leans forward. 'It seems weird, doesn't it?' Her hands and arms come into play as she pulls out the many strands of thought that have been unravelling in her head and tries to straighten them. 'Surely they would have told me? If they hadn't told me when I was little – and I guess I can understand that – surely they would have told me later? Maybe when I went away to drama school. That would have been a good time.'

'There was nothing— When your mother died, there was nothing in her papers?'

'No.'

'No notes, no letters, no correspondence with an adoption agency?'

'No. Nothing at all.'

Karen's puckers her lips thoughtfully. 'I suppose, if you think about it—' she breaks off and glances across at Susie, clearly hesitant.

'What?'

'Well, now you mention it, your folks were older than most of the other parents, weren't they?'

'Yes,' Susie concedes. 'You're suggesting—?'

'Just a possibility. You know. Inability to conceive. Her

41

fault, his – who knows? People didn't talk about such things much back in the Sixties. And then adoption. It makes sense. But Susie – surely it's not possible that you and Archie could have got married without you knowing about this? Don't you have to lodge your birth certificate when the banns are called?'

The practicality is obvious. How has she missed it? Karen is right – of course she's right! Grasping at the straw, she feels relief flood through her. 'Why didn't I think of that? It must all be a nonsense. I knew it! I knew she'd got muddled.' She stands. 'Talk to me while I cook. If I don't eat soon I'll fall over.

'Need a hand?'

'Just keep my glass topped up.'

She heats a skillet, waits till smoke begins to rise from the oil, then tosses in the steaks Karen brought. As they sizzle, she opens salad and empties it into a bowl, quickly shakes together some dressing – oil, balsamic, sugar, salt, mustard – the ritual comforting.

'I knew she'd got it wrong. I couldn't understand how it could be true. I mean, even if they'd not told me when I was younger for some unfathomable reason, surely Mum would have said something after Dad died? Or before she died herself? And you're right – even failing that, surely I would have found some papers, some letters, something among her belongings?'

'Sure. You can't keep something as big as that hidden. What does Archie say?'

'Archie? I haven't told him.'

Karen stares at her. 'O-kay,' she says slowly, and only then does Susie realise how odd this fact is.

'I couldn't believe it was true,' she says, with an edge of defensiveness, 'So there didn't seem any point in bothering him.' The truth, she grasps now, is that somewhere in the dark corners of her mind she's terrified that Archie might actually have known something that she didn't, that for some bizarre reason he might have been told while she was kept in ignorance. The steak in her mouth suddenly tastes foul. She ejects it onto the back of her fork and puts it on the edge of her plate, gazing at it with distaste. She's still clutching the fork because there's something nagging her, something she should remember.

Karen is saying, 'Well, maybe you can put it all aside now. The old woman's clearly barking—'

Susie drops the fork onto her plate. The clatter startles Prince out of his dream and he looks up groggily.

'What?' Karen is startled too. 'What is it?'

Susie is back in 1981, back in her parents' house in Helensburgh, still deeply familiar despite the fact that she hasn't been living there for years. Archie is by her side, they're in the old-fashioned front room. She's sitting in the old sofa, the high-backed one with the floral covering, the roses big and blowsy against their dull gold background. Her mother sits comfortably in her favourite rocker, the chair moving gently back and forward, back and forward. Her father stands, patriarchal and proud, by the mantelpiece. He likes Archie. They both like Archie. They're all drinking sherry from tiny, well-mannered crystal sherry glasses. She can taste its sweetness in her mouth now, even though it's a taste that has passed her by for thirty years.

'We'll need to go and see the minister,' Archie is saying. His hair is black, long at the back and cropped neat on top – a classic mullet – but other than a lack of wrinkles and the fact that black has become white and the length at the back has mercifully been shorn, he's still the same Archie.

'I'd like to do that little job with you, Archie.' Her father, newly retired and already looking old, is insistent. 'My pleasure. There's not going to be much more I can do for my little girl now that she's going to be an old married woman.'

'I'd like to go,' she says, a little surprised at the intervention.

Her father lays his hand on hers, his grip firm and unusually assertive. 'I insist.'

The thirty years that separate Susie from the memory dissolve and the image of the scene comes into sharper focus than she could ever have thought possible.

She is looking across at her mother, who says, 'That'd be best, love.' And – is she remembering right? – there's a look on her mother's face that's more like relief than anything else.

Now Susie's mouth feels dry and unnatural.

'Karen,' she says, 'I've just remembered something.'

Shortly after Karen leaves the next morning, doubtless spraying more gravel onto the verges as she speeds down the drive, the telephone rings. 'Susie? It's Mo, glad I caught you.'

Mo at this time of day is not good news. Conversely, it's possible that it's fantastic news, but she knows the hollow feeling in her stomach has nothing to do with the quantity of alcohol she and Karen downed last night. 'Hi, Mo. What is it?'

'Have you seen *Scotland Daily* yet?'

'They don't deliver here.'

'Of course not, I forgot.'

'What is it?'

'This story with the Rivo Trust—'

'What story?'

'The rumours about mismanagement. I marked up an email for you yesterday, didn't you see it?'

'Uh? Oh, yes, yes I did.' Susie's heart is picking up pace. 'But I don't know what you mean by mismanagement. The charity is struggling a bit, well they all are—'

'According to Justin, things have got so bad that the

charity is teetering on the verge of bankruptcy. There's a rumour that they'll have to sell their properties to pay their bills.'

Susie sits down with a thump. 'No! Surely not?'

'Weren't you at a Board meeting yesterday? Was nothing said?'

Susie casts her mind back feverishly. 'I did ask questions about the accounts. There were weaknesses. Ricky said he was changing the auditors again.'

'You didn't think that was odd?'

'Yes, I—' She did think that, but her head was full of other things and she didn't challenge Ricky in the way she probably should. 'How's he got hold of this story?'

'He must have a mole. Any idea who it could be?'

June Mackintosh, Susie thinks. Out of character, perhaps, but she has a grudge, a justifiable one, and perhaps she thinks that by going to the Press she might be able to salvage something. 'Maybe,' she says slowly. 'Listen, what's in the story? Do any of the other papers have it?'

'Not that I can see. It lists a whole load of so-called facts, castigates the Board, names you specifically—'

Susie groans.

'—insinuates that you've done nothing more than take credit when times have been good but failed in your duty of trust—'

'Damn. What do you want me to do?'

'Are you coming in this morning?'

'I'm almost on my way.'

'We'll discuss it when you get here then.' Mo softens her briskness, 'Don't worry, Susie. It's not the end of the world,' before spoiling that by adding, 'though Coopie's face is thunder this morning.'

Her small snort might have been designed to show that this is a joke, but it does nothing to alleviate Susie's mood. She toys for a moment with the idea of phoning Archie.

45

On any other day in the past thirty years, that's exactly what she would have done, but today it won't help.

She is stopped as she enters the Garden Lobby by a reporter from the BBC. 'Susie? Have you got a moment?'

'Sure.'

'The Rivo Trust appears to be in some trouble, have you any comment?'

Her lips tighten. 'No,' she says, 'No comment.' She sweeps past him, but he follows her. 'As a Trustee, surely it's your duty to—'

She manages to say, 'You know that, as a Trustee, it's my duty not to comment about confidential matters,' then – with relief – she is through the secure door and safely in the private office area. Out of sight, she leans against the wall because her knees are trembling. She should have coped better with that.

Later, she works with Mo on her key words ('Get these in, Susie, if you do nothing else.'). They think about the worst question she might get (an allegation of dereliction of duty at Rivo). Mo is, mercifully, unflappable. Calmness is her great strength, and a necessary one when all the heavy artillery of the media point in her direction.

In the scale of Mo's workload it's a tiny story. Today the Press Director has a cluster of superbug infections in Lanarkshire that have resulted in the deaths of a handful of pensioners, a threatened strike by railway workers and a gathering storm about a change in the school curriculum that is catapulting the Education Minister into the headlines in the least welcome way possible. These all come considerably higher in the ranking of stories to be handled than a side issue about a minor charity.

But this is Susie's problem, her charity, her alleged incompetence and she doesn't have her usual confidence to deal with it. For once, she is happy to consider Mo an ally.

Chapter Five

The clock governs her every action. Six thirty, wake up. *Tick.* Eight, in the office. *Tock.* Ten, Committee meeting. *Tick.* Twelve, constituent meeting. *Tock.* On and on, all through the day, every day. Sometimes Susie resents it – life before Parliament was so much freer. Time is capricious. She sees Time like a snotty-nosed child, sniggering at his ability to drag or fly at will – or to march on relentlessly, pulling aging generation after aging generation in its remorseless wake.

Today, all Susie wants to do is turn back the clock, to the moment before Elsie says, 'This lady's like you, Indira. She's adopted.' Then she'll move aside instead, speak to Jemma, hand out their name badges, anything rather than hear those words, in that moment. If only she'd never agreed to the visit. If only she'd asked Karen to do the tour instead. If only—

'Bad day at the office?' Archie asks sympathetically.

He has seen her car on the drive and already poured her a glass of wine. It's winking invitingly, the deep straw-coloured liquid so chilled that a blanket of condensation has wrapped itself sympathetically round the bulb of the glass. Prince, ecstatic to have them both at home again, nudges her hand insistently, asking for attention. For a few seconds the scenario brings comfort. She takes the wine, closes her eyes and sips. It's rich and buttery.

'Oh – you know,' she says noncommittally.

'What's up, Suse?'

He knows her too well. She can't hide the fact that something is troubling her, but he can't suspect that she's begun to wonder if she knows him at all – and even here,

47

in her own home, where everything is so familiar, she feels she can no longer trust the obvious. The blithe watercolour of glorious scarlet dahlias in its battered frame was her father's. Her father's? But he wasn't, was he, if the story is true?

She looks at the Lladró figurine that has pride of place on the bookshelves to the right of the fireplace, a small shepherd boy, idealised and untroubled. Not her taste at all, but it was her mother's knickknack and her mother's taste, and the shepherd boy was one of the few items she kept after her mother died. It has always seemed to Susie that the small porcelain ornament was the embodiment of her mother – sweet-natured, unsophisticated, honest.

Honest?

She has to ask him. There's no other way. An old cliché springs to mind: 'what you don't know can't hurt you'. But she does know now, or at least she knows partly, and the hurt is there already. She puts her glass of wine down so that he won't see her shaking hands.

'I know, Archie,' she says, the words as simple as she can make them.

But Archie's attention is no longer focused on her. He has picked up the tv remote and is flicking through the channels. Her life is imploding and all her husband can do is hunt through a sea of banality of someone else's making.

She waits. Silence can be as effective as speech.

In the end, he looks up. 'Hmm? Sorry Suse, did you say something?'

'Yes.' She has to say it again. '*I know.*' She invests the words with deep significance.

'Sorry? He asks, confusion on his face. 'You've lost me.'

Is there hope? There's still a tiny window left to her. She can close the conversation now and that will be the end of it. Life will return to normal and the truth –

whatever it is – will remain buried, in the graves of her parents, where it should be. But Susie, eyeing the dahlias, her gaze flickering over the china figurine, knows that the time for simple truths has passed.

She meets Archie's puzzled gaze. 'I had to show someone round the Parliament yesterday, a friend of my mother's around the time I was born. She said – I couldn't believe what she said, Archie, but I heard it very clearly—' Susie lets the words hang in the air, then finishes, her voice breaking, 'She said I was adopted.'

If she has the slightest doubt about the truth of the matter, it's dispelled now. Understanding floods into Archie's eyes like dye dropped into water, curling and spreading until it has changed colour completely.

Until now, there has been one element above all others that Susie can't believe: that Archie knew. But looking at him confirms the story. Like snow triggered into movement by some minor shock, her feelings pick up speed and slither down a bottomless slope. She knows that her life, like the landscape after an avalanche, has changed for ever.

I can't ask him to explain. I don't want to hear.

She stands abruptly. 'I'm going to walk Prince.'

'I'll come with you.' He tosses away the television remote and begins to rise.

'No, Archie. I want to be alone. I'll be fine. It's still light.'

He's going to argue and she knows she's being unfair on him, that in not allowing him to explain she's putting him into the worst of all positions. She knows, too, that he'll be concerned about her feelings and about how this revelation might affect their relationship. She turns away abruptly, angry at these new layers of complication in a world that has already become uncertain.

'Prince! Here boy!' As the dog scuttles eagerly towards her, she reaches for his lead. 'Go to bed, Archie.'

But she knows he won't. She knows that when she gets back, he'll be in his studio, losing himself in his music.

She sleeps fitfully until Archie slips in beside her, when the sheer familiarity of his presence brings enough respite from her thoughts to lull her into a deeper slumber.

It doesn't last long. Susie sees the dawn probe its way through the fabric of the curtains, the fingers of light poking into her sore eyes with an insistence that won't be denied. Ironically, maybe because she isn't trying to be quiet, she manages to get out of bed without disturbing Archie. In the morning light, the whole thing seems unreal once more, its reality grounded only in side-effects, in exhaustion and a mild headache lurking behind her eyes. She pads down the stairs, avoiding the creaky boards so as not to wake Archie. She needs time alone.

Her desk is in the corner of the living room, underneath a window that faces the trees at the back of the cottage. The opening is a deep one and the window itself small, the dimensions evidence of the age of the cottage. A few days ago – before Elsie – she found the time to pick a bunch of snowdrops, but now she notices that she has allowed their water to stagnate and become cloudy and they're already brown. Irritated by her neglect, she grabs the vase and marches through to the kitchen, drops the flowers into the compost bin and returns, without the reminder of her sloppiness, to her work.

She hears a faint creak above her head as she opens her briefcase and tries to settle to her papers. Archie is stirring. She knows she must talk to him because she needs to know his side of the story, but she shies away from the conversation, reluctant to start along the road of discovery.

I don't want to know.
You have to know.
It's too difficult.
You can't hide from the truth, now that it has found

you.

Archie knows how to take care of you. You can trust your husband.

But he lied to you. Her resentment is fuelled by sleeplessness. He's been living a lie.

She bins four brochures and two annual reports, their crisp, colorful, expensive covers gazing reproachfully out of the wicker basket at her. *Listen,* she fires back at them irritably, *I didn't ask for you to be posted to me. I'm too busy for you.* A sheaf of briefing papers from a large charity are more matched to her mood and she glances through them quickly, highlighting a sentence here, a paragraph there with a fluorescent orange marker.

Archie appears. 'You want tea, love?'

'Had some.'

'Ready for toast?'

'Okay.'

'Do you want it at your desk?'

Susie sighs and pushes away her papers. He's trying to be normal – but can anything be normal again? She stands and stretches. 'I'll come through.'

'Last night—' Archie starts when the toast is on the table. He's leaning forward.

She sees his hand start to move towards her arm, the movement conciliatory, and she jerks it back tetchily. *I don't want comfort. I want facts.* Archie's face is weary and she feels compassion but ironically this makes her react more angrily than she might have done.

'Don't—' *Don't touch me. Don't comfort me. Don't ... lie to me any more.* 'I need to know this, Archie. I need you to tell me your part in this story, so that I can begin to understand. I can see that it's true. What I want to know is, why was I never told? Why did my parents—' she breaks off, confused. She can't use that word. It isn't right. 'Why did Robert and Mary—' But that sounds unnatural too, she never called them by their first names, only ever called

51

them – thought of them – as Mum and Dad.

Who were they?

Who am I?

Her gaze drops, the effort of keeping it steady too much. Bizarrely, what she notices is the suit she is wearing – tailored business wear. It's a costume, designed to fit the part she plays every day because she's accustomed to using props. Until now, she's had every confidence in her ability to play her role. This morning, the grey wool looks out of place and unfamiliar. Did she really put it on just an hour ago? The fracturing of her reality has been so great that time itself has warped.

'Just tell me Archie,' she says wearily. 'I can't fumble around any more trying to make sense of this.'

He retracts his hand and crosses his arms as if he doesn't know what to do with them. 'What happened, Suse?'

He's always rational. Archie has only ever done one impulsive thing in his life, and that was to fall in love with her. *If he conspired to hide this from me*, Susie tells herself, clutching at the thought like a life raft, *there will have been a good reason*. Discuss this. Be calm. Archie will sort everything out.

'I had a tour booked,' she says, 'My paren— Their old neighbour, Elsie Proudfoot brought her grandchildren on a special treat. The little one, it seems, was adopted. Mrs Proudfoot told her we had something in common. She obviously thought I knew.'

'I guess it was a reasonable assumption.' He looks the same, sounds the same. But he can't be the same. It's not just the edges of Susie's reality that have begun to blur, but the very heart of it.

'But I didn't know. Archie, why didn't I know?'

He uncrosses his arms and rubs the back of his hand across his eyes. 'I found out just a few weeks before our wedding,' he says. 'Remember when we were going to go and give the minister the paperwork for the banns?'

'As father of the bride, I would like to take it upon myself to perform this last duty of care for Susan.' She quotes the words precisely, her voice lowered in imitation of her father's. Susie has a photographic memory.

'Exactly.'

The small front room in the Edwardian semi in Helensburgh. Neat as a pin, everything in its place, just as her mother likes it. There are flowers on the inlaid marquetry table in front of the window, their most prized possession. This is a special occasion. The wedding is imminent and her folks are in a spin over 'losing her'. Her mother fusses and clucks over Archie ('gaining a son'), her father is proprietorial but always loving.

'He went with you,' she remembers.

'Did you never think it odd?'

'Did you?'

Archie's brow furrows as he considers the question. 'I did, just a little, but what could I say – to my about-to-be father-in-law? I just went with the flow. But I soon discovered his purpose.'

'The birth certificate,' Susie says slowly, putting in place pieces of a puzzle she didn't know existed until a couple of days ago.

'He told me on the way to see the minister the next day. He swore me to secrecy.'

'But why Archie? Why didn't they want me to know? That's the bit that doesn't make any sense to me.'

'Think about it, Susie. You were twenty-five years old. I don't know whether they'd made up their minds never to tell you or whether it just never happened, but by that time it was far too late. They couldn't say anything. Especially not just before such a big event as your wedding. There was no way of knowing how you would react.'

'Is that what Dad told you? And you went along with it?'

Archie sighs. 'Of course I said they should tell you. It seemed absurd to me that you didn't know. But he was distraught, Susie, I'd never seen him like that. He said they couldn't bear for you to know, that it might change everything. He was terrified that you'd stop loving him.'

'How could he think that?'

'You say that, sweetheart, but can you be absolutely sure? How are you feeling now?'

'Terrible, what do you think?' She takes a large gulp of tea. It's almost cold.

'Exactly.'

'But I don't love them less, Archie, I'm just—' she searches for the word that most closely matches her feelings, '—bewildered. Shattered. Adrift.'

'And if that had happened then, just weeks before we married, what would you have felt?'

'I don't know! How could I know that?'

He purses his lips and sits back.

She's irritated with him for being right. 'So what then?'

'Then?'

'Did he have my birth certificate?' Archie is looking at her as if she has said something stupid. 'What? He must have, surely, to give to the minister.'

'Darling, what he gave the minister was an abbreviated certificate.'

Susie feels the blood draining from her face. 'I don't understand.'

'When they adopted you, sweetheart, they were able to apply for a new certificate, which showed the name they gave you, but not the full details of your birth.'

She says, dazed, 'It wasn't my birth certificate?'

'No.'

'So that's ... I'm not good at this, Archie, it's not something I've ever had to deal with. Did they know who I was? I mean, what did they know about my real parents?'

He shrugs. 'Your original birth certificate will be

lodged somewhere, I imagine. I'm not sure how you go about getting it.'

'My passport—'

'I applied for it, same time as I got mine – remember? The abbreviated certificate was fine for that too. Not sure if it would be these days, but back then, it was perfectly acceptable.'

'So you did,' Susie says, her voice limp. 'I never wondered why.'

Archie manages everything – her tax returns, all the household paperwork, the boring nitty-gritty details of life that she finds too tedious and that he takes in his stride. It occurs to Susie that somewhere in the glittering trail she leaves in her wake is a well-oiled mechanism that makes things happen. She should feel grateful, but right now all she can feel is suspicious. He hid this from her. What else might he be hiding? What other little lies – or huge deceits – has he concealed?

Robert MacPherson. Bobby. Her father. Not her father. The thought disorientates her so that she has no idea which way is up. She remembers Robert holding his arm out for her to hook hers through. The creamy lace of her wedding dress is like gossamer on the pale pink of her flesh, tiny pearls glisten in the sunlight through the net curtains. It's her wedding day and her father is so proud of his girl.

Not his girl. I was never his girl.

'Who else knew?'

'I'm not sure.'

'The neighbours?'

'One or two, maybe. They must have known. I assume she came back – your mother – I assume she brought you home one day ...'

'Dear God! Brought me home. Like a mail order baby. Early delivery for a small premium. We make every effort to match your specified colour but cannot guarantee size'

'Try to not be bitter, Susie.'

'Bitter? My whole reality has been turned upside down. Nothing in my life is what I believed it to be.'

Archie says nothing, probably wisely. He allows her to work through her feelings, which she does, until she feels calm enough to speak again.

'So Elsie Proudfoot knew.'

'I guess she must have done. Probably your mother made her friends promise not to say anything. I can only assume she thought you'd have been told at some point.'

'I can't believe they never did tell me, not right until they died. That they didn't even leave me a letter.'

'They loved you, Susie. They were just scared, that's all. They were worried that you'd turn against them.'

'Is that what he told you?'

'Yes. That's exactly what he told me.'

Fury fills her and she jumps up. She doesn't want sympathy, or understanding, or even love. She wants to wallow in her sense of betrayal, grope for its edges and boundaries so that she can begin to understand the extent of the damage.

'I trusted you Archie.' She starts to stride to the window, then turns abruptly and moves towards the door. 'I put all my love and faith in you. How could you have concealed this from me?'

Archie spreads his hands in a gesture of appeal. 'He made me promise.'

'And your promise to him meant more than your duty to me?'

'I did what I thought was best.'

'And you thought that leaving me in ignorance was best.'

He shrugs hopelessly. 'If you didn't know, it couldn't hurt you.'

'That's so facile, Archie.' She berates him bitterly for calling into play the cliché her mind has already processed. That isn't fair, but fairness doesn't seem to be a part of any

56

of this.

'It's not been easy for me—'

But she doesn't want to hear excuses.

Archie, watching Susie driving off, is struggling with the shock of her discovery. It had been a terrible secret to carry but he'd kept it, as her parents did, to protect her.

He walks slowly across the studio, knowing that settling down to work is going to be difficult.

Anger begins to burn inside him. Susie is being judgemental – but what about her secret? The one she believes, quite mistakenly, that she managed to conceal from him?

He smashes his hands down on the piano in a jarring discord and Prince yelps.

Dammit! He has an album to write, but the mood has gone.

Chapter Six

Energy flares off Mannie Wallace like sparks from a Catherine wheel on bonfire night. Restless, impatient, easily bored, she wore her parents out as a toddler and tested their ingenuity to its limits as she grew and demanded entertainment. Where her brother Jonno is introverted but thoughtful, her cleverness takes a different form. She has an unceasing curiosity married to an eagerness to ask questions. She burns to persuade the whole world to her own point of view.

These are all traits that are marketable and her career – quite naturally – took her into sales. Today, seeing Callum McMaster for the first time since his return from Courcheval, she's happy to tell him of the successes she chalked up in the week he was away. She ticks them off on her fingers, one by one, her expressive hazel eyes brimming with vivacity.

'Four weddings, Cal, six conferences – *six* – and three dinners, big corporate ones. Boss man he delighted.'

'No funerals?' Cal asks, the corners of his mouth twitching as he lifts his pint with anticipatory pleasure.

'You can't exactly put them in the forward diary,' Mannie says, her tone lofty, before spotting the teasing glint in Cal's eyes and shoving at him playfully. 'Oh, shut up, idiot.'

Cal grins and wipes his mouth with the back of his hand. He looks fit but relaxed, serenity itself by contrast to Mannie's ebullience. Where Mannie is dressed for business in a smart dark suit, pin thin heels and cream blouse – power dressing personified – he's wearing jeans and trainers and a Scotland sweatshirt. 'I'm just amazed you haven't persuaded the entire Royal Scots to divert their march down Princes Street and stomp in for a pint on the way to the Tattoo.'

'Now there's an idea,' Mannie laughs, tapping the side of her head thoughtfully. 'Note to self, call Army in morning.' She's only half joking because she will consider all ideas for exceeding her targets. Her bonus depends on it and her bonus is an important element of her salary.

'So it's been a good week, has it?'

'Didn't I just say?'

'Missed me, did you?'

His voice is teasing and she can't quite gauge his seriousness. This troubles her, not because she doesn't like Cal, but because she does. She picks up her cocktail and bends her face to the straw. She's beginning to feel edgy about their relationship. Why is that? *Because I'm scared*, she answers herself. *Scared you'll get bored?* No, not that, strangely, not this time. Be honest. *That he'll get bored.*

Callum McMaster is the latest in a line of nice boys she's dated, each one of them sexy and smart and fun. Mannie likes men, she loves great company, but till now, at any rate, she has enjoyed the thrill of the chase more than the slog of maintaining a long term relationship. She gets a kick out of new-minted love. She has made a habit of adoring her latest man, delighting in the pure pleasure of discovering what makes him tick, what he likes to read, what music he listens to, whether he loves (as she does), going for long walks along the beach on a winter's day or climbing Arthur's Seat as the sun comes up. There's nothing that gave her more joy than running her hands under his shirt for the first time, feeling the silkiness of the warm skin that lay beneath, or the hardness of the muscles of his chest.

But there's always a day when novelty palls and she discovers that the man's mind is less agile than her own, that he likes olives and custard, which she hates, or drinks only claret and is disparaging about chardonnay. If exercise between the sheets is the only kind he takes, it dulls the edge of desire. Or if he washes his socks in the bath or doesn't wash them enough, or – worst of all – if he is growing tediously possessive.

Callum is different. Cal has a life of his own. Cal goes skiing with his mates, is a fanatical cricketer in the summer and footballer in the winter and he puts his sporting commitments above her pleas that she hasn't seen him for ages. In short, Cal has managed to keep her interest alive for more than two years now, a fact that perplexes her greatly.

I need to dump him, her built-in alarm system is telling her. *Before he dumps me,* is the uncharacteristic thought she's trying to suppress.

Mannie shares her mother's need to be loved – her outward appearance of confidence can be misleading. She can be bossy, because she likes to be organised. And she's ambitious – which, she's well aware, many people see as pushiness. Underneath all of that, though, it's important to Mannie that people like her. And Callum does care about her, she knows that, though he's only casually demonstrative and not particularly vocal in the expression of his affection. She just doesn't know how much he cares and, right now, she isn't sure about how to answer him.

Seeing her uncertainty, Cal answers his own question. 'Just joking. I know you've been too busy to think about me.'

'Wrong,' she says teasingly, relieved a route has been opened up for her, 'I thought about you all the time, about how hard it must have been giving up all that boring techie stuff just to ski down those mountains every day.'

'I know,' Cal nods seriously. 'It was a difficult decision, but hey, someone has to do it or the ski resorts'll go out of business.'

'Slimeball.'

'Gasbag.'

'Thunderthighs.'

'Gutso.'

'Shut up!' She says it with humour, but she means it. Mannie doesn't have a weight problem – probably because she burns off the calories with her unceasing activity – but she does have a healthy appetite, eating voraciously and quickly. Sometimes she becomes embarrassed about this and Cal, who knows how to press her buttons, is never backward in using the trait to tease her.

She likes this in him. She likes that he's not deferential, that he feels comfortable in risking her possible displeasure, but somewhere there's a niggle that he might actually mean it, that her unquenchable appetite is a turn-off.

'I knew you'd be pleased to see me again.' Cal drains his pint and gestures to his glass. 'Another?'

Mannie nods cautiously. 'Why not? It's only Wednesday night and I've only got a very important meeting at eight thirty tomorrow morning.'

'Taking over the world?'

'Not the world. Just Scotland.'

'Ah.'

'Looking forward to that desk of yours?'

'Actually, yes. It was a great week, but the project I'm on right now is quite interesting.'

She groans. 'Don't tell me about it, I wouldn't understand.'

Callum grins again, the smile revealing pleasingly white teeth and, even better, reaching his eyes so that they fill with amusement. He gathers their glasses. 'Back in a tick. You can tell me your plan to take over Scotland when I've got another pint.'

Mannie watches him as he moves across to the bar, the athletic easiness of his movements reminding her of one of the many reasons she is attracted to this guy. He's sexy, and funny, and knows not to smother her with affection. He lounges against the bar, waiting to be served. He looks relaxed, full of understated confidence, buff. He turns towards her and winks and she feels a surge of desire. *Bugger it. He is bloody attractive.*

'Mind if we don't stay together tonight?' He's back, handing her a V-shaped cocktail glass, its contents pink and opaque, a wedge of lime balanced on the rim. 'I haven't even unpacked and I'm shattered.'

She feels the heaviness that comes with disappointment. 'I'm flattered you had time to see me.' Stop it, Mannie, he'll hate that. She curses herself and adds quickly, 'Don't worry, I was planning on washing my hair.'

Callum shifts closer to her and lays his hand on her thigh. 'So long as it's nice and clean on Friday,' he murmurs into her ear. 'And doesn't need any more attention till Sunday night.'

She giggles, relieved. Everything is fine between them. And that, she discovers, matters.

Later, after they have left the bar and Callum has headed back to his flat, she climbs on a bus to Portobello, where she shares a bright apartment overlooking the sea with her two friends, Jen and Myra.

As the bus trundles down Leith Walk, she notices that the number of Polish delis seemed to have doubled and that café society has reached even this rather run-down part of town. This is the neighbourhood for Asian stores, grocery shops, greengrocers, jewellers – specialists in 24-carat gold necklaces and huge, elaborate earrings. There are bric-a-brac shops and fabric shops, cheap bed stores and shops whose windows are so begrimed with dirt that it's unlikely that anyone actually knows what they sell.

When the bus turns right at the foot of the Walk, things

63

get worse. They're close to the old port, and it shows. Grubby Victorian warehouses, now empty and forlorn, display signs of such dilapidation that collapse seems imminent. Here and there, efforts are clearly being made to capitalise on brownfield sites by the construction of modern flats – too far from the liveliness and clutter of Leith Walk to be appealing.

The bus heads on east and the sea comes into view. This is the part of town she loves, where town meets shore. Here she can slough off the strains and pressures of work and relax.

Portobello, once a thriving small town in its own right, has long since been subsumed into the great city of Edinburgh. It still retains its own character, with its mix of Georgian mansions jumbled higgledy piggeldy alongside smaller period terraced houses, some with pillars, some painted, the paint inevitably peeling in the constant salty winds from the sea. As they near the High Street, Mannie phones Jen.

'You at home?'

'Yup. You on your way?'

'Back in ten. Will I get a bottle?'

'Not unless you're in for some serious drinking. I've only just opened one.'

'Pour me a glass, will you Jen?'

'That bad?'

Mannie laughs. 'Just being sociable. See you.'

She turns into their street exactly eight minutes later, and is in the new block in the ten she promised.

'Hi,' she says to Jen, kicking off her shoes and sinking breathlessly into her favourite chair by the window.

'Hi. Welcome home.' Jen pushes a button on the remote so that the sound on the television sinks to a mumble, while the pictures still flicker garishly. 'How was your day?'

Mannie giggles. 'Christ, we're just like an old married

couple. Good. Yours?'

'Bloody awful. Flaming Sonya's flaming skiving again.'

'What's she done now?' Mannie has heard many stories of the wrongdoings of Jen's temporary member of staff, a slovenly girl with no standards and less ambition.

'What has she not done more like,' Jen grumbles. 'She was meant to tidy up a big report, insert the graphs and tables, check the spelling, make sure everyone's bits were added in – perfectly straightforward stuff, wouldn't you think? She only put everything in the wrong place, ran a spell check that missed some glaring errors and misnumbered all the graphs. Then she stared at me when I told her off and claimed I was bullying her!'

'Sounds grim.'

Jen gulps at her wine. 'Did you see Callum?'

'We just sank a couple of drinks at the Opal Lounge.'

'Good hols?'

'The snow was perfect, apparently.'

'But he's glad to be back, he missed you.'

'Something like that.' She feels oddly reluctant to discuss Cal, but fortunately Jen moves seamlessly on to a topic she loves – herself.

'I splashed out today,' she confides. 'Popped into Harvey Nicks.'

'What did you get?'

'An Armani suit. It's wicked.'

'Let's see then.'

Jen unwinds herself from the futon and sets off eagerly to fetch her prize purchase. She almost collides, seconds later, with Myra Featherstone, the oldest of the three housemates.

'I've got some news,' Myra announces, her plump face portentous.

Mannie sits up, her face flushed in the warmth of the kitchen.

'Do tell. Or let me guess.' She surveys Myra mischievously. 'You're looking quite smug, so you're not about to tell us that you're mother's coming to stay again.'

Myra pulls a face.

'Okay, right about that then. Must be promotion?'

Myra, who totally lacks ambition, has been content in her secretarial job in a small lawyer's office in town for ever.

'No?' She sighs. 'When will you learn to tell people how great you are? They don't value you there. If they won't promote you, get another job. They'll give you a rise faster than you can say Myra Featherstone, bet you anything.'

Jen, coming back in, drapes her suit carefully over the back of a chair. 'She's right. Blow your own trumpet, or Mannie'll be in there blowing it for you.'

Myra looks apprehensive.

Mannie says, 'Has Graham finally popped the question?' Seeing the apprehension replaced with a blush of pride, she leaps over the low coffee table and envelopes her friend in a huge hug. 'He has? Fantastic! This calls for champagne.'

'Have we got any?'

'Always. Get it out, Jen. Then we can celebrate your suit too. Maybe you can wear it at the wedding.'

'Oh no, I'll have to get something new for the wedding,' Jen says, clearly shocked at the idea of missing such a blissful opportunity to shop. 'Fixed a date yet?'

Myra giggles and blushes even more. 'Give us a chance.'

'Where are you going to do the deed? What about the reception? I hope you're not going on a diet, My, you mustn't change a thing about yourself – promise? What does Graham think, is he terrified or thrilled?' Mannie's questions rattle off her tongue, her thoughts – as ever – flitting before her like butterflies that must be chased and

66

captured before they flutter beyond reach.

Jen opens the bubbly with a satisfying pop and hands out three foaming glasses. 'Here's to you and Graham. Let's see the ring, then. An emerald? Wow, I love it.'

Generosity is Jen's middle name, Mannie thinks. It's just a few weeks since her boyfriend of three years announced he'd started seeing someone else, leaving Jen in a state of devastation and offering the explanation for the splurge of retail therapy that is characterising her life at present.

'Bloody hell, Myra,' she bursts out, 'I've just realised – you'll be leaving the flat.'

They stare at each other, aghast.

At last Myra says, 'I suppose I will.' There's real regret in her voice before she adds brightly, 'But hey, nothing stays the same for ever.'

Chapter Seven

Mannie excuses herself and heads for her bedroom. Her mother texted earlier, she is to be on "Newsnight Scotland". Mannie is interested in politics, she and Jonno were raised with social consciences. These have developed depth and become more informed since Susie was elected to the Parliament.

She slumps happily on her bed, picks up the remote for the small set she keeps in there and presses Two. Her mother appears on the screen, the burnt-butter eyes intent, a stray lock of caramel hair falling untidily across her face. Mannie is distracted by it, longs to hook it to one side. She recognises the slightly wrinkled backdrop of Princes Street by night, sees the faint shadow on the street scene cast by the studio lights and deduces that her mother is in the remote studio in Edinburgh. The effect is ramshackle and cheap and she knows that this studio is hard to perform in.

To compound the difficulties, the interviewer is being extra caustic.

'So let me get this straight, Mrs Wallace, you're saying that despite the line your ministers were giving us, you are totally opposed to any cuts at all? Isn't that a bit unrealistic?'

'No, of course not ... I mean yes, I am opposed ... cuts are not ... should be opposed—'

Mannie sits forward. What is wrong with her? She looks tired, which is unusual, but worse, she's falling over her words and appears flustered and ill prepared. This is a subject she's as familiar with as her own navel, for heaven's sake.

'And finally, the Rivo Trust. I believe you are a Trustee? Can you explain the rumours we're hearing that—'

'I can explain nothing.'

Her mother has taught her to read body language and Mannie recognises the signs of defensiveness immediately – the shortening of the neck, the tensing of the mouth, the unflattering tightness around the eyes.

She presses the short dial on her mobile even before her mother is off the screen. 'Dad? What the hell's up with Mum?'

Her father is evasive.

'I expect she's tired.'

'She's often tired, Dad, but she's never like that. It's a poor performance.'

'Perhaps not quite up to her usual.'

'So what's the matter?'

Archie grunts but doesn't speak. He's being diplomatic, as always, but she senses something else too. What?

'How did your anniversary dinner go?' Mannie demands, sliding her questioning gently in a new direction in an effort to glean more clues.

'Fine.'

Fine. The bland catch-all. She recalls her mother's irritation with the words just a couple of days ago. Fine? Fine is all right. Fine is okay so far as it goes. Fine is—

'Da-ad,' she says reproachfully. 'Is that all you can say?'

'We had a nice dinner – though she didn't eat much and wanted to leave before dessert.'

Mannie is perplexed. 'God. Doesn't sound like Mum. Is she ill?'

'I don't think ill, exactly, Mannie.' There's a pause, then he says, briefly, 'Stressed.'

'Yeah but stress, Dad, we all do stress. How's the album?' She's momentarily distracted again, remembering to ask him.

70

'Coming on. I've got this tune in my head, I can't get the words for it yet. It's annoying me that they aren't happening.'

'Hum it.'

He obliges, but the line flattens the sound. 'Sounds catchy. What's stopping you?'

There's another small silence. Her father always gauges his words before speaking, so she's used to this, but it seems that today the pauses are longer than usual, the hesitations resonant with meaning.

'I don't know.' Now he sounds tired. 'Things.'

Mannie's antennae swivel alertly in his direction. Something is going on. She tries another gambit. 'How's Jonno?'

'Working. He's on a late shift again tonight.'

Mannie thinks quickly. 'Listen,' she says, 'I haven't been round in an age. Can I invite myself for lunch on Sunday?'

'Sweetie, since when did you have to invite yourself to your home?'

'I know – but you'll be there, all of you?'

'So far as I know.'

'Can I bring Cal?'

'His place is set already.'

God, her father is nice, she thinks, loving the unfaltering affection she hears in his voice. 'See you then. Make sure Mum gets some sleep – give her a hug from me, huh?'

'Any excuse for an extra embrace.'

Mannie laughs. 'Night then, Dad.'

'Night darling daughter. Don't let the midgies bite.'

The old phrase. Even now, even at the grand age of twenty-eight, she clutches the phrase to her and feels cherished.

On Friday Mannie and Callum meet friends, eat out, go

71

clubbing, but by Saturday she's tired. Cal suggests pizza and they eat it curled up on her bed, watching end-to-end DVDs of 'The West Wing'. Mannie is wearing grey joggers and a pink tee shirt that bear the legend, I love chocolate, Cal has on ragged jeans and a plain black tee shirt. Mannie tears off a slice of dough and fights with the cheese as it forms strings and threatens to slide off altogether.

'Forgot to say, is it okay if we have lunch at my folks' house tomorrow?' She speaks through the food but manages to make it look all right.

'Does that mean roast lamb and crumble?' He looks hopeful.

'I didn't check, but something like that, I would think.'

He munches on pizza and considers. 'But it does mean we'd have to get up.'

'By midday.'

'I guess.' He looks at her calculatingly.

'What?'

'I've been away a week.'

'So?'

'I'm just working it out. Whether a Sunday lunch is more tempting than another couple of hours in bed with you.'

'And?'

He balances his plate on his knees and counts the arguments silently on his fingers. 'Yeah. Lunch wins.'

'Sod!' she squeals, grabbing a pillow and swinging it in his direction. His plate slips onto the carpet, and the cardboard box with the remains of the pizza does a back flip onto the floor beside it as he grabs for her and wrestles the pillow away.

'Witch!'

'Buggering—' her mouth is stopped as he clamps his own down on it and she discovers that his body is pinning hers against the sheet. She wriggles in protest, desire

72

swamping her as she feels his erection against her thigh. Their kiss deepens and she tenses in pleasure as his hand sneaks under her tee shirt to find her breast.

This is what she wants. Callum McMaster mastering her. She thrills in the knowledge that right now, at least, it is what he wants too.

'Fat-arsed b—' she manages to pant as he stops for breath and she's punished for it as he flips her onto her stomach and gives her backside a couple of resounding smacks.

'Sadistic prick!' she squeals, her desire overflowing.

'Wild, wild woman,' he whispers, his voice hoarse with desire as he pulls her up towards him, peeling her tee shirt over her head so that her breasts fall free for his hands to cup. They are kneeling now and he's behind her, his arms pinioning hers so that she can't move, his breath hot on her neck. She throws her head back in pleasure as his fingers massage her nipples.

This is what she wants. This!

And then he is inside her and the intensity of the sensation ripples through her whole body so that she begins to lose all sense of where she is, she only knows that he is her king, her emperor.

Too soon, it's over, and they are sated. He lies along the length of her, gently, breathing heavily, his arms supporting his weight. She can smell the sharpness of his sweat and the sour smell of sex, a heady mix, bringing unexpected sweetness. Her face is on the mattress and she wonders, vaguely, where the pillow is, before remembering.

'More pizza, Vicar?' she asks politely, and he explodes into laughter behind her.

Mannie smiles a small, satisfied smile. She realises in that moment that this is perhaps the nearest she has got to true love in her twenty-eight years and she closes her eyes and recites a small prayer.

'Please,' she says silently to whatever divine being might be listening, 'let him love me too.'

On the small screen, Martin Sheen is dispensing wisdom and chilli.

They make love again, drowsy and hot from sleep, as the sun peeks through the curtain,. This time he makes it last for ever, his clever hands finding her most sensitive places and forcing her to an agony of desire before finally bringing her to a climax.

At eleven she fetches coffee and makes toast. At midday, reluctantly, they rise and shower.

'Will Jon be there?' he asks as they near Hailesbank.

'Think so. He's on late shifts at the moment so he'll probably appear just as Dad's carving.'

'How's the job hunt going?'

Mannie navigates a steep bend in the road. 'Same, I guess. Haven't heard differently.'

'Pretty hard on him. Hard on all kids right now.'

'Yeah. Glad I'm not starting out.'

Cairn Cottage is on a small back road just a mile short of Hailesbank, tucked almost out of sight behind the steep hill from the gateway. Its low roof appears when they are half way up the drive and the familiarity of it tugs at her. This is where she grew up. This is the anvil on which her soul was fashioned.

'The hens are still here, I see.'

'Of course. Bet there'll be eggs in something – sponge cake, maybe, or Yorkshire pudding if its beef. Hungry?'

'What do you think? A man can't live by shags alone.'

'Hush! Here's Dad.' They pull up in the courtyard as her father emerges from his studio. 'Hi Dad! Hi.'

There are hugs and kisses for her and an embrace for Cal.

From the kitchen comes the sound of barking and Prince emerges, his tail a blur, then her mother appears, her thick hair caught up in some kind of clasp, hooked out of the way for cooking.

'Mum! Hi. Can I smell lamb?'

'You can. Come on in. Hello Callum, you're welcome, as ever.'

'Do you mind if we go see the hens first? It's such a glorious day.'

'Do, yes. Jon's down there, mucking out.'

They walk back down the hill, following the curve of the contour so that they wind round the side of the house before turning back towards the hens. Jon is standing in the middle of the enclosure. He isn't shovelling muck or scattering straw, he's just standing, as if his mind is a hundred miles away and Mannie is momentarily concerned.

'Jonno!' she calls and picks up her pace.

He turns and waves. She clambers over the fence and accepts his clumsy, brotherly kiss on her cheek.

'Hi, Sis, what gives? Haven't seen you in an age.'

'Here's Cal.' She beckons him in. 'Great. I'm great.'

She grins at Jonno and watches impatiently as the men greet each other before she blurts out, 'I'm glad I caught you alone, Jonno. What's up, with Mum? I'm worried.'

Jon finishes his work by flinging a scoop of feed to the eager hens. 'Dunno. I don't see much of her. I'm usually asleep when she leaves in the morning and out when she gets back. I heard she fluffed her lines on "Newsnight".'

'Dad hasn't said?'

'Dad hasn't said anything very much. He's spending most of his time in the studio.' Just as they are about to round the corner of the cottage, he halts and turns. 'There's an odd atmosphere. You can't help notice it.'

'Atmosphere?'

'Like they've had a row. They're talking, but it's all very polite. You know?'

This is unusual. Her parents are not given to arguing

75

and if they do, it's a quick blast and then forgotten. Sulking is not in either nature, her mother sails gaily on her course, her father finds a way to make peace.

'I'm going to find out,' Mannie says, determined.

Jon and Callum look at each other and something passes between them, some shared understanding, perhaps, that it's in the nature of Margaret-Anne Wallace to find out and to forge ahead whatever the consequences might be.

She catches the look and says indignantly, 'What? Something's getting to Mum and it's showing. We have to find out so that we can help her.'

'Yes, Mannie,' they chorus and she gives a quick 'Pah!' of contempt as she turns and leads them towards the cottage, and lunch.

She has inherited at least some of her father's sense of diplomacy and waits till after they have eaten. She enjoys the lamb, has seconds, glares at Callum when he mouths, 'Gutso!' at her and tries to kick his ankles with her foot. But the table is too wide and her toes meet only an indignant Prince, who yelps and farts, plods into the kitchen and slumps down onto his bed.

'How's the job hunt going, Jon?' Callum asks, sinking back on his chair and laying an appreciative hand on his stomach.

Mannie glances at her brother with a flicker of apprehension. Jonno hates talking about his continued lack of success.

But Jonno likes Callum and he's smiling. 'As it happens I've got an interview next week.'

Susie exclaims, 'Jonno! That's fantastic. You didn't tell us.'

'Don't get too excited. It's only an interview. Anyway, I haven't really seen you.'

'Where is it, Jonathan?' her father asks.

'One of the big banks.'

'Sounds good,' Mannie says.

'Based in Edinburgh?' Callum asks.

Jon nods. 'Yeah. It's exactly what I want.'

'What's the job?'

'Graphic design assistant.' Jon smiles. It's been too long since he's been carefree and happy, Mannie thinks, not since his graduation. 'I 'spect it means tea-maker in chief, but I don't care.'

'Well, good luck, mate. You deserve a break.'

Mannie demolishes the apple sponge but rejects the offer of custard with an indignant 'Yeugh!' They're winding her up, everyone knows how much she hates the stuff. When their plates are clear, she can contain herself no longer.

'Mum,' she says, pushing her dessert plate away from her and her chair back a few inches from the table, 'What's wrong? You didn't look yourself on "Newsnight". I was quite worried.'

There is silence. Everyone is looking at her mother and her mother is looking nowhere. Mannie panics. I shouldn't have asked, she thinks, whatever it is, it's private. She feels tension in the atmosphere and senses a twisting of a thread between her parents.

'Listen, I—' she starts, but her mother is speaking again.

'You're right, Mannie. I've become distracted. It's very foolish and I'm going to have to concentrate to get through. I'm going to tell them, Archie.' She looks at her father as if she's made a difficult decision and needs support but isn't sure she'll get it.

That's new. Mannie is used to a completeness in understanding between her parents, now she senses – what? Some slight fracturing, perhaps, although her father says nothing, merely tips his head an inch in her direction.

'The other day, Mannie, at the Parliament, I had a visitor, a former neighbour of my parents, back in

Helensburgh. Remember, I told you? From her I learned something about myself, something I never knew.' She pauses, looks from face to face, skipping lightly over Callum's, examining those of her family. 'She told me I was adopted.'

Jonno is the first to speak. 'Adopted? Wow, that's news.'

Mannie can't take it in. 'I don't understand,' she says. 'How can you be adopted?'

Her mother goes on. 'At first I thought it was something I could just ignore. What difference does it make? But I find I can't. There are—' she hesitates and again there's that slightest of glances at her father, '—aspects I find troubling. But I need to get through this and I'm going to need your support and understanding.'

Jonno says, 'Well, it all happened a long time ago. What does it matter? Like you said, Mum, what difference does it make?'

A bubble is growing inside Mannie. A hundred questions need to be answered, myriad emotions have to be addressed. 'You're wrong, Jonno,' she cries, staring at her mother as if she has never seen her before, 'You're absolutely wrong. Don't you see? This changes everything.'

Chapter Eight

More emotion around the subject of her adoption is the last thing Susie needs. Jumping up from the table, she heads for the kitchen, juggling with a badly stacked pyramid of dishes. A plate slides sideways from the middle of the tower and crashes onto the slate floor. Mannie, following her in, stares at it horrified, but recovers in time to rescue the rest of the teetering pile. She slides past Susie to get to the broom cupboard. 'I'll get a brush and shovel.'

Susie is still motionless. 'It's not the plate I mind about,' she says in a dull voice, 'in itself. It's just that it was my mother's. And then when I saw it lying there, I remembered that she wasn't my mother at all.' She lifts her head and stares at Mannie. 'So now I can't decide whether I care that it's been smashed or not. Do you understand what I mean, Mannie?'

Shards of ceramic have to come first because of Prince, so Mannie bends and deals with the task, checking with care to ensure that no jaggy fragments remain that can slice into the dog's soft paws. She closes the lid of the bin and returns the brush to the cupboard, then puts her arms around her mother and says gently, 'It's a plate, Mum.'

In the silent world of the hug, the voices of the three men can be heard from the dining room. They're talking, Susie realises, not about adoption – but about Archie's new album.

'—five tracks pretty much there now—'

'—release date?—'

'—possibly a tour in the States—'

Mannie says, 'Right, Mum. Tell me what you know,' and busies herself with stacking the dishwasher. Prince benefits from a bowl of scraps and demonstrates his gratitude by farting again. Susie grimaces at Mannie and they laugh. If the laughter feels a little forced, they don't acknowledge it.

'As I said, Mannie, I only learned about it the other day.' Susie lifts a saucepan, wipes it with a cloth, and only then realises that it hasn't been washed. 'Damn. Look at this.' Upset, she holds up the tea-towel, smeared with brown. 'How could I do that?'

'It's not a problem, Mum. Just stick it in the washing machine. I'll do the pot in a minute.'

Susie pulls out a chair and sits down heavily, still clutching the soiled cloth. 'You can imagine how I felt. I couldn't believe there was any truth in it.'

'How come you didn't know? Didn't Gran and Gramps ever say anything? Didn't they even leave you a note? Nothing?'

'No, they never told me. And no, they never left me a note.'

'How weird. Why not, do you think?'

Susie shrugs. 'I guess I'll never know the answer to that. Maybe they were ashamed. Maybe they thought it would upset me.' She stretches out the cloth, pulls a face at the dirt on it, crumples it up again. 'But they told your father.'

Mannie whirls round and stares at her mother. 'They told Dad? So why ... Mum, why didn't he tell you?'

Susie shrugs, a small, helpless gesture.

'But—' Mannie turns back and stabs at a crust in the roasting tin. It shifts suddenly and her brush slips into the water with a soft splash.

'Yes,' Susie says, 'but.' In all of this, it is Archie's perfidy that hurts her most.

Mannie's mind has reverted to the wider implications. 'Have you thought about this Mum? I mean, have you really thought about what all this means? Gran and

Gramps weren't my grandparents at all. They were just some random people who happened to bring you up.'

Susie winces. Mannie, perhaps realising how hurtful her choice of words was, tries again, although her voice is thick. 'I mean, sorry, I didn't mean that, of course they chose you and I'm sure they wanted you very much, and I know you had a happy childhood so I guess – well, what does it mean to you? I'm trying to think about it—' she's gabbling now, almost incoherent, '—but there's so many questions, Mum. I mean, who am I? If they weren't really my grandparents, well, who were my grandparents? This *matters*, Mum.' She abandons the roasting dish and clings instead to the edge of the sink for support.

Her familiar world, thinks Susie, is shifting around her. Her own hurt forgotten for a moment, she rises quickly, finds a clean towel and gently turns Mannie towards her, folding her wet hands in the soft cloth. 'Mannie. Leave that, darling. Here. Dry your hands and come and sit down.'

'Mum?' Mannie's voice comes out like a wail. She is like a small child who has fallen and grazed her knee and is looking for reassurance. Susie squats by her side, slides her arms around her daughter and hugs her, wordlessly.

They are still hugging when Jonathan walks in. 'Any chance of a coffee?' he starts, then breaks off, seeing them. 'Oh. Everything okay?'

The sun streaming through the window falls directly on his head and his resemblance to her is striking. His rich brown hair, opulent with russet highlights, is my hair, Susie thinks. But Mannie? Her daughter's dark, sleek locks aren't Archie's wavy brown or her caramel curls. She looks at Mannie through new eyes and it comes to her, forcefully, that the line to her past has been ruptured and that behind her lies only darkness.

Jon puts water in the kettle, switches it on. He joins them at the table. 'Some news, Mum,' he says, his voice genial and untroubled. 'Guess it's been a bit of a shock, huh?'

'A bit,' Susie admits with a small smile.

'Does it matter?' he asks, running his hands through the already rumpled locks. 'I mean, you're still Mum.'

'Thank you,' she says with a touch of irony. 'I'm relieved to hear it.'

Mannie bursts out, 'Jonno! Can't you see? Mum's just found out that the people she thought were her parents weren't her parents at all!'

Jon shrugs. 'Yeah, but they were, weren't they? They wanted her, they loved her, and they gave her everything. And Gran and Gramps were great people. This doesn't change any of that.'

'Of course they were. Of course. I'm not saying that. What I'm trying to say is, well, not only is there a story behind this that needs to be told, but—' Mannie lapses, uncharacteristically, into silence and is rescued by the kettle, which has come to the boil and is hissing steam. It clicks off and emits a silly little whistle. Jon says cheerfully, 'Tea or coffee. Dad? Callum?' he calls out to the room next door, 'Tea or coffee? Mum?'

He takes orders, makes both, busies himself finding mugs.

When he disappears clutching a cafetiere in one hand and three mugs in the other, Susie says quietly, 'I know what you're thinking about, Mannie.' She is still holding Mannie's hand and now she strokes her fingers softly with her thumb. 'You need to know more. And we will find out more. One day.'

'One day?' Mannie looks at her, surprised. 'You mean you're not going to find out now?'

Susie shakes her head. 'Not yet, Mannie. It's all too new. I've got to think about this. There's too many questions—'

Mannie interrupts, fiercely. 'Yes! That's why we have

to find answers!'

'Possibly. I need to think about it all for a bit.'

'You need to think? What about me?' It sounds peevish and childish.

'Sweetheart, slow down a bit. I'm just getting used to this whole shock revelation. As I say, there are so many questions, I need to think it all through before I do anything.'

'What is there to think about, Mum?'

'Well, there are practicalities, like how do I go about finding out who I really am?'

Her voice has a slight tremor, and though she strives to conceal it, Susie's mind is in turmoil. She releases Mannie's hand and pours tea.

'From what little I know, I think it could be very difficult finding out who my mother was, or at least, tracking her down. She may not want to be found. She might have died. She might have covered her tracks. Or take another scenario – what if I do track her down and we don't get on? What if she's resentful, or frightened, or has her own family and she hasn't told them about me? What if she's not a very nice person? How do you think I would feel – we all would feel – about that? Shouldn't we maybe be just thankful that I had such loving parents, who really did want me? What if she has a family, and they are also rather unpleasant? Say she's very ill and wants to come and live here? Would we be able to take that on? It's a minefield, Mannie, all of this. I need to think about it very carefully before I do anything.'

Mannie purses her lips then chews on the lower one. At length she smiles. 'Well,' she says, 'I think the place to start is probably the Register Office. I'll call tomorrow and find out what the procedure is, will I?'

'Tch!' Susie laughs and shakes her head resignedly. 'How did I know you'd say that, my darling, impossibly impatient daughter? Well, just don't expect me to help you, Mannie, I've got enough other problems at the moment.'

On the way home, Mannie can talk about nothing other than her mother's news. Cal, who is driving, grunts occasionally but doesn't otherwise contribute to the one-sided flow of comment.

'Can you believe it, Cal? I mean, I knew she was bothered about something, because I've never seen her do so badly on the telly, but *adopted!* I told her, we've got to find out who her mother was and why she was adopted, we have to see if she's still around.'

Cal stops at a red light and Mannie pauses momentarily. When the light turns to green, she starts off again.

'I've just realised—' her hand flies to her mouth and she gives a small squeal. Callum inclines his head a fraction towards her, the motion showing enough interest to encourage her to continue. 'I could have a whole other family! Christ! I could have uncles, aunts, cousins, grandparents—' she tails off, having run out of relatives to consider.

As they approach Portobello, where Cal is dropping her back home, she's still in full flow. 'So I said to Mum, I'll do the spade work. I've got a few days off soon, I'll do whatever I have to do. I can start by finding out what steps we have to take. I guess it could be difficult, I mean, if her mother hasn't left many clues, but on the other hand, you never know, I could get lucky. We could know in a matter of days who—'

Cal interrupts gently. 'Mannie, slow down will you?' He decelerates for a corner and Mannie looks at him, surprised at the interruption to her galloping thoughts. 'What does your mother say about this?'

'Oh she's cool.' She qualifies this assertion. 'I guess. She just said she hadn't time to help me.'

'Don't you think you should let the whole thing settle

84

for a bit, while you mull it over? You've all survived pretty well for, how long, fifty-odd years in your mother's case, surely you can manage another few weeks while you work out – as a family – what steps you want to take?'

'Oh no, I don't think so,' Mannie says. 'We have to know.'

Cal spots a parking space outside Mannie's flat and manoeuvres the car deftly into it.

'Coming up?'

He switches off the engine, but shakes his head. 'I don't think so, love. I've still not caught up on washing and ironing and tomorrow's going to be hectic at work. I'd better get back.'

She is distracted – momentarily – from her plans by the memory of last night. 'Cal.'

'Yeah?'

'When you said we'd get a hot take-away I didn't realise you meant, like, *hot*.' She grins at him and is rewarded by a glint in his eye and a 'cheeky bitch' before he reaches across the handbrake and pulls her to him.

'Mannie,' he says when the kiss ends. He pulls away far enough so that he can focus on her face.

'What is it?' she asks, her insides still molten.

'Oh —nothing. Just be careful what you wish for, that's all.'

Mannie dismisses his caution with an airy, 'I will be, I promise,' retrieves her handbag and swings the door closed. She gives it a smart slap with the palm of her hand by way of farewell and bends to wave at him through the passenger window as he starts the engine again and pulls off.

As she opens the door to the communal stairway she can't wait to race upstairs.

Christ, she thinks, *just wait till I tell Jen and Myra about this.*

85

Chapter Nine

Susie has been an actress all her life, as far back as she can remember. Even before she enlisted the help of Elsie Proudfoot's son, Jimmy (and later of Karen) she used to line up her teddy bears and dolls on her bed and perform for them. When she was satisfied, she called her parents in and made them sit down to watch.

'I'm doing Cinderella,' she might say, having borrowed a pair of her mother's best court shoes for the purpose. Or, 'I'm Little Red Riding Hood and Daddy, you're to be the wicked wolf. Mummy can be the grandmother.'

Where did all that acting come from? Her mother, Mary MacPherson, endlessly patient, was round and rosy cheeked, with bright little currant eyes and dark hair. She always wore a 'pinnie', Susie remembers a generous floral affair that tied on over her skirt and blouse. The kitchen was her domain, not the stage. Her baking was legendary – not, sadly a trait Susie has inherited, though her standby biscuits, melting moments, have become a household staple.

So: no acting gene, no baking gene. No facility with numbers, like her father, no aptitude for crosswords. She doesn't look like either her mother, small and dumpy, nor her father, pin-neat and big-eared. These aren't matters Susie has ever stopped to think about. Her way of dealing with life is to fly through it at breakneck speed, fill it with people and entertainment and great causes – and why would you pause to consider something that hasn't even occurred to you?

But now everything is different. Her life has turned a

cartwheel, done a back flip, ended in a somersault and has left her sprawled on the floor like a clown doing acrobatics, not knowing which way is up.

'Don't expect me to help you, Mannie,' she said to her daughter. 'I've got too many other problems.' But the discouragement has clearly been insufficient to hold Mannie back, because she calls her at the Parliament a few days later.

'I'm really busy, sweetheart,' Susie says, 'Can this wait?'

'It'll only take a minute, Mum. Listen, I've spoken to this agency. The first thing you've got to do is get hold of your birth certificate, your real one.'

'How do I do that?' Susie can feel herself being dragged along in the wake of Mannie's forcefulness.

'You take this abbreviated birth certificate thingie along to the National Records of Scotland and they cross check it against something called the Adopted Children's Register.'

'Goodness, it sounds daunting.'

'It's all right, Mum, I'll come with you.'

Somehow, the offer doesn't feel reassuring. 'Can I think about it for a bit?'

'Mu-um.' Mannie is wheedling. 'You don't need to go any further if you don't want to, but at least you'll find out your real mother's name. You'd like that, wouldn't you?'

'I don't know.' She is finding the whole situation bewildering.

'Please, Mum? You'll need to get your adoption certificate from Dad. Do you think you can manage that?'

'I don't imagine it will be too difficult, Mannie,' she says, a little acidly.

Mannie apologises at once. 'Sorry, Mum, I didn't mean to be patronising. Or pushy. And you don't need to do this if you don't want to, but—' she lets the pause run on significantly.

'I'll think about it, Mannie.' Susie can see Karen waving at her, tapping her watch and holding up seven fingers. Seven minutes till the vote. She will have to run.

'Come on, Mum,' Mannie pleads.

Despite her daughter's attempts to pretend Susie is the person in control here, she's clearly not going to let this go. Susie is amused despite herself. No wonder her daughter is such a successful saleswoman.

Mannie presses on. 'I can't do this for you. You have to be the one to get the birth certificate.'

'Oh Mannie,' she sighs tiredly, 'I'm due in the Chamber in a minute, there's a late debate after that, then I'm hosting a reception and my email backlog has topped three thousand. I don't know, darling. I really don't. Can we talk about this later? In a week or two?'

'Mu-um. It's important.'

Susie sighs. 'Mannie, important is making sure that schoolchildren still have music lessons. Important is securing funding so that remote communities can still have visits from touring theatre companies. Important is enabling health care to reach people who need it and—'

'Spare me the politics, Mum, just say yes.'

'Sweetheart, I've got to go—'

But Mannie has never been a child to let go once she set her heart on something. 'All right, Mum. Just put me on to Karen, will you?' She says it sweetly, but there is no mistaking the determination in her voice. 'Then you can whisk off to press those buttons or whatever it is you do for the vote. I won't be a bother, honest.'

Maybe it is the wimp's way out but with only four minutes to go, Susie simply hands the phone to Karen and runs.

They're standing on the broad stone steps of the National Records of Scotland in Edinburgh's east end.

It's just a building. I'll just get a bit of paper. That's all.

89

A piece of paper can't hurt me.

She is trembling.

'Okay, Mum?'

Mannie is looking at her anxiously. Susie takes her hand and squeezes it, as much to get reassurance as to give it. 'Fine. Let's do it.'

A piece of paper, that's all.

They walk inside together.

'Have you ever used another name?' The woman at the desk asks the question diffidently.

'My maiden name, of course.'

'Other than that?'

Mannie nudges her.

'Oh – you mean – yes I, well I—' Now that it comes to it, nerves are threatening to overwhelm her.

'Mum knows she was adopted,' Mannie says smoothly.

'That's a relief.' The soft brown eyes flicker upwards, the jaw loosens, the hands visibly relax. 'Sometimes people aren't aware, you know,' the clerk goes on, leaning forward confidentially. 'It can be quite a shock.'

For the first time in weeks, Susie begins to think she has been lucky after all. At least she isn't standing here in this room, being landed with that bombshell.

A phone call. A wait. Another room, a stack of documents, a large ledger, another woman. 'I'm going to show you the Court Order for your adoption,' she says, her voice friendly.

It's going to tell me my name.

A hot hand slips into hers. 'It's okay, Mum.'

Christ, it's stifling in here.

She gathers her thick mane of hair with her right hand and scoops it back to allow what air there is to cool the back of her neck. Mannie is looking at her, excitement bubbling in her eyes. She has wound herself up over this thing like a tightly coiled spring. The energy stored in that coil is explosive, she's scarcely able to contain her

90

feverish anticipation. Just like she used to be before a big treat, Susie thinks, remembering her daughter at five years old, at seven, at nine, sleepless with suspense, almost sick with excitement before a trip to the zoo, the theatre, a sleepover.

The woman opens the ledger. At the top are her parent's names – Robert and Mary MacPherson. So far, so familiar. She can feel the sweat on her forehead, on her neck. Her nerves are strung as tight as on opening night in the West End.

On the next line, for the first time, she sees the name she was given at birth.

The woman points at the first column. 'This is your birth name.' Susie squints at the name. Brenda Miles. My name, Susie realises with a jolt. Brenda? I'm Brenda?

'This is your date and place of birth.' The handwriting is rounded and loopy, the 'R' stylised, as though the person writing the form has been bored, has wanted to fill their days with something more exciting than filling boxes on a form. 'Rottenrow' it says. She studies the word. Place of birth, Rottenrow Maternity Hospital, Glasgow.

'This is your mother's name.'

Joyce Miles, mother.

'And this is her signature, here.'

Susie stares at the page in the ledger, then wonderingly, she reaches out a finger and touches the signature. Her mother wrote this. Her real mother. Joyce Miles went to the Registrar to give this information. Was she there at the time, a tiny infant, wrapped in a shawl perhaps, peeking up at her mother, trustingly? Did Joyce intend to keep her at that moment, or was the decision already made to give her up for adoption? Who was with her? Joyce's own parents, perhaps, irate because of their daughter's illegitimate offspring? Or was she on her own, frightened and defensive? What were the circumstances that had made her give her daughter away?

A million questions teem in Susie's brain; all unanswerable. How could you give away a daughter?

She feels ill at the idea. When Mannie was in her arms, nothing could have separated them. She remembers the anxiety she felt at leaving her daughter for a few minutes, just to go to the toilet or make a cup of tea. Would she stop breathing before she could return? What if she put her little face into the mattress and suffocated? Or just reached out for her mother and found her gone? The complicated anxieties of motherhood, rooted in a need to protect. A primal urge.

Did my mother want to keep me? Was I torn from her arms while she wept – or could she not bear the sight of me, the cause of her shame?

Brenda Miles. The oddness of it shakes her. I am Brenda. I have a mother named Joyce. And I need to know why she gave me away. The need becomes a yearning, the yearning a fundamental necessity. And yet ... it frightens her. Susie feels overcome by an emotion so profound she cannot look it in the face. She is floating, falling, like an autumn leaf on the wind. Will she hit the ground lightly or fracture with the impact? So many unknowns, too many to contemplate. Her head is bursting with imponderables.

'Wow! You were called Brenda! How weird is that?' Mannie giggles. 'What else is there? No father. Bother. I hoped—'

'There was never likely to be a father's name, we knew that.'

'Yeah, I know, but still. Anyway, we've got Glasgow. That's something. I mean, you could have been born anywhere, I suppose.'

I could have been born anywhere.

A sense of identity, it comes to Susie, is fundamental to one's understanding of self. She already has a new set of parents and a new name – if she had discovered she was a different nationality as well, what might that have done to

92

her psyche? If she'd been French, perhaps, or Irish? Is it possible to feel any more insecure than she does already?

She glances at her watch and smiles at the official. 'Thank you so much for your help.'

'You can order a full certificate if you like.'

'Yes. Thank you. I expect I will, but I'm afraid I've got to go. I've got a Committee shortly.'

'Oh.' Mannie looks crestfallen. 'I hoped we'd have time for lunch. There's so much to talk about. I mean, we've got to decide what to do next.'

'Right now, nothing,' Susie says firmly, making for the door.

'Nothing? But we need to find out if Joyce Miles is still alive. Then we can find out your real story.'

'Suppose I don't want to know?'

'Of course you want to know!'

She is striding out briskly now, whirling through the building with fiendish energy, bestowing smiles and thanks on the security staff at the door, checking the time, desperate to just not think about it any more. On the steps outside she pauses, envelopes Mannie in a hug, then turns briskly and says, 'We'll talk soon, Mannie, I promise. Only not now, okay?'

She sets off briskly, striding across the junction and up South Bridge as if a horde of demons is after her and leaving Mannie staring after her and biting her lip.

The show must go on.

An old cliché, perhaps, but the adage is one that actors live by and now she is drifting like a twig in a fast-flowing current, Susie is able to draw upon the discipline of years of professionalism in order to get through the days – and not just edge through on a whisper of a prayer. By pulling on her skills, she is able to give performances that dazzle almost more now than at any time since her election.

It's a febrile beauty, like a last flare from a firework

93

before it fizzles out and dies. In the days following the discovery of her identity, she delivers a blistering speech from the floor of the Chamber, attacking the generally disliked Shadow Culture Minister; she appears on Question Time, where her responses are greeted with warm applause; and she speaks at a School conference where she seems to be idolised. It's heady stuff.

At home, the story is a very different one. Far from being brilliant, her relationship with Archie has deteriorated into a series of sullen silences punctuated by the kind of humdrum exchanges necessary for the smooth continuation of everyday life.

'Have you got any washing?'

'Did you pay the electricity bill yet?'

'What day do they come for the plastic recycling?'

Other than that, their paths seem to cross less and less. Susie is putting in ever longer hours at work, caught up in a whirlwind largely of her own making, and Archie is spending more and more time in his studio.

'Do you want to shower first?' Archie asks when they retire one night, unexpectedly, around the same time.

'No, no, you go,' Susie says, thinking back on the times when they would have squeezed in deliciously under the hot jet of water.

'It's okay, I'll wait,' Archie counters, coldly polite.

So she sighs and gives in. When he joins her in bed, the weird courtesy continues across the five feet of mattress. He climbs in, turns out his light and rolls on his side with a grunt, facing away from her. After half an hour of listening to his breathing and trying to work out whether he is awake, she reaches a hand out tentatively towards his shoulder. It's only half way there when she retracts it again, awkwardly, as the now familiar sense of betrayal overwhelms her.

Discussing the adoption has become deeply difficult, with Archie turning defensive if she raises the subject. His wariness piles up wretchedness and it has become easier not to talk about it at all.

One Sunday morning a few weeks after the visit to New Register House, Susie is sitting at the kitchen table in her dressing gown, jotting notes for a speech. Archie, who had gone into Hailesbank early to pick up the papers, pushes open the kitchen door and tosses a heavy bundle onto the scrubbed pine surface.

'Everyone's talking about you.' The papers land with a thump, the draught lifting her notes.

She sighs at the disruption and reorganises the papers into a neat pile. 'Dare I ask why?'

He extracts one of the magazine supplements and holds it out to her. On the front cover, she sees her own face staring back, her dark gold eyes unfathomable, her creamy skin shining against a cloud of brown-gold hair. The photographer has made her look like a pre-Raphaelite angel. It's an oddly fey look.

'Where Her Heart Is: Susie Wallace on Life, Love and Politics'.

She snorts. '"Life, Love and Politics"? What do I know about such things? That interview was done ten weeks ago'

'Great photograph.'

Susie is overcome by irritation. She snaps back at him, 'Great photograph of the actress known as Susie Wallace. I don't think it reflects anything at all about the person called Brenda Miles.' She bends to her notes again, her hair falling forward so that it masks the deep lines etched on her forehead and the troubled look in the notorious golden eyes.

'Oh come on, Susie.'

Something cracks. 'Come on?' She seizes the magazine and shakes it at him. 'What do you think I feel like, Archie? Hmm? Seeing this? This—' she searches for the word, '—this arrogant nonsense?'

She opens the magazine, thumbs through the pages until she gets to the feature, scans down the columns, begins to read. '"I like nothing better than to sit round a table with my husband Archie and my two fabulous children. Family means everything to me." Ironic don't you think? Or this – "In Susie Wallace's sweet little cottage home, there are treasured mementos of her parents, who sadly did not live to see her become a Parliamentarian. Her heritage, she says, is of huge importance to her. She likes to think of her past, and where she has come from, and what she, in turn, is handing on to the generations to come."'

She tosses the magazine onto the table. 'Jesus, Archie. Such crap. What does it all mean? What does anything mean any more?'

'There are plenty of things that haven't changed, Susie. We're still all here – your family.'

'You? My trusted husband, you mean?' Her voice is rising with mounting hysteria and she is ready for a row. A big blow-out might serve to clear the air. Until now, her way of dealing with the situation has been to hide behind activity, lots of it. She has thrown herself into the role of politician, has hidden – as she does with such practised ease on stage – behind a mask of contrivance. No point in concealment from Archie. He knows her too well. But does she know him? Has she ever really known him?

Archie sighs resignedly. 'Susie, we've discussed this. What was I to do? I was caught in a trap—'

She doesn't want to hear the voice of reason. She doesn't want explanation, excuses, common sense. She wants an argument. She raises her fist and thumps it down on the table so hard that the mugs and teaspoons jump and rattle.

'You *lied* to me.'

'I didn't lie.'

'You lied by omission, Archie, for Christ's sake let's

not split hairs.'

Archie stands perfectly immobile. She knows him of old, he is about to turn and leave. He hates arguments, he will walk away every time. Exasperated, she starts to move towards him, meaning to force him to stay and engage with her, when another voice brings her up short.

'Mum? Dad? what's up?'

Jonathan is standing in the doorway of the kitchen, his hair rumpled, his face flushed from sleep. Susie stops on the spot, her bubble of anger popped as she takes in the anxiety on his face. He's a small boy again, six years old and fresh from a nightmare, needing cuddles and reassurance. She wavers uncertainly. Her need is for exorcism through confrontation, but her men cannot bear this.

While she hesitates, Archie turns to the door. 'I'm going to the studio.'

Jon looks from one parent to the other, distraught.

'It's all right, Jonno,' Susie says heavily. 'Just a spat, that's all. You want some tea?'

But her son shakes his head and swings away. 'I don't think tea's going to help.'

Susie slumps back onto her chair and tries to focus her attention on her work, but she'd dropped the magazine across her papers and has to move it. She glances at the offending cover, then flicks to the inside again. It's not just about her, she realises, it runs across a number of pages and is a broader feature about Scottish actors headed 'Six of the best'. The journalist's choice starts with an actor called Jimmy Scirocco, the Irish-born madcap who made Scotland his home and whose once dazzling career was blighted by drink and womanising. A charmer, a wit, an actor of scintillating talent – and a wasted soul. The corners of her mouth lift a little, because being linked with this man is a real tribute. Ewan McGregor features, naturally, alongside Sean Connery and Alan Cumming.

Who is the sixth? She turns the page.

Maitland Forbes.

At once she is back in time. It's twenty-nine years ago. She has been married to Archie for only a year and she's away from him, filming. It's her chance for a breakthrough – this film has the potential to make her a star. It's a costume drama about the Highland Clearances and they're on the island of Mull, on a beautiful beach, its sands pure white in the summer sun. She hasn't yet met her co-star, though she knows who Maitland is. His face is for ever in the press because of some mad escapade, a drunken night out with the boys or – more recently – the news that shattered his army of fans: his wedding.

He'll be fresh from his honeymoon. Will the glorious Serafina be with him? Susie anticipates arrogance and is prepared to dislike him. She expects disdain. She is prepared for pretty much anything – except for falling wildly, crazily in love.

She slaps the magazine shut and tosses it onto the recycling pile.

Has Archie seen the article, or did he only look at her photograph on the cover?

She pulls her work towards her determinedly. It was a long time ago and anyway, Archie never knew.

The angry exchange that day marks the beginning of a further decline in her relationship with Archie. In a lifetime of being close, Susie finds the growing estrangement between them difficult to live with, but she has no idea how to bridge it.

Archie takes a duvet and some bedding from the spare room and decamps to the studio.

'The worst thing is,' she confides to Karen over a coffee in the Garden Lobby of the Parliament, 'I hate sleeping on my own. We've never been apart for more than a few days when he's been away on a gig, and I hated

98

that. I feel bereft.'

They're snatching a brief break between meetings. Karen stops burrowing through the stack of files she has piled onto the low coffee table and gazes at her, the cool grey eyes appraising. 'Can't you talk to him?' she asks sensibly.

But good sense doesn't come into it. 'No,' Susie says flatly. 'Sadly, I can't.'

'Talking about it really seems the only way forward. I know you feel he kept something really important from you, Susie, but I'm sure Archie sees it differently. I mean,' she rocks back in her seat and holds Susie's gaze, 'Archie's the straightest man I know. He must have had good reasons for keeping it from you, don't you think?'

'Oh sure. But they all seem to weigh on the side of my parents – my adoptive parents, I mean. And rest on the glib assumption that if I didn't know...' her voice trails away.

Karen glances at her watch. 'We've got ten minutes before your Cross-Party Group meeting. Can we talk about this later? I need to go over these papers with you.'

'Of course.' Susie takes another gulp of coffee, tries to focus on the job.

Maybe Archie was right.

Chapter Ten

Jonathan has a headache. It feels like the beginnings of a migraine, but it could be a side effect of the ill-tempered atmosphere in the house.

He wanders into the bathroom and opens the cabinet, searching for his migraine pills. If the thing blows up, he'll have to call off work tonight, and that will be bad news, because if he doesn't work, he doesn't get paid. Not that there's much to spend cash on at the moment, since he split with Claire he hasn't had another girlfriend.

There have been a couple of parties where he managed to hook up for a one-nighter. Good for the ego to know he can still pull when he exerts enough effort to charm, but hardly satisfying.

My fault, he thinks. How can I even begin to care for someone else when I can't stand myself?

He dismisses the thought. It's not down to me: it's all down to my circumstances.

He swallows a couple of pills and prays he's taken them in time. Most of his friends, he reflects, have jobs already, some have moved away, others are in long term relationships. He's left with itinerant Aussies and the odd student. Not that he's desperate for a girlfriend, but a bit of congenial company would be nice.

He closes the cabinet door and scowls at his reflection in its mirrored front. Like his father, he analyses what he sees with logic and reason.

a) I look a bit like Mum.
b) I think more like Dad.
c) I thought I inherited my caring side from Grandma

MacPherson, Mum's mother – but it turns out she wasn't her mother after all.

So d) who was? And e) what was my real grandmother like?

Fuck it.

He turns away. His first instinct was right. What does it matter anyway? What is, is. We are who we are.

Outside, the weather has changed and what looked to be a wet morning has transformed itself into a sunny one. Jonno grabs a paperback and decides to sit in the sun. Perhaps a little warmth on his face will burn off the migraine. He'll give it twenty minutes and see if the pills work.

On the bench outside the kitchen door, he can't concentrate on reading. Instead, he ponders the question of inheritance. He isn't much given to talking about his thoughts or feelings, but this stuff has been subtly eating away at him ever since the great revelation.

It's been affecting them all in some way or other. Take Mannie, for instance – she's gone absolutely mental, pushing Mum to find out about her birth mother with typical Mannie impatience. Mum's refusing to do anything at all and worst of all, she seems to have fallen out completely with Dad.

Jon swishes at a fly that's buzzing irritatingly round his head. Being jobless is bad enough, but having his parents at war with each other is much worse. Not even at war – if they'd just shout at each other and make up, it'd be a lot better. But that isn't their way, and never has been. His mother has a temper. It can flare suddenly and magnificently, and is a thing to be feared, but it'll die just as quickly, and hugs and tears and declarations of love will follow. You know where you are with that kind of temper.

But his father is different. His father hates arguments. He would rather put on his jacket and head off for a long walk than face confrontation of any kind. With his father, temper turns inward and morphs into moroseness.

Just like me.

Jon closes his eyes. Half an hour and he'll have to set off for his shift. Bar work doesn't faze him, but he doesn't get much out of it either. He wants to put into practice all the technical expertise he learned at college and he yearns to find an outlet for all the ideas that buzz round his head. Even though he sits at his computer for hours, he's frightened he'll lose his hard-earned Photoshop skills or forget the intricacies of Illustrator and Dreamweaver.

He wants a challenge, not mindless pint pulling. And how can he even think of looking for a new girlfriend until he has some self respect?

A light toot of a car horn rouses him from his reverie. He opens his eyes, squints into the sun and prays the pills will take their effect soon. The postie's van is coming up the drive.

'Hi, Jon!' Mike, the postman, is a cheerful guy who is for ever trying to persuade Jon to give up bar work in favour of the postal service. He steps out of his van with a bundle of mail and leans on the roof to watch Jon sift through it. Any break from tedium. 'Saw the letter there. Franked by the Bank.'

His curiosity is evident as Jon lifts the envelope in question out of the pile.

Jon slits it open and scans the letter, tosses it aside. 'Shit,' he mutters.

'Another rejection?' Mike guesses sympathetically. 'Give up that lark, Jon, I keep telling you. Join the Royal Mail. Good hours, pay's okay, no worries to take home with you. And you won't be stuck in an office. What more could you want?'

'I'll think about it, Mike,' he promises.

Right now, it sounds like a good option.

He gives up on the idea of going to work and flops into

bed with a blinding headache. By the time his mother comes in much later, he has managed to emerge from his pit and curl up on the sofa.

'Hello, Jon,' he hears her call, her voice surprised. 'Not working tonight?'

He's channel-hopping, holding the remote out in his right fist and flicking randomly up and down the air waves, not settling long enough on any one programme to assess whether it might be of interest.

'Jonathan?' her voice goes up a notch, clearly unsure whether he has heard her.

He grunts briefly to acknowledge her presence. His migraine has lifted, but has left a ghost of discomfort which is eased by minimising movement. He hears his mother drop her briefcase on the kitchen table and come into the living room. 'I said, aren't you working?'

It has been a long day. Somewhere about six his migraine receded but it left him deeply pissed off in every way – health-wise, job-wise, financially and romantically. Weakened with the pain, he abandoned all efforts at fortitude and resorted to the bottle. Not the best answer, but hey—

He has a beer in his left hand and there are three empties lying messily on the carpet. He watches a trifle groggily as his mother stoops to pick them up, then perches on the arm of the sofa.

'—built with typical German precision—' comes the unmistakeable voice of Jeremy Clarkson, before Jon flicks the remote again and some gem-shopping channel appears.

'Nope.' He doesn't mean to be so curt, but it's all he can manage.

'Not on the rota?'

'Didn't feel like going in.'

'Are you unwell?' He sees her eye the empties.

All he can manage is a grunt. He is dimly aware of her walking to the kitchen and putting the bottles in the

104

recycling box, then coming back in. God, he thinks fuzzily, she's going to quiz me.

Apparently he is right, because she crosses to the television and switches it off at the set, then turns to face him.

'Hey!' he grunts crossly, propping his body up onto his elbow so that he isn't completely supine.

'And don't tell me you were watching it, because quite clearly you weren't,' she says. 'So are you going to tell me what's up?'

How does she do that? Put her finger on things so accurately. Is it a thing all mothers do – or just his mother? He says, 'Nothing,' not meaning to be surly, just unable to find the right words.

'Did you hear back about the job at the bank?'

'Yeah.' He'd dismissed things lightly to Mike the postie, but the rejection has cut more deeply than he cares to admit. On another day, he might have tried to discuss it with his mother, but today that's beyond him.

'I take it they didn't offer it to you.'

'They said I didn't have enough experience.' He turns his face towards her, aggrieved. 'How am I meant to get experience if no-one will give me a job?'

His mother sighs. 'You'll get something, love. You just have to believe it.'

He purses his lips, turns his head away from her, says nothing.

'Jonathan. Is that it? Is that all that's troubling you?'

'I'm bloody tired of the atmosphere in this house.' The words come out in a rush, with a greater vehemence than he expected. 'You and dad – what the hell's wrong with the two of you? Can't you just, I dunno, kiss and make up, for fuck's sake?' He feels like a petulant child, wanting everything to be perfect between the two people he loves most in the world, knowing that life isn't like that.

'Oh sweetheart,' she sighs, sinking down beside him

105

and enfolding him in her arms, 'There's nothing I'd like better.'

Grown man though he is, Jon allows himself to be hugged. His solidity feels like a deception: flesh and bones covering a fragile soul.

'Saw you last night on the box, Mrs Wallace.' Danny Robertson, one of the security guards, grins at Susie as she comes into the Garden Lobby. 'Great stuff. Irene was in floods.'

'Thank you, Danny.' Susie stops to acknowledge the compliment.

'That bit where you were thrown out by your family – shocking. How could they do that to you?'

'Home, Where My Heart Is' is based on a book of that name, set in the 1930s, about a young woman from a slavishly respectable middle class family who was thrown out when she found herself pregnant. It was dramatised as a series of five episodes, filmed more than twenty years ago. Susie played the role of the young mother, Jessica Playfair. After a lengthy wrangle over repeat fees, the drama is finally being rescreened.

'Changed days,' Susie smiles. 'Doubtful if it would happen now but—' She's desperate to go. Danny means well, but the last thing she wants to do is talk about the series. 'Home' is proving too close to home by a long way. She can feel emotion welling up in her as she speaks and she turns away from Danny and resumes her brisk stride. 'Give my best to Irene,' she calls over her shoulder.

How many people today will mention the drama? And how can she school herself not to react emotionally?

Upstairs, Karen smiles as she turned into her office. 'Morning, Susie.'

'Have you been here all night?' Susie asks dryly. 'What's new?'

'Four invitations to receptions, half a dozen magazines

for info, a note from the Presiding Officer about conduct in the Chamber and a couple of nice thank you cards for the launches you did last week. Oh – and a reminder from Facilities about the unseasonably cold weather. All on your desk.'

'What's Facilities saying?'

Karen laughs. 'The usual. Reminding us to use the temperature controls properly. Are you remembering your meeting with the Theatre Trust people at nine?'

'Yup. What else mustn't I forget?'

Karen reels off the list of her appointments for the day. 'Oh, and I've already taken a call from Hugh Porteus at Rivo.'

'About?'

'He wouldn't say.'

Susie sighs. 'I guess I'd better find out what he wants.' If there's one good thing about her job it is that it takes her mind off everything that is happening at home. She has to keep concentrating on what she's doing, because slips and trips can be horribly public.

'Hugh? It's Susie. How can I help?'

The chairman's voice coming down the line is a little less relaxed than normal. 'I'm calling all the Board, Susie. It's not great news, I'm afraid. I was concerned about things after our last meeting—'

'Yes, there's been a few rumblings in the media. I'm afraid I didn't handle them perhaps as well as I should have.'

'—no, no, you've been a model of discretion, as ever. But I know you were concerned about this second change of auditors, as were some other Board members. Possibly we should have pursued it a bit more vigorously at the time, but of course, Ricky was so reassuring.'

'What's the problem? Don't tell me the grant isn't going to come through?'

'I think it will, though it's not through yet. No, I'm

afraid there seem to have been some irregularities. I had a friend of mine look through the accounts, I do hope you don't mind, but as I said, I was a little uneasy. We had something similar, one time, hmm, with a verger, I recall.'

Hugh Porteous is a decent enough Chair, Susie thinks, but liable to tell long stories that have no clear ending. She tries to get him to focus. 'Irregularities?'

'Yes, indeed, as I was saying. Of course, my friend has no locus on this, we'll have to take the matter through the auditors, but he did flag something up. It rather looks as though some funds have been, shall we say, hmm, diverted.'

'Diverted? What does that mean?'

'We're not entirely sure yet. We think that the money given to us for the Youth Literacy Project was switched to do that roof repair. It may have been done with the best of intentions, of course, but it's quite irregular and there's now a possibility that we may be asked to return the grant.'

'How on earth could that have happened?'

She can almost hear him shrug. 'Truths, half-truths and lies. We were told an officer had been appointed and had started, but it seems that's not the case. I had a long session with June Mackintosh—'

'I thought she'd been made redundant?'

'Indeed. But she came to me in great distress, with some tales that I should have listened to much earlier. June's a very loyal person, but it does look, hmm, as if the redundancy was perhaps the result of her threat to expose mismanagement.'

'Goodness. How dreadful. This is Ricky's fault?

'Possibly. We need to do a lot more work, I'm afraid. I'm just flagging it up. It was June who has been dropping hints to the media, apparently.'

'Really?' It seems her instincts might have been right.

'Hmm, yes. She feels she wasn't being listened to.

However, rather than go any further, she decided to try to get my ear again and I'm very thankful she did. There may be a chance we can rectify the situation. It will mean a lot of meetings with the new auditors, I'm afraid, and probably some rather difficult meetings with Ricky.'

'Oh how dreadful. Do you want me to do anything?'

'Not for the moment, I'll keep you informed, of course. But I'm afraid there's one more thing. And it's not good.'

'Oh?'

'It seems that the Trustee Indemnity Insurance policy has not been paid up.'

'What?' Susie is appalled.

'There may be some exposure to the debt.'

'By us? The Board?'

'The trustees, yes.'

'What are we talking about? Hundreds? Thousands?'

'I don't really know at this point. I'm sorry, Susie. It's a pickle we should never have allowed ourselves to get into. Let's hope we can get ourselves out of it without too much damage, hmm.'

'Right. Well—' What can she say? 'Thanks for letting me know, Hugh. Keep me posted, will you?'

'Of course. Goodbye.'

Susie puts the phone down, dismayed.

'Bad news, I gather?' Karen asks from across the room.

'Not good.' She glances at her watch. Five to nine. 'I'd better go. I'll fill you in later.'

She flees in a wild cloud of russet-gold hair and with an energy that is more frenetic than useful. So much for work providing a welcome diversion from problems at home – her life seems to be going down a thorny path at the moment. Well, like Hugh Porteous, all she can do is pray she can get herself through it without too much damage.

That night, Susie can't find rest. She thinks of her father, calm, sensible, kind, and wishes she could talk it all over

109

with him, before remembering that he never was her father. She runs her fingers through the thick tangle of her hair and presses her knuckles against her forehead. Why did they never explain?

It hurts.

Jonathan is unhappy. Mannie is eager to understand where she has come from. And she needs to find a way of communicating with her husband again.

No more blame. This is not how she wants her life to be. Maybe the only way of uniting her family once more is through confronting her own fears and insecurities.

The darkest hour of the night passes, and with its passing comes a new resolve. She will try to find Joyce Miles.

In the morning Susie sits down at her desk, checks the number she has written down and lifts the phone. She clears her throat. She is unimaginably nervous. Why? It's just a phone call.

'Hello, yes. I'm looking for my mother,' she says, her voice coming out like sand scratching on pebbles. 'Goodness, how silly that sounds.' She laughs edgily. 'As if I'd inadvertently left her in the supermarket or lost her at a funfair.'

The woman on the other end of the phone is sympathetic. 'It's all right, we get this all the time at Birthlink. I'm Helen, would you like to tell me your name?'

'Susie.' Susie hesitates, considers adding her surname, then chooses to shelter in anonymity. Gathering up all the courage she can muster, she blunders on. 'I understand you might be able to help.' God, she sounds unhinged.

'Of course.' The woman makes the request sound as matter-of-fact as if Susie is reporting a mislaid umbrella. 'That's what we're here for. Can you tell me–what details you have? Your full birth certificate?'

Susie clears her throat. 'Yes. Yes, I now have that. I only discovered ... I'm fifty-five ... quite recently ... you must think this very strange, sorry—'

'It's fine. It doesn't sound strange.' The voice is very gentle. 'So, you have your birth certificate – have you been able to get any more details?'

In a week when pressure at Parliament has been high, Susie has somehow found time to drop in to the Records Office. Constrained by the weight of work and the endless demands on her time, she rushed in, checked her sealed record, obtained a copy of the court order finalising her adoption and was back out before she had time to examine what she was feeling.

Every word of the birth certificate is etched into her mind, the rounded Rs, the names Joyce Miles, Brenda – Brenda! Her passport to the truth. Another lump of apprehension has clogged her throat and she clears it again.

'I have copies of the Court papers.'

'Good. That's all excellent.' There's the briefest of pauses, then the voice says sympathetically, 'Would you like to come in? Tell us about your story? Sometimes people find this easier face to face.'

Tact and understanding envelop Susie.

'I'd love to,' she says.

Chapter Eleven

Mannie flies into City Airport in the early evening. Gazing down from the small aircraft at the winding loops of the Thames far below her, she reflects that the contrast between the huge skies of Scotland and the heavily developed square miles of stone, concrete and brick that house some nine million people in Britain's capital city could hardly be greater.

London. Love the place or loathe it – and Mannie does both in almost equal measure – she is already looking forward to the buzz that is the annual Confex fair. Soon the pleasure of striding yesterday with Callum along Yellowcraigs beach in an ambitious early spring sun fades into little more than a delightful memory.

Mannie's world revolves around financial goals, customer satisfaction measures, brand standards, and above all, targets, targets, targets. Her normal week – if such a thing exists, consists of a dozen or more calls to drum up new clients, a great deal of talking and listening, a lot of schmoozing with new and existing customers and far more meetings than she cares for.

As sales director, she also has to line-manage a small and ambitious team, all of whom are in London this week. They are good. Mannie makes sure of that. Her manager, co-ordinator and two researchers are as sharp and efficient as she is. Though she'll need to manage their ambition too, she thinks as she inspects the stand they have put together in the ExCel centre. Hungry salespeople can be ruthless and in her job the demands – and the rewards for success – are high.

'What do you think?' Sylvia Collingwood, the youngest member of her team, looks anxious as she surveys their handiwork.

'Fantastic. Great job,' Mannie says warmly. She pats the small fan of smart hotel brochures laid out prettily on the pristine damask cloth. 'Are there plenty more of these in the back? And presumably the flowers will be changed daily?'

The stand design is simple, yet it looks sophisticated. A table is laid for dinner, complete with silverware, crystal glasses, candles and fresh flowers. A slide show projected onto the screen at the back shows diners enjoying their meal, conference delegates in session, the leisure facilities at their city centre hotels and the glorious gardens and fabulous settings of the chain's more rural locations. Although this trade fair is designed to attract conferences, pretty scenes never go amiss, in Mannie's experience – and you never can tell, perhaps some pre- or post-conference bookings might result.

'They'll be delivered at eight every morning.'

'Good. And there's coffee and wine in the back?'

The stand – a large one – has enough room for a private area behind the screen.

'All set up.'

'You've done a great job.'

'Thanks, Mannie.' Sylvia looks pleased. 'Everyone's gone for dinner, but we were all here most of the day.'

'I know.' As she will be doing the longest shifts all week, Mannie has delegated the work of setting up to others. She hooks her arm through her young assistant's. 'Come on. Let's go. You've earned a drink.'

It seems hard to believe that just yesterday she and Callum rambled across Yellowcraigs beach hand in hand. London seems a world away from that experience, in every sense. There, she enjoyed the simple pleasures of a day spent in

114

wide open spaces, content in the company of the man she loves. Here, everything is brick and concrete and glass, she is alone, and she has to work.

At least Docklands is surrounded by water, she thinks as she strides the next morning from the hotel to the trade centre as briskly as her neat skirt and precarious heels allow. If the sun isn't the clean, pure sun that blessed her and Cal yesterday, at least she can watch it playing on the rippled surface of the water in the dock for a few minutes. It's warm here, much warmer than in Scotland, where a brisk wind had whipped capriciously through her hair and goaded spots of colour into her cheeks.

Reluctantly, she turns towards the entrance to the exhibition hall. There will be little time to delight in small pleasures for the next few days.

She is right – the madness starts as soon as she steps inside, where a man-sized white rabbit sticks out its paw and thrusts a leaflet into her hand.

Ten yards into the hall, two men dressed in trench coats and trilbys take a flash photograph of her and hand her a business card.

Further down, she can see three girls on a raised dais dancing a cabaret routine.

I'm Alice, she thinks, in Wonderland. All this needs is the Mad Hatter.

It only gets worse as the crowds arrive and the stallholders fight to grab attention. The buzz is fantastic, the networking excellent – but the number of buyers dismal. Everyone, it seems, is cutting back. The lavish conferences of the past are being eschewed altogether or are being replaced by modest, workmanlike sessions: in, do the business, out. Mannie and her team have to work harder than they have ever worked to attract visitors to their stand – and, more importantly, to convert interest into contracts. The seductive chic of her stand feels understated compared with the colour and exuberance and sheer ingenuity of many others.

It's as well, thinks Mannie as she smiles fixedly at a woman who stops to pick up one of her brochures then wanders on uninterestedly, that approaching complete strangers and doing the sales pitch is something I'm really good at.

By the last day she's flagging. A week of being on her feet, talking all day and entertaining potential and existing clients in the evenings, is taking its toll. She can't even be sure about her conversion rates. Of those she talks to, will half eventually book? Thirty per cent? Ten percent? The odds could mean the difference between meeting her month's targets and failing. With the end of the fair in sight, Mannie is desperate to secure a good deal. Around ten thirty, she finds herself turning on the charm to a large German from a bank based in Frankfurt. He speaks hesitant, heavily accented English but seems perfectly capable of driving a hard bargain. It's taking all Mannie's ingenuity and powers of persuasion to draw him into a contract on her terms.

She sits in the private, screened area and pours him yet another coffee.

'Herr Leeuwen,' she says, 'what can I say to persuade you?'

He beams at her, his large chins wobbling. 'Throw in ze dancing girls,' he smiles.

'Oh Herr Leeuwen,' she chides him, her voice full of mock remonstrance. 'I would if I could, you know that.' Her face is alight, mobile, the hazel eyes expressive and full of laughter, but focused. Something of her mother's acting ability has, thankfully, come her way.

He sighs, settles his hands on his rotund tummy, and shakes his head. 'Fraulein Wallace,' he says gustily, his accent making the W into a V so that it emerges as Vallace, 'Fraulein Vallace, you greatly the charm have.' He leans forward, his watery blue eyes, their lustre diluted by years of over-indulgence in schnapps, staring closely into hers. 'I tell you vot, you give me the forty protsent, we a deal call it, yes?'

It isn't a good enough deal. She pretends that the watery gaze is appealing, flutters her dark eyelashes a little and flashes a great smile. 'Herr Leeuwen,' she beams, 'Two hundred guests for four nights, plus a banquet for four hundred on the Friday? I can give you fifteen percent discount – and a promise that I, personally, will look after your party. Do we have a deal?' She sticks out her hand in the hope that he won't be able to resist the contact.

Her strategy pays off. He shakes on it. Mannie tries not to flinch at the touch of his soft, sweaty hand and maintains her smile. She's a professional, clinching a deal. And in fairness, Herr Leeuwen isn't an unpleasant man, merely a grossly overweight and slightly seedy one.

Her mind hops back to Callum and the touch of his skin, so very different in its smoothness; satin and velvet under her fingers. And he loves her! He has said so! The magic of this comes fresh and fragrant into her mind.

She emerges from the screened area with Herr Leeuwen. They have completed the paperwork and both parties are content. She shakes his hand once more, fighting the impulse to dry her palm surreptitiously on her skirt, but as soon as he turns away, she does exactly that. Then she lifts her eyes to meet the gaze of another man, one she hasn't seen before. He has observed the gesture and is clearly amused.

Sweet ... Jesus.

Mannie inhales sharply, her breath taken away by this man's presence. She feels his scrutiny like a branding iron. Her skin prickles and grows hot. She can feel a blush rising from her neck and travelling up her face so that her cheeks, become suffused with blood and grow red. After a minute she remembers to breathe, but motion seems difficult.

The man is smiling. He is holding out his hand to her in greeting. Her colleague, Sylvia, is at the far side of the stand talking to a woman with platinum blonde hair. Mannie recognises her as the events manager for a large oil company. She can't demand Sylvia's support, she has to deal with this herself.

But what is there to deal with? A pleasant-looking, ordinary man has arrived at the stand. It's a perfectly normal situation. She opens her mouth. Closes it again. She finds she is unable to speak.

He seems to have no such problems. 'Hi.'

His hand is still extended and Mannie realises that she has lifted her own towards it. He grasps her fingers. His grip is warm and friendly, but at his touch she feels a shiver run the length of her spine, as if something fundamental is shifting.

'Good morning,' she croaks, her mouth dry. She clears her throat and tries again. 'How can I help?'

He releases her hand. You couldn't call him handsome, Mannie's racing brain decides. He isn't particularly tall and he certainly isn't young – maybe fifty? He has a round head and a round face and his hair is sparse. He is stocky, though not obese, and he's wearing a crisp business suit and a tie whose vividness speaks of some character and individuality. Or perhaps bad taste. He's certainly sure of himself. His eyes, hazel like hers, hold a sparkle that she finds irresistible. Is he flirting with her? She isn't sure, but behind the sparkle there's a connection that he's intent on making, she's sure of that. He is holding her gaze with some intensity.

Christ, he's hypnotised me, Mannie thinks, riveted. She can't pull her gaze away because she is unwilling to tear the thread that binds them together.

But he has looked away. He doesn't seem to have noticed her discomfiture. The brochure for the hotel is in his hands and he's riffling through its pages. 'I know the hotel in Edinburgh, of course,' he's saying, 'but I'm not familiar with the facilities. How many can you feed, for a banquet?'

'Four hundred,' she croaks. She clears her throat. 'Four hundred.'

'Still with a stage for a band?'

She nods.

'We'd need to set it up with screens, projectors, all that kind of thing. I assume that's possible?'

'Of course.' Whatever it is that has swept over her, she has to overcome it, because quite clearly it's a nonsense. She coughs lightly. 'We are one of the premier hotels in Edinburgh. I'm delighted to say that we can offer more or less anything you need. Even dancing girls.' Recklessly, she offers him what she refused Herr Leeuwen.

He looks puzzled. 'Dancing girls?'

She giggles, then says quickly, 'Sorry. Silly joke. May I ask what kind of event you are thinking of, and when?'

He asks, 'Do you have a card?'

She reaches to the table and picks one up off a small stack. 'Margaret-Anne Wallace, Sales Director' it reads. She holds it out, takes the card he is proffering with the other hand, reads it. 'Brian Henderson, Managing Director, CommX Corporate Communications Ltd.' Mannie passes a hand across her forehead. She detects a faint sheen of sweat and feels a little faint.

'Are you all right?" There's concern in his voice.

'Yes. Thank you. Shall we sit down? Would you like a coffee?'

Brian glances at his wrist, the gesture brisk. 'A quick one, perhaps. I've got a few more stands to see, then I'll have to get back to work. We're short-staffed at the moment. I'm just looking at possible venues. We'd need a good deal.'

'Everyone needs a good deal.' She glances down at the business card he gave her. 'CommX. Remind me – what do you do, exactly?'

He grins. 'We're not, as many people assume, telephone engineers,' he grins. 'We work with large companies, doing media work and employee communications. Consultancy, web design, graphic design, basically. But it's not CommX I'm thinking of – for the conference, I mean. We're far too small. It's for my professional institution.'

Recklessly casting professionalism aside, Mannie ignores the business hook and seizes on a phrase. 'Graphic design? That's what my brother wants to do. He's got a degree, but he can't get a job.'

'Oh?'

'It's so unfair. He's clever, he's really talented, and nice, but it seems to be so difficult to get a job when you're straight out of college.'

Brian says, 'We have a job going for a graphic designer. I'm not sure, but I believe it was advertised in the press, either yesterday or today. It's in Scotland though.'

'That's not a problem – we live in Scotland. Thanks so much – Jonno will be thrilled.' Is he being helpful because he feels the same as she does? The connection between them seems to her so strong it's inconceivable that he doesn't feel it as well.

'I can't guarantee anything, he'd have to apply through the usual channels.'

'Of course.'

He stands. She gets up too. Her head nearly collides with his as she unbends. They laugh and he reaches out a hand to steady her so that once more she feels the shock that runs between them, buzzing and spitting.

'I'll be in touch if we decide we can use your hotel for our reception,' he says.

'I hope we can be of service,' Mannie smiles as she trots out the usual formula, but inside, she is churning.

The CommX ad is in the paper. Graphic designer required, Stirling. She calls Jonno.

'It sounds just right for you, why don't you apply?' she says encouragingly.

'In Stirling? It's hours away.'

'Come on, Jonno, less than an hour.'

'I'd prefer Edinburgh.'

'You don't want a job?'

'Hey Sis, you know I do.'

'So—'

There's a sigh and a reluctant, 'You're right.'

'You'll get it off today?'

'What's got into you, Sis? You're not normally so concerned for my well-being.'

'I am,' she says indignantly, 'I just don't show it all the time.'

'I'll get it off. Okay?'

'Okay.' She's about to ask him about their parents, whether anything has improved at home but he has cut the call.

Chapter Twelve

Archie is, in his own way, a strong man, and not without resources. A lifetime of living with Susie has taught him strategies to help him manage his wife's ebullient personality. He learned – a long time ago, the hard way – that jealousy is exhausting. These days he is fairly sure that his wife's habit of hugging everyone enthusiastically is no cause for it. 'Darling' is a universal greeting and can be used equally when addressing people she is sweetly reprimanding and the lucky recipients of her praise. He has learned how to hold Susie back from agreeing to every engagement she is asked to undertake, and he has learned how to manage her mood swings.

Susie's personality is like a seesaw – with himself, he sometimes thinks, as the fulcrum. Generally favourably tipped to the skies, sunny side up, there have been a few notable occasions when something flipped the weight seriously downwards. 'Calgary Bay', he thinks, then forces himself to move on. After Jonathan was born; when her second West End show bombed; and once for no apparent reason at all (a long winter? too much chocolate – or too little?).

Archie deals with his own low periods by either playing music or writing it. The cadences and rhythms of sound soothe his soul.

Only this time, it doesn't seem to be working.

The studio is a spartan environment in which to be living – not that this bothers him. Apart from the musical equipment, there's only a sofa and a small table and chair, plus a basic shower room at the far end. There isn't even a kitchen, so he still wanders across to the cottage for his meals, usually waiting until Susie has headed off to the Parliament. However, there is a deep woollen rug on the floor and he has hung thick curtains at the windows to help absorb the echoing edges of the sound. It is these curtains that allow him to sleep late, long after the sun has started playing peekaboo through the scudding clouds of this March morning.

He hears the tap at the door while he is still three-quarters asleep. Or was it a tap? Edging slowly into consciousness, Archie isn't quite sure.

The door opens and Jon appears.

'Dad? You okay?'

Prince reaches him first. He smells his doggy breath and hears the pleased panting before full alertness arrives.

'Huh? Jon? What time is it?'

'Nearly midday. I was worried about you.'

'What?' Archie swings his feet onto the rug and sits up, shocked.

'Bad night?' Jon sympathises.

The worst so far. Unused to sleeping alone, Archie has allowed himself to be governed by his increasingly erratic body clock.

'I brought you tea.'

'Genius.' Even the thought picks him up a little. He holds out a hand and takes the mug gratefully. Jon pulls back the heavy curtains and bright shafts of sunlight stream in.

'Aargh!'

He throws the other hand up to shield his eyes, slopping a little tea from the mug with the violence of the movement.

'Da-ad,' Jon says reproachfully. 'Christ, this is weird. It's like I'm the parent around here, trying to deal with two sulky children. What is wrong with the two of you?'

'Where's Mum?' Archie asks carefully, feeling the

124

justice of Jon's words.

'Where do you think?'

'What day is it?'

'Saturday. Christ, Dad, don't you even know that?'

'You're right, Jon.' He sips the tea and begins to feel more human. 'I'm being pathetic.'

'Just talk to her. You two were always so good at talking.'

Archie grins at that. 'Your mother was good at talking, I did the listening.' The smile fades. 'Only this time, I feel I have a point of view too. Trouble is, she's too darn touchy to listen to me.'

They sit together in the puddle of light, grey head and brown, father and son. It is, Archie reflects as the tea works its way into his system, usually a good relationship. And it isn't fair that his son is still adrift in life. Thinking this, he makes an effort.

'Worked last night, did you?'

'Yeah. I'm not long up.' He glares at Archie reproachfully. 'But I didn't get back till three so I have an excuse.'

'Okay, okay. You've made your point.' Archie smiles to show he harbours no ill feelings. 'Claire still on the scene, is she?' It's been some time since Jon brought a girl home and he has to search for the name.

'Claire and I split months ago.'

'Oh. Sorry. I hadn't registered.' He's slightly shocked. How could he have become so turned in on himself that he's neglected to show an interest in his son? 'Is there a replacement?'

Jonathan sighs. 'Not really. It's difficult meeting people, when all I do is work at the bar and sleep. And write job applications.'

Jon's shoulders are sagging – a sure sign, Archie thinks, of lack of confidence. And low confidence makes people unattractive. Something has to be done.

'You'll get a job soon, son,' he says sympathetically.

'Don't patronise me, Dad,' Jon snaps back.

Ouch. Archie tries again, more carefully. 'Have you spoken to the agency recently? What are they saying?'

'I've spoken to all of them. There's nothing much around at the moment. You know what the world's like, Dad. Cuts, cuts, cuts. And no future for young people.'

'Don't talk like that, Jon. I know it's hard, but you've got to stay positive. Believe in yourself. Your mother and I believe in you.'

'You and Mum?' He snorts derisively. 'Don't give me that. You and Mum do nothing collective these days, least of all support Mannie and me.'

'Jonathan! That's not fair. When have either of us ever neglected to be there for you? I'm not sure what else we can do, right now. And in any case, you're not very open to help.'

Jon's anger subsides as quickly as it flared. 'Sorry. That was a stupid thing to say. It's just ... well ... horrid. This atmosphere. It's not like home any more. Can't you just try to speak to Mum? Please?'

Archie leans forward and pats his son's hand. 'You're right. This situation is untenable. Is she across at the house?'

He nods dumbly. 'Making soup.'

'I'll shower and come across.'

Jon pushes back his chair and stands. 'Thanks, Dad. Sorry to be a grump.'

'It's me who's the grump. Fed the hens yet?'

'I'll do it now.'

Archie leans down and rescues his trousers from the floor, where he dropped them wearily the night before. He fishes out his wallet and hands Jon a note. 'Thanks, Jon. Appreciated.'

He means for everything, but he doesn't need to spell it out. He can see from the flash in his son's eyes that Jon understands.

Susie is in the kitchen. making soup. Archie stands on the threshold of the open doorway, observing her, watching the familiar movements, the sway of her body, the curve of her hips.

She catches sight of him, perhaps feeling his presence more than seeing it.

'Hi.' Her voice is neutral, not warm, but certainly without the coolness it has held of late.

'Hi. That smells good. What is it?'

'Butternut squash and red pepper.'

'Am I allowed any?'

'Don't be ridiculous, Archie, of course you're allowed some.'

Wrong thing to say. Stupid. Put myself on the defensive and allowed her to find a weak spot. 'Do you need anything? Bread? I could go and get some.'

'Everything's under control. Thanks.' She puts the pot on the stove and busies herself in tidying up.

'Susie?' He wants to hold her, to bury his face in her hair, to feel at one with her again. How would she take that? Should he try?

'What is it?'

She scrapes the peelings from the chopping board into the compost bin and turns an enquiring face towards him. Bugger this, he thinks, she's my wife, and I love her. He takes two swift steps across the kitchen and gently relieves her of the board and knife, placing them by the sink before wrapping his arms firmly around her and folding her into a cuddle. She feels stiff at first, resisting his embrace, then he senses her flesh soften and relax. She turns her head and lays it on his chest in a gesture of affection, one that is so familiar to him that it takes his breath away. From somewhere down the garden they can hear Jonathan calling, 'Prince! Here boy!' and the friendly sound of hens

127

fussing and purring.

My family, Archie thinks, my home. And my love.

'Hey.' Edging away half an inch, he puts his hand under her chin and tilts her face gently up towards him so that she has to look into his eyes. What can he read there? A plea? Affection? Not anger, at least, not right now. 'Love you, missus,' he says softly.

'Love you too,' Susie says as he bends to kiss her.

Then she pulls away. 'I love you, Archie, but that doesn't make anything better. I still feel hurt and bewildered.'

'Yes. I know.'

Damn, damn, damn. Jon would be disappointed.

'Do you want to come back and sleep upstairs?'

Does he want to? Do hens lay eggs?

'You know I'd like that, Susie. Of course. But I think I need to know—' he says it hesitantly, cursing that he can't make things easier for himself, '—I think I need to know if you've forgiven me first.'

He sees her eyes cloud over and knows that nothing has been resolved.

'It's not about forgiveness, Archie. It's about ... understanding. And there's just too much I don't understand about any of this.'

'I wish I could help.'

Behind her, the soup is starting to boil and she turns to deal with it.

'Come back or stay away, whatever you think best.'

He can't bear her indifference.

'All right,' he says dully as Jon comes back into the cottage.

He sees his son looking from one face to the other, his expression hopeful, and he wishes he could look more positive. But Susie has turned away to deal with some washing up, and the atmosphere has become emotionally charged again. He can feel it and so, it seems, can Jon

128

because his son's smile fades and he pushes past Archie, the ire and hurt clearly returning.

Each one of them seems angry and hurt. What a mess.

The lunch he anticipated with some eagerness turns into a fragmented, hurried affair.

'I'll just have mine in the sitting room,' Jon says, ladling out some soup and grabbing a hunk of the crusty brown bread Archie has hacked into pieces. 'I'm off to meet some mates down the pub to watch the home derby.'

'I'll take mine on the hoof,' Susie says, blowing on a spoonful as she dashes around the kitchen, straightening, neatening, tidying. 'I'm giving the prizes at the fair down the road at three.'

'Okay,' Archie says tiredly, sinking onto one of the chairs at the kitchen table and opening the paper. 'DIVORCE STATISTICS SOAR', reads the headline. 'ONE IN THREE MARRIAGES ENDS IN FAILURE'.

Cheer me up, he thinks morosely, why don't you?

The worst thing is, he still can't get the words to the melody he has dreamed up two months ago. It's a sweet and poignant run of notes and the tune haunts him. He knows it holds the promise of being one of the best things he has ever written, but a tune on its own is one thing: married to words that echo and add to the sense, it becomes something else entirely. His failure to complete the thing is the source of a frustration that is mounting to such huge proportions that it's threatening to block all useful activity.

He sits for two hours at his keyboard, but produces nothing. In the end, he whistles for Prince, throws on a jacket and goes for a walk. At least, he reasons, if I get some exercise, I might sleep tonight.

Jon lies sprawled across his bed, playing a time-wasting game on his iPhone. Through the small dormer window, he glimpses a flash of red and a blur of black out of the corner of his eye and looks up in time to see his father heading out of the gate with Prince.

He tosses the phone onto the bed.

Sod it, he thinks, everything's wrong. No career, just a cruddy job in a bar; no girlfriend and therefore no sex; an overhyped sister who seems to be going mental about discovering this new family; and a catastrophic decline in relations between my parents.

He docks the phone into his speakers. The sound of Adele fills the room and the shadow of depression lifts an inch. He sinks back on the bed and lets the glorious voice wash over him.

We so nearly recaptured it, Susie broods as she lies sleeplessly in bed in a still empty bedroom. Perhaps I didn't invite him warmly enough. Was it my fault? But then, he could have been more eager. I did leave the door open.

Failure bites deep. Having his arms around her was so completing that she'd been tempted to opt for an easy solution. It would have been easy to utter bland words of absolution and welcome him back into her life, but her spirit baulked at the final hurdle. Her faith in his integrity has been deeply damaged and restoring that is not something that can be done in an instant – because how can she change what he did in the past?

It's not just the rift with Archie she regrets. She saw disappointment written all over Jon's face as he rushed through the kitchen. Did he set Archie up to try for a reconciliation? Her son hates conflict, just like his father.

Still restless, Susie sits up and switches on the light again. She throws on a cotton dressing gown and pads downstairs. She hasn't told anyone, but she found time to call Birthlink during the week – and discovered that her birth mother has registered on the database.

'It's that simple?' she said incredulously to Helen.

'You're one of the lucky ones. Now, you should think very carefully about the next steps. We advise starting cautiously. Exchange a few letters. Just give what information about yourself you're ready to give and ask the questions you'd like to ask. There's no need to rush.'

Susie smiled. 'I have a very eager daughter,' she said.

'It's not unusual for the children of adopted people to be the most eager to find the birth family. But this is your story and you should control everything that happens.'

For four days, she has sat on the news. Now, contemplating the devastation that has engulfed her family since she first heard about her adoption, the decision she has been evading for so long comes to her with clarity and certainty.

Now is the time.

She picks up a pen and starts to write. She isn't even nervous.

Dear Mother —

Chapter Thirteen

The garden at Cairn Cottage is more rustic than cultivated. Only the cobbled courtyard has plants that need tending and although this is Susie's job – and her pride and joy – she realises as soon as she looks out of the window that she has been neglecting her duties. The winter pansies are sagging pitifully.

Stirred by guilt at her neglect, she fills a watering can and pads across the cobbles, still in the furry zebra-striped slippers Jonno gave her for Christmas. How they laughed at them as they emerged from their snowman wrapping paper! What a glorious, trouble-free time it was. She and Archie—

Susie turns her mind away from Archie. The awkwardness between them is too awful to brood about. She lifts the watering can and watches as the silvery drops fall lightly onto the thirsty plants. The glorious purple of the pansies deepens as they slake their thirst gratefully and their beauty touches her. The air still holds the freshness of early morning, but it's almost April now and the day promises to be fine. Surely today is a day for mending?

She picks a few stray weeds out of the tubs and lays them in a heap for later despatch to the compost bin. Prince is nowhere around, he has taken to sloping off to the studio to be with Archie. Susie tries not to think of it as a betrayal, but it feels like that right at this moment. She hooks her fingers through her hair and tries to calm its unruliness. The air is cool and she contemplates running in to fetch a coat, but settles instead for pulling her light negligee tighter around her and knotting the belt.

On the far side of the chicken coop, an overgrown path winds down to a glade on the fringes of the garden. Here, she and Archie constructed a small pergola (or rather, she corrected herself, Archie built it at her suggestion), facing out to the rolling countryside. It boasts the prettiest view from anywhere in the property and has the bonus of catching the early sun. She strolls past the chickens and makes her way down to it, zebra slippers ridiculous on the stony path. As she rounds the large rhododendron bush that shields the pergola from the cottage windows, she spots Prince lying on the grass.

'Hello, old boy,' she calls, surprised. 'You haven't been out here all night, have you?'

The dog shambles to his feet and trots towards her, clearly pleased at her appearance. Susie bends to pat him as the wagging of the tail redoubles.

'He's been with me.' The voice comes from somewhere behind the leafy foliage of the clematis that has colonised the wrought iron work of the pergola. 'I got up early, for a change.'

'Oh! Hello.' She scans Archie's face and is shocked by how drawn he looks. 'Problems with the composing?'

'Why don't you come and sit down?' He shuffles along the seat to make room for her.

Susie hesitates. 'I hadn't thought about stopping. It's a bit chilly. I'm only in my nightwear.'

'I noticed,' Archie says dryly, making Susie blush – so ridiculous, when they've been married for thirty years. 'Here.' He takes off his fleece and holds it out to her. 'Put this round you. I'm warm enough.'

'Okay. Thanks.' She drapes it around her shoulders and sinks onto the bench. His warmth lingers in the garment. Its smell is faint, but achingly familiar.

They sit for a while in a silence that feels companionable rather than awkward. In the sky far above them a buzzard wheels magnificently, intent on some hapless vole or mouse hundreds of feet below. If only we were blessed with sight so extraordinary, Susie thinks. If only I could see even further – into the minds and feelings of my children, for example.

As if catching her thoughts, Archie asks, 'Does one ever stop worrying about one's children, d'you think?'

'You feel it too?'

'Of course. I feel responsible.'

'You always wish you could suffer something yourself rather than watch your kids go through it, don't you?'

'It would be much easier.'

They are talking. Susie feels the pleasure of it with sweet delight. 'Jon's problems will all disappear, I'm sure, as soon as he gets a job.'

Archie's hand is on his knee, inches from hers. It seems completely natural to reach out for it. At once, Susie finds her fingers encircled by the familiar clasp of her husband's grip. They sit side by side, gazing quietly at the view over the valley and woods below them, just as they sat here before they built the pergola, just as they have sat here for years. Despite their children's troubles and her anger at what has seemed like a long betrayal, it feels to Susie as if her world is being restored to her.

She lays her head on his shoulder and feels his own rest comfortably on hers.

'Archie—' she starts to say, thinking it is time to welcome him back into her life. But for some reason she slips her fingers into the pocket of the fleece and feels something in there, some paper. She draws it out idly and glances at it. An envelope, partly opened, addressed to her.

'What's this?' she asks curiously.

'Oh sorry, I meant to give that to you days ago. I completely forgot. I started to open it, but saw it was for you and shoved it in my pocket.'

'You kept my mail?'

'I got distracted, love, that's all.'

135

There aren't many handwritten envelopes these days. Susie removes her hand and uses a finger to slit open the rest of the seal. Inside is a sheet of A4 paper, ruled. She can see writing covering both sides, and a signature: *Your ever loving mother, Joyce.*

'It's from my birth mother,' she says, staring at it. 'I've been waiting on tenterhooks for this, thinking that after all she couldn't want to know me or she would have written. And all the time you've been hiding it from me!'

'I wasn't hiding it, sweetheart, I just—'

'Just stuck it in your pocket and forgot it.' The anger that seems to have become so much a part of her feelings for Archie is resurfacing. All the tension that has been wrapped up inside her ever since she penned her own note to her mother explodes like a bomb, with Archie as the target. 'How could you Archie? As though keeping my adoption secret all these years wasn't enough!'

'I – darling—'

'Don't darling me!' She stands up and shakes off the fleece, gripping the letter so firmly that the paper crackles in her fingers. 'It's too much, Archie, really it is!'

Shaking with anger and disappointment, she turns and marches back round the rhododendron bush and up the overgrown path to the house. She's conscious that she may be doing herself a disservice as well as doing a wrong to Archie, but overshadowing this insight is the notion that has embedded itself in her head. *Once again Archie has tried to keep the secret of my birth from me.*

Susie showers and dresses before she can pluck up the courage to look again at the letter. At last, with no more excuses to procrastinate, she sinks down on her bed, opens it again, smooths out the crinkles she made and turns it right side up. The words are clearly written, the writing almost childlike in its simplicity.

To my much-missed daughter

I am shaking so much I can hardly write this letter. For all these long years I have dreamed of this day and now that it is here I don't know where to start. The agency says that we should not say too much at first, just tell each other a few things about ourselves, so here goes.

I am now seventy-three years old. I was just seventeen when I found I was pregnant with you and eighteen when I gave birth. I wanted to keep you – oh, how I wanted to keep you – but there was a great deal of pressure from my family and I knew there was no way I could afford to look after you. It wasn't like it is now. No free council flats or benefits. And they told me they would find you a good home, so I did what I thought was best for you, even though it broke my heart.

Anyway, later I found a nice boy and even though I told him everything, he still wanted to marry me. I was lucky.

I had two more children of my own, though Andrew and I never did tell them about you. Now I suppose I have to tell them. I'm not ashamed, but it will be difficult to come out with it now, after all this silence.

Maybe it will be a relief.

My husband Andrew died eight years ago and I really miss him. My daughter lives in Australia but my son lives not too far away. He has two children of his own— my grandchildren – so I've done quite well after all, maybe better than I deserved.

Anyway, they told me don't say too much at first, get to know each other bit by bit, so I'll sign off now. I just want you to know that there hasn't been a day gone by that I haven't thought of you and wondered whether I did the right thing.

Your ever loving mother,

Joyce

PS I always think of you as Brenda, but they tell me

you are called Susie now. It's a pretty name.

Below her, in the courtyard, Susie can hear voices. She glances out of the window and sees Archie talking to Jon.

My husband. My son. My family. But now I have another family as well. How strange that is. A woman called Joyce is my new mother. And she was only a teenager when she gave birth to a small, lustily howling, illegitimate baby. Ten years younger than Mannie is now. She must have been frightened, maybe alone, certainly her pregnancy was not a time of joy and celebration.

Susie scans the letter again. She was loved, that seems clear. Words and phrases jump out at her. *I did what I thought was best for you, even though it broke my heart. ... There hasn't been a day gone by that I haven't thought of you ... Your ever loving mother ...*

It's a step, and she knows she will write back. Hopefully, she'll soon meet this new mother and that is important – but is meeting her more important than making up with Archie? Is a family she has never known more important than the one she has now? Will it be possible to retract her angry words or has she just created another gulf between them?

The phone by Susie's bed shrills brutally. Blearily, she reaches for it. 'Hello?'

'Christ, Suse,' Karen sounds very much awake, 'You sound rough. You okay?'

Susie peers at the clock on the bedside table. It feels like five but the dial reads eight thirty. She has slept in.

'I'm fine,' she says, her voice hoarse with fatigue.

'I take it you haven't seen *Scotland Daily* yet?'

'Not yet. Why?' She doesn't feel prepared for a new week. A few months ago she lived and breathed politics, loving every minute of the work – meeting her constituents, talking at conferences, opening fairs, even the media work. Especially the media work. That's where she feels at the top of her game – after all, it brings all her skills into play, and she adores being in the limelight. But now? Everything has spun topsy turvy, all the things she used to love doing have become a chore.

'You'd better brace yourself.'

'Oh God. What now?'

'Let me quote: "MSP DENIES SHE IS A LESBIAN. Susie Wallace, Member of the Scottish Parliament for Lothians, is not a lesbian, she claims. Despite reaching stardom in a role that lent scorching credence to rumours of her sexuality, her long term partner said yesterday—" '

'What?' Susie breaks in, incredulous. 'What is this crap?'

' "—her long-term partner said yesterday—" '

'Karen. For heaven's sake, what is this? Who's written this drivel?'

'Byline is Justin Thorneloe. It goes on—'

'I don't want to know how it goes on,' Susie says wearily. 'What is it with Justin Thorneloe? The story's utter bollocks and he know it.'

'I know that. You know that. But no smoke—'

'What does Mo say?'

'She's not here yet. Are you coming in soon?'

'I'll be there in an hour.'

'Did you talk to him over the weekend?'

'Justin? No.'

'Did Archie?'

'I've no idea. I don't think so.'

She can't believe that Archie would have made any kind of comment to any journalist, but she's beginning to wonder if she knows her husband at all. He concealed her letter, didn't he? Maybe not deliberately concealed, but he'd 'forgotten' about it. Perhaps he 'forgot' to mention a conversation with Justin Thorneloe too?

She puts the phone down tiredly. She misses the warm

comfort of Archie's presence in her bedroom and she misses being able to chew difficult things over with him. The ache is not alleviated by a nagging sense that she was the one who drove him away. One way or another, she has become pretty good at messing things up.

'What do we do about it?' she asks Mo Armstrong an hour later.

'Nothing.'

'Nothing? But the story's outrageous.' Susie has worked herself into a state of righteous anger on the drive in from the cottage and is now in combative mood.

'And completely fictitious, yes?'

'Of course!'

'Then we ignore it. There's nothing to back it up. The other newspapers might poke around a bit to see if there's anything in it, but it'll disappear. I give it three days, max.'

'Three days! I've got to live with this garbage for that long?'

'Just get on with other things, Susie. Don't talk to the press, let me deal with it.' Mo smooths back her red hair then asks, 'Anyone got it in for you, Susie? Apart from this journo, I mean?'

Susie shakes her head. 'God knows. In this game, there's always someone, I guess.'

Karen says, 'There's a few people quite jealous of your popularity. In the Party, I mean.'

'Really?' Susie, who is a conviction politician rather than a career politician, is sublimely unaware of internecine struggles. 'Why? I mean, I'm not exactly jostling for a ministerial post or anything.'

'You're the first person the press call on for all kinds of media appearances. Especially since the repeats of "Home" started. There's a lot of people would kill for that kind of exposure.'

'You think someone's planted the story?'

'It's a possibility,' Mo says. 'Listen,' she sweeps up her notebook and the folder of the morning's press clippings and stands up, 'I've got to get on. Leave this with me, but don't worry about it, I think it'll just go away.'

When she has gone, Susie says, 'That Thorneloe guy's got it in for me.'

'Ignore him.'

'Easier said than done, Karen.'

'I know. But you've got a busy day. Let's get started.'

Immersion in work is the answer, because Susie doesn't have time to think about the headlines. And any time it looks as if she might have a slight lull, Karen finds something that requires urgent attention. By the evening, she's exhausted. At six she switches off her computer and says rebelliously, 'If I have to do another email today I'll murder someone. I'm off home.'

'Not yet you're not,' Karen says with grotesque cheerfulness.

'Why not?'

'You've got a reception.'

'Really? Where? Who?'

'Garden Lobby. Now. Creative Scotland. They're launching a new strategy.'

Susie groans. 'Another one?'

Karen laughs. 'Just go on down. You'll enjoy it once you get there.'

'I'm bone tired.' Susie considers confiding in her about Joyce Miles.

'Suse?' Karen picks up on her hesitation. 'Something wrong?'

But her foray into her past still feels too private to relate, even to Karen. 'Nothing,' Susie lies. 'I'll go and grab a drink and schmooze a bit. I'll probably perk up. You get home now. See you tomorrow.'

'Okay. If you're sure.'

'Has Mo said anything?'

'About the lesbian story? No. Well actually, yes – apparently one of the gay and lesbian organisations you've helped in the past has sent a message of support.'

Susie smiles wanly. 'Well that's comforting I guess.' At the door she turns. 'They do know I'm straight, don't they?'

'Susie my love, everyone knows you're straight. Now go.'

The Garden Lobby is already full of people. In one corner, a string quartet is playing – students probably. She spies the new Director of Creative Scotland, a controversial appointment. On any other evening, she might have felt compelled to confront him, but tonight all she wants to do is move round as quickly as possible, make sure her presence is noted, then retreat to Cairn Cottage.

'Susie!' Across the room, someone is waving. She can't see the face, but heads in the direction of the wave anyway, threading her way expertly through the throng. A gap in the crowd opens and she stops, dead.

It's Maitland Forbes.

Maitland is standing directly under one of the spotlights in the ceiling of the Garden Lobby, and although he's now a huge star and must surely be tonight's guest of honour, he is, in this moment, completely alone. Susie stares at him, slack-jawed with shock. The past rewinds itself before her eyes like some speeded-up movie and she realises that her heart is pounding. She hasn't seen Maitland since—

'You haven't changed one bit,' he says softly, and although he barely whispers the words and the noise around them is high, she hears them as clearly as if he has shouted them.

'Nor you,' she says stupidly, and she knows they are both remembering the same thing.

Someone jostles her and the moment is gone. She is in

public, at a reception, and the secret they have both kept for so long must remain a secret. She takes a step towards him and holds out her hands, bracing herself for the touch of his skin and saying with forced gaiety, 'Maitland Forbes, by all that's miraculous!'

He is still with Serafina, she knows that. She knows everything about him, she has read it over the years. The madcap youth may have defied Hollywood odds on marriage but he still makes headlines. 'Still flying high? What did I see you in last? That Spielberg film? What are you doing back in Scotland? I thought you were a permanent fixture in Hollywood these days.' She's babbling. It's nerves.

'I've been bribed to be a front face for this thing.'

'Really? The Creative Scotland strategy? It must have been a big bribe. You're surely not so down on your uppers you have to stoop to this kind of appearance these days?'

Now she's teasing him, which is a good sign – talking to him is getting easier with every minute. She knows, of course, that Maitland has made it big in Hollywood, that he finally broke free from the stereotype of the sardonic Brit abroad and is now playing more complex roles suited to an aging actor with real star quality. But she herself is now playing a role and she has to play it better than anything else she has ever done because to risk discovery of what happened all those years ago is unthinkable.

'Let me look at you.' She holds him at arm's length and studies him. 'You've worn well.'

'Darling Susie, you're the real star. Look at you! That hair's as glorious as the day I met you –and those *eyes*! What are you doing buried away in this place?'

Susie manages to laugh. 'It's a vocation. Like acting, but with a different kind of audience.'

Maitland sighs. 'That old social conscience thing. That's why I'm here too, I guess, to do something for the

143

homeland. I've been away too long.' He pulls a wry face. 'Of course, as soon as your First Minister found out I was taking a vacation here, he wanted to trot me out for public inspection.'

'And here you are.'

'Here I am,' he agrees, his chiselled features breaking into a perfect grin.

He's had a lot of dental work done since she saw him last. Only in America, Susie thinks, amused, are teeth as perfect as that.

'So tell me about all this,' he sweeps his wine glass out in a dramatic arc, taking in the whole of the Parliament. 'Enjoying it?'

'Mostly,' Susie says dryly. 'There are good days and bad days.'

His laughter rings out. 'I read the headlines this morning. I thought it was hysterical. Susie Wallace, a lesbian!'

'Not that funny,' Susie says sourly. "Actually, it's not being called a lesbian I mind, it's the idea that I would conceal it if I was.'

'Would a big snog help?'

He's teasing *her* now. Her heart races, but she keeps her voice steady. 'Well, that would certainly make a different kind of headline.'

'How's that man of yours? Still making music?'

She had thought that over the years the memories would have faded, but he has remembered and she's touched by this. 'Oh yes. He hit the big time a few years back.'

'Celtic Rock. I've heard them. Great band.'

'You've heard them?' Then he must have followed her career too.

'They've got quite a following in the States.'

'He's working on a new album.'

'I'll look out for it.'

He moves closer to her. He's about to say something, but they are joined by someone, an oil executive Susie thinks, eager to meet the big star. They smile at him and nod, adjust their stance to admit him, but Maitland keeps on talking to her.

'Remember Calgary Bay?

'Of course.' Her heart is pounding madly. How could she ever forget?

'What was that island called again? The one where we did all the filming.'

'Mull. Off the west coast of Scotland. '

'That's the one. Perfect paradise, apart from those pesky midges. Ever been back?'

'We took the children there a few times.' She'd made Archie go. It had been a kind of test, the first time at least, a check to make sure it was all right, that she'd made the right decision, that the past was safely where it belonged. 'I became really fond of it,' she says honestly. 'Tobermory. Iona. And Calgary Bay itself, of course.'

She hasn't seen them coming, but the First Minister and the new Director of Creative Scotland are suddenly upon them, surrounded by a press pack – and right at the front is Justin Thorneloe. That little snake gets everywhere, Susie thinks, surely he must have heard our conversation. She glowers at him and is profoundly thankful for the presence of the oil executive – his arrival certainly prevented a more confidential chat.

'I'd like to introduce Maitland Forbes, First Minister,' the Director is saying ingratiatingly, butting into their conversation and completely ignoring Susie. 'He's kindly agreed to say a few words to our guests.'

Creep, thinks Susie, taking an instant dislike to the man. 'Listen, Maitland,' she says quickly, 'You're going to be busy. Give me a call will you? Maybe we can have lunch while you're in Edinburgh.'

'Honey, I'll do that.' Unfazed by the overbearing

145

efforts to monopolise his attention, he envelopes Susie in a bear-hug. 'What a wanker,' he murmurs into her ear.

Susie stifles a giggle. She's on safer ground now because she knows that although the memory of what happened is still vivid, each of them has long since moved on. The past is locked where it should be and she can take delight in the fact that he's still the glorious, irreverent Maitland she once fell for – and finally resisted.

Maitland releases her and turns to the Director and First Minister. He says smoothly, but loudly enough for the press pack to hear, 'Forgive me, but I've known Susie for ever. And by the way—' he invests deep meaning into his voice, '— I can vouch for the fact that she's no lesbian.' Susie feels her diaphragm tighten, but Maitland goes on smoothly, 'She's an actress, you know.'

The First Minister guffaws, the Director smiles tightly and Susie sees the look on Justin Thorneloe's face and almost laughs aloud. Thanks to Maitland, her day has just got a whole lot better.

They meet the next day. Is it a good idea? She has turned the matter over in her mind since his early morning call and is comfortable with her conclusion. It's lunch, it's public, their affair was a long time ago and in any case, almost no-one knew about it.

They are in Hadrian's restaurant in the Balmoral, where he is staying. The Maitre d' has found them a quiet corner, and although already one tourist has not been able to resist asking for an autograph, they are being left pretty much in peace.

'So, Susie darling, bring me up to date. You're saving the world with your passionate protection of the arts—'

'Saving Scotland, Maitland. Only Scotland,' Susie protests, laughing.

'Scotland, then. What brought you to it?'

'I could see things happening all round me that made

me angrier and angrier. All the time Margaret-Anne and Jonathan were growing up, I witnessed services being cut, the things that seemed to me the most important being dismissed as if they didn't matter.'

'Like drama, you mean?'

'Like drama. And music, and painting, and poetry. And singing. Do you know, hardly any schools have choirs any more. Singing is so liberating. We're failing our children.'

Now it's Maitland who's laughing. 'Darling, you've got my vote, I promise you. If only I had one.'

'Sorry. I know I get carried away. Of course, it's not just arts I get passionate about. It's the many injustices I see, all the time. Petty bureaucratic decisions that ruin people's lives. Wrapping everyone up in cotton wool to avoid lawsuits, so that no-one dares to risk anything any more and all we do is sit around getting fat. The rich creaming off profits and dodging taxes, while all the time blaming all the woes of the world on benefit scroungers.'

'Quite the little socialist, aren't you?'

'I don't define myself in those terms. I just deal with things as I see them.'

When the waiter fills their tiny coffee cups, then discreetly leaves them the pot, Maitland says unexpectedly, 'What's troubling you, Susie?'

She is startled. 'What do you mean?'

'Honey, I may not have seen you for years, but I know you well enough to see that you're edgy. That article wasn't the first little bit of nastiness, was it?'

Susie stares at him, amazed. 'How do you—?'

'I've seen it happen before, believe me. These people drop in more and more idiotic stories in the hopes that eventually their quarry will crack. Either it's just malicious, or they're really trying to get a bigger story they think is lurking there somewhere.'

'Oh, God.' It hasn't occurred to her that this might be what's happening.

'Am I right?'

'I'm not sure,' she says slowly. 'There is a journalist who's being particularly troublesome, but—'

'He doesn't know about us, does he?'

'Heavens, no!' Horrified, she imagines the headlines screaming across huge spreads, the salacious gossip, speculation dressed up as fact, and the impact of it all on her family and her Party.

'Does Archie?'

She shakes her head dumbly.

'You never told Archie?'

'No. By the time it was all over ... when we'd decided ... I saw no need. Did you tell Serafina?'

'I tell Seri everything. I guess it's why we've lasted.'

Susie weighs this. Archie has not been such an honest communicator, or he would have told her about the adoption.

'Is there something else, Susie? Something this journo might know about?'

She shakes her head. 'No!' It comes out more forcefully than she intended.

'You don't have to tell me, darling.'

Maitland is outside it all, he's only here for a few days and she knows she can trust him. She says, hesitantly. 'I found something out recently. And ever since, things seem to have been going wrong. But I'm sure it's just coincidence.' She finds that talking is a huge relief.

'Jeez, Susie,' he says when she has stopped, 'that's some story. So have you met her? Your mother?'

Susie shakes her head. 'Not yet, no. I've started writing to her a bit.'

'And?'

'It's difficult.'

'I guess it must be. Do you want to meet her?'

'I'm not sure. I ... ought to want to.'

Maitland says softly, 'What are you really afraid of,

148

sweetie?'

Goodness, he's perceptive. It occurs to her that Maitland is extraordinarily clever and that perhaps his madcap persona was deliberately constructed from the beginning. She says, hesitantly, 'Maybe that it would make me a different person, in some way – and that I won't like that person? It's already made me look at Archie differently. Everything feels as if it's shifting. The whole landscape of my life is unfamiliar. Sometimes I think I have to meet her, so that I can resolve everything that's going round and round in my head. Other times I think I can't bear the idea of meeting her because that would diminish all that's happened in my life so far.'

Maitland goes to the heart of the matter at once. 'I do think you've inadvertently opened Pandora's box, darling, and now it's impossible to stuff everything back into it.'

She thinks about that for a long time. At last she says quietly, 'I guess I'm going to have to face my demons.'

'Good girl. Is this story what's at the bottom of all this newspaper stuff, do you think?'

'Oh no,' Susie says. 'No, I don't see how it could be.'

They part affectionately. Meeting him has been good, she has laid to rest one ghost. Now she knows she must face another spectre.

At Cairn Cottage, Archie takes time out to fetch the newspapers from Hailesbank. He's exhausted with the strain of composing, but particularly drained because he still has no inspiration for the words to his tune. He pours coffee and sits at the kitchen table, determined to enjoy half an hour's tranquillity before Sandie arrives.

A headline on page five catches his eye. CREATIVE SCOTLAND STRATEGY LAUNCH BOOSTED BY PRESENCE OF STAR. Susie will have been at that launch, it's square in the middle of her territory. He scans the story with scant enthusiasm, then his eye stops dead, arrested by two

149

words.

Maitland Forbes.

So Maitland is back.

'Scots-born Hollywood star Maitland Forbes created a sensation last night by appearing at the launch in the Scottish Parliament of the new Creative Scotland strategy. Forbes, who is in Edinburgh only until Wednesday evening—'

Today is Wednesday. Hating himself, Archie thinks of a pretext and dials Susie's number in the Parliament. It's Karen who answers. 'Hi Archie, good to hear you. How's the album coming along?'

'Not bad, Karen, thank you. Is Susie there by any chance? I wanted to check whether she's remembered she has a dental appointment this afternoon?'

Karen sounds puzzled. 'This afternoon? I don't think— oh I see it, Archie, it's next Wednesday. Just as well, because she's gone out to lunch with someone.'

'Oh really?' His heart sinks, but he is compelled to probe further. 'Business or pleasure?'

'I haven't a clue, Archie. Sorry. She didn't say.'

'It doesn't matter.'

But it does matter. To Archie, it matters very much.

Chapter Fourteen

Susie edges towards the meeting with her mother with caution. There are more letters, more doubts, more urgings from Mannie. The Easter recess comes and goes and this year there's no quick trip with Archie to Prague or Nice or to a cottage in the Highlands, because their relationship has dwindled to the politeness of strangers.

Susie sometimes feels as though she's fighting on all fronts. She's at war with her Party on funding cuts, she's struggling to help Rivo Trust to find a way out of its mess and she's drowning in the sheer number of emails that require her daily attention.

Eventually, she decides that her apprehension about meeting her mother is like a festering wound – it has to be dealt with. Once it has been swabbed clean, she'll be able to tick it off her Things To Do list and get on with her life. So a few weeks after lunching with Maitland, Susie finds herself standing in her bedroom in an agony of indecision.

Business suit or jeans? The neat green knee-length *broderie anglaise* skirt teamed with a cream cardi and pearls? Or perhaps just black trousers and the white linen jacket with the tiny flowers embroidered on it? What is most appropriate?

Meeting your mother for the first time, she reflects with a growing sense of panic, must surely be the most important day in your life. For most people it happens on Day One: your birthday. And then you spend the rest of your life learning to love her or loathe her; testing the boundaries of her love; vowing never to grow into the person you think she is; making your own mistakes with her but, above all, whether she's a rock, a yardstick, an irritant or your best friend, in the safe and secure knowledge that she is your mother. But this is not so for her. She has so many things to learn, and to unlearn. So many lost years to recapture. So many secrets to uncover.

The pile of discarded clothing on the bed grows while Susie struggles to work out how to present herself to this new mother of hers. She settles in the end for the black trousers and white linen jacket, adding a simple black tee and the pearls. Easy dressing. Presentable but not over the top. Neutral. Because the truth of the matter is that she has absolutely no idea what kind of person her mother is, what she looks like, what her tastes are, her background, her life – nothing.

'Are you certain you're ready for this?' Helen at Birthlink asked when they made the arrangements. 'We do suggest not meeting if you are in any way stressed about anything in your life.'

Stressed? Susie just laughed.

In her mind, her hopes are well defined – that this meeting will in some magical way resolve all her emotional turbulence.

She takes a last look at herself in the bedroom mirror, sees the billowing caramel-gold hair, the amber eyes so many people described as 'extraordinary', the heart-shaped face, still presentably pretty even in middle age. Will she look like her mother? As the reality of the imminent meeting takes hold, her nerves ratchet up a gear. She has enlisted Mannie's support, but it's Archie she longs to confide in. She even hopes, as she runs downstairs, that he might be in the kitchen and that she can bridge the ridiculous gulf between them, that he'll hold her and kiss her and tell her everything is going to be all right.

But he isn't in the kitchen. Instead, a note is propped against the kettle:

'Sandie's here. We're composing today. Please do not disturb.'

The surge of disappointment almost swamps her.

The café on the first floor of the bookshop at the west end of Princes Street has stunning views over the Gardens and south towards the Castle. It's a pleasant and popular spot for a break from browsing and buying. Mannie has settled at a table right by the window and Susie spots her daughter's dark hair and pale, perfect face right away.

'Hello, darling.'

'Hi, Mum.'

'Thanks for coming. Was it difficult? Taking the time, I mean.'

'No problem.' Mannie indicates her laptop and the ever-present mobile. 'I can work while you're meeting her. Joys of modern technology. There's no such thing as escape.'

Susie grimaces. 'Don't I know it.'

'How long do you think you'll be?'

'Not long, I shouldn't think. It'll be—' she pauses, overtaken by uncharacteristic anxiety, '—a little difficult. Best to keep it short.'

Mannie says, 'It'll be brilliant. I'm sure it will,' and places a reassuring hand over her mother's.

'Yes. Thank you. You will wait for me? Afterwards?'

'Of course I'll wait. That's what I'm here for. '

Susie glances at her watch. 'Thanks. Well. Better go, I suppose.'

'It's not the dentist, Mum. It's a joyous occasion.'

She manages a smile. 'I know. I'm really looking forward to it.' In a way this is true, but her apprehension is great nevertheless. 'Back soon, then.'

'Don't worry, Mum.'

Birthlink's modest premises are in an unlikely spot above the Golden Dragon Chinese restaurant in Castle Street. There are a few stone steps, a white painted door in need of some attention, then a winding staircase that leads up a narrow entryway to the first floor offices. In these humble rooms, Susie thinks as she mounts the scrubbed stone stairway of the interior with ever-increasing apprehension, dreams are realised or broken, lives mended or ruined for ever.

'We'll ask your mother to come a little early,' Helen has told her. 'We'll get her settled comfortably. We've found that it's not a great idea to meet for the first time by bumping into each other on the stair.'

Susie senses years of experience, deep sensitivity, calmness and perception. The staff have been so good to her. Everything has been done just as it should be – the careful beginnings, the letters delivered through their mediation, the painstaking arrangements for this meeting. Still, the apprehension is indescribable. Only one thing mitigates the sense of mounting panic – the understanding that her mother, waiting inside the room at the back of the office, must be feeling something very similar.

'Hello, Susie.' Helen is smiling, calm, reassuring. 'Ready for this?'

'I think so.'

'Sure?'

'Let's do it.'

Her mother is looking out of the window. She's fidgeting with the cord of the blind, twisting it between her fingers, and her back is rigid with tension. What kind of being has Susie imagined? The eighteen-year-old who gave her away? Some little old woman, twisted by regret and bitterness? Some aged reflection of herself? Her mother turns, and Susie realises that she's none of these things. She is small-boned and slight, a little shorter than Susie, her hair a glorious silver, her eyes the colour of sage and bright as shiny buttons. She has an impression of tidiness and a blur of aubergine before she finds herself locked in a fierce embrace. She is filled with hope and

154

confusion – but not love, not the overwhelming visceral feeling she has longed for and feared in almost equal measure.

There are tears – a few – and hankies, and anxious laughter and at some point, Susie realises, Helen has discreetly withdrawn so that she is alone with her mother.

'I knew you must be Susie Wallace,' Joyce says when they break apart at last.

Susie has kept her full name private until now, fearful that knowledge of her celebrity might influence her mother's decisions and feelings.

'Really? What made you think that?'

She studies her mother, looking for something familiar that might tie her to this person. There's something about the way she carries her head, perhaps, upright and a little defiant? Maybe the way her mouth curls and moves as she speaks is a bit like her own?

'You're so like— I can see—' Her voice tails off and she shakes her head. 'You're my daughter, that's all that matters to me.' She repeats the word with a kind of wonderment. 'My daughter.' Her eyes are still bright; tears near the surface, pride holding them back. 'All these years. Every day, thinking about you, thinking about my baby, not knowing – not daring to believe – that I would ever see you again. And here you are. Here you are.'

She sits down gingerly on a low chair, her back straight as a pencil and her body just as slim. The suit, Susie now sees, is a classic, nicely cut and neither old-fashioned nor trendy. Her mother has a sense of occasion. Susie takes a moment about her choice of seat. To face each other or sit side by side? To be close enough to touch, or a little further removed while they each make their assessment? Space and time to examine, with care, the tender surfaces of exposed emotion?

She settles back, just out of reach. For her part there's caution, certainly. Curiosity, perhaps. Maybe there's love

155

in the mix, maybe there's still anger – a deep-seated fury at what this woman has done to her, how some moment of irresponsibility has caused her to be brought into the world, then given away for fate to treat as it would.

'I need to know things,' she says.

'Of course. Where do you want me to start?'

Susie draws a deep breath. 'Tell me about my father.'

There's a pause. It's so long that she wonders if Joyce might, even now, baulk at giving her the information she craves. At last she says, 'You've got his hair. When you walked in the door, my breath was taken away by that.'

'Did you love him?'

Joyce gives a short laugh. 'It was fifty years ago and the world was a very different place. I was seventeen years old and I was working in a tea room near the theatre in Glasgow as a waitress. It was a summer holiday job with long hours and poor pay, but I was happy because the money gave me some small kind of freedom.

'And I liked the actors. They came in for their tea before the show quite often. High tea, we served in those days. Poached egg on toast followed by bread and jam, pancakes and scones, with a big pot of tea to wash it down. Fish and chips on a Friday. Mutton pie and beans instead of poached eggs some days.

'There was one of the actors took a shine to me, a young lad. Jimmy, his name was. He had glorious red-gold hair and honey coloured eyes and he was quick and funny and teasing. All the girls were a bit in love with him, but it was me he fancied. I was proud as punch when he asked me out.'

Susie finds she hasn't been breathing. Her father was an actor? Maybe one bit of her life is about to make sense. As Joyce pauses reflectively, she inhales deeply. Her story is about to unravel.

'He had difficult hours, of course, being in the theatre and all, but I used to wait for him at the stage door and then we'd be off out, to the dancing, to a party at some friend's flat, then eventually to his own room.'

She glances across at Susie. 'It was very different then. To go with a boy like that was chancy. I relied on Jimmy ... We thought we were being careful. We had such fun. What a boy he was! He made me feel like a queen, even though we had no money. He had the gift of the Irish for talking. Oh, he was a charmer. Did I love him? Yes, at the time, I thought I did, I was besotted with him.'

She stops talking for so long that Susie has to prompt her.

'And then?'

'He moved on. The season came to an end, he was out of work and he went back to his family until he found another job. I didn't know I was pregnant then, but I'm not sure what he'd have done if I'd known. He was a sweet talker, all right, but commitment was not a word he knew.'

'So you—'

'When I found out, my parents went mad. I'd brought shame on them, I'd brought disgrace to my family, I'd ruined my own life. They wanted him to marry me, but I knew he wouldn't. And I didn't want to mar the perfect happiness we had enjoyed with an endless future of argument and disillusionment and probably poverty. Marriage wouldn't have worked, not with Jimmy. I knew that. I wouldn't even tell them his name. So they sent me away, to a place on the other side of Glasgow, a hostel.'

'You were only seventeen!' Susie is appalled.

'Eighteen by the time you were born. Yes. And it was a difficult birth. The hostel had to send me to the hospital.'

'Rottenrow.'

'That's right. Rottenrow. I wouldn't let you out of my sight, you know. When they came to take you a few days later, I screamed and screamed, but in the end, I had no choice.'

Telling her story seems to have lent Joyce some

semblance of calmness; it has been a part of her for years, nothing is new, except the telling of it. For Susie, living it for the first time, the picture is bleak. Her cheeks feel wet. She puts a hand up, touches them, is forced to rummage for a hankie, all determination to remain calm undermined. 'You wanted to keep me?' she whispers, the need to know greater than anything.

'Brenda – Susie – my daughter.' At last the veneer of composure cracks and the look of fathomless anguish in Joyce's eyes tells Susie everything.

Susie reaches out her hand and grasps her mother's. And this time, the touch feels like some kind of answer to the multitude of questions that have weighed her down for so many weeks. They sit in silence, their clasped hands forging a primal link after half a century.

At length Susie speaks. 'You didn't say his name. My father's. Jimmy ...?'

But before Joyce can answer, there's a discreet tap on the door and Helen pokes her head round. 'Everything all right?' she asks brightly, then comes into the room. 'I can see you two are getting on well, but we do suggest that perhaps the first meeting is kept quite short. There's so much to tell, so much to learn, so many feelings to be explored, that we find it can all be a bit overpowering. How are you feeling?'

She looks inquiringly at Susie. 'A bit odd,' she admits with candour, 'but I feel happy to have made this move.'

'And you, Joyce?'

'Overwhelmed,' she admits. 'It's all happened quite quickly. But I'm overjoyed. I can't begin to put it into words.'

'Could I suggest,' Helen says diffidently, 'that perhaps the two of you make another arrangement to meet? Now that you've made a start, you can think about everything for a bit, maybe make a list of all the questions you still need answered. How do you feel about that?'

'Sounds good to me,' Susie says. It's true – her reservoir of energy has been drained by emotion.

Joyce, too, is looking exhausted. 'I think it's a good plan.'

Susie is just about to leave when she remembers that Joyce still hasn't told her who her father was. 'You were saying,' she says, 'my father—?'

'Yes. Sorry. It's quite odd – I'd seen you in films and things, but I couldn't be sure, not till you walked into the room today and I saw you for real. I told you he was an actor. He made it big, bigger than I thought, but the weakness I'd sensed in him was there all right. Maybe you even met him? His name was Jimmy Scirocco.'

Chapter Fifteen

Jimmy Scirocco.

Jimmy Scirocco!

Susie's head feels as though it's bursting. It has been a morning of such intense emotion and so many revelations, and now this – her father was the actor, Jimmy Scirocco.

Her mind flashes back to the article in the magazine. How ironic that her name has already been so publicly linked with his. Jimmy has been dead for ten years, overtaken by an excess of high living and a blind refusal (or perhaps a complete inability) to reform – but what a parcel of personal history to be handed!

Susie makes her way back to the bookshop where she left Mannie. It explains so much about her – where her acting came from, for sure, but also the more mercurial aspects of her personality, and perhaps her tendency to depression as well. It's a genetic bundle that includes genuine flair and a whole package of vulnerabilities – and they have been handed to her own children as well.

Mannie, vivacious and persuasive, is brilliant at her job, but her energy can turn all too easily into hyperactivity and her enthusiasm into excess emotion. And Jonathan, her talented young son, unwaged and apparently unwanted – it's no wonder he's on the verge of depression. She'll have to keep a careful eye on his drinking, she realises with shock.

What was it Mannie said, the night she told them all about her adoption?

'You're absolutely wrong, Jonno. Don't you see? This changes everything.'

Mannie's email inbox is brim full. Organised though she is, she'd always rather be talking to someone than staring into the unwelcoming screen of a computer. However, she's committed to sitting here for the next hour or so and it's a good opportunity to deal with her correspondence. She sips her Americano and launches herself vigorously into the task.

At the counter, a sturdily-built man with a receding hairline puts his mug on a tray, pays his bill and looks around.

Booking inquiry: a large dinner.

Complaint: room service tardy and inadequate.

Meeting 1: time confirmed.

Meeting 2: cancelled. Damn, damn, damn for the last one – a potential client she has been gently trawling for a while and is desperate to land. A slippery fish, it seems. Mannie clicks on the email and ponders what bait she can use on her hook.

<Dear Angela, I was so sorry to hear that you are unwell and trust that you will feel much better soon. Can I propose that we postpone our meeting till the 6th? We are opening our new coffee shop within our Princes Street hotel the following day, so you could join me for a test drive. Of course, assuming you are fully fit and back at work— >

'Is anyone sitting here?'

The voice, breaking in on her concentration, seems as familiar to her as if she has known it all her life. She looks up.

Jesus. It's him.

'Hi!' Mannie feels the blood rising to her face in treacherous betrayal. She bends forward so that her hair falls in a curtain across her face while she recovers and moves her laptop quickly to make room for him. 'No. Sit down. How extraordinary.'

'Oh, hello again. I didn't realise it was you. How

lucky.' Brian Henderson takes his coffee off the tray and sets it down carefully on the table. 'The coffees they serve in these places are always so huge, aren't they?'

She nods. 'Gross.'

Lucky? He said it was lucky! She can't pretend that she hasn't thought about him, but she has tried, in the period since she encountered him in London, to convince herself that the inexplicable feelings she experienced were some weird aberration. She has conquered them.

Or so she thought, until this moment of seeing him again, when she knows, beyond doubt, that she has never put him aside and that she will never be able to remove him from her thoughts. He forms an essential part of her. She *adores* this man.

She wrestles with the impulse to seize his hand so that she can stroke his skin and feel his fingers curl round hers. Something tells her this is odd behaviour, but she's utterly helpless in the grip of emotion. She desires him, but not in the way she desires Callum. She tries to define the sensation that fills her. It's something absolutely necessary, like breathing. The urgency of her need to be part of him overwhelms her absolutely.

He's invaded my soul.

She watches his Adam's apple move as he speaks. His neck is no longer young. Small folds of skin hang above his collar. She can't honestly describe them as attractive, but at the same time something deep within her is compelling her to bend her face towards them, smooth out the wrinkles with her kisses, feel the roughness of the stubble of hair that grows there against her lips. Lunacy.

She shakes her head to clear the feelings and says, as steadily as she can, 'This is a surprise – seeing you in Edinburgh, I mean.'

He sips his coffee, flinches at the heat, puts it back on its saucer and she notes that he drinks it black and as hot as possible, just as she does. She notices, with something akin to irritation, the gold band on his ring finger.

Married.

Of course he is, damn it.

'I'm in Edinburgh quite frequently. We have a number of clients here.'

'But your office is in Stirling? Isn't that a little unusual? Not being in the capital, I mean.'

'Stirling is better situated than you might think. We have clients in Inverness, Aberdeen, Glasgow.' The smile becomes mischievous and his next words make Mannie laugh. 'And believe it or not, our Glasgow clients would rather come to Stirling to see us than to Edinburgh.' The old rivalry between the two big cities is notorious. 'And I happen to live there, so it's a great base. Our head office is in London, of course.'

'Of course.' She's curious. 'Are you meeting someone?'

'I could ask you the same thing. Actually, my mother called on my services.' He glances at his watch briskly. Mannie, unconsciously, does the same thing, her slim hand mirroring the gesture. 'She's going to call me when her meeting's over.'

He lays his mobile on the table. Irrationally, she instantly hates its presence there because its ringing will drag him away from her. She tenses in anticipation.

'Working?' He nods at the laptop, then leans back and crosses his legs. He is nonchalant and relaxed – the polar opposite of the way Mannie is feeling.

'Yes. No. Well, yes, but nothing that won't keep. I can do it later.' She closes the lid.

'I haven't got back to you about that conference.'

'No hurry.' *Yes there is. I want to see more of you – a lot more.*

'I've been away on business.'

'Are you away a lot?'

'Sadly, yes. London, of course, all the time, but the

164

Middle East and America too. We have clients there.'

'Sounds glamourous.'

He grimaces. 'Travel always sounds glamorous, but living in a hotel room is far from – oh, sorry!' He laughs, realising.

'Don't worry. I know. Hotel rooms are bleak unless you're there for pleasure.' God, shut up, Mannie. 'We try our best to make them comfortable of course.'

Time races. Her coffee grows cold. She pushes it aside. Coffee doesn't matter, only talking to Brian matters, only being with him.

He's been abroad, he tells her. He has meetings in Edinburgh today, will be back in London tomorrow. He dislikes London, prefers the country. Likes long walks, if only he can find the time.

Just like me.

But time is always at a premium, with a business to run. He's ambitious, always has been.

Just like me.

A shaft of sunlight, edging round the frame of the huge windows, settles onto his face, picking out fine details. The laughter lines spreading from the corners of his eyes. Their colour – hazel.

Just like mine.

The soft folds of flesh under his chin. What was he like when he was my age? Cal's age? Good-looking, for sure. His face has lost the definition of youth, but he still has charisma. How else can she account for her feelings?

Her head is swimming. All thoughts of work have long since vanished.

'Mannie?'

'Sorry?' Christ, he's been chatting away and she hasn't even been listening. What must he think of her? 'I missed that. What did you say?'

'Your brother. Did he apply for that graphic designer job?'

'I think so. Yes.'

'Well, good luck to him. I hope he gets it.'

'Thank you.' Mannie is floating in the deep, powerful current of desire. It's as if he's a part of her, that she can't be complete without him. She wants, more than anything in the universe, to curl up within his comfortable embrace, be restored to a kind of entirety she hasn't known she lacked.

But I love Callum, she thinks, bemused.

The mobile on the table vibrates, then rings. Brian picks it up. 'Hello, Mother? Yes. Yes, fine, I'll be there in five minutes. Sorry—' to Mannie, '— duty calls.' He flashes her a smile.

Jesus, I want to drown in that smile.

'Of course.' Her flesh is tingling, as if it has been awakened by some unfamiliar force. It's a fabulous feeling, deeply luxurious. The thought of him walking away is unbearable. 'Will you call? About the conference, I mean?'

'Of course.' Again the hand is extended, a gesture far more formal than Mannie desires, but she takes it anyway.

This is what I need. This touch.

'Mannie? You all right?'

'Oh, hi, Mum.'

'You look rather flushed. Are you feeling all right?'

Mannie puts her hands up to her cheeks. They burn under her fingertips. 'It's a bit airless in here. I'm fine.' She waves at the chair Brian has just vacated. 'So. Tell me. How'd it go?'

She tries to listen. She is interested – truly – but her mother's words hold no meaning. All she can think of is Brian, and when she can see him again.

'Difficult day?' Jen asks that evening.

Mannie kicks off her shoes and sinks into her chair,

groaning. 'Unimaginable. Everything's such hard work at the moment. Getting a contract from anyone's like squeezing breath from a corpse.'

Jen hands her a glass of wine. 'Poor duck. Is Callum coming round?'

'No. He suggested it, but I'm too bushed.'

She doesn't want to tell the truth, which is that she can't face Cal, not now, not till she gets her head sorted out. For the first time since her encounter with Brian, Cal's face becomes vivid in her mind. She can see his clever, amused eyes and his expressive lips. She can hear his voice in her head, teasing her into a sharp, funny exchange. Cal has learned how to handle her restlessness, how to challenge her physically and emotionally. She finds him endlessly stimulating.

But now there's Brian.

She's drawn to Brian Henderson like a small shard of metal in the vicinity of a powerful magnet – she can't resist his pull. At the thought of Brian's smile, his compelling eyes, his aura of brisk efficiency, she becomes aware again of something deep and raw inside. She longs to discuss the encounter with Jen, but something stops her.

Jen is saying, 'Myra's getting a dress with a red top.'

Mannie stares at her. She couldn't connect with the words.

'Her wedding dress, Mannie,' Jen explains patiently. 'She's found one with a scarlet bodice, she says. She thinks it's wonderful.'

'Christ.'

'I know.'

'Red?' Mannie tries to clarify. The vision of the plump and slightly florid-faced Myra in a wedding dress with a red bodice is alarming.

'Can we talk her out of the idea, do you think?'

'We have to try. Has she set a date?'

'September.' Jen's face drops a little as she

167

contemplates this. 'You'll be going with Callum, I guess.'

Even in her current state of emotional turmoil, Mannie understands what the comment means. Jen is unattached. She will have to attend the wedding alone. Mannie has been in this position herself and she knows that going to weddings as a single woman is difficult. There's a deep sense of loneliness because everyone else is matched up in blissful coupledom. Either that or the bride places you helpfully with one of the groom's single mates – unattached because he has serious body odour, or can only talk about football, or is a complete geek – and what starts out as a mildly depressing day descends into grim martyrdom. It becomes impossible to wait to see the last dance – but as a close friend of the bride, you have to. She extends a sympathetic hand towards Jen. 'Bet you've got a great guy by then.'

Jen shrugs. 'Not sure I can handle a relationship right now anyway.'

Mannie isn't certain she can handle a relationship either. Despite everything she is trying to do to stop it, the recent vision she has begun to nurture of a life that delightfully includes Callum has started to fracture round the edges. In the space of a mere day, she's no longer excited by the thought – in fact, she finds it confusing. She loves Callum, but thinks only of Brian. She opens her mouth to tell Jen about the encounter, then closes it again, because what can she say? How can she describe something so irrational?

'Anyway, I've made a decision,' Jen says.

'Yeah? What?'

Mannie is expecting her to say, 'I'm going to join an internet dating agency,' but instead she comes out with, 'I'm going to buy a flat for myself. I'm going to grow up, finally!'

Mannie's jaw drops open and she gapes at Jen. Buy a flat? With Myra getting married and Jen buying her own

168

flat, Mannie will be on her own, a thought that appalls her. Much as she has enjoyed her many relationships, she is comfortable in the company of her girlfriends. They understand her. They share her interests. They clean up after themselves and don't leave things all over the floor to be magically tidied away.

'Wow,' she says, her voice feeble. Her support system is crumbling – just, she thinks, as she might need it most.

Jen pulls out a copy of the weekly property list and points to some flats she has circled. 'Will you come and see them with me? I'd ask Myra, but she's all wedding plans right now. I know you're busy, but could you spare an hour or two on Sunday? I'd be ever so grateful.'

'Sure. Love to,' Mannie lies. Myra holds the lease of the flat. She thinks it runs out in the summer. What is she going to do? Already she has noticed that Myra is spending less time in their company, presumably now that she has a ring on her finger she has granted her man some premarital rights. And – has she been aware of it? – she realises that Jen has also been less in evidence. Where has she been? Maybe spending more time with her parents. Her father has recently been ill, she's a dutiful daughter.

'Are you going to move closer to your folks?'

'Possibly. It can take for ever getting across town sometimes and I'd quite like to be nearer Mum.' She doesn't say it, but she means if anything happens to her father.

'Of course.' Mannie is sympathetic, but inside she's devastated. Myra will be married. She'll move away. Jen is going to move too. Days ago – heavens, hours ago even – this might have seemed to her the perfect opportunity to float some ideas to Callum. To take on the lease? To discuss the possibility of purchasing a property together?

But now? Where does her future lie now?

A few days later, Jonno calls. Mannie is at work, deep in a

dispute about disabled access ramps.

Jonno never calls her at work. 'Hey,' she says, alarmed, 'What's up?'

'I've been asked for an interview.'

Her anxiety subsides at once. 'Great. What for?'

'That job. The one you suggested I apply for. In Stirling?'

Mannie abandons the computer and sits back suddenly. *Brian Henderson has come through for me.* Memories of the hazel eyes and animated smile flood over her like a wall of water breaching sea defences. She is so intensely overcome that she has to cling on for her life. She's clutching the edge of the desk, her knuckles are already white, pain is shooting up her arm.

'Still there, Sis?'

'Sure.' She clears her throat. 'That's great, Jonno. When's the interview?'

'Monday. I'm getting nervous.'

'Don't be. You'll get the job.' She's absolutely certain of this, but she can't tell her brother why.

'There'll be loads of competition. I'm lucky to be getting an interview even. I mean, now there's people getting made redundant, people who've got loads of experience.'

'Stop talking yourself out of it, Jonno. They may not want someone with experience. They might want someone they can mould.'

'Like putty? Meek and malleable? Not sure that's me.'

'That's not what I meant.' Mannie is struggling to hold on to the conversation. She's trembling. The thought of Brian is making her feel hot and cold and shaky, all at the same time. 'They might want someone with new ideas and with no preconceptions, and they're sure to want someone hungry for the chance. Whatever, you've got what it takes, bro. Sock it to 'em. Mum and Dad pleased?'

'Haven't told them yet.'

'That still not good, huh?'

'Not great.' He sounds cautious. 'How's Cal?'

'The cricket season has started. I've not seen much of him recently.'

'Right. You okay?'

'Fine,' she lies. 'Let me know how it goes, hey?'

'Sure. Will do.' And Jonno has gone, leaving her alone with her emotions.

Mannie sits at her desk for what feels like forever. She's fighting against her inclinations, because what she wants to do – all she wants to do – is see Brian Henderson.

She'll call him – she has his card. Or text him? Perhaps a short email might be the best approach.

Or maybe she shouldn't get in touch at all, because she loves Cal.

She reaches for her handbag, stowed in its hiding place underneath her desk. Opens it. Finds her purse. Feels for the card Brian handed to her. It's in her hand. She stares at it, even though she has already memorised the telephone number. What she needs is to hold it, because he once held it. It's her connection to him. She puts it to her nose and sniffs it. The card seems to hold the essence of his particular odour, warm, slightly musky, very male. She puts it to her mouth and brushes the card with her lips.

Above her, on the wall, a clock is ticking. Six minutes have passed since Jonno ended the call.

Chapter Sixteen

Mannie spends a week fighting the impulse to call Brian Henderson. His business card becomes grubby from frequent handling. Finally, she succumbs and dials his number.

'Is Mr Henderson there please?'

'May I ask who's calling?'

'My name is Margaret-Anne Wallace.'

'From—?'

The secretary sounds protective. Her job is to shield her boss from nuisance callers and she's determined to fulfil her duties. Mannie hesitates. 'It's personal,' she says shortly.

'Hold on please, I'll see if he's available.'

Mannie rolls her eyes and tries very hard not to make her tut of impatience audible, but it takes only a few seconds for the call to be put through and once again she hears the voice she's been imagining in her head for the past eight days.

'Ms Wallace. Hello. How nice to hear from you again. What can I do for you?'

The formality of his greeting shocks her. What did she expect? In her head she's been creating a much more intimate scenario and now that she's on the phone, she realises that she hasn't thought this through. She doesn't want to talk about Jonno, that must take its course. In truth, she only wants one thing, which is to see him again, and as soon as possible.

Impulsive to the core, she blurts out, 'I was wondering ... next time you're in Edinburgh? I thought we might meet for dinner.'

God, what must he think of me?

She adds hastily, 'I mean, there's so much more I can tell you about what we can offer here at the hotel, I'd love to discuss it more informally than I was able to at Confex. Or I could come to Stirling?'

'Well, I—'

Of course he's taken aback. How idiotic she is!

Mannie is cringing at her ineptitude and still trying to work out her next line when Brian says, 'Actually, I see I'm in Edinburgh next week for a meeting that should finish around six. Would Thursday be any use to you? I don't have any reason to rush home, I dare say we could fit in a quick meal. If you're free that day, that is?'

She feels her face flush. *Am I free?* 'Thursday's fine,' she says neutrally, although inside she's dancing a jig.

They arrange a venue. After he rings off, she checks her diary and discovers she has a prior engagement, a meeting with an important client. She'll have to ask Sylvia to deputise. The client won't be pleased, but needs must – seeing Brian Henderson has to take priority.

The week passes slowly. Work is a chore, she feels weighed down and heavy, drugged, almost. It's as if she's lacking some essential element in her life blood. She considers a doctor's appointment (maybe she's anaemic?) but decides to wait.

'Meeting someone nice?' Myra pokes her head round Mannie's door and shouts above the noise of Mannie's hairdryer.

'Sorry?' Mannie stops brushing, switches the dryer off and lifts her head.

'I said, are you meeting someone nice, or just Callum?' Dimples appearing in her plump cheeks as she roars with laughter. 'Oops, sorry! I didn't mean Callum wasn't nice, I meant—'

174

'It's okay, I've got you,' Mannie smiles. Her hair, almost dry, shines softly in the light streaming in the window and swings, thick and smooth, round her shoulders. 'I'm meeting a client.'

'Oh, poor you. You do so much evening work, it's a shame.'

'I don't mind. I'm sure I'll enjoy the evening.' *Enjoy it? I'm going to cherish every minute.* 'How are your plans coming along? Have you got the dress sorted out? Did you go for the red?'

Myra snorts and giggles. 'No! Thank heavens. Jen talked me out of it. She was quite right, red would have reflected up onto my face and made me look like a beetroot. I've gone for ivory, with a lace top, just like Kate Middleton's.'

Mannie feels a pang of guilt. She has been neglecting Myra, while Jen has been spending time with her. She berates herself for selfishness, she hasn't been a good friend. She smiles warmly. 'Oh, that sounds lovely!'

'So this client – what's his name?'

Again the tiny flutter in her chest. 'Brian Henderson.'

'He's a big business prospect, is he?'

'I'm going to try to secure a contract,' she keeps her voice casual.

'What a shame. Bet you'd rather be looking at Callum across a dinner table, any night.'

She shrugs. 'Cal's training anyway. And this guy's nice.'

Nice. Such a dismissive word. So ordinary. Yet no way is Brian Henderson ordinary, not in her eyes. Put Brian Henderson side by side with Callum and there can be no comparison – no girl in her right mind would choose the older man, pleasant though he is. But what does sense have to do with anything? Brian is essential to life. To her life, at least. And that's that. She can't put it more simply. He is the missing element in the structure of her DNA, the

175

gene that is needed to complete her.

Leith is full of restaurants. Like waterfront areas in many cities, the area is still a mixture of the seedy and run-down and the vibrant and trendy. Mannie has arranged to meet Brian in one of the many eateries that line the small river that runs into the sea at this point.

The evening is unusually still, there's hardly a breath of air to roughen the surface of the soft-flowing water and as Mannie walks towards the rendezvous, she can see the serried rows of white-painted, crow-step-gabled houses reflected on its surface. By the bridge, a swan paddles lazily upstream, barely hampered by the current. Further down, a small crowd has spilled out of a pub onto the broad pavement and is noisily and happily exchanging gossip, jokes, snatches of song.

Mannie glances at her watch. She has ten minutes to make it to the restaurant. Plenty of time. She slows the ferocious pace she has set herself. It will not look good to be early. Better to let Brian wait a civilised few minutes.

By the bridge she stops and leans on the parapet to stare into the slowly swirling water. It's dark and unfathomable. The surface acts like a mirror, so that Mannie can see her own face staring back up at her against the blue of the evening sky. It's disturbingly unfamiliar – dark, shadowed, unreadable. And beneath the surface? Weeds, unchecked and untended; small pockets of rubbish, carelessly and wantonly discarded; a dark secret, perhaps – some rejected ring, or a knife, thrown in haste to avoid discovery. It can be a rough area in the dark of the night.

Sucked into her thoughts, it's some minutes before Mannie jerks back to Leith on a Thursday evening in early summer and to an encounter that beckons deliciously. She hurries round the corner.

She pauses on the threshold of the restaurant, overtaken by doubt. What if it's a disaster? What if she has been imagining her feelings? What if he doesn't feel the same way? What if he isn't even there? Mannie takes a deep breath and pushes open the door. There's only one way to find out.

He is there, waiting for her, sitting in a dimly lit corner. His head is propped on his hand as he reads the menu. The angle of his head lights a bonfire in her soul.

Ridiculous.

But true.

Her breathing has almost stopped and it feels as if her heartbeat has doubled in pace.

'Hi!' He lifts his head, he sees her, he's looking at her, smiling, waving.

'Hi!' The word emerges as a croak, but it doesn't matter because her voice could not be heard across the hubbub of the restaurant.

She winds her way between the tightly-packed tables towards him. He's standing now and she thinks for one dizzy moment that he's going to encircle her with his arms, but instead he extends his hand. She clutches it eagerly, desperate to feel his skin against hers, luxuriating in the feel of his warm fingers, his dry palm.

'Lovely to see you again.' He releases her hand and pulls out a chair for her.

Mannie, reeling from his touch, tucks away the memory of it in her soul. 'And you.'

Then it's all small talk, menus, decisions about food (two courses or three? meat or fish?) and about water (still or sparkling?). Wine – red or white, Bordeaux or Burgundy? She goes with the flow, reading the new language of his face and eyes, trying not to stare rudely as she drinks in his presence.

'Thanks for giving Jonno an interview,' she says as she picks at the glistening pink flesh of the smoked salmon in front of her. She's starving, but excitement is also making her feel nauseous. She moves the fish around her plate, puts her fork down and reaches for her wine.

'He's been asked to come, has he? I didn't know.' Brian's appetite is clearly unaffected by her proximity – he shovels his starter into his mouth with obvious appreciation. 'I'm glad.'

Mannie experiences a momentary disappointment. Brian has not been involved in the decision. He hasn't done her a special favour, as she has imagined. Still, she smiles. 'He's really excited. And nervous.'

'I'm sure he'll do very well. You'll appreciate I can't get involved?'

'I wouldn't expect it,' Mannie lies. Every thread of her being is drawn towards him, like tendrils reaching to a branch for support. She yearns to reach out to touch him. In her head she can hear her manager's voice: 'Inappropriate behaviour'. But is it? How can it be when it feels so right?

'Tell me about yourself.' His eyes are bright, alert, full of humour.

The intimacy of the question thrills her. 'Oh I'm just—'

What is she? Who is she? Is she the same person today, now, sitting at this table with him, as she was last week, in bed with Callum, telling Callum she loved him?

'—just me,' she finishes lamely. 'I'm the sales director for a hotel chain – well, you know that, of course,' she adds, flustered. 'I like walking, sport, talking – I do that quite a lot,' she grins, beginning to relax more in his company. 'I live with a couple of girlfriends in a rented flat, which I quite like, because I do like a good gossip. But I'm almost ready for something different,' she adds hastily, lest he should think her immature.

'Boyfriend?'

'Yes. No. Well, sort of.'

How can she betray Callum like that? Mannie hates herself for the words, but can't help them. She doesn't want Brian to think there's any barrier to them being

178

together.

'Sort of?' he's smiling inquiringly, the flirtatious look back in his eyes.

He likes me! This is more than a business dinner after all.

The main course comes and goes. Dessert comes and goes. She barely touches her food. All she can think is, *This man completes me.* Every word, every gesture, each opening and closing of his mouth seems to confirm and reinforce her feelings.

But by eight it's over. They are finished and Brian is saying, 'I must go.'

Outside, in the sudden chill of the evening, she says, 'Thank you for dinner.'

'My pleasure,' he smiles, his face friendly as he gazes down towards her.

He takes her hand as though he's going to shake it, then just as regret is washing over her, he pulls her close to him and bends his head to hers and they're kissing. The softness of his lips is delightful and her mouth goes slack with pleasure. A breeze, sneaking round the corner of the building behind them, lifts her hair and wraps it round the two of them, a curtain of privacy. As his lips move gently on hers, desire passes through her like a surge of a thousand volts and she arches her body towards him.

It's over almost as quickly as it began. Brian steps back sharply, his hand gentle but firm on her arm, pushing her away. 'No need to thank me,' he says neutrally, turning briskly to walk on. 'Listen, I'll drop you home.'

Is it an opening? Will he come in? Is he playing with her? Why has he kissed her? He must feel the same as she does, surely? She says, a little shakily, 'It's out of your way.'

'No trouble.'

For once, Mannie wishes Portobello was further from Leith. A ten-minute drive is not enough. She wants to be in the car with him for hours – for ever. She wants to inhale the musky warmth of him and swim in the rich, dark waters of his voice. 'Coffee?' she asks brightly as he pulls his Audi up to the kerb outside her front door.

'Sorry, I must go. It's still an hour's drive home and I'd like to see the kids before they go to bed.'

Kids. Of course. He has kids. He has a wife, he told her so. What is she thinking? What is he thinking, because she didn't imagine that kiss.

'You're a lovely girl, Margaret-Anne Wallace,' he says softly, reaching across the gear stick and running his hand down her cheek.

Her breathing quickens and she thrills at the touch of his skin.

'So pretty.'

He takes her hand, runs his fingers across hers, rubs his thumb in her palm. It's incredibly sensual, deeply arousing.

'We must meet again.'

She says, 'Yes,' feeling the inevitability of it.

He releases her hand and she lifts it to her head. She can feel the blood pumping at her temple, the force of it threatening a headache. Is he suggesting an affair?

'Come in,' she says, pleading.

'I can't. Not tonight. Be patient.'

So she has to get out of the car and leave him to go home to his wife and his children. She feels the parting keenly, watches as he speeds round the corner of the street, stares at the vacuum he leaves behind. As the space left by his car expands and fills the sky, Cal's face comes into her mind and, with it, confusion returns.

Chapter Seventeen

'Got that contract with the German signed yet?' Callum's voice down the phone is thin and unreal.

She hasn't seen Callum in the past fortnight. It is, possibly, the longest period they have been apart since they first met.

'Today, as it happens.'

Miraculously, in the midst of emotional turmoil, she has nailed one contract, at least. She doesn't want to think about work.

'How's the cricket?'

Callum groans. 'I'm not as fit as I'd hoped. Every muscle aches. How about supper?'

'I'm really busy at the mo.'

'Are you avoiding me, Mannie?'

'No. Why?'

'I haven't seen you for ages.'

'You're really busy. So'm I.'

'We could've met at the weekend. Sunday.'

'I had to go in and do some budget forecasts.'

'So you said.' Callum's voice is heavy with scepticism.

'So—'

'So you can't have been all day doing budgets.'

'I was.'

'And all evening? You said you'd call after you were done.'

'I was shattered.'

For the past couple of years Callum McMaster kept her keen by having other interests and other friends, so that she sometimes felt she had to book herself into his diary like a business meeting. Now she's the one being evasive.

'You could have called to tell me.'

'I did. I left a message.'

'Then hid behind your voicemail.'

'I didn't hide. I went to bed early and turned the phone off.'

There's a pause. Mannie, curled up on her bed with her mobile to her ear, is only half engaged in the conversation with Cal, another part of her is wondering what Brian is doing right now. Seven fifteen, Tuesday evening. Is he at work? In his London office? Or at home, having dinner with his wife? The last thought chills her.

'So have supper,' Callum is saying. She can hear the challenge in his voice.

For a minute, Mannie's whole mind switches to Cal and she can see his sharp cheekbones and teasing smile. She thinks longingly of the closeness they developed. *I want to tell him about Brian*, she thinks, absurdly. *I want to get his advice. I need to know what's happening to me, because I don't understand.* The fact is, however, that she is utterly powerless to resist them. And she can't confide in Callum. She hasn't even been able to tell Jen.

'Okay,' she says reluctantly, in answer to his question. 'When?'

'Tomorrow. There's no nets. I'll come round. I'll bring a Chinese and some beer.'

'Fine.' She knows her voice is unenthusiastic so she repeats the word, this time with brio. 'Fine!'

After he rings off, Mannie sits for a moment, staring vacantly into space. Her mind, however, is far from vacant. She looks down at the mobile phone in her hand as though it's something magical that has just appeared in her hands, like a rabbit pulled from a hat. It's a means of communication. With Brian. Why hasn't she thought of that before? The phone is smooth under her fingers. It's time to make contact.

She starts to text.

<Hi Brian. How r u? Loved dinner. Must meet again soon.>

She selects Brian's mobile number and presses send. And waits.

Nothing.

Maybe he's switched it off. No harm in trying again.

<Forgot to say, loved ur tie.>

It isn't entirely true, but she's desperate to keep all channels of communication open.

Still nothing.

She plays idly with the touchpad on her phone, composes the text she really wants to send.

<PS I love you.>

She looks at the shape and form of the words. So short and simple, yet so deeply sweet. There's a book of that title, isn't there? And a film? She must find it and watch it. Still, even though she might think the thought, she can't send this message to Brian. She reaches for the delete button.

Shit! She has pressed send by mistake.

Mannie looks at the phone in horror. Christ! What will he think? Too late to undo the deed. Best compose another text to explain.

<Sorry! Didn't mean 2 send.>

But does she really want to deny it? Why not be open and honest? There shouldn't be secrets between them. She keys in another message, her thumbs tapping the screen in short, staccato movements.

<True tho.>

A rap on the door and Jen pokes her head round. 'Drinkie?'

'Why not?' She hasn't had a good chat with Jen for ages. Absently, she presses send again.

'You're not working?' Jen indicates the phone.'

Mannie tosses it away. 'No, no, nothing like that.'

'And Callum's not on his way, is he?'

'No, not tonight.'

'I'll pour then.'

'Be right there.'

As Jen closes the door behind her, she reaches forward and picks up the phone again, peering at it as if a message might have – by some supernatural means – have appeared silently, without announcing itself. A ridiculous notion, of course. There's no answer from Brian. She picks her phone up again and scrolls through her sent messages, re-reading what she's written. Good grief! Has she really told him she loves him? She'd better rectify that.

<Soz for last msgs! Mistake. Let's talk.>

There. That will reassure him. She tucks the phone into the pocket of her jeans and squirms off the bed. Passing the mirror, she pauses to run a brush through her hair. He called her pretty. The thought pleases her and she is smiling as she walks into the living room. 'Hey.'

'Hey. Nice to see you looking happy for a change. Here.'

Jen hands her a glass of white wine. 'Cheers.'

'Oh. Yeah. Cheers.'

As they sink down on to their chairs, Jen says curiously, 'You've been really odd recently, Mannie. Something up?'

Up? Nothing much. Merely the fact that I've fallen in love with a man old enough to be my father. Even thinking the words gave Mannie a jolt. Not only is Brian Henderson as old as her father, but he's also quite ordinary, and middle aged, and balding. He's got a spare tyre and a wife and kids. And she has Callum, who is gorgeous and who loves her, and who is, besides, a Really Nice Guy.

'Mannie?'

She takes a deep gulp of the wine and feels it course down her throat. 'Yes?'

'Is something wrong?'

Mannie tries to convince herself that she can talk to

184

Jen, that she's safe. Nevertheless, she proceeds cautiously. 'I've been worrying. See, there's this girl at work—'

'Do I know her?'

'Er, no, I don't think so. Anyway, it doesn't matter. This girl, she's having an affair.'

Jen laughs. 'Nothing new there then. Is it with her boss?'

'No, not her boss, but with a much older man. Old enough to be her father.'

'Yeugh, gross.'

'He's a very nice man.'

'Whatever. Why doesn't she look elsewhere? Is she crazy, or what?'

'Crazy.' Mannie considers the word. 'I suppose she might be. Depends how you define crazy, I guess. She seems to be pretty fixated on him. Anyway—'

She pauses, considering. She isn't entirely sure, now that she has started the conversation where it's going to end up.

'Anyway, what do you think I should do? Tell her to give up on him, or tell her to follow her heart?'

'Oh, tell her to give him a swerve, for sure. Plenty other guys around.'

If only it were that simple – but there's nothing rational about her feelings for Brian Henderson. All the arguments are against pursuing a relationship with him, but something inside her is driving her to him.

'Don't you think it's a bit weird?' Jen is saying, 'I mean, why would you?'

But now Mannie doesn't want to talk about it. Jen's reaction is enough to warn her off the topic. 'You're right,' she says. 'I'll tell her. Now listen, what about you? Any news on the flat front? Thought about that one in Musselburgh we saw?'

'Yeah. I've decided it's too far out. You free tomorrow to go round more?'

185

Mannie shakes her head. 'Sorry. Promised to see Cal.'

'Right. I'll go myself then.'

'I'd love to Jen, honest.'

'Sure.'

Mannie can hear her phone buzzing through in her bedroom. *Brian!*

'Hang on, Jen, sorry, I need to get that.'

He's answered me! I knew he would!

But it isn't Brian. The message is from her mother, suggesting lunch.

Mannie ponders Jen's reaction to her story as she lies awake in bed. She is right, of course. The very idea of having a relationship with such an old man is bizarre. And in any case, who is she fooling? Brian has shown no desire to see her again and apart from that one brief moment when they kissed, he has shown no sign of finding her particularly attractive.

Best to put all thoughts of him aside.

But is that possible? she asks herself.

Back comes the answer: not only possible – essential.

By the time she falls asleep, her mind is made up. She won't contact Brian again.

Chapter Eighteen

Supper is to be a private affair – Myra is at her future in-laws for supper and Jen is out. Mannie makes an effort. She showers and washes her hair just before Callum arrives, so that her dark locks shine and ripple across her shoulders as she moves. She even puts on her red dress, the one Cal really likes.

I am going to forget Brian, she vows to herself. *I really am.*

Cal arrives, smiling and handsome and bearing a bulging carrier bag of food, and she knows she had made the right decision.

'Singapore-style noodles, scallops with ginger and cashew nuts, egg fried rice and some Tsingtao, nicely chilled.'

He unloads a series of foil containers from the paper carrier bag.

'Brilliant. I'm ravenous.'

He laughs. 'You're always ravenous, Mannie. Got some bowls?'

She pulls them out of the cupboard, and glasses for the beer.

'So. What's new?'

'Nothing really. Just loads of work. You?'

'Work. And cricket, of course.'

'How's it going?'

'Pretty well. Except for the screaming muscles.'

Cal helps himself to a large bowlful of food and attacks it with the chopsticks Mannie has laid out.

'When's the first match?'

The scallops are good and she eats them with relish, but

as she asks the question, it occurs to her that she should know the answer already, that they're talking like relative strangers. This is Cal, for heaven's sake!

'Week on Saturday. Going to come?'

'Of course I'll come,' she says reproachfully, and feels guilty that he has to ask.

Callum is smart and talented and nice – and he is hers. That is what she wants. So why does she feel so ridiculously awkward with him? She feels almost as if she has been unfaithful and is frantically trying to cover her tracks – which is so not true. Or is it? Because in her head, she has come perilously close to being unfaithful.

'I'll stay tonight, if you like.'

'That would be great.'

Mannie tries to say it with enthusiasm. *I am keen, for goodness' sake.* She thinks of his smooth skin and the hollow plain of his stomach, the way she fits together with him, like exactly the right jigsaw piece slotting into place. He is the best lover she has ever had, not just because he's deliciously sexy, but because she loves him. She holds out her hand, across the kitchen table and lets it nestle inside his big one.

Myra appears, opening the door and stumbling in awkwardly, dropping her bags clumsily in her usual ungainly way.

Cal leaps to her aid. 'Hi, gorgeous bride to be.' He kisses her cheek.

Myra blushes. 'Ooh, Cal, you are lovely,' she giggles. 'Isn't he, Mannie?'

'Lovely,' Mannie agrees, wondering why she isn't melting inside at the thought of him sharing her bed tonight.

'Shall we head?' Cal nods towards her bedroom.

She knows what he's thinking. He wants privacy. He wants to hop into bed and cuddle up. He wants all the things she wanted too, just a week or two back. *I do want them*, she tries to convince herself. *Of course I do.*

But when the door is shut and he turns and pulls her into his arms, she tenses, and when his lips came down on hers, she turns her head away.

'What?' He senses the resistance and moves back. 'What is it?'

She bursts into tears.

'Christ, Mannie, what's up? Is it the time of month? What? I've never seen you like this before.'

Mannie rolls into a ball. Callum, perching on the edge of the bed beside her has his hand on her shoulder. He's trying to uncurl her, to get her to look at him, to coax her to tell him what it's all about. She knows it, she can feel the contact, loves him for trying, hates herself for being like this.

'What?' Callum repeats. 'Have I done something? Mannie—'

His voice trails away uncertainly.

She hears it and the guilt redoubles. Uncertainty so isn't like Callum, and he's done nothing to deserve this. Nothing at all. It's her fault, everything is her fault. But I can't not tell him, Mannie thinks, as the great, wracking sobs begin to ease into something less all-consuming. What will he think? Will he be like Jen was? Revolted? Critical? Hurt?

She uncurls slowly and twists round so that she can bury her head on his chest – anything rather than actually face him. And yet that has to be done. She has to look into his eyes and confess her feeling, because unless she does, there can be no moving forward.

It takes ten minutes, maybe more, and Cal's patience in that time nearly breaks her heart. He holds her, soothes her as you might comfort a child who has fallen over.

'There, there. It's all right. It's okay. Everything's going to be fine,' he repeats over and over again, whispering softly into her hair so that all she is aware of is a sweet susurration of sound, like a breeze in tall grasses.

She thinks of the day they spent on the beach down the coast – before London, before Confex, before Brian – when they lay on the dunes and heard the wind make just this noise.

It works, up to a point – up to the point when she knows she can avoid it no longer. She edges out of his arms, accepts a tissue and blows her nose.

'So,' he says, the corner of his mouth lifting a fraction, a twitch that reads more like wry resignation than humour. 'I think you'd better tell me. Or no, let me guess.'

He puts a finger to his chin and tilts his head to one side. 'Just nod or shake. Okay?'

She nods.

'You've been sacked for gross misconduct.'

Shake.

'Herr Leeuwen's cancelled his contract?'

Shake.

'Okay, but he's sticking with the dancing girls request?'

Shake, this time accompanied by the tiniest of giggles.

'Good. You've lost weight?'

Shake, shake.

'You've put on weight?'

Shake, shake, shake.

'That leaves illness, an illicit affair and pregnancy.'

He says it jokingly, but faced with three options, Mannie hesitates. It's enough to alarm him.

'Don't tell me you're pregnant.'

'I'm not pregnant.' She manages a whisper. In her hand, the balled tissue feels soggy and unpleasant.

'You're ill? What? You haven't got cancer or something, have you?'

'No, no – no, I'm not ill.' Her voice dies as she realises what is left.

Cal is staring at her, his eyes filled with disbelief.

'You're having an affair?' His voice rises sharply at the end of the sentence. 'Mannie?'

'I'm not having an affair.' She can hear her own voice, the words choked and half strangled, sounding unnatural. 'Not even close.'

The relief on his face is obvious, and that made her confession even harder.

'I give up. You'd better tell me.'

Prevaricating, she reaches for a clean tissue, blows her nose again, wipes her eyes, sniffs, then – finally – begins.

'I've met this man.'

'I thought you said you weren't having an affair?'

'I'm not.'

She thinks of the kiss and dismisses the memory. The lie is only a tiny one.

'The thing is ... the thing is—' This is it. Here goes. 'I met him one day. Accidentally. I was at that trade fair, the same one I had to deal with Herr Leeuwen, and he just came by the stand. And I ... got these strange feelings for him. I didn't mean to, Cal, honest, I couldn't help it, it just happened and I can't stop thinking about him but nothing's happened, honest it hasn't, I mean I haven't done anything, but I'm obsessed with him and I can't help it and —'

The words are gushing out now, unstoppable, and the sight of Callum's face, the open mouth, the incredulous look in the eyes, just makes her babble more. 'I know it's ridiculous, Cal, I've told myself a dozen times, a hundred times, don't think I haven't, but I can't stop thinking about him.'

'I don't understand.'

'I've said.'

'You met a man at a trade fair and you've fallen for him. Just like that.'

'Yes.'

She can't bear to look at him. She can't bear what she is doing any more than she can understand why she is doing it.

'Why, Mannie?'

She shrugs, a tiny lift of the shoulders. It isn't meant to appear unfeeling, but the gesture is enough to infuriate Cal.

'Is he handsome? Funny? Rich? What?'

'None of these things. He's as old as Dad, and he's going bald.' She can hear the absurdity of it.

Callum is just staring at her. It seems he has lost the power to speak.

'I don't know what it is, Cal.' She spreads her hands pleadingly. 'I know it's stupid, but I ... can't help it. I want to be with him. Sometimes it seems to me that's all I want in the whole world. It's like my whole being has been invaded by something and I can't fight it.'

She reaches out for his hand, wanting to explain, but he snatches it away and folds his arms. His lips are pursed tightly, and a deep frown has appeared between his eyes.

'I still love you, Cal,' she says beseechingly. 'And I don't want this to happen. I want to fight it. But I can't. I can't.'

The tears are threatening to start again and her throat is swelling with the effort of fighting them. Cal's arms are folded tightly across his body, forbidding approach. He stands up and starts pacing around the room.

'Christ, Mannie, if you'd told me you'd turned lesbian I couldn't be more stunned.'

'Cal, can we talk about—'

'What is there to talk about, for heaven's sake?'

'I haven't done anything! Cal, please, you've got to believe me! It's just how I feel and I can't help it.'

'I thought you loved me, Mannie, I had begun to think we could make it.'

'Me too!'

'I laid my heart on my hand for you.'

'Cal—'

192

'And with your pals moving out, I thought we might even talk about living together.'

'Sweetheart, I—'

'Sweetheart? What are you talking about, Mannie? You can't be in love with two people at the same time. And certainly not when one of them is me.

'Please try to understand—'

But Cal is reaching for his sweater. 'You're a great talker, Mannie, but don't try to talk yourself out of this one. '

She is heavy, weighed down with it all. She can't move. Even raising a hand to try to stop him seems too difficult. All she can do is watch, her eyelids leaden with shed and unshed tears, as he slams out of the room.

She hears Myra say, in startled tones, 'Everything all right, Callum?' and his growled reply, and then the front door bangs closed and he has gone.

Christ. I messed that up.

'You okay, Mannie?' Myra's head comes round her door, her kindly face full of concern.

'Fine,' Mannie says, in a voice that tells exactly the opposite story. 'Just fine.'

It's a wretched night. Why did she have to tell Callum? Couldn't she have kept the whole thing to herself until she'd sorted her head out? Sleep doesn't come to her till dawn, and even then it's fitful and brings little respite. The first thing she does when she wakes is check her phone.

Mannie hates herself for that, because in truth what she wants to see is something from Brian, not Callum. The memory of Cal's face, the look of shock, and hurt, and wretchedness, and confusion, of his usually kissable lips slack with barely controlled emotion, hurts her inside like a reamer scouring her guts – but it's Brian she wants to text her.

Frantic with longing, she flicks her way through the

193

messages, wondering if she has missed something in her eagerness. But there's nothing. Against all rational judgement, she texts him again.

<Morning! Call me from work?>

She goes to wash.

Makes herself a coffee.

Forces herself to wash last night's dishes before she checks again. Still nothing.

<I'll leave my phone on. Call any time.>

By the time she leaves for work, she has sent eleven texts. Nothing unusual in that. Just making sure he knew she wanted to talk to him. Just normal, friendly texts.

She's in a client meeting first thing and is forced to put her phone on silent, but she leaves it on the table in front of her.

'Expecting an urgent call,' she says with an apologetic smile. 'Hope it doesn't disturb us. Sorry.'

If he calls, she'll have to excuse herself, there can be no other choice.

But he doesn't call. With an effort that feels almost superhuman, Mannie forces herself not to text again. A dozen times she picks up the phone, her fingers itching, then makes herself lay it down again. He will think she's mental. She isn't, of course, just ... just what, Mannie? Just obsessed? Not that, surely not that? Just friendly, just wanting to know he's all right, that he has been thinking about her.

Don't kid yourself, Mannie, a voice in her head keeps telling her. You're crazy about him.

What, then, of Callum?

And so it goes on, round and round her head until she really does feel crazy – but Brian doesn't call that week. Neither does Callum.

Chapter Nineteen

Home, even for a nearly thirty-year-old, is the place to run to when life gets rough. At home, Prince will greet her with unequivocal, non-judgemental devotion. At home, her mother will fold her in her arms and hug her to bits just as she used to when she was a kid. At home, her father will kiss her eyelids and the tip of her nose and call her, 'Treasure.'

Mannie heads to the cottage at the weekend, carrying – unusually – an overnight bag and thinking longingly of the small room she grew up in, still painted pink, still ready for her return at any given moment.

'Hi!' she calls, stepping out of her car.

It's unusual not to be greeted by someone – her father normally, sometimes Jonno, always Prince. She calls again, uncertainly, 'Anyone at home?' The door is unlocked and she steps inside. The cottage feels curiously vacant, as if its heart has slowed and its pulse is failing. She drops her bag and sniffs. No cooking smells, no enticing aromas.

Unsettled, she stomps through the hall to the kitchen. She relies on her parents to supply routine and normality in her life, to be there for her, no matter what.

'Hello?' Her voice is almost quavering now. This is so not what she needs.

'Hello, pet.'

Her father comes through the back door and opens his arms wide. Prince, gruff and excited, his tail flapping like a sail in full wind, barges past him and catches the back of her knees with full force so that she buckles and laughs.

'Hello, Daddy. Hello Prince, old thing.'

'Your mother will be back shortly. She's at some reception or other.'

'So what's new?' Mannie grins. 'Is Jonno at the pub tonight?'

Even as she asks it, her question is answered because her brother comes into the kitchen, still wearing wellies and carrying a dirty bucket.

'Hey, Sis.'

'Hey, Bro. Heard from CommX yet? How did the interview go?'

He puts the bucket down with a clatter and hold up his hands in warning. 'Don't hug me, I'm covered in chicken shit,' he grins. 'It went okay, I think. Haven't heard yet.'

'Who interviewed you?'

'Two women – the editorial director and one of the client directors. They normally have the managing director there too, they said, but he was in Dubai, apparently, meeting with an important client.'

So that's why Brian hasn't answered! He must have gone off to Dubai right after they met for dinner. The skin of misery that has been hanging over her all week peels back. She could whoop with elation. He hasn't been ignoring her! He has just been busy! He has been abroad!

'So when will you hear?'

'They said a few days. They're going to run everything past him when he gets back.'

'Which is when?'

'Thursday.'

Thursday. Two more days. That's all she has to endure. Two days, then they'll be back in contact again. He'll reply then. She can text him – when? – maybe tomorrow. Surely he'll be back home a day before heading back into the office?

'Cuppa, Mannie?' her father asks. 'Or are you ready for a glass of wine? I'm in the middle of a song, I'll get back to it till your mother gets home, if that's all right. We can catch up over supper?'

'Tea would be great, Dad. Thanks. Stop me from drinking for another hour,' Mannie says. She doesn't need a drink, she can't stop smiling.

'Me too,' Jonno says, disappearing into the utility room with the bucket. Mannie can hear him swilling it out as her father drops tea bags into three mugs and busies himself pouring hot water over them.

There's a gray pallor on his face that doesn't look normal, and the line that runs vertically between his eyebrows seems to be etched deeper than usual. 'You okay, Dad? You look tired.'

'Just the deadlines,' he says, stirring busily, not looking at her. 'That's all.'

'Really? Hey—' she remembers, '—that tune you wrote. Finished the song yet?'

He shakes his head. 'Stupid, isn't it? But the words need to be perfect. I've got a feeling about this tune. It could be a biggie.'

'If you get the words.'

'Yes.'

He isn't his normal, calm self. She can sense a kind of vulnerability about him that's disturbing. She would like to probe, but Jonno comes back in, asking, 'Any biscuits, Dad? Where has Mum hidden them?' and the moment is lost.

'In the flour tin,' Archie grins. 'I came across them this morning.'

'You mean, you were frantically hunting for them,' Jon laughs.

The fondness Jon and Archie share for Susie's home-baked Melting Moments is a standing joke in the house. Years ago, her mother started to look for ever more inventive places to hide the latest batch so that they wouldn't disappear in ten minutes flat, and the habit has continued. In the Wallace household they call the biscuits

197

'Melting Nanoseconds'.

'Here.' Archie opens the flour tin and hands the cookies round. Then, 'See you later,' he says, and he's out of the door with his tea before Mannie can stop him.

'He looks tired,' she observes through a mouthful of crumbs. 'Is he all right?'

Jonno scrapes a chair back and flops down onto it. 'Not really. It's pretty crap here at the moment, to be honest.'

'He's not still sleeping out there, is he?'

''Fraid so.'

'That's pants. What's eating them?'

'Still this thing about Dad not telling her about the adoption, I guess. And she's been busy. There's a load of stuff going on at the Parliament.'

'But there's always loads going on at the Parliament. It's never made her like this before. And I'm sure Dad meant it for the best. Not telling her, I mean.'

'Sure. Anyway.' Jonno shrugs away all discussion of emotion and takes another biscuit. 'Cal not with you?'

'He's tied up with his cricket.'

Mannie is struggling with the weight of her secret. She hesitates. Jonno might be crap at feelings, but he can usually be relied on to be discreet. It'd be nice to be able to talk to someone about Brian.

'Jonno,' she says slowly.

'Yeah?'

'If I tell you something, will you promise to keep it secret?'

'Depends.' He grins. 'If it's got sale value, I know a journalist who—'

'Beast! Promise?'

'Hmm. Go on, tell.'

'There's this man.'

'What man?'

'That's what I'm trying to tell you, idiot. There was this man who came by our stand at the trade fair.'

'Who?'

'Just a businessman.'

'What about him?'

'Just shut up and listen, will you?' She clears her throat. 'I've got feelings for him.' Her brother is staring at her as though she's barking. 'What I mean is, I've fallen for him. I'm crazy about him, Jonno. It's driving me nuts.'

'What, you've split up with Cal? You met a guy at a trade fair and you've fallen in love with him and finished with Cal?'

'No! Well, yes, maybe. I don't know. I don't want to finish with Cal but when I told him about this he ... well, he just walked out,' she finishes lamely.

'Well honestly, Sis, can you blame him?'

She shakes her head numbly. 'Not really.'

'What does he do?'

'He runs a business,' she says vaguely.

'What kind of business?'

'Not sure exactly,' she lies. 'It's in Stirling, I think.'

'So how long have you been seeing this guy?'

'I'm not really seeing him. I had coffee with him, but that was an accident, I was waiting for Mum. And I had dinner with him. He's like ... he's married.'

'Married? You've ditched Cal and started an affair with a married man?' Jonno is incredulous.

'I'm not having an affair with him. He's loads older than me and I've only seen him once since then. He's not even answering my texts right now.'

'I don't get it.'

'No.' Mannie wells up. 'Neither do I. I just adore him. It's a mess, Jonno. A complete mess.'

Behind them there's a flurry of movement and a rustle. Prince barks softly and lumbers to his feet. Mannie looks round to see her mother standing in the doorway, her face concerned. 'What's a mess?' she asks.

'Nothing.' Mannie dashes the back of her hand across

her face and runs to her mother, opening her arms for a hug.

'Mannie says she's—' Jonno begins.

Mannie cuts across him quickly. 'Jonno, no! You promised not to say anything!'

'I had my fingers crossed.'

'Shut up!'

'Children, children,' Susie says, amused. 'This is just like the old days. Calm down.'

There's a silence, then Jonno says, 'Sorry, Mannie, but I think Mum ought to know.'

'Know what?'

'No!'

'It's Mannie. She's—'

'Tell tale tit, your tongue will split!'

'Children!' Susie says again, laughing.

Jonno ignores them both. 'She's only gone and dumped Cal, Mum – the soundest guy she's ever gone out with. And she's started an affair with a married man.'

'I have not!'

'What? Mannie? You haven't finished with Callum have you?'

'You're such a pain, Jonno,' Mannie cries, pushing past her brother angrily and storming out of the kitchen. 'I'll never tell you anything again.'

Behind her, as she grabs her case and runs up to the sanctuary of her room, she can hear their voices, discussing her.

She's furious with them. But she's even more furious with herself.

Chapter Twenty

The girl appears from nowhere, round the corner of the building, and almost trips face forwards over Jon's feet as he leans back against the wall, legs extended.

'Christ Almighty!' She rights herself quickly. 'Sorry, I didn't expect anyone.'

He shoots out his hand and catches her arm. 'Are you okay? I'm the one who's sorry. It was my fault. I was just a bit early.' Jon doesn't like to admit he's been waiting for twenty minutes outside Ashley House, home of CommX, short for Communications Excellence: his new employer.

'I'm fine. Really.' The girl turns to face him. 'You're new.'

She looks so assured that Jon feels ridiculously gawky, like a five-year-old starting school. 'Jonathan Wallace. Jon. It's my first day.'

'Welcome to the bear pit. I'm Alex Townsend.'

She's tiny, like a little sparrow, brown-haired and dark-eyed, with quick, energetic movements and a chirpy friendliness. She's wearing dark jeans, rolled up a couple of times to below her knees, flimsy leather pumps and a flowery cotton top in brilliant purples and pinks. Her hair is shoved up at the back with some kind of clip, so that he can't tell how long it is.

Alex punches a few numbers into a keypad, pushes open the door into Ashley House, where CommX has its home, and halts in the slate-floored entrance lobby. 'You must be taking over from Mark. Sorry. I've been on holiday. I'm a bit out of touch with news.'

'What happened to Mark? Thrown to the bears?'

She laughs. Her smile is wide and even, and her teeth

are pearly against tanned skin. 'Nothing so sinister. He landed a job with one of the big banks.'

One of the jobs I went for no doubt, Jon thinks. There's a brief moment of bitterness as he remembers the dozens of applications, the equal number of rejections, the very few interviews, before he recalls, with a small glow, that it doesn't matter any more, because he's here now. He has made the impossible leap. He has set out on a career.

Another door. More numbers on a keypad. A big open office, full of desks and computers.

'I don't know where they'll put you. Mark's desk was over there.' Alex points to a space near the kitchen area, clearly one of the less desirable locations in the big open-plan office where they're now standing. 'It's not too bad,' she adds quickly, 'People come and talk to you there.'

'Where do you sit?'

'The designers are all in this block.' She gestures at the area just to the left of the now-no-more Mark's desk, where dull PCs have been banished and gleaming Macs, huge-screened and elegant, reign supreme. 'I guess they'll resurrect Mark's Mac for you, if it hasn't been cannibalised for parts already. Just joking,' she adds, grinning at his despondent face. 'Listen, want a coffee? Or tea? I need to get started, I just know there'll be a thousand emails, that's why I came in early.'

She's twitching, eager to get going, wanting to be friendly but unwilling to waste time.

'Why don't you let me make you something,' he offers, and sees the glimmer of relief, swiftly hidden.

'Thanks, cool. Tea please, I don't do coffee. Milk if there is any that's not off, otherwise black for now.'

She turns away, settles at a desk by the window, unslings her bag and presses a button on her Mac so that it gives a melodic boom and glows into life. Jon fumbles his way round the small kitchen, finds mugs, tea, a fridge with a half pint of milk that seems acceptably fresh, and has just filled the kettle when voices cut into the room behind him.

'Morning Alex. How was France?'

'France? Have I been in France? Seems like I've never been out of this damn place.' Laughter. 'Catch me up on the goss in a mo, Stu. Just scanning the emails. Oh, there's a new guy in the kitchen, by the way.'

A face appears, young, round, pleasant, the head completely bald. 'Hi. I'm Stu. We met when you came in for your interview.'

Hot on Stu's heels came Rob, Gus, Andrea, Jane, Frank, Eva, and a dozen more. New names, new faces, a blur of new impressions. Within ten minutes, there are fifteen people in the office. He greets them, smiles till it begins to feel mechanical, counts them, sees that the only spare place is, indeed, the desk Alex indicated half an hour ago. Finally, he puts his mug on it. The tea is cold.

'We have a Monday morning meeting,' Stu tells him. 'The Boss is here today, so he'll cover the weekly business. If he's not here, Maris does it. Someone will give you an induction. It's usually Sara,' he points to a pallid girl with mousey hair and an insipid air. 'Don't be fooled,' Stu grins, seeing Jon's doubtful look. 'She's the most organised person around here, by a million miles. And bossy with it, although you wouldn't know to look at her.'

The two senior women who interviewed him arrive, deep in conversation.

'Welcome, Jonathan,' says the one with red hair, extending her hand. Jonno remembers her as Maris Jay. 'So pleased you've decided to join us.'

Decided to? Jon nearly laughs out loud. Decided to? He would have crawled all the way from Cairn Cottage on his knees for this job. 'Thanks,' he says diffidently.

Seventeen. Only 'the Boss', as Stu has described him, to come. He is curious to meet the man who founded CommX eight years ago and who has built the business up so quickly. It takes a certain kind of magic to make a

design agency thrive because this is an overpopulated area
– competition is cut-throat and a strong reputation difficult
to establish.

Around half past nine, the door opens and a man enters.
Late forties, perhaps, slightly balding, but with lively hazel
eyes and an air of relaxed confidence. Something about the
eyes, and the energy, remind him of Mannie. He's wearing
a beautifully cut grey suit, teamed with a very white shirt,
open to show a well-tanned neck.

'Morning everyone!' Friendly, assured, in charge.

There's a rapid-fire volley of good mornings and
greetings, the odd wave from those who are already on the
phone, then he disappears into a glass-walled office at the
far end of the room.

Jon sits at his desk, feeling faintly awkward. What is he
to do? What are his duties to be? How is he to start this
new job? Everyone seems busy, intent on organising the
week ahead, already coping with problems, finding
solutions.

'Hi.' The girl Stu pointed out as Sara is by his desk.

'Hi.'

'We'll be having our meeting in a minute, then I'll do
your induction. The Boss wants to see you after that.'

'Okay. Thanks.'

'No worries.'

She wanders off, leaving Jon once again alone.

An hour later, his head is whirling. He stares at the
notes in front of him. CommX has twenty three clients
with current projects. Some have three or four projects
running, making, so far as Jon can tell, thirty seven live
jobs. There are three divisions – magazine design, web
design and consultancy. Brian Henderson has run through
the lot in the course of the meeting, asking questions about
project status, clearly expecting smart answers. Problems
are flagged and fixes discussed. Upcoming work
opportunities are debated. Pitches, they are called

officially. Beauty parades is the slang. He tries to keep his mind on it all, but the sheer volume and complexity of the information is bewildering. Twenty-three companies. Multiply the key contacts within each company by, say four, and that means a minimum of ninety-two people whose names, jobs, personalities and preferences he will have to get to know, quickly. The prospect both thrills and terrifies him.

Sara takes him round the office, shows him the toilets, the kitchen, the fire extinguisher and assembly points. She runs through some of the main systems and processes, does a quick tour of the stationery cupboard and explains the filing systems and how projects are stored on the server and how they can be accessed. By midday, Jon is exhausted. He thinks longingly of the chickens and of Cairn Cottage and of the simplicity of life as a barman, and wonders whether he has made the right move.

'Right,' Sara says. 'Got that?'

He jerks tensely. What? What does she mean? The point she has just been making about marking files in use, or all the points of the induction? 'I think so,' he says cautiously.

'Good.' She must see his expression because she softens a little and adds, 'Don't worry. It is confusing at first. But you'll get used to it. Now,' she glances at her watch, 'The Boss said he wanted to see you at midday. Let's see if he's free, shall we?'

Jon has done his research on CommX pretty thoroughly, and on its managing director, Brian Henderson, in particular. The man has earned a healthy degree of respect and has won various industry awards. An article Jon downloaded from one of the trade magazines filled in the detail. Fifty three years old, educated at Stirling High and Oxford University, worked as a journalist on regional newspapers, then moved in-house, becoming public relations manager for a small pharmaceutical research company. Headhunted by one of the biggies a few years later, but made redundant after a decade of service. Married with two children, he needed to earn a living, and he boldly used every last penny of his redundancy money to set up CommX. It paid off. The rest, as they say, is history.

I want to be like you, is Jon's first thought as he is ushered in to the Boss's office: successful, knowledgeable, respected.

'Hi. Have a seat.' Brian Henderson looks up from the papers he is studying and waves Jon to a chair. 'Sorry I didn't have time to say hello properly before. Things are always mad in here on a Monday morning, and I've been in Dubai and New York, so there's some catching up to do. What do you think of it so far?'

Jon clears his throat. 'H-hmm. I'm delighted to be here,' he hedges, not sure quite what he can say in response to the question. The workings of CommX are, so far, a bewildering mystery.

Brian smiles. 'Pleased to have you. It was a lucky chance.'

'I'm sorry?'

'Well, you might have missed the advertisement if I hadn't ... or did you see it advertised yourself?'

'Advertised?'

'The design post. Of course, it would normally have gone through the agency, but I believe there was an administrative hiccup and the agency didn't get briefed until very late in the day. So meeting ... someone who knew you were looking,' he nods at Jon meaningfully, '... was lucky.'

Jon's confusion must have been reflected on his face, because Brian adds, 'I didn't take any part in the selection process, of course. That was conducted by my team here. I wouldn't like you to think you were here without merit.'

Jon's head is buzzing with so many booming alarms that he hardly knows which one to consider first.

Someone who knew you were looking.

Mannie. It was Mannie who'd phoned him about it. *My sister organised this job for me.* Anger mixed with mortification at the thought. How dare she patronise him like that? Putting in a word for him as if he wasn't capable of getting a job on his own?

Then the second implication of Brian Henderson's words wallop into him and take his breath away completely.

He runs a business ... It's in Stirling, I think.

He isn't sure how he got out of there – or indeed, how long he was in there after Brian Henderson's bombshell. He supposes there was some discussion of his duties at CommX, but he prays that someone else will brief him because he can't recollect a single word. Maybe it doesn't matter anyway, Jon thinks as he paces the car park in his lunch break, because how can he possibly stay here after this discovery?

Mannie has fallen in love with his new boss. And whatever she says, he can't believe that there hasn't been some encouragement on Brian Henderson's part – because how could someone as bright and pretty and young as Mannie turn her back on a great guy like Cal for this middle-aged slap-head, however smart and smooth and successful he is?

Jon forgets his earlier admiration and respect for Brian Henderson and is swamped by a growing fury. He pulls out his mobile and punches Mannie's number into his phone. He has to talk to her. Now.

'This is Mannie Wallace. I'm sorry I can't speak right now, please leave a message and I'll get back to you.'

Fuck.

Fuck, fuck, fuck.

'I need to speak to you Mannie. Call me back. It's

207

Jonno.'

There are strict rules about mobile phone use, he does remember that part of the induction, but he doesn't care. A stiff breeze swirls round the car park, stirring the dust that has accumulated in the corner of the building and whipping the leaves on the small rowan trees that have been planted in an attempt to soften the stark lines of the new-build block. Jon turns his face to the wind and feels it ruffle his hair. One gust, stronger than the rest, blows some grit into his face and he closes his eyes, almost welcoming the discomfort. The bleakness of the place echoes his mood perfectly.

His break comes and goes, but Mannie doesn't call. Nor, he realises as he retraces his steps reluctantly back into the office, has he eaten. And if he felt gawky in the morning, he feels miserably uncomfortable now. Every instinct tells him he should just go home and forget about the job. Then he remembers his long battle to secure work and he rebels against the prospect of renewed unemployment.

In the face of his gloom, however, the afternoon disconcerts him by becoming interesting. It transpires that he is to shadow Stu for a few days while the new computer is in transit, and they go out to a meeting with the national agency that looks after Stirling Castle. As they walk across the ancient esplanade and enter the precincts of the Castle itself, a sense of excitement quells his unease.

For the moment.

'How's it been, then?'

Back in the office, Jon is engrossed in filling in a meeting report form and is only peripherally aware that someone is standing by his desk. As he's on a main passageway to the kitchen, he has already grown used to comings and goings and has begun to filter them out.

'Hello?' The sing-song note of inquiry finally

penetrates and he looks up to find the girl, Alex, standing next to him, laughing at his concentration. 'Anyone in?'

He sits back in his chair and smiles. He can't help smiling at Alex. She's like a little bobbing robin, bright-eyed and spirited, hop, hop, hopping from one foot to another with a delightful vivacity. She reminds him of Mannie at her nicest.

'Sorry. Hi.'

'How was your first day?'

'Everyone's been very friendly,' he says, truthfully.

'I'm all in. The first day back after a break always seems endless. Fancy a drink?'

The prospect of a pint is enticing. 'Do I just.' He glances at his screen. 'Can you hang on five minutes? If I don't finish this I'll forget what I'm supposed to be filling in.'

'Sure. No hurry. I need to finish up myself.'

The pub Alex suggests is in the local village of Bridge of Allan. 'Less likely to bump into the others,' she explains. 'Not that that's a bad thing, I mean, they're a nice enough bunch, but if you want to escape from work talk, it's better to go further afield.'

Jon has no complaints. He's had as much new information in one day as he can handle and besides, getting Alex to himself is rather a pleasant prospect.

'Let me get the drinks.'

'No, not at all.' It doesn't seem right for a girl to buy the first round on a date. Is it a date? Probably not, probably just a friendly gesture, but even so—

'I insist. My personal welcome to CommX. A thanks for making tea this morning.' She grins mischievously. 'Even if it was cold.'

Jon blushes furiously, and hates himself for it, but it's a hazard with his coloring. 'Sorry. So many people stopped me to introduce themselves—'

'I was teasing, Jon Wallace. Here's your pint. Do you think we might sit outside?'

'Great.'

It's May, and the weather has turned clement. The stern breeze that played havoc with the dust in the car park earlier in the day has died away completely, bequeathing a pleasingly warm early evening sunshine.

'So. What do you make of us all?' Alex takes a long swig of her pint. Jonno watches her with a deep sense of pleasure. Her hands are small and tanned, the glass looks ludicrously large and heavy in them, yet she handles the drink with ease. The beer leaves a small moustache of creamy foam on her upper lip and he has to repress the urge to kiss it away.

'People are very friendly. It's a lot to take in.'

She wipes the foam away with the back of a small hand. 'I always think if you can handle working in an agency like this, you can handle anything. It's very high pressured. Be warned.'

'I don't mind that.' *If I can stick it at all.* 'What do people think of the Boss?' he asks casually.

'He's good. Very polished. Some people call him Innocent because he's such a smoothie.'

'Innocent?' Jon's short laugh is more a cynical bark. 'Really? That's funny.' He thinks about it for a moment, then says carefully, 'And maybe not very apt? I heard he was a bit of a womaniser.'

'Did you? He's married.'

'Yeah.'

Alex surveys him thoughtfully. 'You shouldn't listen to rumours.'

'Are they wrong?'

She takes another long pull of her beer. 'Let's just say, I've heard that he appreciates a pretty face.'

'Has he ever come on to you?'

Her laughter is like a bell, clear and true. 'I'll take that as a compliment, will I? No. He's not daft. He's not going to set himself up for a sexual harassment case. Anyway,' her shoulders lift in dismissal, 'So far as I'm concerned, what he does out of the office is his own business.'

Jon takes the hint. 'How long have you been with CommX?'

She's a couple of years older than him, she has been working as a designer for five years and she's currently single. Glory be – because by the time they part an hour later, Jonathan Wallace is well smitten.

He turns the Volvo towards Hailesbank and mulls over the many unexpected twists and turns the day has taken. These feelings, he realises, make the choices and decisions that lie in front of him all the more difficult.

Chapter Twenty-one

In Edinburgh, Mannie is having problems of her own. She pushes her way through the heavy revolving door into the hotel and crosses the shiny marble floor of the grand lobby. She's in a hurry. She's always in a hurry, but today her mission is especially pressing. At the reception desk she stops abruptly. 'Seen Freddie?' she asks, perhaps more sharply than she intended.

'Not recently,' says Agnieska, the receptionist on duty, but her eyes flicker to somewhere over Mannie's shoulder and she swivels sharply to catch sight of the hotel's head of operations scurrying through the door into the grand salon.

She glares at Agnieska, but the girl has ducked her head away and is studying something intently. She's always too protective of the man.

'Freddie!' Already Mannie's heels are snapping on the tiles, businesslike pops of intent. She catches up with him in seconds. 'Mosse Harbinger Fund Managers. They need twenty-two tables, not eighteen. And they've changed their minds. They want an option on desserts for the dinner rather than just the parfait au citron.'

'Four extra tables? At this notice? The dinner's tonight!' Freddie Blackman has been at The Acanthus Hotel for less than a year and still isn't used to the stringent demands Mannie makes in order to please her clients and meet her targets. It's what makes her supreme at her job – but feared by her colleagues. 'How are we meant to do that for heaven's sake? The room'll be bursting and the Wyllie Room is booked so we can't move

213

them in there!'

'Your problem,' Mannie says callously and turns on her heel. She has other headaches.

'And a second dessert? Chef'll go ballistic!' Freddie calls after her retreating figure.

She doesn't even bother to reply to that one.

She picks up Jonno's message. Heavens, he sounds angry. This is his first day at CommX and she knows he's really excited. She hated sending him in cold because finding out about Brian is inevitable, but there hasn't been an opportunity to explain things. And anyway, how can she explain? Better to let things take their course and deal with the fallout afterwards.

Three times that afternoon she picks up her phone with the intention of calling her brother and three times she lays it back down again. The longer she leaves it, the more time there will be for things to shake down at his end. She considers switching her phone off, but although she's not looking forward to a conversation with Jonno, she really has to face it this evening, because he has to go back in there tomorrow. She can't risk him throwing in the perfect job because of any stupid, misplaced notions.

One thought overrides all others: Jonno has seen Brian. She's jealous of her brother for that, because she hasn't seen Brian since their dinner in Leith.

He has called, though – just the once, but every word is etched onto her heart as if she has taken a needle and tattooed them there herself. They echo down the days and replay in her head.

'Hi. It's Brian.'

'Hi! Wow, hi, I mean, it's great to hear your voice, where are you?'

'New York.'

'New York?' Disappointment at learning of the vast distance that separates him mixes with a sense of glamour. He's calling her from New York! He's making the effort to call her from half way across the world!

'I'm over here for a couple of days. Business.'

'Sounds really glamourous.'

'Maybe, but transatlantic travel is pretty exhausting.'

'Where are you now? This minute.' She longs to picture him, exactly.

'In my hotel room.'

'Wish I could be with you.'

'That would be nice. Listen, Mannie—'

'God, if I'd known you were going, I could have come with you! You should have told me.'

'Whoa, Mannie, stop.' She can hear him laughing. 'You know, it's very flattering to have a gorgeous girl like you making the running, really, really wonderful.'

'I can hear a but coming.'

'Mannie, I'm married. I told you that.'

'That doesn't mean we can't see each other, does it? I'll be really discreet, I promise. I won't say a word to anyone. I'll do anything you ask, Brian. Have you thought about me? Since we had dinner?'

'No. Not once.' That shocks her into silence, then he laughs. 'I'm lying. Of course I've thought about you. I've tried not to, but Christ, Mannie, you're bloody irresistible, do you know that?'

Yes! 'Tell me you want to be with me.'

She thinks he isn't going to say it, but then the words come, across an ocean and a continent. 'I want to be with you, Mannie.'

He says her name so sexily she wants to cry. 'Oh God,' she whispers. 'Oh my God.'

'But Mannie, Mannie, Mannie – lovely girl – please, stop texting me, will you? Anyone could see these texts. At work. My wife. Just ease off. No texts. I'll call you when I can. I'll fix to see you when I get back.'

'Promise?'

'I promise.'

'We can spend a night together?'

'If I can fix that, I will. If you stop texting.'

'I will stop.' *If I can.* 'Now that I know you care. Will you be back when Jonno starts?'

'Hopefully. Mannie, someone's at the door. I've got to go. I'll be in touch next week.'

'All right.' She longs to say *I love you* but the desire to say the words for the first time to his face is stronger. They will be her gift to him, the perfect gift for her perfect partner. The lump of unspoken words in her throat grows and becomes painful, so that she can hardly even say goodbye.

'Bye Mannie.' As suddenly as he made the call, he cuts it.

Mannie holds the phone for a long time. It makes it feel as if the connection is still there.

He wants me.

He has feelings for me.

He thinks I'm irresistible.

He wants to be with me.

It isn't that she has stopped loving Callum, his absence still hurts like a nagging wound. But she can't think about Callum now. She won't allow herself to think about him. That's over. It's sad, but inevitable in the face of what she feels for Brian, and now that he has confirmed his feelings for her, the future has a very different shape to the one she has imagined – but it's a glorious, shining, magnificent shape.

She needs Jonno to be cool about it. There's no way what she and Brian feel for each other should come in the way of Jonno's career. They're quite, quite separate, especially as (for the time being, at least) she will be keeping her affair with Brian quiet. Until he sorts himself out, of course, and decides to leave his wife and come and live with her. Which he will do, Mannie has absolutely no doubt of that.

She sighs. That's for the future. For now, she must deal with her brother.

'Hi, Bro. How was your first day?'

'Mannie! At last.' He's still cross, then. 'It's him, isn't it?'

She laughs, hoping it sounds nonchalant. 'It's him, what?'

'Brian Henderson. He's the man you're having an affair with—'

'Hey, hey, stop there, Jonno. I'm not having an affair.' It's true. Just.

'Whatever. You've fallen "in love" with him.'

He says it sneeringly, as if the words cover something demeaning. She smarts at his tone, but chooses not to pick at it. 'Brian's the man I met at the trade fair, yes,' she says neutrally. 'How is he? How was your day? You haven't answered me yet.'

'My day, Sis, was a revelation. You wangled the job for me.' This time the voice is accusing.

'You say that as if getting a start on the career you've waited for so long was a bad thing.'

He starts to interrupt, but she cuts through him.

'No, stop right there, Jonno. Whatever chip you've got on your shoulder, I suggest you remove it, right now.'

She speaks authoritatively, the voice of a manager experienced at dealing with problem staff.

'You got this job yourself. All I did was point you towards the opportunity. Brian played no part in it whatsoever. So stop being a big wuss and get on with your life. Okay?'

'How the hell can I get on, as you put it, when I know my sister's having an affair with my boss? My married boss. And he must be encouraging you, Mannie, because why else would you fall for a guy like that, instead of Cal McMaster?'

He's right, she'll have to be careful – but she can play a long game. There's plenty of time to get to know Brian and make their plans for the future. And in the meantime, anything might happen at work – Jonno might move on to another company, the landscape all around could look very different. 'No, Jonno,' she says circumspectly. 'I haven't even seen him since I told you about him.'

'Really?' The word is pregnant with doubt, but she hears hope there – hope that there's something that can justify him staying at CommX.

Obligingly, she gives it to him. 'Really. I promise.' *I would have seen him, though, given half a chance. Oh God, I would have seen him.*

'Well—'

'So. Tell me. How was the rest of the day?'

'A bit bewildering, they have so many clients. Everyone's very nice. I'm shadowing a guy called Stu. We went to the Castle.'

'Edinburgh Castle?'

'No, no, Stirling. It was brilliant.'

She lets him run on for a few minutes, hearing the excitement in his voice, then she says gently, 'So you will go back tomorrow.'

There's still hesitation. 'You can see how difficult it would be for me? And I don't like it, Mannie. Cal was the best. Tops. You've really shafted him and I don't understand why.'

'I don't understand either, Bro.' And that's the truth.

'You won't pursue Brian Henderson?'

Mannie sweeps back her dark hair with her hand and starts twisting it at the back of her neck. She frames her answer with care. 'I promise I won't embarrass you.'

'Okay.'

'Let me know how the rest of the week goes.'

'Okay. Bye, Sis.'

She lets go of the bun and her hair swishes forwards,

218

shielding her eyes. There's no-one looking at her, but if there had been, they might have seen a kind of dark joy, exhilaration – and pain, because deep inside, Mannie knows that she has pushed a button that is marked 'Self Destruct'.

But it glows brightly – and it opens a door labelled 'Paradise'.

Chapter Twenty-two

Susie is finding it odd not to see Jonno's car in the courtyard when she comes down in the morning. Now that he leaves early for Stirling, she misses his presence, even though he used to be deep in slumber at this time of day.

She misses Archie, too. She aches for him. Last night she heard the band leave the studio late, high on their music, and longed to be a part of that exhilaration, as she always was in the past. She even got out of bed and went down to the kitchen, hoping that Archie would come in for a drink or a mug of tea. Forlorn hope – he has all he needs in the studio. Even the dog has deserted her.

She shakes her head in an effort to rid herself of negative thoughts.

'Smile,' her mother used to say, 'and the world will smile with you.'

Such a cliché, Mother, but worth a try. She smiles. Around her, the stillness of the kitchen seems like an insult to her endeavours. She picks up her briefcase and opens her diary. Petitions Committee at ten. *Tick.* Meeting with a constituent at twelve thirty. *Tock.* Briefing in the Committee Room Four – a theatre group aimed at disabled actors that has run into financial trouble. *Tick.* She sighs. It's all money, money, money, at the end of the day. Most of her work ends up being about money. At three, another meeting with her mother, before getting back for the vote at five. *Tock.*

She puts the thought of the meeting with Joyce Miles aside. Meet when you feel ready for it, Birthlink advised. Keep the meetings short at first. Have an agenda, if it helps

– some questions you need answered, perhaps, or maybe bring some photographs of your own family to show, or of your house, or your pets.

How was a picture of a guinea pig likely to bond mother and child? Or a fish? A stick insect?

Silly. She's creating ridiculous scenarios in order to push aside the real issue: she has not yet felt the flood of love and emotion for her birth mother that she thinks she should – and with that, comes guilt.

Stop it. Smile. She opens a side drawer in her small desk in the front room and eases out a folder of photographs. Archie. Their wedding day. Margaret-Anne, at a week old, at three, at eight. Jonathan, the same. There. Homework done. And now she will put aside all thoughts of the meeting with Joyce, because her duties beckon.

In the Parliament, the Lobby is already getting busy. Susie has developed a habit of peering past the security desk to check for lurking journalists before venturing in. It might look odd, but she can always find some excuse for ducking back out again if Justin Thorneloe is anywhere in sight. A detour might lose her ten minutes, but that's better than allowing herself to get needled by the man and upsetting her equilibrium for the rest of the day.

Thorneloe seems to bear a grudge against her. What has she done to merit that? In vain, Susie racks her brains for the answer to that riddle.

Today the way is clear and she scuttles across to the office block unhindered. The sun is streaming down through the boat-like windows, casting sharp-cornered shadows at prow and stern. In the small courtyard garden on her left, a gardener is already at work, weeding. She pauses for a moment to watch him, envying his aura of peacefulness. Such satisfying work, gardening. So utterly tranquil.

'Morning, Susie.'

She turns, her short reverie broken. 'Good morning, Tom.'

Smile.

She smiles, and is rewarded in return by a slight lifting of the lips at their outer edges that might – just – be described as a smile. From Tom Coop, it is a milestone.

The brief feeling of elation doesn't last. As she walks into her office, her telephone is ringing, and although Karen's jacket is on the stand, her PA is nowhere in evidence. She reaches for it automatically. 'Hello, Susie Wallace.'

'Hmm.' The throat-clearing tells her in an instant who is calling. Her heart sinks, because she suspects that the more than usually diffident start heralds bad news.

'Morning, Susie, it's Hugh Porteous here.'

She makes herself sound bright. *Smile.* 'Good morning, Hugh. What news is there?'

'Hmm, mixed news, as a matter of fact. I've taken advice, but – well, the fact is, we've had to dismiss Ricky.'

'Oh!' Susie sits down on her chair heavily. 'I see. Because?'

'We uncovered, shall we say, shortcomings in his work.'

'Dishonesty?' She is deeply disappointed. Ricky Waring has always seemed so committed, and so straightforward.

'Shall we just say, hmm, incompetence.'

'Oh.' It's better, but not a lot. 'We're watertight, are we? On sacking him? I mean, we're not going to end up at a tribunal.' Her stomach is heavy at the thought – it's not a scenario that would bring good publicity.

'As I say, I've taken advice, so yes, I believe we are, as you put it, watertight.'

'So what's next?'

'Not good, I'm afraid. We have a shortfall of some twenty-five thousand in the short term, and to continue in

223

operation, we'd need to find a similar sum, in the medium term.'

'Fifty thousand pounds.' The sum sounds huge. 'And dare I ask ... the insurance?'

'Ah well,' the voice becomes almost jovial, 'in that regard the news is better, I'm pleased to say. The insurance is valid until September.'

Relief can be indefinable. Sometimes you don't know how deeply worried you are about something until the pressure of it is lifted from you. 'So the twenty-five thousand—' she seeks clarification, unwilling to be falsely seduced into reassurance.

'Won't be recoverable from the Trustees, personally. However, we are still in the very awkward position of having to dredge that sum up from somewhere, or explain to the funding body that it has been misappropriated. Hugely embarrassing, hmm.'

'Right. I'm with you. And where might we find such a sum?'

'If you know, Susie, I'd be terribly grateful if you could tell me.' He gives a small laugh. 'For myself, I intend to pray.'

'Ah. Excellent.'

She has never been the praying sort. Sunday mornings spent in Bible classes in a chilly outbuilding while her parents worshipped at the cold, grey stone church near their home in Helensburgh have left only one legacy: a promise to herself that she will never voluntarily enter the gates of such a place again.

'I'll certainly give it some thought. Is the news being released? About Ricky?'

'We're going to try to sit on it for the moment. I don't think he'll be running to the press, so we may be all right. Of course, it's not something we can hide for long, hmm. Nor would that be right. But we might just buy a little respite in order to come up with a solution.'

'Solution. Of course.'

It seems an impossibility. Starved of their usual sources of funding, many charities are being squeezed into closure, and Rivo's work is seen by many as peripheral because it isn't putting roofs over heads or food in mouths.

'I'll give it some thought, Hugh.'

'Thank you, Susie. Hmm. Goodbye.'

She puts the phone down heavily. What price saving my own skin, she thinks, if I can't save those souls who can rebuild their future through Rivo's work? She's shaking – not with relief that she won't after all, have to remortgage the cottage to cover the debts she has incurred as a Trustee, but with fury. Fury at Ricky Waring for covering up his feeble mismanagement instead of bringing the problems to the table so that they could all work towards a solution. Fury because it has made her unable to do what she pledged to do for the many souls who turn to Rivo for help. And above all, fury with herself, for failing in the duty of care she undertook.

'Morning, Susie.'

'Morning – oh, bless you, Karen,' she exclaims, as Karen places a large carton of frothy latte in front of her. 'How did you know I'd be in need?'

Karen taps her forehead as she places her own coffee on her desk and slips her scarlet jacket onto the chair behind it. 'Just had a feeling. Who was that?' she indicates the phone.

'Hugh Porteous.'

'Rivo?'

'They've sacked Ricky.'

'Great. And?'

'And I'm not personally liable.'

Karen pulls out her chair and settles herself into it. 'Good. You remembering your meeting with—'

'My mother? Yes.' Susie is momentarily irked at Karen's easy dismissal of Rivo's problems – because they

225

are all still there – but the breakneck speed of Parliamentary business necessitates organisation and concentration. Her able assistant has launched with iron firmness into the business of the day, dragging her – willing or no – unbendingly in her wake.

It's almost half past two before she is able to give any further thought to the impending meeting with Joyce. They are to meet, on this occasion, in the Palm Room at the Balmoral Hotel on the corner of Princes Street and South Bridge. It's an imposing place with soaring ceilings that lend it a cathedral-like feel, while at the same time offering niches created by swaying greenery and an almost architectural tracery of fronds and leaves.

The sun, more delicate now than earlier in the day, lights the expanse between floor and cupola, while motes of dust swirl dimly in the air – stirred, no doubt, by the breath of gossiping guests.

It's a good place to meet. It has its own kind of anonymity. A public space, but more inhabited by foreigners drinking in atmosphere and tea than by Edinburgh locals, and handily located – just fifteen minutes' brisk walk from the Parliament and a short taxi ride, if time necessitates, back again.

She sees Joyce before her mother sees her. For a few seconds she stands motionless, observing. Her mother's silver bob shines in the light from above as if burnished and buffed, the small features are alert, eager, searching – for what? For the love of a daughter? For the love, Susie thinks, biting her lip, that I'm not ready – or able – to give her?

'Hello!' She sees the greeting rather than hears it, sees a slim hand raised in salutation. Sees it hesitate in the air, pause, drop to the lap in a gesture of apprehension. Her mother is scared about this meeting. Maybe she fears coolness.

'Hello, Joyce.'

Smile. You're good at acting.

She kisses her mother, senses the unfamiliar fragility of elderly skin under her lips.

The thin hand grasps hers and holds it.

'Susie.'

That's all – Susie. But the word is invested with a world of meaning, with love and longing, with hope and despair and humbleness.

'It's good to see you, Joyce.' She can't call her Mother.

Her hand is released. 'I've ordered tea. Is that right?'

'Terrific.'

Joyce's rigid uprightness relaxes a fraction, and she feels rewarded. This is a journey. We have a long way to travel, this new mother and I, at least we can be comfortable on the way.

'I've brought you some photographs.'

Joyce revisits old ground. 'How could I never have seen it before? Your likeness to your father, I mean?'

Her father: Jimmy Scirocco. His name is a waft of wind – and a deceit. She knows his real name, everyone knows Jimmy's story. He was born in Ireland, in a bothy in a heathery valley, so he told the world, though the story might have been as much a fiction as the rest of his life. 'Sheamus Dhonnchadha was too much of a mouthful for anyone,' he told an interviewer once, the gleam in his eye ferociously comical, 'especially for a young illiterate like myself.'

'Jimmy' was self evident – but why Scirocco?

'Sure, with Dean already taken, what was left for a young rebel but a wind that wreaks havoc?'

It was an answer, and no answer, but it was like Jimmy himself, you could never pin him down or make a reality of him. He was actor incarnate, always inhabiting someone else's skin, and so skilfully that you believed every breath of him.

227

'On television, on film even, it's not the same,' Joyce is saying, 'there's something about the presence of you that reveals it.'

'He never knew about me?'

'No.'

There it is, in a word. Two letters of finality and denial. Jimmy Scirocco never knew he had a daughter. Or – the thought strikes her forcibly – perhaps he had other children too, seeds of his faithless loin scattered into a dozen willing wombs. Jimmy Scirocco might have been a great many undesirable things, but his charm was legendary. She shakes her head – impossible to follow that thought. Here, Susie, is your mother, think about her.

'Right. So, after I was born—' She lets it trail, the sentence unfinished, its intention clear.

'I met up with a lad I knew back in school, Eric Henderson. I was pregnant when I first saw him again, still playing with deception, wearing a cheap brass ring and pretending I was married, like. We got on well and I was tempted to confess everything to him then and there, but he jumped to the obvious conclusions and although we had a great night out, he left me at the end of it with a warm wish for good luck and good fortune and he was gone again, out of my life.'

She sighed, a small, tight exhalation of breath.

'How many times I've kicked myself for my pride. If I'd confided in him that day – well, we might have got together then and I might have been able to keep you.' She shakes her head regretfully.

Susie is appalled. Wearing a cheap ring was such a small attempt to preserve dignity, but it had had a profound effect on the course of her life.

'I met him again a few months after you were adopted. I told him everything then, but of course, it was too late.'

Susie is wordless until tea arrives on a tray and splits the silence.

'So what happened to Eric Henderson?' she manages finally.

'I married him. Just a year after you were born.' This is the easy part of her story. This is where everything is resolved, where she begins the happy-ever-after part of her life. As Susie is kicking, then crawling, then making baby steps into the fiction that will sustain her life, her young mother is creating a new world of her own.

Susie murmurs, 'That's nice.'

'I was lucky.' Joyce seems oblivious to her pain. 'I got pregnant again almost straight away. Eric was wonderful. He supported me completely. He knew how I'd suffered, having to give you away.'

How I'd suffered. 'Right.'

'Yes. I had my little boy, Brian, two years to the day after you were born. Isn't that funny? To the day.'

'I have a brother?'

'He's a lovely boy, Brian. Not a boy any longer, of course. He's married. He's got two children. Teenagers now, Cheryl and Antony. Ant, he likes to be called.'

'Have you got any photographs?'

Joyce leans down and lifts her handbag from its position near her feet. 'I brought them specially. Here.'

A family photograph. A man, slightly balding, his face pleasant, a little rounded. The woman pretty, a brunette, petite and tidy. Two children, nice looking, bright kids.

This is my brother. These are my niece and nephew, Cheryl and Ant.

'I have another daughter, too, Sharon. She lives in New Zealand now. Here.' Another photograph, another family. 'That's Alan, her husband, and Stacey, her little girl. She's eight in a few weeks time. Of course, we don't get to see them so often, with them being so far away.'

And a sister. It's too much to assimilate.

'Brian, he's local. He stays in Stirling, to be near me. He's really kind.' Her back straightens, she is glowing with pride. 'After my Eric died, he said he'd be sure to take care of his Mum, because Sharon had already gone off. She was always an adventurer, that one, but Brian runs a big business, you know, he's done really well for himself. Of course, he worked hard, he always was ambitious.'

'What kind of business?'

'I never really understand it myself, but they do design work. On computers, he tells me. Internet stuff. Magazines. That kind of thing.'

In the battered, overwhelmed area of her head that Susie normally likes to think of as a brain, something resonates. 'A design company? In Stirling? It's not called CommX, is it, by any chance?'

Joyce beams. 'That's it. Yes. CommX. Do you know it?'

Chapter Twenty-three

Family conferences are not in the Wallace tradition, but it's time, Susie thinks as she drives home that evening, to tell her family about their new relatives. Archie too, if she can drag him out of the studio.

'Sunday,' she says to Mannie on the phone. 'No excuses, I want you here for lunch.'

'Sunday lunch,' she tells Jon. 'I don't care how tired you are. You can tell us all about your first week at work.'

'Lunch is at one on Sunday. The children are coming. Please be there,' she writes on a note for Archie. She shoves this under the door of the studio.

The cottage is silent when she rises at eight. The calendar has tipped into June and the sun has demurely followed its prompting, obligingly turning up its thermostat so that the kitchen, when she descends for her habitual cup of tea, is deliciously cosy. She opens the back door and allows the light to flood over the stone slabs of the floor.

One day in a week to call my own.

It's a fatal thought, because just as she sinks onto the bench in the courtyard to enjoy the peace, the phone rings.

'Radio Scotland here, Mrs Wallace,' says a cheerful voice. 'We understand that the Education Minister is under pressure to resign – are you willing to talk to us?'

It's news to her. She gives a holding response while she tracks down Maureen Armstrong and fills herself in on the background. Her own constant criticism of the cuts in funding for school arts projects have not, Mo tells her sternly, helped the case and she should not, repeat not, agree to an interview.

She calls the station back. 'I'll talk to you,' she says, knowing it's suicide, but Party loyalty or not, she is determined to remain true to her cause. The Arts must come first. And children. Children are the future and their hearts and souls must be nourished and fed – and how is that going to happen on a diet of literacy and numeracy targets?

It's a busy morning and consequently when Mannie drives up the gravel drive at midday, her work in the kitchen isn't nearly done. So it's, 'Will you peel the spuds, love?' and 'Could you possibly set the table, darling?' – knowing the men won't turn up till lunch is steaming on their plates – and there's no time for talking.

Jon is first to show, his hair rumpled with sleep and his eyes still bleary. Mannie laughs. 'What a sight,' she teases. 'Homo laboro. Working man at his worst.'

'Piss off,' Jonno says, still grumpy with tiredness, but he doesn't say it unkindly.

Archie's shadow falls across the floor. 'Where will I put these?'

He's standing in the doorway, the brightness of the sun behind his head making his silvery hair into a kind of halo. His arms are full of flowers –a gesture that touches her heart. He has been picking these for ages, he must have been, because some of the flowers grow not in the garden but deep in the nearby wood, where the small loch spills onto the heather, checked only by some rough, moss-strewn boulders.

'How lovely. Thank you Archie. Mannie, could you put them in a vase? Archie, open some wine will you please? Jonathan, the roast is ready to take through, your father will carve.'

It's almost like the old days. Jon is more or less cheerful, Mannie is a blur of motion and energy, Archie is stolid and quiet, but there.

'So, Mum. What's this all about, huh?' Jon says as he

lays down his spoon and fork. 'Great crumble, by the way.'

'Thank you, Jonathan.'

She settles back in her chair and looks round her family.

'I want,' she says, 'to tell you about your cousins.'

It isn't, as it turns out, the cousins that have the real impact on her audience. Susie thought she had it all planned, but it's not at all straightforward. She'd imagined that unveiling the identity of her true father would be the highlight, but in the event, there's only mild interest in that.

'Jimmy Scirocco?' Jonno snorts. 'That'll make the news.'

'Christ,' says Mannie,' That explains a lot.'

Archie says nothing, merely folds his arms and slumps a little further down in his seat. She can't read him. This disconcerts her, because in all the years they have been together, she has never found Archie difficult to fathom.

'What do you mean, Mannie?' she asks her daughter.

'Well. You know. The acting. The hair. All that energy. I guess I've got a bit of that, too,' she adds, realising.

Susie says, 'He never knew about me.' She becomes unexpectedly emotional at this point and is forced to swallow back tears, although no-one seems to notice. 'Joyce married an old school mate, within a year.'

Mannie observes, 'She can't have been that much in love with him then.'

'And she had another child, quite quickly. He was born two years to the day after me.'

Jon, never renowned for his sensitivity, says, 'Really? That'd cheer her up.'

'What about poor old Mum?' Mannie says reproachfully. 'Given away, handed over to heaven knows what fate.'

'But Mum did all right,' Jon protests. 'She did really well, in fact.'

'I did all right,' Susie acknowledges. 'Joyce had a daughter a few years later. She lives in New Zealand now, apparently. I've got photographs.' She stands up and goes to her small desk, lifts out a folder. 'Here.'

She hands a photograph of Sharon to Mannie, who scrutinises it. 'She's got a kid. She's what, eight or nine?'

'Almost eight.'

'They look nice.'

'Yes.'

'What about the boy?' Mannie asks. 'Did he move away too?'

'No, actually, he still lives locally, in Stirling.' Susie pauses. This will be a surprise for Jon, she knows. She draws out the next photograph. 'In fact, you might recognise him.' She turns it over. 'His name's Brian Henderson.'

Jonathan's eyes grow round. He picks up the photograph and stares at it intently. 'Jesus Christ,' he says weightily.

'Let me see,' Mannie says, her voice taut. She snatches the photograph from him and Susie watches in astonishment as all the blood drains from her face and her hands begin to tremble. The photograph falls to the table and slides across the glossy surface, coming to rest against the stem of Archie's wine glass.

'No!' Mannie cries, in a voice Susie barely recognises. It sounds more like the cry of a beast in agony than anything human. 'No! It can't be!'

'What?' Archie, she notices, has roused himself from his passivity and is sitting bolt upright, concern writ large on his face. 'What is it, Treasure?' he asks gently, and tries to take hold of one of Mannie's hands.

She pulls it away violently and stands up. Her chair clatters to the floor, its back hitting the flagstones with a

234

crash. Mannie spins on her heel and turns to the kitchen, running to the sink, where she is noisily and violently sick.

Susie is appalled. 'What's wrong? What is it?'

Jon stands too, his face almost as white as Mannie's. 'The photograph,' he says. 'It's Brian Henderson, my boss.'

'Yes,' Susie says puzzled. 'I know that. I thought it was quite funny, you ending up there just as we discover we're related.'

'That's the problem,' Jon says. 'He's your brother, isn't he? Which makes him Mannie's uncle.'

Susie nods.

'Brian Henderson is the man that Mannie's obsessed with. Mum – she's in love with her uncle.'

The retching in the kitchen turns into a wail.

Susie's response is immediate and irrational.

'This is your fault, Archie,' she says, tartly, all the anguish of the past months rolling into one bitter accusation. 'If you'd just been honest with me, we'd have known about my history and discovered my birth family years ago. None of this would have happened and poor Mannie wouldn't be in this mess.'

The moment the words are out of her mouth she regrets them, but it's too late. Archie is on his feet, his lips pursed tight against the possibility of making any retort. He marches towards the door.

'Wait! Archie!'

He halts, but doesn't turn to look at her. Then, very deliberately, he continues walking.

Archie whistles for Prince and opens the back of the old Land Rover so that the dog can jump in. He has to get away from here, he has no idea where to, anywhere will do. He is appalled and he's worried, but most of all, he is furious – because after all, who is Susie Wallace to talk of secrets? His mind catapults back across the years, to how close he came to losing her.

Calgary Bay is ten weeks into filming and Archie has known from the start that she has met someone. Susie's honesty can be a painful thing, but her dishonesty is excruciating. He hears it first in the forced levity of her voice, detects it in the uncharacteristic half-heartedness of her protestations of affection then realises, with debilitating numbness, that there is one person she has completely omitted to talk about: her co-star, Maitland Forbes.

He visits Mull one weekend, when they're shooting on location, and his suspicions are confirmed. There's an unnatural tension between Susie and Maitland. She avoids his eye and Maitland is excruciatingly jovial. The crew exudes uneasiness in Archie's presence and he knows that they know, or at least that they have guessed. Each signal is small by itself, together they provide him with a devastating dossier. He's certain that his instincts are sound.

He has to return to Glasgow, where he is teaching in a secondary school. The autumn term has just commenced, so he's no longer free to travel to Mull, to gauge whether things are the same, he has to agonise alone. He and Susie have been married for just one year and he's still hopelessly, tormentedly in love with her. He wonders, daily, why this glorious, bewitching woman chose him when there were so many more tempting suitors.

With his suspicions come a deepening loss of self esteem and he struggles to get through the days, his mind a quagmire of questions. How should he deal with this? Should he abandon everything and cross to Mull for a confrontation? If he forces the issue and she chooses him, will she always resent his actions and regret her decision – and what will his marriage be worth then? If she doesn't, then he will have lost her, for ever.

In the end, he knows in his heart that he has to leave it

to Susie to make her choice. He says nothing, just waits in agony.

Susie comes back to him the day the filming ends and tells him that she adores him. She lavishes affection on him as if she needs to make atonement. She buys him a guitar he has pined for and declares her love incessantly. Perhaps such things could be taken as cover for wrongdoing, but there are no signs of secrecy or dishonesty, no furtive phone calls or letters hurriedly tucked away and Archie gradually becomes secure in the knowledge that whatever she felt for Maitland has been put aside and that Susie has made her decision. It's over.

Eight weeks later, she announces that she is pregnant.

At the crossroads, Archie pauses. Straight on into Hailesbank, left towards Edinburgh or right, deeper into the countryside? It isn't so much a choice as an instinct; he turns right, the Land Rover taking him towards the farm where Sandie Alexander lives with her partner, Jim Gibson. He can drive past of course, but ten minutes later he finds himself pulling into their yard and fervently hoping she's there and willing to talk.

'Afternoon, Archie.'

It's Jim who appears at the door of the farmhouse, his florid face all friendliness. When Sandie moved in with the big, gentle widower five years ago, it was the talk of the neighbourhood and viewed as the most unlikely match imaginable, but there's something in the counterpoint of the two personalities that works perfectly.

'You for a cuppa? Sandie's in the kitchen.'

'Got a moment, Jim, have you? I'm not intruding?'

'Sure, sure. Good to see you. Want to take the dog in with you?'

He lets Prince out of the back and finds Sandie stacking the dishwasher. The quiet domesticity of the scene is disturbingly at odds with the Sandie he knows, the rock

237

queen with the sultry voice who can whip an audience of thousands into a frenzy.

'Hi. Jim's promised me tea.'

Sandie's pale face breaks into a broad grin. 'Just tea? He's fucking mean. I'll get him trained one day.'

Jim, who has followed him in, moves up behind his wife and folds her in an embrace of surprising tenderness for such a big man. 'I'm the one who should do the training. Language lessons.' He beams at Archie. 'It's no use. I've given up. Listen, you two will have things to talk about and I need to get up to the top field to take a look at a sheep I'm worried about.'

'Sure? I'm not driving you out?'

'Not at all, not a bit of it.'

Sandie sets out two mugs. 'Really tea, Archie? Or something stronger?' She looks at him speculatively.

For all her edgy appearance, Sandie is astonishingly intuitive, but he says, with the ghost of a smile, 'Tea's fine. I'm driving.'

'Well.' She pours. 'Is it the album?'

Prince flops comfortably at his feet and closes his eyes and Archie feels the comfort of his presence. He takes a moment or two to respond to Sandie's question, and when he does, it's with one of his own. 'You and Jim – you're sound, the two of you?'

Sandie picks up a packet of cigarettes and pulls one out. 'So you've had a row with Susie?'

Archie doesn't normally take sugar in his tea, but he picks up a teaspoon and loads it with a small, glistening mound. 'We've been married thirty years, you know.'

'Fuck me. I was ten back then.'

'I used to see her at the college, so beautiful, always surrounded by admirers, absolutely unattainable. I never thought I'd be the lucky sod who'd land her, the biggest catch of the decade.'

'She's the fucking lucky one, Archie,' Sandie says

238

softly, putting the cigarette to her lips and inhaling deeply.

He goes on as if he hasn't heard her. 'She was always a passionate person. Always had her causes. I think it was the passion that made her such a great actress. When Susie acts, she becomes that person. She can make you empathise with the character so much that each agony is your agony.'

He has been tipping the sugar into his tea grain by grain. Now he watches as the last of it slides off the spoon, then he dips it back into the bowl and reloads it.

'She could have been a much bigger star, you know. She could have been as big a name as—' he forces himself to say the name, '—Maitland Forbes. Bigger. But when the children came along, she started turning down the parts that would have taken her away from us – the big films, Hollywood.'

He lowers the spoon slowly into the tea, watching as the crystals absorb the liquid and turn brown, layer by tiny layer. *Mannie.* He ignores that line of thought and forces himself to go on.

'I think it would be true to say that the politics started because of the children. Susie couldn't bear to see how little time was given in schools to art, to drama, to music. She couldn't simply stand by and let it happen, she had to do something about it.'

'Like you said, she's a passionate person.'

'And stubborn. Once she's made a judgment she won't move on it. Like falling out with her own Party because their policies don't match up to her exacting standards.'

Like believing he had betrayed her trust and hating him for it.

'Don't tell me this is about fucking politics.'

'What?' He lets the sugar sink into the liquid and stirs it vigorously.

'This visit, Archie. Not that I'm not pleased to see you or anything but it's bloody unusual. Do you want to tell

239

me about it instead of flaming wittering on?'

Archie picks up the tea and takes a big sip. It's unbearably sweet and he grimaces and sets it back down on the table.

That day Susie had done the early morning television interview. He'd seen Brian Henderson, on the item just before she appeared. It was the mouth that had been the clue. *Susie's mouth.* Put that mouth into a slightly softer mould and frame it in a woman's face, and you had Susie.

He'd had a bad feeling then. If he'd listened more carefully, perhaps he would have heard that he was a director of CommX, perhaps he could have found some way to avert all this.

'I'd better go,' he says, suddenly desperate to be on his own.

'Right. Good to fucking talk,' Sandie says, her voice heavily ironic.

'Yes. Good. Thanks, Sandie, Thanks,' Archie says, oblivious to her tone. He's at the door already, but he turns. 'This tune.'

'Which bloody tune is that, Archie?'

'The one I wrote on our wedding anniversary.' Archie looks at her impatiently, as if she should know. Or has he even told Sandie about it?

'Oh, that one.'

'I did tell you?'

'Nope.'

'Oh.'

'What about it, anyway?'

'It's driving me mad. I can't find the words.'

'Want me to write them?'

They have a fruitful collaboration and Sandie often writes the words to Archie's music, but on this occasion it feels wrong. 'No. Thanks Sandie. I need to do it myself. But something's stopping me. I'm climbing the wall.'

'Sort out your problem with Susie and the words'll

240

come.'

He stares at her. What an odd thing to say. 'Right. Thanks.' He turns and goes out, Prince at his heels. 'Thanks for the tea,' he calls over his shoulder.

In the kitchen, Sandie looks at the virtually untouched mug and pulls a face.

He's still three miles from Cairn Cottage when the engine coughs, splutters, and dies. He manages to coast in to the side of the road and comes to a final halt with the nearside wheels half in a ditch. The fuel gauge shows empty. How the hell has he forgotten to fill the thing? He's been so preoccupied recently it's clean gone out of his mind. Bugger it. He'll have to walk.

'Here boy, out you come.'

He opens the tailgate and sets off along the road, deep in thought. *Sort out your problem with Susie and the words will come.* Maybe Sandie is right, but there's much, much more in his life to worry about than she can possibly know. He kicks at a small branch that has fallen across the road as Prince leaps to and fro, barking for it to be thrown.

'All right, old boy, here you go.' He throws it and watches as Prince chases along the lane to retrieve it. The dog is getting old, his movements are becoming ponderous and he lacks the bounce he used to have. I'm getting old too, he thinks – too old for dissent.

There's a drip on the back of his neck. The sky has darkened and there's rain starting. Blast. He hasn't brought a jacket. Prince is at his feet, his face upturned, the stick in his mouth ready for throwing again. Well, so what if he gets wet, what does it matter, in the scale of his problems?

Brian Henderson. As he trudges towards the cottage the breath whistles through his teeth in sheer disbelief. What a twist! For Jon to end up working for the man is an odd coincidence, but for Mannie to fall for him is frankly bizarre.

Archie thinks of himself as a simple man – music is his sphere, not emotion. For years he has schooled himself to write any feelings he might have into his music rather than let them fester in his heart. Twenty-nine years ago he nearly lost Susie. When she came back to him, he promised himself he would be grateful for every moment they spent together, and that he would do anything he needed to in order to keep her by his side – even if it meant accepting the child she was carrying.

Even if it was Maitland's.

Archie has never expressed his doubts to anyone, certainly not to Susie, and he has loved Mannie with all the passion a father can bestow on a daughter. Mannie is her mother's daughter, there's no doubt of that. She has all Susie's boundless energy, her impulsiveness, her enthusiasm but she doesn't have Susie's colouring or features. Nor does she have his. Her hair is dark and straight, her eyes are hazel.

Like Maitland's.

For nearly thirty years, Archie has carried the burden of not one secret, but two and now the subject of genetic inheritance has thrown up a boxful of trouble and left him with an impossible decision. Should this, too, be laid on the table?

At a wooden stile he turns off the road and clambers over it onto a narrow path. He can take a shortcut from here back to the cottage. Now he's soaking. The long grass at the sides of the path drags at his trousers so that the sodden flaps of cloth cling to his legs. Through the discomfort, the melody he has written plays itself in his head, the refrain insistent. It irritates him beyond belief.

The path comes to a small burn. Archie has been down here quite recently, but he sees that recent rain has dislodged the plank that had been thrown across it by way of a bridge. He'll have to jump. He pauses, rocks back on his heels, and leaps – and finds himself lodged firmly in two feet of squelching mud at the bottom of the stream, his ankle twisted beneath him. He is stuck, and although it's June, the water is extremely cold. He allows himself to swear, while on the bank Prince runs to and fro, barking himself stupid.

It takes Archie ten difficult minutes to drag himself out of the burn. Every stitch of clothing he's wearing is soaked through and heavy but at least his ankle, though painful, doesn't feel broken or sprained. The softness of the mud must have cushioned the impact of the twist. In this condition, it takes him another hour to stride back to the cottage, discomfort and despondency permeating every bone. Even the tune has deserted his brain.

Mannie's car has gone and from the grateful chattering of the hens he guesses that Jon is feeding them, now that the rain has stopped. The back door is open and he can see Susie, standing by the sink.

She glances out.

'Oh there you are Archie,' she calls. 'We wondered where you'd gone. Trust you to get out of washing up.'

He stands stock still in the middle of the yard, too angry to speak. *I could have died out there. Drowned in that fucking stream. And no-one would even have noticed.*

He turns, hunches his shoulders, and limps across to the studio. If there's to be any comfort this day, it will only be found in music.

From the doorway of the kitchen, Susie watches him, furious with herself for her flippant words. She'd hoped to defuse the tension between them with a light-hearted joke, but instead she had clearly made things even worse.

Chapter Twenty-four

Jon spends the whole of Sunday afternoon and evening mired in contemplation of the mess. He can't go back to CommX, everyone will know – and yet it's what he wants more than anything in the world.

Shame cripples him to the extent that he can't make a clear decision and he finds himself, bleary-eyed and feeling rough, half way along the road to Stirling before he has thought it through. One thing drives him forward – not his new career, not the money: Alex Townsend.

He can see her face now, her dark eyes bright and intelligent, her skin lightly tanned and smooth. He finds her cheerfulness immensely attractive and she makes him feel at ease. It's as if he's known her for years, she's like an old pair of slippers.

Sod it, that's hardly flattering! Is this the best he can come up with by way of a chat-up line?

His mood darkens as he nears the front door. He's here, but will he stay? He enters the office realising that he has been praying that Brian Henderson is in London, or Dubai, or New York – anywhere other than Stirling – and his prayers are answered. The morning meeting is taken by Maris Jay, though it proves scarcely less bewildering than last week's in terms of the number and complexity of their ongoing projects.

'That's it. Sara will type up the notes and put them on the server. Oh, and Brian will be here tomorrow,' she adds, shuffling her papers together and standing up, 'with news, we hope, of a contract win in London that will impact on us here.'

'Do we know we've got it?' someone asks.

'No. But the signs are positive. Okay folks, on with the work. Jonno,' she turns to him, 'you all right? Know what you're doing?'

He nods. 'Yes. Thanks.'

'Your Mac up and running okay?'

'Yes. Thanks.'

'What project are you working on?'

'I'm doing some posters for an event at the Castle, a storytelling series for kids.'

'Great. Okay.' She turns away, leaving Jonno to his work and his thoughts. Tomorrow. One day's grace. And it's clear that no-one knows – that's the only fact that offers him any comfort.

He sits all day at his computer, perfecting his concept for the posters, sourcing the images, clearing the idea with Stu, working on the complicated Photoshop montage. Sitting in a corner is all right, he can manage this, but tomorrow will bring another challenge and he still doesn't know what to do.

'Hi Jon.'

He glances up. His thoughts have been preoccupying his mind to the exclusion, even, of Alex Townsend, but now she's here by his desk and his heart thumps with pleasure at her nearness. 'Hi. Good weekend?'

'Catching up. Doing the washing, seeing the folks. Nothing glamourous. You?'

'I—'

Can he tell her? Can he trust her?

'Something happened,' he says. He saves his document and looks up at her. He sees concern in the bright eyes. Old slippers? God, no. This girl is pure gold, one in a million. Trusting his instincts, he says impulsively, 'Later, Alex, after work – would you mind having a drink with me again? There's something I'd value your opinion on.'

Don't be busy. Don't be rushing home for keep fit or

246

singing or French class or whatever you do on a Monday. Please God, be free.

'Sure. Love to. See you later, then.'

'You don't mind coming here again?'

'Not at all.' The pub in Bridge of Allan has figured prominently in Jon's mind for the past week. He will never forget the first drink they'd had together, it was the best pint he'd ever tasted.

'So.'

Again her top lip is rimed with foam. It's the way she drinks beer. He watches, entranced, as her tongue emerges to lick it off, delicate as a cat's.

'So. This is nice.' Lame.

'There was something you wanted to talk about.'

Desperately – but now that they're here together, he can't find the words.

'What's up, Jon? Is it something I can help with? Something to do with work? Home? Girlfriend problems?'

'No, no, I'm not seeing anyone at the moment,' he blurts out, not wanting her to think he's romantically involved. 'It's a bit delicate, actually.'

Alex puts her glass on the table and leans forward on her elbows. The fabric of her cotton top stretches taut across her small breasts, a fact that Jonno, despite his mental turmoil, can't help noticing.

'Oh goodee. Gossip.'

His face falls. It's not the reaction he hoped for. 'No. It's nothing. Forget it.'

'Come on, Jon!'

'No. I shouldn't have said anything. It's too – I'm ashamed.'

'Ashamed? Why? What have you done?' She leans back and puts her hand over her mouth in mock shock. 'You didn't nick Maris's chocolate doughnut, did you?'

There was an outcry from the manager earlier in the

day when she went to the fridge to recover the anticipated treat, only to find someone had already scoffed it. No-one has owned up.

Jon finds a smile. 'No. I'm not into chocolate doughnuts.'

'Some other vice, then.' She leans forward. 'Do tell.'

They're not on the same wavelength. He can't confide. He's disappointed – but seeing this, she turns serious and catches hold of his hand. The unaffectedness of the gesture and the warmth and dryness of her touch are intoxicating.

'Sorry, Jon. I shouldn't have been flippant. Listen, I'm here. I promise you, I'm good at keeping secrets. And I'd like to help, if I can.'

'Okay.' He clears his throat and looks around nervously, but the bar is almost empty. It's still early. Across the far side of the room, two workmen are downing pints thirstily, but they aren't in earshot. The door swings open and they're joined by half a dozen mates. The noise levels rise, adding to his safety. They won't be overheard. 'It's about my sister,' he says cautiously, 'and the Boss.'

Alex's eyes widen. 'Is this related to your question last week?' she asks. 'About Brian being a womaniser?'

Christ, she's quick on the uptake. 'Sort of.'

'Jon – is she having an affair with Brian?'

His shoulders slump and he buries his face in his hands. He shouldn't have started this. He should have found some other way of dealing with his problems. Now Alex is involved – and what will she think of him?

'It's not the end of the world. It happens. I won't tell anyone. Probably it'll all blow over in no time and that'll be that. I hate to say it, but she's not the first – but you knew that, anyway.'

He lifts his head and stares at her. 'It's not that,' he says wretchedly. 'Not just that, anyway.'

'She's pregnant?'

'God, no! Actually, I don't think they've slept

together.' The thought makes him feel bilious.

'Then – what?' Alex looks puzzled.

'If I tell you—'

'Jon, come on, we've been through all that. Just spit it out, for heaven's sake. The suspense is killing me.'

'We just learned the truth yesterday. Brian Henderson is my mother's brother. My uncle. Mannie's uncle.'

'You just found that out? How can you just discover an uncle?'

He groans and rubs his hands in his eyes as if to clear his vision. 'We learned a couple of months ago that Mum was adopted. Her parents had never told her. Dad knew, but he didn't tell her either and that's caused all sorts of ... never mind. Anyway, she's tracked down her mother, her real mother, I mean, and last week her new mother told her. Her name's Joyce Henderson and Brian is her son. Born two years after she gave Mum away.'

Alex sits back in her chair. 'Christ. That's some story.'

'There was a family summit yesterday. Mum knows that Mannie split with her boyfriend and that she'd started seeing some married man – of course, she isn't happy about that, you can imagine – but she had no idea that the man she was seeing was Brian.'

'Stars above. Isn't that incest?'

No-one has said that word, though Jon imagines it has been on everyone's mind. He shies away from it, even now.

'Mannie's reaction was extreme – shock, throwing up, hysterics. Mum blames Dad for everything, like if he'd told her about the adoption they'd have sorted everything out years ago and this would never have happened. Dad marched out and went for a long walk in the rain, nearly drowned in some stream, apparently. Mum didn't care, he told me. They're not talking, haven't talked much for ages but this seems to have finished it.'

He runs his fingers round the rim of his glass, which is

empty. He should offer to buy her another drink—

'What about your sister?'

'Mannie screeched off in her car and God knows how she's handling it because her mobile's off and she didn't go in to work this morning. And I—' he pauses and stares at her, desolation all over his face, '—how can I go on working here, Alex? I land the job I've been desperate for then this happens. How can I stay, knowing what I know?'

'Hey, hey.' Her voice is soothing. She reaches for his hand again. 'Take it easy. Let's just take time out, shall we, and think?'

'Think? I've done nothing else. I wouldn't have come in this morning except for—' He stops, embarrassed. Except for you he'd been going to say, but it's too early in their relationship – if they're going to have a relationship – for such admissions. 'I don't know what to do,' he ends forlornly.

Across the bar there's a burst of laughter. The men are enjoying themselves.

Alex is looking puzzled. 'How did she meet Brian? Why did she fall for him, do you think? You said she was seeing someone before it happened?'

'Yup. A really great guy, Callum. I thought – I think we all thought – that this was it. She's had loads of boyfriends before, she's kind of cute I guess, but she always gets bored. Callum had her sussed and she seemed smitten. Anyway, she met Brian at a trade fair in London and that was that.'

He glares at Alex.

'They both promise me he wasn't involved in the decision to give me the job or I would have walked out last week.'

'Heavens, Jon, anyone can see your talent. Of course you got the job on your own merit.'

That feels a bit better, at least. 'Finding that out was bad enough, but then the penny dropped that this is the guy she's obsessed with. I couldn't believe it, honest to God, I nearly died. My sister – and my boss!'

'I don't imagine it's all one-sided,' Alex says with a grimace. 'I was trying to be diplomatic last week when you asked about Brian, but to be truthful, everyone knows he's a bit of a sleazebag. He'll have come on to her, no doubt about that.'

It's mildly reassuring to think the fault is not all Mannie's. 'You think? Still, whatever. It doesn't change anything, does it?'

'But now that she knows he's related?'

'You should have seen her, Alex. She was hysterical. She kept shouting, "Nothing will make me give him up. Nothing!" There was no talking any sense to her.'

'But perhaps we could talk sense to him.'

Jon stares at her. 'Talk to the boss?'

'Someone's going to have to.'

He pondered this idea. How could he talk to Brian Henderson about such a desperately delicate matter? His *boss*?

'I couldn't!'

'Think about it.'

'No. No, no, no.'

Walking into that glass box and telling Brian to stop coming on to his sister? His face grows bright at the thought.

'It needs to be dealt with, Jon.'

Again there is laughter across the room. Jon glances at the men, so carefree and happy. Can he ever laugh again? Not, certainly, unless this mess is cleared up – if that's even possible.

'I guess you're right,' he concedes reluctantly. 'Maybe my mother?'

'I expect that will be on her agenda. But this is your job, Jon, your situation.'

He downs the rest of his pint, but it tastes like

dishwater.

Alex says, 'I've just had a thought.'

'Yeah?'

She stands up. 'Something I read recently. Listen, I'm going home.'

'Aren't you going to tell me?'

'I want to check up on it first. Can you get in early tomorrow? Eight?'

'Sure. But—'

'If I'm right—' she smiles up at him. '—well, it might help a bit. Go rest, Jon. We'll sort this out. Promise.'

By her car he takes her hand. He longs to crush her close to him, but not here, not like this, not yet. His free hand steals up to her face and he moves a tendril of hair from her eyes with great gentleness. 'You're quite something, Alex Townsend.'

She grins. 'You're not so bad yourself. See you in the morning.' And she's gone.

He spends hours thinking about her. She's so feisty. He loves that she's determined to solve the insoluble. He imagines he'll be awake all night, remembering that wisp of hair, but he sleeps as soon as his head hits the pillow, worn out by the emotions of yesterday and the tensions of today.

At a quarter to eight the next morning, he's back in the CommX offices.

She's already there.

'Hi.'

'Tea?' She has it ready for him.

'Thanks.'

The office is empty, waiting for the day to start. There's something pleasing about its readiness and its willingness to accommodate them now.

Alex says, straight out, as if it's the only way she can do it, 'I've been doing some reading. I think your sister has

252

fallen victim to something called genetic sexual attraction.'

'What the hell's that?'

'People tend to shy away from it because it's about incest, but when you told me your story something clicked in my head. I read an article in a magazine recently about a couple who couldn't have kids so they decided to adopt – this was years ago – and they adopted a boy and a girl. The boy was never any trouble, he was good as gold, while the girl was always a pain. But when the boy was in his twenties, he got engaged and they started to plan the wedding.'

Jon fidgeted. Where was the connection with Mannie?

'Bear with me, Jon. Everything seemed to be going really well, then one day the boy's sister – his real sister, I mean, not the adopted girl – got in touch. She'd been fostered out and ended up being adopted by a couple who emigrated to Australia. The girl had managed to track him down and was planning on coming to visit. They were all really excited – until the girl arrived.'

'Why? What happened?'

'The boy and his real sister fell in love. Just like that. Completely and obsessively in love. The engagement was broken off and they moved in together. End of. '

'Brother and sister? In love?'

'Nothing would stop them, nothing anyone said could change their minds. They had different surnames, they didn't tell anyone outside the family, they just went off together.'

'Christ Almighty.'

'When you told me yesterday about your sister, I remembered the story and wondered whether there might be any kind of similarities. I did some research on the net to see if there were any case studies, and there are. There's some theories about why this kind of thing happens.'

'Theories? Justifications, you mean?'

'No, just attempts to get under the surface in an objective way. Apparently, when you grow up with someone – a parent, a brother or sister, whatever – they reckon there's some kind of built in inhibitors that stop you being attracted to them sexually. The old familiarity breeds contempt thing. You know they pick their noses, fart when they eat sprouts, whatever.'

'And if they don't grow up together—'

'The inhibitor doesn't kick in. You meet someone and maybe recognise something in them that's really familiar and nice, maybe because you're like that too or something, and you think, wow, this person's like, the half of me I never knew I had. It's strong stuff.'

'And it can convert into sexual attraction?'

'Yup. Not with everyone, of course. But yes. Mothers often feel an overpowering need to feel the skin of their son next to theirs, maybe something they never felt when the guy was a baby.'

'Mothers sleep with their sons?'

'There's plenty of case studies, yes.'

'Gross.'

'That's what I thought. But they can't help it. Don't you see, Jon, maybe Mannie can't help it.'

Jon's tea sits on the desk next to him, untouched. Alex's explanation is startling, but the more he thinks about it, the more it makes sense. Why else would she give up a guy like Cal for Brian Henderson? What was it she said, the day she confessed? *It's a mess, Jonno. A complete mess.* He says slowly, 'You might be on to something.'

'So – next steps?'

'No idea. How do you deal with something like that?'

'Well for one, you go to the boss and tell him he's her uncle – or does he know already?'

'I don't think so. Mum's only told the family.'

'That's probably a good thing. Maybe when Brian realises, he'll back off.'

'That depends, doesn't it? What if he's got it too? This genetic whatsit.'

'Then it'll be harder. But it's not always reciprocated, apparently. We have to hope it's just Mannie. That way it'll be easier to break.'

Jonno's shoulders sag. 'Jesus,' he says, appalled. Then, 'Jesus,' he repeats lamely.

The door bursts open and half a dozen staff appear, chatting and laughing. The day is about to begin.

'I need to think about this,' Jonno says quickly.

'Sure.'

'And Alex—'

'Yes?'

'Thanks.'

It was all he has time to say, but the look she gives him buoys him up all day.

Chapter Twenty-five

Susie is in trouble again. Maureen Armstrong is fizzing with rage. 'I thought we agreed, Susie. No off-message interviews.'

'You agreed, Mo,' Susie says with every outward appearance of calm. Frankly, in the scheme of what's happening at home, Mo's rages seem insignificant.

'Tom's incandescent.'

'I imagine he is.'

'Don't you get it, Susie? You're making our education policy look ridiculous.'

'That's because it is ridiculous.'

'Susie, you can't head off unilaterally in your own blessed direction, not if you want to be a member of this Party. Your constant criticising is doing us no good at all. I'm going to have to forbid you to talk to the media.'

Susie smiles sweetly. 'That's going to look great, isn't it? I can see the headlines now. "Party gag on Scotland's National Treasure".'

It's an unfair trick, but she's quoting an article that appeared in one of the Sundays, where she was – amazingly, in her opinion – featured in a list of 'National Living Treasures'.

She can almost hear Mo growl in frustration. 'Susie, how can I put this any more clearly? Joe Shearer's job as Education Minister is seriously at risk. I've heard rumours that the opposition is going to force a vote of no confidence next week. It could bring down the government. We'll need every vote to save the day – including yours.'

'I hear what you're saying, Mo, and I do understand the concepts of collective responsibility and Party unity. But arts education matters to me. Really matters. I'm not simply spouting words and I'm not just being awkward about this. I care.' She sighs. 'Actually, I'm not sure I *can* vote with the Party on this one.'

Mo runs her hands through her crop of flaming hair and back again, leaving it standing up like a cockscomb. 'I know you care. Joe knows you care. The First Minister knows you care. But there's such a thing as the greater good.'

'And what, pray, is the greater good in this instance?'

That silences Mo, as she knew it would. The Media Manager turns on her heel and stalks off, frustrated.

'That was something to behold,' Karen says cheerfully.

The day she was elected to the Parliament was one of the greatest days in Susie's life. Politics isn't a career she prepared herself for, or trained in, or really gave very much thought to until passion for her cause drove her here. It's been fun – but the best part has always been getting home from work each day and talking it all over with Archie. No matter how late the hour, he has always been there, waiting for her, eager to learn about who she has met, what she said in the Chamber, the ideas she has had, who she's been able to help.

Today, steering the car the last couple of miles from Hailesbank to the cottage, weariness seeps through her bones. The Rivo debacle is still troubling her deeply. It's all very well sacking Ricky Waring, but that won't solve their problems, not by a long way. The challenge, as always, is money.

The best way to make amends for only half keeping an eye on the job she committed herself to do by joining the Board is to raise fifty or sixty thousand pounds, and quickly – but who does she know who can flash around that kind of money?

Jonno has retired to bed. Archie, presumably, is in the studio, because he's not in evidence in the cottage. Susie opens the fridge, takes out a bottle of white wine and squints at the level. Not bad. Jonno's drinking has dropped since he started working and that, at least, is something to be thankful for.

She pours herself a glass and goes through to the sitting room. She has just flopped down on the sofa when the phone rings. She's tempted to leave it, but thinking that perhaps Jonno is sleeping already, she heaves herself up again and goes across to her desk to take the call.

'Susie? That you?' The Scottish accent tinged with American is unmistakeable.

'Maitland? Hi! Are you in Scotland?'

'Sadly, no. This a good time to talk?'

'Excellent. It's great to hear you. What's new?'

'I've made a bit of a breakthrough, actually. Did I tell you about the movie I wanted to make? The historical based on the final days of the Jacobite rebellion?'

'No. Tell me now.'

'It's by a young playwright, a girl. I saw her work a few years ago at the Fringe in Edinburgh, a short drama about Bonnie Prince Charlie. It made him out to be a bit of a fool.'

Susie laughed. 'Well, he was in many ways, though you might make a few enemies by showing him in that light.'

'He was idealistic too, I guess. But what I really liked about her interpretation was the way she'd done Flora MacDonald, really challenging, a teenager who spoke her mind, even in front of the Prince. She wasn't cowed or intimidated. So I asked the playwright for a treatment with Flora at the heart of the story, not as an add-on, and took an option. And the funding's come through to make the movie! I'm so excited.'

'That's fantastic, Maitland. Are you going to star?' She couldn't see Maitland as Charles Edward Stuart and besides, he was too old by far.

'No, no, darling, I'm going to direct. My debut.'

'I'm so excited for you.'

'Thing is, Susie, I'd love you to be in it.'

'Me? Really? I'm way too old for Flora.'

'Sure. But there'll be something else. Her mother, perhaps, or a lady at Court. Not a big part, maybe, but a return to the screen. It's long overdue, honey.'

'Maitland, that sounds delicious. But I have a career.'

'Politics? Call that a career? Darling, you're an actor, born and bred.' The sound of coughing splutters down the line. 'Maybe that wasn't the best choice of phrase, huh? But you know what I mean. It wouldn't take long. We could fit your shooting round your schedules.'

'I'll give it some thought, I promise. It's certainly a very attractive idea.'

'Good. Do that. Anything else new, darling?'

Maitland is one of the few people she has confided in. She's tempted to tell him about the latest developments, but the line isn't great and the complexities are too major to convey properly in a long-distance call. 'Too much to talk about. But Maitland—' she hesitates. She's had an idea but it's a bit cheeky.

'What is it, honey?'

'Nothing.'

'No, there is something, do tell.'

'Well—' Nothing ventured ... 'You know you were saying you wanted to do something in Scotland. For Scotland, I mean? There is something that might appeal.'

'Yeah?'

'Remember we talked about community arts, schools, all that stuff?'

'Sure. You were pretty passionate about it. Converted me. Not that I really needed converting.'

'There's a small community-based organisation I'm on the Board of. It helps young people who've lost their way to find meaning and purpose through the arts. But there's been a problem with the Director, he mismanaged funds, I won't bore you with it, but the upshot is we need to find some money. Rather quickly.'

'How much?'

'Fifty thousand. Pounds. Minimum.' The whistle down the line tells her all she needs to know. 'I know. Sorry. I shouldn't have asked. It was just an idea.'

'No, hold on, darling, I was just a bit surprised is all. Tell me more.'

She fills him in on the details and plays her rapidly improvised masterstroke at the end. 'I could perhaps persuade the Board that we could rename it. After you, I mean. The Maitland Forbes Foundation, something like that—?'

He chuckles. 'It's got a certain ring, hasn't it? You clever thing, you know how to tempt a guy. Listen honey, I've gotta go. I'm not saying yes, but I'm not saying no either. I'll get back to you in the next couple of days. Is that okay?'

'I can't ask any fairer than that. Thanks, Maitland.'

'You'll think about the film?'

'Likewise.'

'Bye, sweetie. Take care of yourself now.'

'Bye.'

She replaces the receiver thoughtfully.

'Who was that?'

'Mannie!' She swivels round to see her daughter hunched in the doorway. 'I didn't hear you come in.'

'I heard you on the phone, so I tried to keep quiet.'

'Are you all right? You look terrible.'

'Oh Mum—' It comes as a wail, and then her daughter is in her arms, wracked by sobs.

'Goodness, Mannie. Here, come and sit down.'

261

It's all she can do to calm her. It takes ten minutes, perhaps more, for the hysteria to subside and to make any sense of the incoherent words that are stumbling out of her daughter's mouth.

Hate myself...

Callum ...

Can't understand ...

Falling apart ...

Work's a disaster ...

'Shhh. Shhh. There, child. Hush now.' She cradles her like a baby, rocks her to and fro, holds her close so that her warmth and nearness might lend solace and comfort. 'You drove all the way here? Darling child, you look exhausted. Now,' she commands more authoritatively as Mannie gradually gains some semblance of control over herself, 'tell me everything.'

She knows most of it already. The chance encounter with Brian Henderson in London, the feelings that were aroused even then. Meeting him again – while they were both waiting, Mannie has worked out now, for their mothers. 'It was that day I waited for you in the café in Princes Street, Mum. He said he was waiting for his mother, too. I didn't know, then, that his mother was Joyce Henderson. How could I?' Her voice is beginning to rise again, the hysteria threatening to return.

'You couldn't have known.'

'I really fell for him. I couldn't help it.' The tear-stained face is turned up to hers pleadingly. 'I didn't want to. Everything was going so well with Callum. But I couldn't leave it alone. My feelings for Brian were like a scab that just had to be picked at. I started to text him, like, all the time? Then I met him for dinner and that just made it worse.'

Her fists are balled tightly and she thumps them down on her thighs. 'I made him fall for me, Mum. I know I was bad and that it was wrong, but he did encourage me.'

'You haven't – Mannie, tell me you two haven't—'

'We haven't slept together, no, if that's what you're asking.' She turns her face up desperately. 'But I would if he asked me to. I'd do anything he wanted.'

'But he's your uncle! And now that you know—'

'I know that in my head, but here,' she places her hands over her heart, 'it doesn't make any difference. I know it should, but it doesn't. None at all.'

'Mannie—'

'Don't preach at me. Everything's bad enough already. I know it's not going to be possible, I just want it to be so badly. My life's falling apart, Mum.' She shoves her sleek, dark hair back over one ear. Susie watches it slide forward, as it always does. 'I missed my targets this month.'

'Really?'

'I can't seem to keep my mind on things long enough. If I miss them next month too, they say they'll have to consider my position.' The face turned to her is tragic. 'I can't seem to cope, Mum. What am I going to do? I just want to be with him.'

'I don't know, pet. I don't know. We'll get through it.' Feeling inadequate, she brews tea and makes sure that Mannie drinks it. 'Will you stay over?'

Mannie, a little calmer, shakes her head. 'No. Thanks, Mum, but I'll have to get in to work really early. I need to start impressing again, and it might take my mind off things.'

'Sure? Are you all right to drive?'

'Certain sure. Thanks for listening. And for not laughing at me.'

'No-one's laughing, Mannie.'

Susie stands in the doorway until the red of the tail lights have disappeared behind the contours of the garden.

How has everything fallen apart so badly? A few months ago she was riding high, confident in her beliefs, secure in the love of her husband, proud of her two

263

children. Her stock in the country was good. 'Home, Where My Heart Is' was back on the small screen and was boosting her popularity. National Living Treasure. More in demand by the media than the First Minister. She could do no wrong – and now look at her.

She closes the cottage door and climbs tiredly upstairs to her empty bedroom. On her dressing table, a family photograph thrusts at her like a jibe. They're all there: Jonathan and Margaret-Anne, Archie and herself – even Prince, looking deceptively loyal – hugging and laughing, a loving family. Frustration, anger, loneliness, and self-pity flood through her. She spends her life caring for others, but does anyone care about her?

The generous curves of her lips pinch into a hard, straight line.

'Loving?' she cries to the ceiling. 'In all this mess, who the hell is loving Susie?'

She sweeps her arm across the dressing table in a vicious, jabbing movement. The photograph flies off the dressing table amid a meteor shower of lipsticks and brushes, mascara and jewellery. The earrings Archie gave to her one Christmas jet across the carpet and the eternity ring he bought her when Mannie was born arcs towards the wall and slithers down to the skirting board.

She stares at the mess blindly.

I can't stand this any more. I can't stand it!

She runs downstairs, unlocks the door, and hurtles into the courtyard. Above her, the stars have clouded over and she feels the first drops of rain splash on her hands. She lifts them to the skies as the shower gathers momentum.

How can I protect my daughter?

Rain soaks into her hair and runs down her face.

How can I be true to my Party as well as everyone else who has put their faith in me?

Water courses down the back of her neck, saturating her blouse.

How can I salvage the wreck of my marriage?

Puddles have formed in the courtyard but Susie splashes through them heedlessly. There's a simple answer to all her problems. How could she not have seen it? How could she have so resolutely, so stupidly, turned her back on it all these weeks? Her feet, now, are as wet as her clothes, but it doesn't matter. Her mind is filled with a kind of blinding joy and it's focused on one thing, and one thing alone.

I need to talk to Archie.

Chapter Twenty-six

By mid morning, the battering rain of the night before has stopped and the skies are clear – but Archie hasn't yet stepped out to admire them. He is still surfacing from the deepest sleep he's managed since he decamped there.

Late last night the band finished recording the album.

'That's it!' Jake shouted as the last reverberation of the guitar strings died out. 'We've done it!'

He high-fived Archie, he high-fived the rest of the band, they all whooped with glee and Archie cracked open the first bottle in the crate of bubbly he'd kept for the occasion. After they'd got through six bottles, he slept.

Something nags at him as he begins to clamber into uneasy wakefulness. He props himself up on his elbow and surveys the mess. Jake, Sandie and the rest of them are all still there. He dimly remembers throwing them blankets and they appear to have more or less lain where they dropped. Jake is on his back, snoring gustily, his beard thick with drool. Colin's bony frame pokes up from the floor like the broken spokes of a rusted bicycle. He can hardly be comfortable. Drew is curled like a cat, his head tucked under an arm. And in the corner, uncaring about privacy, Sandie sprawls, her hair spread around her like Ophelia floating downstream.

They'd been right to celebrate, but for Archie, the task isn't over. There's one tune he hasn't been able to finish and it still inhabits his head like a toothache.

He needs coffee.

He struggles to his feet and picks his way between bodies and instruments to the door. The rain has been heavy. At his feet, the notice he'd tacked up, 'STRICTLY NO ENTRY. RECORDING IN PROGRESS' has fallen, limp and sodden, into a puddle. He picks it up and watches the drips run off the useless paper.

Susie wouldn't have come near the studio anyway, what does it matter?

The rain is over and the clean, fresh air is a welcome assault on his befuddled brain. He leaves the door open as he trudges across the courtyard to the cottage kitchen. Let the others benefit too.

There are no cars there. Susie and Jon have both gone to work. Not surprising, because the sun is already high in the sky. He fills the kettle and glances up at the clock. That late? Midday already?

The shrill sound of the telephone slices through the silence. He's tempted to leave it, but the ring tone is flat and has always offended his ears, so he crosses the room and lifts the receiver.

'Hello? Archie Wallace.'

His voice rasps like a file on slate. Too much singing, too much celebrating, too much latent inhaling of Jake's and Sandie's filthy fags.

'Archie! Thank heavens I've reached you at last.'

'Karen? What's up?'

'Is Susie with you?'

'Susie?'

'Your wife, Archie. Susie Wallace?'

'I don't think she's here, Karen. At least, her car's not here. I'm just up.'

'Can you check?'

'Sure. Of course. She's not with you?'

'Would I be calling if—'

'No, sorry, stupid question. She didn't turn up this morning? She hasn't just gone straight to some meeting or other?'

'She was due in here for a meeting at nine. At ten she

268

had a very important meeting with the Chief Whip, but she didn't show for that either. She was scheduled at eleven to—'

Okay, okay, I get the picture.' Archie is as wide awake now as if he'd plunged into an ice cold loch stark naked.

'I was about to start calling round the hospitals and the police.'

'Hospitals? Police? You're that worried?'

'Aren't you?'

'Well I wasn't, but you're beginning to make me concerned. Listen, give me five minutes, Karen, I'll call you back.'

The cottage is small and there really isn't anywhere to hide. Might he find her slumped on the floor in the bedroom, unconscious? Has she slipped in the shower and injured her head? The rational side of Archie tells him that these scenarios are unlikely, because her car isn't in the yard, but even so—

Jonathan's room is empty. So is Mannie's old bedroom. He stands at the top of the stairs and listens. The silence is broken only by the steady ticking of Susie's old grandfather clock and the distant clucking of the hens, their contentment unaffected by his tension. He pushes open the door to their bedroom, uninhabited by him for so long.

Christ. It looks as though a burglar has been in. The bed is tumbled, there are clothes everywhere and across the floor lies a trail of debris. Archie bends down and picks up a photograph frame. The glass is shattered. The faces of his family stare up at him, unblinking. He places it back on the dressing table, carefully, gathers the shards of splintered glass, one by one, and lays them in a pile by its side.

He spies the earrings he gave Susie on their first wedding anniversary, half hidden under the rug. The brooch that was her mother's favourite is behind the waste basket, its small rubies winking from their gold setting. Something is down the side of the carpet next to the skirting board. He stretches to pick it up. It's the eternity ring he gave her when Mannie was born.

What the hell has happened here? What was Susie going through when she did this?

Archie sinks down on the bed and clutches the pillow to his chest. The scent of his wife on the linen is overwhelming.

When he has exhausted all the possibilities, he calls Karen.

'She's not here. It looks as though – I don't know, I just get the feeling she was a bit upset last night.'

'Upset? Archie, listen, is her briefcase there? Her laptop? Her mobile?'

He should have thought of these things himself, he isn't thinking straight. 'Hang on, I'll look.'

Two strides and he's at the small desk where she bases herself in the cottage. The laptop is plainly visible, still plugged into the power socket. Her briefcase lies on the floor, its top open, papers spilling out. He bends down and rummages through it quickly, but there's no sign of her mobile. 'Karen? Laptop and briefcase here, mobile – I can't see it.'

'Very odd. Why would she leave without her briefcase? She doesn't always carry her laptop, so that's no great help. What about her handbag, Archie?'

Idiot. What's he thinking of? He looks around – sitting room, kitchen, both bathrooms, the bedrooms. 'No sign of her handbag.' Possible scenarios grow and multiply in his imagination. 'Do you think she's had an accident?'

'Has she left a note? Where would she have left a note?'

The kitchen table. Why hasn't he thought of that? He glances at it, but it's empty, save for the coffee tray he'd been preparing for the band. He glances across to the

270

kettle, which is where they tend to leave notes for each other, knowing they'd be likely to head there first. Nothing. Of course, he has already filled the kettle, he'd have seen it earlier.

He thinks of the fridge. Had she stuck some clue in there? A note wrapped a note round a bottle of wine, perhaps, in some kind of ironic comment on his drinking habits?

But no, nothing.

'What about your mobile, Archie?' Karen asks. 'Has she left a message on your mobile?'

Again, he is being stupid. Checking his mobile should have been the first thing he did. 'Hold on. No, listen, I'll check it and call you back.'

His mobile is in his shirt pocket – and there is a message from her, left this morning, early.

'Listen Archie, it's all too much. I've had to go away. You mustn't ... tell ... so don't—'

That's all he can make out, the rest is static. Then it goes dead. He replays the message, hoping to get more.

'Listen Archie, it's all too much. I've had to go away. You mustn't ... tell ... so don't—'

It's impossible to make out anything else. It sounds as though she is somewhere windy, but it could be anywhere.

He calls Karen. 'Hi. She's left a message.'

'She has? Thank heavens. Where is she. What did she say?'

'It was really broken up, the signal was appalling. All I could make out was "it's all too much, I've had to go away." And, "you mustn't tell—".'

'That was it?'

'No, it was obviously a longer message, but that was all I could make out.'

'Do you think Mannie and Jon might know anything? We have to find her, Archie, and quickly. It's going to be impossible to keep this quiet.'

271

'I can call and ask them.'

But he doesn't want to disturb Mannie and Jon at work and besides, the idea that she might have told them something she hasn't told him is painful.

'Archie, listen, let me make some calls. I'll get a team onto it here, we can cover the ground quite quickly. I'll get back to you when I have anything to report. Meantime – why don't you do some phoning? Is there somewhere she might have gone? Someone she might have turned to, if she felt she needed support?'

Me, she should have turned to me.

'Honestly, Karen, I would have thought either us, her family, or you. She's pretty close to you – but she didn't get in touch?'

'No. I find that quite worrying, I must admit. Why don't you start going through her address book? We'll do the police and hospitals.'

'Police and hospitals? Oh surely not. She doesn't sound that depressed, Karen.'

'Just in case.'

'You will call me at once if—'

'Yes. Bye Archie.'

'Bye.'

He listens again to the long-familiar tones of the woman he loves so deeply. What was her mood when she left that message? Despairing? Suicidal? Or merely self aware? Is it the voice of someone who knows she's at her limits and just needs to retreat for a while? With Susie, sometimes, it's hard to tell. If she has thought her plan through, she could put anything she wants into her voice and make you believe it.

He stands for a few minutes, deep in thought. Where has she gone? What's happened? Why hasn't she turned up at work today? What is she thinking? Archie, the most prosaic of men, reaches deep into his soul and tries to make a connection with his wife, but he gets nothing.

Prince, trotting in from the courtyard, whimpers uneasily. He is catching something in the atmosphere.

'All right boy. All right.'

He pats the old dog.

'Here. No need for you to go hungry.'

He opens a can of dog food and spoons it into Prince's dish. The dog eyes Archie mournfully.

'Off your food, huh? Don't blame you, Prince. Don't blame you at all.'

He turns his attention to brewing the coffee, then takes a moment to gulp some and feels his head clear a little. Karen is doing the horrid bit, the police and the hospitals, although he doesn't seriously think she'll find anything, because if anything has happened to Susie, surely he'd have heard by now? There'd have been a knock at the door, a phone call – something. Susie is very well known. Hell, it would probably be on the news by now, not that he's had the news on, but Mo Armstrong monitors it constantly.

So – plan of action. The logical Archie is beginning to come back. One, get the band up and away, no reason they should be involved in all this. Two, sit and think. What has triggered Susie's disappearance and where might she have gone? Three, make some calls. Old friends? The children, obviously, but maybe not just yet. If either of them knows anything, they'd have alerted him already, so there's no reason to disrupt their working day.

He hacks a loaf of bread into rough slices, forages in the fridge for butter, cheese, cold meat, marmalade, and makes his way back to the studio bearing breakfast for five, on a tray.

'Hey, Archie, that smells good, pal.'

'Surprised you can smell anything, Jake, through all that nicotine up your nostrils,' Archie teases, his voice as normal as he can make it.

A groan comes from the spiky pile of bones. 'Uuurgh.

This floor's hard.'

The cat-like figure uncurls, stretches luxuriously and says, 'Waiter service. Excellent.' From the corner, the petite form of Sandie Alexander sits bolt upright and her sexy, rasping voice declaims, 'Fuck me, Archie, I need that caffeine.'

'Right, guys.' He places the tray on the low table by the window and pulls the curtains open, grinning at the universal groan as light slashes mercilessly into sleep-rimed eyes. 'You've got fifteen minutes to get out of here. The cleaner'll be in here with her mop and bucket and I've promised her complete peace. She's a demon if she's crossed.'

It's an outright lie, they don't have a cleaner, but it's the best he can come up with.

Jake groans. 'Aw right, pal. I get the message.'

They don't need to dress, because they didn't undress. Drew, clearly the best-slept of the five of them, grins. 'I'll drive you all back to town. Just give me coffee first.'

'Great night, lads.'

It's universal practice to treat Sandie as one of the lads. It's what she wants and expects from them. She says, 'So it really is a wrap?'

'Bit of mastering to do, but it'll be on target to meet the contract.'

'We'll talk about it soon,' Archie says, standing up. 'Sorry folks, but I do need to do stuff.'

They pack their instruments into the van. The last he sees of them is Jake's long, hairy arm waving lazily out of a window as the van rounds the bend in the drive where the hill hides it from view. A honk of the horn is followed by a blast of Colin's small cornet. Archie smiles affectionately. Celtic Rock was formed by lucky chance and the band has validated his music. They're a great team.

The smile fades as he considers that. What validates Susie?

Answer: her family and her career – and both have let her down recently.

Drama queen.

Archie yanks the door of the studio closed with a bang that echoes round the courtyard and stomps back to the cottage. Criticising him about honouring her parents' wishes is so unfair. She has spurned every effort he has made at reconciliation. And when it comes to the bit, she's hardly been honest with him, has she? In the scale of dishonesty, whose deceit has been greater?

The first shock of her disappearance over, he's sorely tempted to let her stew.

Chapter Twenty-seven

Karen appears at the cottage a couple of hours later. 'Any joy?' she asks as soon as she gets out of her car.

'Nothing. I've made a few calls to friends but no-one's heard from her. I don't want to start rumours running.'

'There already are rumours. When an MSP doesn't turn up for key meetings, questions are asked.'

'But surely you've been able to cover?'

'To a certain extent, yes. We can tell constituents she's poorly, make apologies. But the Chief Whip's a different matter.'

'The delightful Mr Coop.'

'Tom, yes. And Mo, of course, is in a terrible panic. It's almost impossible to stop the staff gossiping – the more you ask them to keep secrets, the more likely they are to get out. And even the most disciplined of Parties has its moles. At least the hospital and police calls haven't turned anything up.'

'I didn't think they would.'

'You seem calmer, Archie. Do you know something?'

'No, I don't. But I'm pretty certain she's all right.'

'Well that's something. Have you talked to Margaret-Anne and Jon?'

'No. Not yet.'

'No? Archie, why ever not? Surely—'

'If they were worried about their mother, they'd have phoned me. I've been holding off talking to them because Jonno has a new job and I don't want to make waves—' Leave aside all the complications there '—and Mannie's always rushing around, doing deals. I wouldn't like to distract her.'

'Okay,' Karen says doubtfully. 'Let's run through everything else, then. There's nothing among the papers in her briefcase?'

'Help yourself. You're more likely to spot anything vital than I am.' Archie indicates where it sits, next to her desk.

Karen rummages through the contents quickly. 'Just the usual, so far as I can see. What about her mobile? Not found it?'

'Nope. Must be in her handbag. That's definitely not here.'

'The laptop?'

Archie waves at it. 'I wouldn't know where to start. It's password protected anyway.'

'Let me have a go. I know some of her passwords.'

'Help yourself. Tea?'

'I'd love some. Thanks.'

He brews a pot as she boots up the laptop.

'I'm in,' she calls.

'That was quick.'

He finds a batch of melting nanoseconds in a polythene bag stuffed behind the cookery books on a shelf, an old hiding place. He breaks off a piece of biscuit and tastes it. It's fresh, so she has baked recently and she couldn't have baked if she'd been over stressed. Something must have happened since then that has tipped her over the edge. What is it?

He puts the biscuits in a dish and adds them to the tray. 'Sugar?'

Karen is tapping away at the keyboard. 'Just milk. Thanks.'

'Anything?'

'A load of emails. She obviously didn't check last night, or this morning. They haven't been opened since she left the office yesterday.'

'Any clues?' He doesn't say it hopefully.

'There's an email from Maitland Forbes.'

A shiver of dread passes through Archie's heart.

Karen says, 'I'll read it.'

He doesn't want to hear and starts to say so, but she's already reading it out. 'Hi Susie darling. As agreed in our conversation earlier this evening, here are the details of the movie. It will be called "Flora MacDonald" (working title only) and I'd love you to play the part of Flora's mother. As I promised, I'd do my utmost to shoot round your schedules. Regarding the other matter, I will give it my best consideration and will get back to you within the next couple of days. Hugs to you, honey. Maitland."' She eyes Archie quizzically. 'Darling?'

That, at least, he can shrug off. 'It means nothing. All actors call each other darling. Does that get us anywhere? What was "the other matter"?'

'No idea. Could have been anything. We should give Maitland Forbes a call.'

'He's in California. What's the time there?'

She does a quick calculation. 'It's two o'clock here. It'll be six in the morning.'

'Maybe leave it a couple of hours, then.'

'This is an emergency, Archie.'

'Not yet,' he says. Since his earlier panic, an odd calmness has settled on him.

Karen swings round in the chair and thumps her hand on its arm. 'Archie, the world's going mad around the disappearance of your wife and you just sit there like the Sphinx and smile. What aren't you telling me?'

'Nothing. Honestly, Karen, I promise you, I'm not hiding anything. I don't know where Susie's gone, I just know she hasn't jumped off a cliff. And the world isn't in freefall, a few politicians in your Party are a bit worried, that's all.'

'I don't think you understa—' She halts in mid word,

slouches back and smiles wryly. 'You're right, Archie. I guess we all get a bit caught up the in Holyrood bubble. For those of us who work there, it's the only thing that matters.'

Then the seriousness is back.

'But Susie's one of those people too, Archie. Her politics matters to her, her constituents matter, her beliefs matter. That's what makes this so difficult to understand.'

'I'm not denying that Susie's in a bad place in her head. I just don't think she's in danger. Physical danger, that is.'

'There's a vote on Thursday. It could bring down the government.'

'I don't care about the government.'

'Susie cares.'

'Does she, Karen? Does she really? Or is that part of the problem?'

'I know she feels trapped between her Party and her constituents.' She looks at him directly, her cool grey eyes level. 'But she matters to me, Archie. She's my best friend and I care about her.'

Silence falls. All Archie can hear is the ticking of Susie's grandfather clock, measuring out the hours as it has for centuries. Past, present, future – sometimes, Archie thinks, each one is as much a mystery as the other.

'I know you do,' he says at last. 'I care too. Very much, as it happens. I'll find her, Karen, I promise.'

Karen stands up. 'Thank you, Archie. There's nothing more I can do here, just keep an eye on her emails, will you? I'll leave the laptop on. And call me if you find anything.'

After she has gone, Archie sits and thinks. The days when Susie Wallace trusted him and depended on him are past. He doesn't doubt that he can find her – but can he reach her? He cares about her more than he can possibly express, but has he lost her again – and this time, for ever?

And finally, the sixty-four thousand dollar question: is

he prepared, this time, to fight for her?

Jonathan arrives home around six. Archie tells him everything.

'Christ. Gone? *Gone?* Mum?'

He looks so like her, his hair a perfect match in colour, his eyes a replica of her bright toffee and gold, that his heart twists inside him.

'I suspect that she simply needs some time to herself.'

'You're not worried?'

'I've done nothing but think about it all day, Jon, and I honestly believe she's just taken time off. She did leave a message on my mobile, after all.'

Jon isn't stupid. He knows how bad things have been between them. He says, 'Do you want to find her, Dad? Or is this just another step in the weird dance you two have been doing?'

He says, honestly, 'I don't think she's playing games.'

'Bet the Party's in a tizz.'

'There's some huge vote in a couple of days, so yes, tizz is probably a pretty good description. But if I go looking for her it's got to be for me – for us – not for the Party.'

'Oh, agreed,' he says fervently. 'Have you spoken to Mannie?'

'Not yet. I didn't want to disturb you guys at work.'

'Thanks Dad, appreciated. But you needn't have worried about disturbing me, I've been disturbed ever since Mum told us about Brian Henderson being our uncle.'

'I can understand that. It's almost as hard for you as it is for Mannie, isn't it?'

Jon rubs his hand restlessly through his hair, leaving it sticking up in spiky furrows. 'I was going to resign, Dad.'

'Resign? Oh, Jon, don't! You've worked so hard to get this job. You need it. You *deserve* it. Don't resign, for

281

God's sake.'

'That's what Alex says.'

'Alex? Who's he?'

'She,' Jon corrects him. 'She's one of the designers at work. She's brilliant.'

Admiration and affection shine so clearly out of his eyes that Archie's heart contorts. *He's found someone. Good.*

'Alex says, hang on in there. I told her, Dad, about Mannie, I mean, and Brian. I wasn't going to, because, well, she's at work and she knows him, he's the boss, and it could be difficult. It is difficult, it's hellish, but I felt I could trust her.'

'I'm glad there's someone you can talk to.'

'More than talk to, Dad. When I told her about Mannie, and about Brian being our uncle, she went and did some research.'

He outlines what Alex has discovered.

Archie says, 'It sounds horrifyingly plausible. Are you going to talk to Mannie about it?'

'I suppose so. Can't say I'm looking forward to that conversation. Anyway, I'm not going to do it tonight, I'll need to do it face to face.'

'Okay, but we should call Mannie now in case she can tell us anything about Mum.' He pats Jonno's shoulder. 'I'm really proud of you. You know that.'

'Thanks Dad. But it's really down to Alex.'

'Then I can't wait to meet Alex. Let's call Mannie, shall we?'

How quickly Jon has grown up, Archie thinks. Tonight he's the strongest member of the family. The potential was always there, of course. Throughout the long slump in his fortunes, when unemployment dragged at his son like seaweed round an anchor, he kept going. He refused to get sucked under, he worked in the bar, he fought loss of confidence and depression and battled with the temptation of drinking to ease the darkness. He found himself a job at last.

And now, with Mannie on the end of the phone in floods of tears because she believes she is the cause of her mother's disappearance, Jon is taking over. He's calm and in control and he's reassuring her that it isn't her fault.

'I'm just checking – can you think of anything else, anything at all, Mannie, that might give us some clue about where she's gone?... No? Nothing? ...I see – no, don't come racing over here, there's nothing you can do from here, we've searched everything. Call if you think of anything else.'

Archie smiles wryly at the role reversal. Normally it's Mannie who's in charge.

'Yes of course we'll call you back, sis. ... Okay? ... Yup, 'night to you too. Bye.'

Jon turns off the phone and looks at Archie. 'What now?'

Archie shrugs. 'Get some sleep, I guess. Go to bed, Jon. She's okay.'

'How do you know that?'

'I just feel it. Don't panic. We'd have heard if there'd been an accident.'

'Okay then. 'Night Dad.'

'Good night.'

He's alone in the kitchen.

I'll sleep in our bed tonight, he thinks. I'd like to feel Susie's presence there with me. I'll smell her on the sheets and the duvet, and I'll find hairs, long and golden brown, on the pillows. The closer I get to her, the easier it's going to be to sense where she is. He pats Prince's head absently as he mulls over the events of the day. There must be a clue somewhere. She must have left something, inadvertently perhaps, but something.

And then it comes to him.

Where do they keep important things? Tickets, vouchers, notes, reminders?

On the dresser.

He looks up. It's right in front of him, three steps from where he sits. How can he have been so stupid? He's there in an instant, pulling the small stack of papers from the shelf where they are stored, where Susie keeps everything that's current.

He shuffles through the pile, but there are no clues. Nothing.

The Council Tax bill.

The leaflet about recycling.

Invitations from the Lord Provost of Edinburgh, from the University Chancellor, from the Royal Society of Edinburgh.

Tickets for a jazz concert at the Queen's Hall and for a youth production of 'The Boyfriend'.

An empty stamp book.

Nothing else.

He stands there, baffled. He'd been so sure.

The dresser is an old thing. It came from his parents' house, and his mother's parents' house before that. Susie liked its sense of history. Besides, as she said at the time, 'We can't afford anything else.' It was imported into the cosy kitchen and there it stayed, accumulating family detritus and memorabilia for almost thirty years because cleaning round the back of furniture is not their strong point.

A triangle of white catches his eye. Something is protruding from a crack in the back panelling. Gingerly, he reaches for it and slides it out. If it had slipped right through it would have fallen to the floor under the dresser and might have lain there for years.

This looks new. He unfolds it. Susie's writing. A hasty scrawl.

Dear First Minister

I have given this a great deal of thought, and it is with much sadness and regret that I write to you to tender my resignation as an MSP. As you know ...

Archie lets the paper slide from his grasp onto the table. This he didn't expect. He checks the date. Yesterday. But why is it still here? Is it just a draft? Why didn't she post it?

Of course – the book of stamps is empty. He remembers using the last one himself, sending away for something trivial, he forgets what now. He meant to replace them but – preoccupied – forgot.

So she wrote it, went to the dresser to get a stamp, found there were none and was distracted by something. Why else would she leave the letter behind? Surely she'd take it with her to post as soon as she could? Instead, she must have stuffed it with some agitation onto the shelf, so that it slid into danger of disappearance.

Because she saw something else on the shelf perhaps? Picked it up before ensuring the letter was safely lodged? What? What could be so interesting that it diverted her attention from something so important?

And then he remembers a gift from the children – the hotel voucher – and he knows, with utter certainty, where she's gone. But far from feeling relief, his heart sinks. It makes his decision about whether to go and find her much, much harder.

Chapter Twenty-eight

Mannie looks around the room. There are four people present – Jen, Jonno and his new friend Alex, and herself. Her eyes are scratchy with tiredness. She has hardly slept for days. Her mother is still missing and she feels utterly responsible. Work today was a massive challenge, but one she knew she must rise to, or lose her job.

The worst thing is being unable to master her feelings. All her life, Mannie has been in control. Smart, efficient, focused, she gets what she wants. She's well aware that some people at work think she's high-handed and arrogant. She doesn't mind that. These are the weapons she needs in her armoury in order to succeed, and success is her goal. Her colleagues know that outside of the workplace she's different, softer. Yet now that she needs her armoury as she has never needed it before, all her shields and protectors seem to have deserted her.

And what is this all about? She looks at the girl – Alex – that Jonno has brought with him. There's an electricity between those two. He has found someone special.

'Thank you,' Jonno starts, 'for agreeing to this, Mannie. Thanks, Jen, for being here. And Alex,' he turns to her, a spontaneous smile lighting up his face, 'for doing the research.'

Mannie is curled up on her favourite deep chair near the window in the living room of her flat. She has kicked off her shoes, but otherwise she's still dressed for work in a knee-length straight skirt and white silk blouse. She hasn't been back home for long and she feels haggard. Her hair, usually lustrous, is dull and lank. Her hand clutches a

287

balled-up tissue, which she keeps squeezing convulsively. She can see Jen, bless her, watching her with concern.

'Myra says sorry,' Jen says to Jonno, 'but she and Graham have something important on tonight otherwise she'd have been here.'

'Thanks, Jen. Mannie,' he says, turning to her, his expression serious, 'Alex would like to tell you what she's been researching. Okay?'

Mannie shrugs listlessly. 'Okay,' she said dully, 'but I can't imagine how anything's going to help me.'

Alex says gently, 'It's something I discovered after Jonno told me your story.'

Mannie shifts restlessly. How many people has Jonno discussed her with? She'd be angry if she had the energy.

It seems that Alex has guessed at her thoughts, because she says, 'I hope you don't mind? I promise you, I haven't told anyone else, and I never will, not unless you want me to.'

Mannie relents grudgingly. *I'm beginning to quite like you.*

'Something about your story rang a bell with me and—'

The sound of a bell ringing comes right on cue.

'That's the front door,' Jen says, puzzled, 'who could that be? Will I send them away?'

'See who it is,' Jonno says, an odd smile on his lips.

In her dreams, Mannie would not have dared to expect the visitor who appears a few moments later. She leaps to her feet, her hands to her mouth, her eyes round with astonishment.

'Cal!'

'Hi.'

Callum McMaster stands framed in the doorway, lithe and sturdy, his bright, intelligent eyes surveying Mannie a little warily, but his expression friendly.

There's a moment's awkwardness, which Jonno breaks

by explaining, 'I asked Cal to come, Mannie. I hope you don't mind. This is something I believe we all need to pull together on and Callum's agreed to come and talk about it.'

'Here, Cal.' Jen gets up from her seat next to Mannie and offers the chair to Callum. 'I'll move to the bean bag.'

'I can sit there,' Cal says, smiling at her.

'No, you're all right.' Jen slumps down comfortably before Cal can preempt her.

He kisses Mannie's cheek. 'Hello fat-face,' he whispers.

Fat-face! He called her fat-face! He doesn't totally hate her then!

'Hello thunderthighs.'

It's barely even a whisper, but he hears it and grins, then subsides on the chair beside her.

'Okay, as I was saying,' Alex resumes, 'when Jonno told me about Brian being your uncle, and about your feelings for him, Mannie, it rang a bell. I read a story in a magazine recently about a couple who had an adopted son, who basically fell in love with his sister. He'd never met her before, because she'd been adopted too, and she'd been taken to Australia.'

'Shit,' Jen shakes her head. 'He fell for his sister?'

'Apparently, it's a lot more common than you'd think. And as our families get more and more complicated, it seems to be getting more frequent, although it's not often talked about.'

She looks round at each of them.

'I believe that what has happened to Mannie is that she's fallen a victim to something called Genetic Sexual Attraction.'

'Sounds like chlamydia,' Jen grimaces.

'Thankfully not, but it *is* a medical condition. It's quite widely recognised now. It can happen when you meet someone – a relation, I mean – when you're grown up,

289

someone you didn't know when you were young. I'm not making this very clear.'

Jonno takes up the explanation. 'Apparently even mothers and sons can get it and end up sleeping together, setting up home together even.'

Mannie squirms uneasily.

'But it's not always reciprocal,' Alex chimes in. 'It can be a one-sided obsession.'

Callum says slowly, 'And you think that's what Mannie's got?'

'Think about it, Cal. She's getting along perfectly well with you, in fact, I've never seen her so happy with anyone.' He grins. 'And I've seen her with a few,' he adds irrepressibly.

Mannie is indignant. 'Shut up!'

'Then suddenly, wham! Instead of a fit guy like you, she's lusting after a pretty ordinary middle-aged man, balding, building up fat round the midriff, and married. Not exactly a likely quarry, is he? Not really a prospect for a girl like you, Mannie.'

Mannie says nothing. What is there to say? She can hardly deny it.

'Mannie,' Cal looks at her steadily, 'Is it reciprocated? Is this guy as obsessed with you as you are with him?'

Christ, this is hard, Mannie thinks. 'I don't know. He seems to like me.' What was it he said? God, you're bloody irresistible, do you know that?

'I hope for all our sakes that he isn't, because if he is, it's going to be very difficult to work on this. From what I understand, this thing's really powerful.' Jonno looks at Alex, then adds, 'But from what I hear he's a bit of a womaniser and my suspicion is he's maybe been a bit flattered by Mannie's interest in him.'

Mannie's face is burning. She hides it in her hands. This is horrible, horrible, horrible. If the floor could open beneath her she'd happily fall through it, anything to get away from this analysis, this probing, these judgements.

'Mannie.' There's a hand on her shoulder, gentle, but firm. 'Look at me, Gutso.'

She presses her hands harder over her face and shakes her head. 'I can't,' she groans, her voice muffled by her fingers.

'Look at me.'

She moves one finger aside. Callum is looking at her with such sweet concern that she could weep.

'We can work on this, Mannie. Come on. We're all here to help.' He prises her fingers away from her face and imprisons her hand in a firm clasp. He turns to Jonno. 'This is all very well, Jonno, but where does it take us?'

'Alex thinks I should talk to him.'

'Does he know? That you're his nephew?'

'I don't think so. Mum wanted to tell us first. Maybe when I tell him, he'll back off. That's my hope, anyway.'

'This has put you in a really difficult place, hasn't it? There's no way of knowing where it'll end up.'

'I could be out of a job.'

Mannie is roused out of bleakness. 'I can't allow that, Jonno. You mustn't put your job at risk.'

'I can't see any other way. Anyway, unless we get this sorted, I'm not going to be able to work with him.'

'Then you need to let me come with you.'

'No, Mannie. I think it's best if you keep away completely. I'm going to find out about counselling for you.'

'Counselling! I'm not a psycho.'

'Being able to talk this through with a trained counsellor might help. I dunno, it might flush it through your system or something.'

Jen says, 'I know someone, Mannie. She's really good, and if it's not her thing, I'm sure she'd be able to recommend an expert.'

'An expert in this genetic sexual attraction stuff?'

291

Mannie snorts. 'Right, so they get loads of cases, do they?'

'Try not to be bitter, Mannie.'

'Oh Christ. Listen to yourselves. It's so bloody easy for you, isn't it? Let's all sit around and decide what's best for Mannie. Well it's not that easy for me, so you can all piss off, do you hear me?' She uncurls furiously and stands up. 'Just fuck off, the lot of you!'

It's fifteen strides to her bedroom door and she makes it in three seconds, slams the door behind her, flings herself onto the bed and pulls a pillow over her head.

She doesn't expect company. They'll be staring after her and saying, 'My goodness, Mannie's in a mood, isn't she?' before they sit round and discuss what they might do about it for a bit longer.

But it's only a matter of seconds before she hears the door open, and shut again, and Callum sits down on the bed next to her.

'Is Miss I'm-Not-A-Psycho Wallace going to come out and play?'

'Fuck. Off.'

He's laughing. 'Come on, Mannie. I'm just relieved to see your spirit hasn't left you completely. I thought you'd been possessed by a creepy love bug but I see the real Mannie's still in there somewhere.'

'I said leave it, can't you?'

He stops laughing and after a few moments he says, his voice kinder, 'It will pass, Mannie.'

She sits up, infuriated, the pillow clutched to her stomach. 'And if it "passes", what then, Callum? Will I be able to turn back the clock? Will you come back to me? Will you love me again? Or will I always be soiled goods?'

'Never that, Mannie.' He eases the pillow out of her grasp and drops it onto the floor. 'Listen, if Alex and Jonno are correct, you're a victim in all of this, not a perpetrator, but much as I think they're right, I still can't answer your questions.'

He draws a light finger down her cheek to the corner of her mouth. 'My feelings have been knocked sideways by this too. I loved you, Mannie, and that love was kicked into touch. Okay, so I understand now that you couldn't help it, but it's not just a simple matter of clicking a switch and making everything better.'

The hurt that fills Mannie is absolute. Nothing seems to function, not her breathing, not her movement, not her sight. The room is a blur, and she realises that her eyes have filled with tears and that she's powerless to stop them. Another weakness, she thinks despairingly – then, hopelessly, I've lost everything.

A hand wipes the tears away, clumsily, and she realises that it's shaking almost as much as she is.

'I can't make everything come right, Mannie. I suspect it may be some time before your world stops rocking on its axis and I'm not sure when the sun will shine again in mine. But I will promise you this: I'll be here for you. If you need to talk, you can talk to me. If you want to scream, you can use my sweater to muffle the sound. If you need to cry, I'll have a hankie ready, a whole boxful of hankies. I won't abandon you, Mannie.

'And one day – I don't know. We'll see. I think we have to take it one day at a time, don't you?'

From Callum, it's quite a speech. It's all she can hope for and it's more than he needs to give. Gratitude sweeps through her, and with it comes a faint ray of hope.

'Thank you, Vicar,' she says, and manages a smile.

Chapter Twenty-nine

The air on the island is sweet and balmy. It's one of those June mornings when you know that spring is over and that the long, seductive days of summer are finally beginning. It can be a deceitful seduction, of course, in Scotland, on the west coast, on the island of Mull. The wind can change direction, pick up moisture, drop it with some vitriol on the lump of volcanic rock known as Ben More, drenching every moving being in its path as it moves on its malevolent way to the mainland.

Today glitters with promise and Susie, stoutly shod, is trudging up the long, rough path to the summit of the Ben with an odd sense of euphoria. It isn't that peace has broken out in her mind, but perhaps hostilities have eased a little, a ceasefire has been called. In this place, in this weather, and putting all problems to the back of her mind, she's able, for the space of a few hours, simply to exist.

She stops, breathless, and makes the view an excuse for the halt. It's excuse enough. From her elevated position, the island is like a map spread at her feet. Below her, as blue as the skies above, lies Loch na Keal. A huge sea inlet, it rolls westwards, almost splitting the island in two.

At the mouth of the loch is the island of Ulva and its more famous infant companion, Staffa. Mendelssohn, drawn here, was inspired to compose his Hebridean Overture and so set the fashion for visitors to flock in their thousands to the dramatic cave.

Below her, to the west, is the grim remnant of the cottage at Gribun – just three low drystone walls surrounding a massive boulder. Susie shivers, remembering the story – a young couple were killed here on their honeymoon night when a storm loosened the boulder and it crashed down the mountain and demolished their home.

It's an unforgiving landscape and an ancient one, the rocks among the oldest in the world. Forgetting the inherent dangers of the place, Susie laughs aloud because it's indescribably magnificent, the most beguiling landscape in the world. It punctures self importance and puts you in your place. It's unarguable: in the face of its scale and age and majesty, nothing else has significance.

And that's what I need to remember.

'Amazing, is it not?'

She turns. A young couple, descending the mountain unnoticed by her, have stopped to share the moment. 'Stunning. Where are you from?'

'We are from Germany,' the girl says. 'We are so loving your country.'

'Thank you. I'm so glad you are getting the weather.'

'We have the mountains near us too, bigger mountains than this, yes. But this is—' the man halts. He can't find the word he's searching for and simply ends, '—very special, *ja*?'

'Very special,' Susie agrees. 'But if I'm to get to the top I must press on.'

'Not far,' the girl beams. 'Half of one hour, yes?'

'Thank you. Enjoy your holiday,' she calls after them, because they're already bounding down the mountain with goat-like athleticism.

She pulls a face. What would she give for half their fitness?

You are what you are, Susie.

She ponders that thought as she trudges the last few hundred steps to the summit. Surely that's one of the lessons she has to absorb: you are what you are – and you are *who* you are.

She puffs her way upwards, steeped in thought. It's what she came here for, after all – to get some distance, to escape from the burden of political responsibility, to consider her past, present and future.

When she stumbled across to the studio, a mere thirty-eight hours ago, to find Archie's notice firmly tacked onto the door, its capitals shouting their instruction 'STRICTLY NO ENTRY. RECORDING IN PROGRESS', she refused to take the prohibition seriously. She had to talk to Archie, she was going to talk to her husband. She tapped on the door, then hammered on it, then pounded as hard as she could – but all to no avail. The soundproofing he had installed was too efficient and inside, no doubt, the band was giving it everything.

That was when she cracked.

Enough.

Every emotion she could name seemed to course round her body. Angry, hurt, and bewildered, she felt abandoned and distressed.

She cursed Mary and Robert MacPherson for their secrecy about the truth of her identity.

She blamed Archie for covering for them all these years.

She felt helpless in the face of her daughter's anguish and concerned for her son's position.

She'd met a new mother and hadn't quite found it in her heart to either forgive her or love her and that made her angry.

And she already hated the brother she still hadn't met for what he had done to Mannie.

To cap it all, her political career had nosedived. There was a journalist who seemed intent on destroying her reputation and her Party was forcing her to act against her beliefs.

She retraced her steps with burning fury across the courtyard to the kitchen. A least she could deal with the last thing. She pulled out some paper and a pen, sat down at her desk, and wrote.

Dear First Minister

I have given this a great deal of thought, and it is with much sadness and regret that I write to you to tender my resignation as an MSP. As you know ...

Now she can see the cairn that marks the summit, just yards away. She's nearly at the top. One last effort – and here she is, queen of the world.

What a good idea this was. She has achieved something. She has climbed a Munro, all three thousand one hundred and sixty nine feet of it – nine hundred and sixty six metres.

And that, Mr First Minister, is worth all your votes of confidence and then some.

There were no stamps so she wasn't able to post the letter. But the upside was she spotted the hotel voucher Mannie and Jonno gave to her and Archie for their wedding anniversary. Perfect. Why not? Just go. Archie won't even miss you.

She threw a few things in the car and drove.

After a while Susie's breath recovers and she allows herself to sit in the shelter of the small ring of stones and survey the view she has earned. Oban is a three-hour drive from Cairn Cottage, so she arrived in the middle of the night and parked the car in the queue for the Mull ferry. Boarding in the morning was easy. The magic started to work as soon as she stepped out of the car and onto the deck. The wind in her hair, the sun on her face, the sea blue and calm below them – and the island of her memories drawing closer and closer.

She called Archie soon after she landed, to put his mind at ease. 'Listen Archie,' she bawled down the phone, battling the wind around her, 'it's all too much. I've had to go away. You mustn't worry about me, I'll be back in a few days. Please tell the children and please don't try to find me. I need this time on my own. Bye.'

She should call Karen and explain her absence – but not yet, an inner voice murmured. *Archie will tell her. I need this time to myself. There are still things I need to think through.*

On her second morning on Mull, she hears her father's voice in her head when she wakes. She can almost see him, grey hair, grey trousers, grey sleeveless V-neck, dark, thin, featureless tie, and kind, gentle smile.

'You can achieve anything you want, love. Never settle for doing less than your best.'

His mantras might have been clichéd, but they were her guiding principles all the days of her childhood.

'Be the best you can be.'

She's so firmly in her past that she opens her eyes gingerly, unsure of where she actually is. She knows she's not in her childhood home, the pin neat, old-world, much cared-for terraced house in the small town of Helensburgh, nor is she in Cairn Cottage, the home she and Archie so lovingly created together. The room, when she sees it, comes as something of a surprise.

It's neat and impersonal. Heavy drapes mask the light from the bay window, two small armchairs by a low coffee table add a touch of informality. For the rest, two sets of drawers topped by a teak slab resemble a dressing table and a flat screen television is anchored to the wall above it. To her left, a door, slightly ajar, opens to a tiled bathroom. A hotel?

She remembers: Mull. I'm in Mull. I've run away.

She almost laughs at that. Yesterday, on top of the mountain, everything seemed so simple but now, with the voices of her past echoing in her head, she understands that escape is not going to be easy. There are duties, responsibilities, loyalties and because it's in her nature and her upbringing, she'll have to do her best to answer to them all.

She draws back the curtains to reveal the sweeping panorama of Tobermory Bay, then retreats to bed.

My nature and my upbringing.

There's the key. For weeks now she's been beating herself up because she doesn't feel an immediate affinity with Joyce Henderson. Then again, she thinks, why should I? I spent the whole of my young life with Mary and Robert MacPherson. It was Mary who changed my nappies and fed me when I was a baby. It was Mary who read me stories and cuddled me and taught me to cook. And it was my father – Robert, not Jimmy Scirocco – who instilled in me the values I've held dear all my life.

My wee treasure. My wee giftie.

Again his voice is echoing round her skull and she can feel herself being lifted above his head, tossed screaming with delight and apprehension towards the ceiling, caught again safely. 'Again, again!' More screams, more laughter.

That's it – the essence of her childhood. Being taught about adventure and danger, then being pulled back to safety and security. That's what my parents gave me. The leaden lump that seems to have inhabited her heart for months begins to ease. She registered downstairs at Reception as Brenda Miles, needing to feel what it's like to be Brenda.

'You look like that actress,' the girl on duty said. 'You know, the one on the telly in that old soap thing. What's her name again? Susie something. Susie ... Williams!' she ends triumphantly.

'I'm not Susie Williams,' she said, truth made easy by the girl's confusion. She signed the name, Brenda Miles, with a flourish. 'But I do believe she might be a distant cousin.'

'Ooh, how exciting. Imagine being related to someone on the telly.'

Does the past matter? Well, yes. Every day since she first heard the word 'adopted' she's been driven to think about things she's never considered before, about identity, personality, genetic inheritance. She's had to think about the Miles inheritance and the Scirocco legacy.

She met Jimmy Scirocco once. He was a legend, then, back when she was in her twenties and fighting to emerge from the bit-parts and make her name as a leading actress. He had magnetism, dear heavens, the charisma of the man. Poor Joyce. A young waitress, and pretty, she must have been helpless in front of the tsunami of young Jimmy's charm. What chance would she ever have had? Jimmy was never a man for restraint or responsibility. Has she forgiven him? Because whatever the effect his carelessness had had on her life, it had been equally traumatic for Joyce Miles.

A sleek yacht, its sails taut in a brisk breeze, scuds across the bay in front of the hotel. She knows she'll have to talk to Joyce. Apart from anything else, she has to talk to her about Brian.

She showers and pulls her fingers through the tangled golden masses of her hair. The aches in her muscles are easy to cope with compared with what's waiting for her.

She has to go back. However enchanting these days of freedom are, there's no escaping the life she has back in Edinburgh. Reality is setting in and the time for action has come. She must square things with Karen and the Party. She has to give Maitland his answer about the film and press him about Rivo. Above all, she needs to start talking to Archie, because in the end her husband and her family matter to her more than anything.

She finds her mobile, but the battery is flat and she has no charger. She'll have to pay the premium for the hotel line.

One ring, two, three, four. The call trips onto the answering machine at four. Archie must still be asleep in the studio, another late night at the music, no doubt.

So much for missing her.

She draws breath to leave a message, changes her mind.

She starts instead with Karen and gets through right away. 'Karen? It's Susie. Hi.'

And then it's excitement and relief and chaos, and a discussion with Mo Alexander about the plot she's hatching in her head, with a promise to call back after she's talked to Joyce.

Susie has made some decisions and in one part of her life, at least, she's regaining a semblance of control – but if she's to become whole again, she has to put things right with Archie.

This day is as glorious as the last. She winds her way along the single-track road through the forests south of Tobermory until she reaches the small village of Dervaig. From there, it's a small hop to Calgary Bay. She parks by the beach.

This was where she filmed with Maitland. This was where she played with fire and risked everything she had with Archie. For what?

For sheer, unbridled lust.

A light breeze ripples the waves and races through her hair, lifting the curls so that they move and glisten and echo the motion of the sea. There's no-one in sight. Amazing that a beach this beautiful can be so empty. Transport it to France and there would be sun loungers and parasols as far as the eye can see, a beach café would be selling drinks and ice creams at exorbitant prices, children would be running into the waves, screaming with delight and men would be smoothing oil into naked, bronzed flesh of their girls. Yet here, although the day is pleasantly hot, there's only a man and his dog and, on the road behind her, a distinctive scarlet post-van meandering on its way.

Twenty-nine years ago it all looked very different. An

array of large trailers dotted up the road where the post-van had just disappeared, causing considerable inconvenience to the locals for the duration of the filming. The dunes behind the beach were a muddle of cameras and cranes, lights and sound equipment. The film crew seemed to be everywhere. And in the middle of the mayhem, she met Maitland Forbes for the first time and her world had trembled on the brink of collapse.

Susie blinks. The man is crossing the beach, his dog running gleeful rings around him, this way, now that, now back again, covering five times as much ground as his master. Such energy. It was Maitland's dog she met first, she remembers. A wet nose on her hand, a curious muzzle in her crotch, embarrassment and laughter and her first glimpse of that notoriously handsome face. The lust had been instantaneous and mutual and completely, absolutely irresistible.

She picks her way across the marram grass to the pristine white of the beach. Maitland was newly married, photographs of the event were still wet on the pages of the current magazines. How could he have been so disloyal? How could he have desired her when he was fresh from the sublime Serafina's bed?

And how could she – how *could* she – have betrayed Archie like that?

Susie settles on a rock at the far left of the beach and stares into the deep turquoise of the water, so clear that she can see a crab scuttling across the sandy bed, and a sea anemone opening and closing, opening and closing, fish-like in its pulsing movements. There's another world down there. Pleased with her thoughts, she becomes lost in them. Here's a school of small fish, darting and weaving round the stalks of the seaweed. Here are the treacherous, opaque ribbons of a jellyfish.

One wave, bigger than the others, splashes on the rock in front of her and spume flies up and onto her skirt.

Smiling, she looks indulgently at the patches of damp. In this heat, they'll dry quickly.

Back then, it took them both a few weeks to surface from the dream and understand how terribly they were deceiving not only themselves but also the partners they truly loved. At once, the decision to end the affair became easy. Filming finished, Maitland flew back to London and Serafina (and later to Hollywood) and by mutual agreement they didn't stay in touch. Susie, stunned by how she could have so easily gambled her marriage, returned to Archie. It was a decision she never regretted because Archie means everything – has always meant everything – to her.

On the road above her, a car coughs its way up the hill. That engine needs attention, she thinks idly, admiring the ridges formed by the tide in the sandy sea floor. So pretty.

She becomes aware that the car has stopped. Another walker, perhaps – it doesn't much matter. The beach is huge and there's room enough for others. Her peace won't be disturbed.

But she's wrong. Someone calls her name. It reaches her across the expanse of marram grass and sand, across the rocks and the seaweed.

'Susie!'

Her heart lifts. Archie has found her. She always knew he'd come. She stands, turns, begins to wave, but as the figure draws nearer, she sees that it isn't Archie.

It's Justin Thorneloe.

Chapter Thirty

Justin scurries across the beach. His skinny legs are encased in tight jeans and a tee shirt bearing the legend 'World Domination' clings to his torso. He's clearly delighted with himself. 'I've found you at last.'

'What—' Susie is lost for words. 'What are you—?'

'Good to see you, too, Susie,' he says equably, his sharp features twisted into a self-satisfied rictus.

All Susie's worlds are shattered in an instant. The mountain, the beach, her own silent underwater world, the gift of respite that nature and beauty have given to her, all snatched by this man, this *ferret*.

'Were you invited?' she says coldly.

'Now don't be like that. I've worked bloody hard to track you down, you didn't make it easy. You could at least be a bit more welcoming.'

'And just how did you find me here, Justin?'

'Ah well now—' He flashes a grin and taps the side of his nose in a gesture, she supposes, designed to indicate knowingness. Then he relents, obviously keen to show off his investigative skills. 'You'd gone missing. Everyone was talking about it. Mo Armstrong, bless her, was madly keen to cover your absence, but it was too good a story to stay secret for long.'

His sharp, knowing eyes drill into her. 'Anyway, your disappearance intrigued me because it seemed to me that you have quite a lot to hide. So I started digging. Your assistant, Karen, she was tight as a monkey's arse. Your researchers were getting nowhere. I called your man a dozen times—'

'Archie?'

'He is your man, isn't he? Or is there another?' he says sneeringly.

He's insufferable. Susie looks around for escape, but he's on the only rock between her and dry land and she's trapped.

'But he was saying nothing. Seemed to me, though, that he was running scared. It wasn't that he was covering up, he didn't know where you were either. I was stuck.

'Then I remembered two things. The first was a conversation I heard you have with Maitland Forbes, about that film you shot together. "Calgary Bay". You seemed really taken with the place, said you'd had some great holidays here since. That was a start. Then I remembered that that daughter of yours, Margaret-Anne, works for that big hotel chain, the one with a hotel on Mull. It didn't seem an impossible guess that you might have headed for here. So I started phoning around. First call was to the hotel, but you outsmarted me there, didn't you?' He leers at her. 'You didn't register under your real name. That threw me off the scent for a bit.'

Oh, but I did, Susie thinks, *my real name is Brenda Miles.*

'I was going to give up, but I'm not one for being defeated.' He puffs his skinny chest up importantly. 'I've got a contact, see, works for the ferries. I put in a call to him, gave him your car registration. If you really want to disappear, Susie, hire a car next time, it'll make it much harder for the likes of me.'

'I'll bear it in mind,' Susie says grimly. 'So, Justin, now you have found me. And what, may I ask, are you hoping to get from all this exertion of yours?'

'For one, I've got a cracking story now, haven't I? The man who found Susie Wallace. Pretty good in itself, your disappearance has caused quite a stir round the Parliament. But more than that, I want to find out what made you take

306

off, because that's the real story, isn't it?'

'I've nothing to say.'

'No comment? Really?' He laughs. 'You're just so perfect, aren't you, Susie? That's why I've been pushing you all these months. Nobody can be that perfect, there's got to be some dirt in there somewhere and I wanted to be the one who finds it.'

'Pushing me?' Susie latches onto one phrase.

'Well, yeah. The lesbian story? I enjoyed that one. Pity your man from Hollywood managed to quash it because we could have had fun with that for a while.'

My man from Hollywood? It's an odd choice of phrase – does he know something? Has some crew member leaked some tittle-tattle after all this time? Can this horrible little man drag something up that might still damage them both?

'Rivo Trust? That's much closer to home, now, isn't it? There's real meat there. "MSP mismanagement fiasco." "Trustee of charity fails in duty of care." Oh yes, I still scent blood there, I've just been biding my time on that story.'

Susie says nothing, but her mind shrieks, *Failure, failure!* He's closer than he knows but she won't give him the satisfaction of seeing it.

'Then there's the biggie, isn't there? The one no-one else has come near yet.'

Her heart seems to have stopped completely and she holds her breath while her world hangs precariously from this man's meddling fingers.

'Susie Wallace was adopted. Not a scandal, I grant you, but still, a great story to break.'

She's so surprised that he knows about this that she's startled into blurting out, 'You know about that?'

'Oh yes. I was there. I heard it all.'

'Where? You heard what?'

'I got lucky, Susie. I just happened to be passing by

307

when that old woman let it slip. "This lady's adopted, Indira, just like you".'

She remembers now – Justin Thorneloe was behind her when Elsie Proudfoot let the truth slither out. She didn't think anything of it at the time, she'd barely registered it. He must have sharp, sharp little ears.

'Well and so what? Hardly earth-shattering, is it?'

'Depends.'

'On what?'

'On what happened. Why you were adopted, who your parents were. There might be a nice, dirty little story to be told.'

She can no longer contain her fury. 'How dare you! How dare you dig your grubby little paws around in my business! Even as a member of Parliament, I'm entitled to some privacy—'

'That's a matter for debate. If someone's past has an impact on—'

'And what in my past could possibly impact on the way I act and behave now? You're a contemptible little shit—'

He's laughing at her. Laughing! The rage inside her swells to such enormous proportions that she doesn't notice that another car has driven up the hill and another figure is running down the beach.

'Leave her alone! Get out of here, you stinking little toad!'

Justin turns, alarmed, as Archie races towards him, fury written all over his face.

'Stop it—' he starts to shout, as the seventh wave of the seventh wave rolls in. With the seaweed now slick and oily and the water dragging at his feet, Thorneloe's scrawny frame hasn't the strength to retain a purchase on the slippery surface and he topples, in glorious slow motion, into the sea.

Archie stops in his tracks. Susie, wide-eyed and slack-jawed, stares at him in astonishment. Justin, tossed between the rocks on a rising tide, screams, 'Help! I can't—' before his head goes under and all that can be seen is one white hand scrabbling in vain to get a grip on the rock. For a long minute they look at each other.

'I suppose we'd better—'

'Here, I'll do it.'

Between them, they manage to grab his wrists and pull the journalist onto the slimy boulder he just slipped from. He lies there, floundering like a beached whale, gasping and spluttering, stripped of all dignity.

Susie's gaze meets Archie's across the spectacle. She never could work out who started to laugh first – was it her, or was it her wonderful, loyal, tenacious husband?

'He's all right—'

'More's the pity—'

'Are you—?'

'I'm fine ... how did you ... I didn't hear ...'

'I thought he was going to attack you.'

'More like the other way round.'

'He's ... wet.'

'Very.'

A small voice comes up from the rock. 'Do you fucking mind. I'm still here, you know.'

Susie flops down onto her rock, higher than the others and still dry enough to sit on. Laughter overcomes her, her ribs ache with it. Archie is bent double, clutching his sides.

'Oh ... oh ... oh, stop, this is hurting.'

'I'm bloody hurting too,' Justin reminds them.

In the end, they help him off the rocks and onto the safety of the strand. The tide has been coming in fast. Despite their amusement, his fall could have been serious because the pull of the waves has grown very powerful. Her peaceful underwater world has become a murky swirl of seaweed and sand and spinning pools of grit and slime.

'You didn't need to fucking shove me,' Justin says, aggrieved.

'No-one was near you, Justin. If anything shoved you, it must have been your conscience. That's if you have one, which I doubt.'

He's grumpy and resentful. 'I'm bloody freezing.'

'Get your clothes off then.'

'What? Not bleeding likely.'

'Haven't you got any spares in your car?'

'Might have something,' he admits grudgingly.

'So go and change. Then, if you're prepared to talk in a civilised manner, come back down and we'll talk.'

They follow the trail of drips as he trudges up the hill to where he parked his car.

'Archie,' Susie says, turning to him. 'You are a miracle.'

He pulls her to him. 'I can't stand it, Susie,' he says, murmuring into her hair. 'I can't bear not being your friend. I hate the emptiness in my life where you should be.'

'I'm sorry, Archie.' She pulls back so that she can look into his eyes. 'I'm sorry for everything. Only can we talk about it later, because the skunk approacheth.'

'What on earth is he wearing?'

As Justin Thorneloe winds his way carefully back down the path to the beach, it seems that the only dry clothing he's been able to find is an outsized and completely shapeless hand-knitted sweater with a reindeer on the front and a jaunty Santa on the back, and a pair of very short swim shorts.

'*Do. Not. Laugh,*' he shouts as he approaches.

They bite back their mirth. It can be saved and relished later.

'It's all I've got with me,' he says aggressively. 'My mother knitted it. I keep it in the car so I can wear it when I visit. It keeps her happy.'

'Ah yes. Mothers,' Susie says, her face straight. The idea of Justin Thorneloe with a mother who knits sweaters and has to be kept happy is almost too delightful to contemplate.

'Talking of which,' he produces a notebook from a canvas satchel strung across his shoulder, 'yours.'

Susie says nothing, merely wishes she'd let this rat drown.

'I've done quite a lot of research,' he says, 'and I've got a lot of information. I'm going to publish. Anything to say?'

'Go ahead.' But please, please, please, don't let him have discovered anything about Mannie and Brian.

'Really?' He looks surprised. 'You don't mind?'

She shrugs, trying to look more nonchalant than she feels.

'Right.' He sounds a little less confident. 'Rivo,' he changes tack, certainty back in his voice. 'Breach of trust, wouldn't you say? Failure to spot fraud. MSP clearly not up to the job.'

'If you say so.'

Adopting the effect of calmness is clearly the best line she could have chosen. It isn't easy, but she can see that it's working – her indifference is disconcerting him.

'Right. Well. And then the vote. There is to be one, you know, on Thursday. Will you be back for it, Mrs Wallace?'

Oh, Mrs Wallace now, is it? His pencil is poised above his notebook, he's going to take down this quote verbatim.

'I'll be back,' she says quietly.

'And what way do you intend to vote?'

But she won't give him the satisfaction of that one. 'That, Mr Thorneloe, you will have to wait and see.'

He can't get any more out of her, although he tries, and when he spots that Archie has pulled out his mobile and is pointing it in his direction he runs off, shouting, 'Don't you dare take my photograph! Don't you dare!'

They watch with mounting hysteria as his spindly white

legs scamper up the path and he wrenches open the door of his car.

'The hunter hunted,' Archie says, choking back his laughter.

'I wonder if we dare put it on You Tube,' Susie chortles. 'Or I just might slip it to Mo and let her do her worst.'

As Justin's car shoots off up the road, Archie says more seriously, 'You were very calm, Susie, but what damage can he do? Really?'

'I hope very little.'

They wander across the sand to find a seat among the long grasses of the dunes. She feels the softness of the sand under her and the warmth of Archie next to her, where he belongs. 'I've known all along I'll have to vote with my Party and try to make it up with my lobby in some other way. He can make of that what he will, it's not going to damage me too much, whatever he does.'

'Don't betray your voters, Susie.'

'Believe me, Archie, I've struggled with that thought.'

She lays her head on his shoulder, then straightens.

'I feel it will be all right though, heaven knows why. I'm more worried about the adoption story, but only because of Mannie. I should tell you, Archie, I spoke to Joyce this morning, and to Mo. The story's going to be published in *Scotland Daily*, with her blessing. I hope you don't mind.'

'It's your story.'

'I'm not worried about the story itself, I'm just praying that he hasn't got hold of the one thing that could hurt us all.'

'Mannie?'

'Yes. Mannie and Brian.'

'There's quite a lot happened on that front since you left, Susie. Jon's been fantastic. Jon and his new girl, Alex, that is.'

'What? How long have I been away? Jon's got a new girl?'

Archie smiles. 'And they've been making strides.'

He tells her about Alex's research, fills her in on what happened at the meeting at Mannie's house and finishes on the more sober analysis of what might happen when Jon talks to his boss – his uncle – the object of Mannie's obsession.

Susie says, 'That'll be all right, I'll see to that, even if I have to go and confront Brian Henderson myself. I haven't met him, Archie, but there's no way Joyce would let him sack Jon, she'd be horrified. She's already ultra proud of her new family.'

She hooks her arm through Archie's and snuggles close.

'I've found this all very hard, darling. Joyce doesn't feel like my mother to me. In my head and in my heart, Mary's still my mother. But all the same, I've begun to have a lot of respect for Joyce. She's honest, and straightforward, and loving. Whatever she did to me by having me adopted, she did it for reasons she thought were best at the time. Probably they were the best, I just wish I'd known about it and been able to come to terms with it years ago.'

A cloud crosses the sun and immediately the temperature plummets.

Archie says, carefully, 'I wish you'd let us know where you were going, Susie. We've all been frantic.'

'Really? But I left you a message saying I'd be back in a couple of days and not to worry.'

'You left a message that was pretty much indecipherable.'

'Was it? Oh.'

'Where did you call from?'

'Once I landed on Mull.'

'It sounded very windy and the signal was really bad.

313

All I got was "Listen Archie, it's all too much. I've had to go away. ... Don't ..." Or something like that. I thought perhaps you'd headed off for good.'

'Oh heavens, I didn't mean to be that elusive. I said not to worry, tell the kids I'm fine. This wasn't a ploy to punish you, Archie.'

'I thought—' He starts to say something, but chokes on the words.

'What?'

'I couldn't help remembering – Mull. "Calgary Bay". Your affair with Maitland Forbes.'

'My what?' Susie pulls away from him, shocked.

'I thought I was going to lose you then, Susie.'

Archie is scanning the horizon, looking at the hills, looking anywhere rather than at her.

'I didn't think you knew.'

'I couldn't bear to talk about it. I thought you were going to leave me for him. I thought of rushing in and punching him, but I realised that if our marriage was to be worth anything I had to wait until you decided.'

Susie is speechless, shocked by the realisation that Archie has known about Maitland for years.

Archie's eyes are closed and pain is etched on his face. She can see it in the tightness of his lips and in the line between his eyes, the furrow that deepens when he's worried.

'It was the worst time of my life.'

She gulps. *He never told me.*

'Susie—' He murmurs her name, so quietly she barely catches it.

'Darling, I'm so sorry—'

'I need to know the truth, Susie.'

'About Maitland? It was a silly crush, that's all. We worked out pretty quickly that it was only lust, both of us—'

'Not that. I know that, or I would have left you.'

314

This possibility has never occurred to Susie and she's stunned by it – but the words he utters next rock her to the core of her being.

'Is Mannie my daughter?'

'What?'

'It's a simple question, Susie. You were pregnant just after you came back from filming and I was never sure—'

'You thought Mannie might be Maitland's?'

His lips are so tightly pursed they have almost disappeared and she sees that his hands are clenched into tight fists. In an agony of pity she puts her own hands around them and tries to prise them open.

'You thought the baby might be someone else's and you were prepared to accept her anyway?'

'I would have done anything for you, Susie, knowing you'd made up your mind to stay with me. *Tell me.*'

'Mannie is your daughter.'

Tears are running down Susie's face. She's appalled by the damage her behaviour has inflicted on Archie across the years, how her thoughtlessness and selfishness has caused him so much pain.

'Oh Archie, she's yours, without a shadow of a doubt. She was my gift to you, my declaration of commitment.'

She can't bear to think about the doubt he's lived with all these years, the way that he has suffered in such stoical silence.

His eyes are screwed tightly shut, she feels him shuddering and realises with distress that he's sobbing too, noiselessly. It wracks her soul. 'Archie, she's yours, darling, your own daughter.'

'Her hair—' she can barely make out the words, '—her eyes ... hazel ... not yours or mine ... I thought—'

'You thought—?'

It's true, Mannie has neither her colouring nor Archie's. Her straight dark hair is more like Maitland's, her hazel eyes nearer to the shade of his than her amber or

Archie's blue. Her mind is racing.

'It never occurred to me, Archie, I never gave it a single thought, she was always just our baby, but don't you see? Mannie doesn't have your hair and eyes, nor mine, her coloring comes from Joyce Miles. She has inherited her grandmother's genes.'

She sees the tension in Archie's shoulders relax a fraction and his hand uncurls enough to allow her to slip her own inside his fingers. They sit together, wordlessly, too full of emotion to speak.

At last Susie says shakily, 'Mannie said that knowing about my adoption would change everything. She can't have known how right she was – but if it's brought your doubt to light and let me set your mind to rest, then I'm glad, Archie. I'm so glad.'

For all these years, she realises, Archie has carried the burden of not one secret, but two. She drops her head into her hands and rubs her hand through her thick curls.

'You know, ever since I discovered you knew about my adoption, my trust in you was destroyed.' Archie's hand stiffens and she adds quickly, 'But now I understand at long last that keeping the secret wasn't a betrayal but a supreme act of love.'

How can she convince him how much she loves him?

'You know I came over to the studio before I went away? You know I was desperate to talk to you?'

'Why didn't you, then?'

'It was locked and there was a huge Keep Out notice. The only person in the world I needed to be with was you, and you'd barred my way. I felt utterly alone.' She tightens her grip on his hands. 'I can't function without you, Archie. I never have been able to.'

Archie jerks his hand free, finds a handkerchief and blows his nose noisily.

He says, 'I'm glad,' and she understands he means, *for everything.*

How long passes? Five minutes? Ten? Half an hour?
Tick. Tock.

For the moment, time is vanquished because the peacefulness seems to last for ever.

Archie breaks it at last.

'There's something else you need to explain, Susie.'

He pulls a folded piece of paper out of his pocket and passes it to her.

Dear First Minister

I have given this a great deal of thought, and it is with much sadness and regret that I write to you to tender my resignation as an MSP. As you know ...

'Heavens, Archie, where did you get this? I thought it was in my handbag.'

His voice is still thick, but he's speaking more normally now. 'My guess is you left it on the dresser when you found there were no stamps – and saw the hotel voucher Mannie and Jon gave us for our wedding anniversary.'

'*Eh bien*, M. Poirot, have you wax enough for the moustaches you disguise as antennae?'

'Well?'

He looks at her appraisingly. She can read relief there and a love so deep it makes her want to wail.

'Will I give you a stamp?'

She takes the letter from him.

'Would you like me to resign, Archie? Politics is a grimy business, with every Tom, Dick and Justin poking their nose into your private life and trying to make it public. Maitland has offered me a part in his film, you know. I could take up acting again.'

'Susie, you do nothing but act. Do you want to do the film?'

'Yes – and no. It's mostly being shot in the States and I don't really want to start all that peripatetic living out of suitcases again. It's bad enough that you'll have to do it when Celtic Rock hits the charts again, as it will when you release the album. If I were to go back into the business too, we'd never see each other.'

'And you enjoy the work in the Parliament? Despite the pressures?'

'I did enjoy it when I felt I was able to make a difference – and before weasel-face Thorneloe started poking his pointy little nose in. I found it absolutely hellish when I couldn't come home and chew the fat with you, Archie.'

'And if I make the great sacrifice of giving up my lumpy sofa bed in the studio and move back in with my wife?'

'Then perhaps your wife might carry on for a while.'

She folds the paper again, then tears it in strips.

Somewhere in the depths of his pocket, Archie's mobile buzzes. 'Karen? Hi. Yes, I found her. She's here. Want to speak to her?'

Susie takes the phone. 'Yes. Yes, everything's fine. Do you know who was just here, hounding me? Justin Thorneloe. Yes. Yes I am serious. I'll tell you all about it later. Did Mo get my stories off okay? Great. Yes. What? What?' She starts to laugh. 'Really? You're joking. You're not joking. Yes. I'll call him right away. Yes, I promise. Bye.'

She hands Archie's phone back to him.

'What was all that about?'

'I don't have to rush back. The First Minister has side-stepped the confidence vote with a reshuffle. Joe Shearer's been downgraded to Communities.'

'Don't tell me he's made you Education Minister. That would be funny.'

'Not Education, no. He wants me to call him.'

Susie's mind is whirling. This is Tom Coop's revenge – not to sideline her, but to muzzle her in a different way.

'Karen says the rumour is out that he wants me to be Culture Minister.'

Archie starts to laugh.

Hearing his laughter fills Susie's heart with blind joy, but she says, 'Stop it, you horrid man. It's not funny!'

'Culture Minister,' he chortles. 'Culture Minister! You!'

'Beast!'

But it's too infectious to resist, and in minutes, Susie's laughing too.

'Susie Wallace, oh, ow,' Archie is howling now. 'A Minister! Ow, oh!'

She's hitting out at him and laughing and angry and annoyed and unbelievably relieved all at the same time.

'Beast, beast, beast!'

He tries to catch her wrist and she ducks under his guard to attack his ribs, and then they're tangled on the dunes like teenagers in love. The relief at rediscovering Archie is profound.

'Archie,' she says at last, detaching herself from his embrace with some reluctance.

'Mmm?'

'I do hope Skunk Thorneloe hasn't got a long lens.'

He reaches up and pulls her back down. 'Even a politician is entitled to a private life,' he whispers.

Susie rolls onto her back, her head on Archie's shoulder, his arm tucked round her with comforting familiarity. Above her, small wisps of cloud scud across a blue sky that seems to stretch for ever. All she can hear is the sound of the waves rolling across the sand and splashing onto the rocks and the bubbling call of a curlew, calling to its mate.

They are mere dots, she and Archie, in the enormity of mountain and moorland and shore.

Privacy it isn't.

She smiles and squeezes his hand. Let Thorneloe take photographs if he's still around. Let him publish pictures if a fond embrace with her husband is what the world really wants to see. Nothing can hurt her now that Archie is by her side again.

Some months later

Be careful, Callum said to Mannie once, *what you wish for*. Would things have been different if she'd heeded him, if she'd reined back her impulsiveness and let her mother take things more slowly?

Mannie pours herself a glass of cold white wine and sits down at the kitchen table in Cairn Cottage. A plateful of melting nanoseconds has been set out in the centre, where a jugful of late summer roses, heavy with scent, hang red and rich above the polished wood.

You can't change things. A few short months ago she had a job she excelled at and a boyfriend she adored and life seemed full of promise. Now she's struggling to achieve her targets and keep on top of her work, and Callum is ... well, the best she can say is that the nature of her relationship with Cal has changed.

She reaches for a biscuit and bites into it.

I wanted to know about my genetic inheritance and all I got was heartbreak.

It doesn't seem fair.

The biscuit is finished. Absently, she reaches for another.

What cruel chance led Brian Henderson to my stand at the trade fair in London?

Mannie still hasn't entirely conquered her feelings for him. Understanding that you have been swept away like matchwood in the ferocity of a flood you are powerless to resist is one thing: being able to swim against the tide is another completely.

I don't love him. I never have. But I was obsessed by him.

She polishes off two more biscuits in quick succession and glances at the clock on the wall. Where is everyone? They'll have to leave soon, surely.

There's a stir on the stairs and she hears the sound of Jonno's voice.

'I know we've all got to meet up tonight and okay, he's crap as an uncle,' Jonno is saying, 'but you've got to admit, it was brilliant that he wouldn't let me resign.'

Mannie's heart lurches and the old nausea returns. They're talking about Brian. She still hates herself for what happened. *I should have been able to control it.*

Alex appears, her hair hanging loose this evening and falling around her shoulders like soft ripples in a pond. The friendship between Alex and her brother has blossomed into a relationship that's promising to become a fixture. Alex seems lit by an inner radiance and Jonno, following her into the room, looks more relaxed and happier than she has seen him in years.

'Oh sorry,' Jonno says, 'didn't see you there, Mannie.'

Alex smiles apologetically at Mannie, understanding. She's good at intuition. 'That's all over now.'

'Thanks to you,' Jonno says, his eyes like a dog's, loving and happy.

'Bleh,' Mannie says dryly, miming retching. 'Pass me the sick bag.'

Jonno ignores her. 'Any sign of the old folks yet?'

Mannie shakes her head. 'Should we shout?'

'Let's give them five minutes.' He opens the fridge and examines the bottle nestling in the door. 'Mmm, Sancerre. Want one, Alex?'

It's business as usual – except that it used to be her and Cal raiding the fridge, now she's sitting there like a gooseberry while her brother makes eyes at his girl.

In the whole of her life, she has never felt lonely, until now. It seems to Mannie that she had lost everything: Callum, Brian, even her job is hanging by a thread.

Knowing, as she now does, that she can never be with Brian Henderson, she is battling as valiantly as she can against the ferocious power of her feelings. Sticking a label on them has helped, a bit. It makes her feel marginally less insane, but does little to lessen the intensity of her emotions.

Perhaps catching something of her thoughts, Alex asks, 'You going to be okay, Mannie? Is Cal coming?'

Is Cal coming. *Cal.* The kindness her ex has shown makes Mannie's heart hurt, but she still doesn't know whether they will ever get back together – really together – or be able to recapture the love they once knew.

'I don't know,' she admits. 'He said he'd try.'

She's sick with nerves. The whole family is going to be present at tonight's celebration. The whole family. Including Joyce Henderson and her son, Brian. She feels herself trembling and tries to still it. She hasn't seen Brian again and the last time she spoke to him was when he telephoned from New York, flirting with her, responding to her advances, more or less opening the door to an affair. And then had come the revelation.

Before Brian, after Brian.

Before Cal, after Cal.

Phases of my life.

Sanity, insanity, the wilderness of the space between them.

Jonathan thinks, Sis is still looking peaky.

His big sister. He remembers her aged – what? – ten? He'd have been five, just starting school and scared as hell, though it was only the village school and he knew other kids there. She held his hand that day, led him through the gates and right to the door of his class room, promised to be there at break time. She looked after him. Mannie has always looked after him. Perhaps because of the age gap and the gender difference they never developed the intimacy some siblings have, but they never squabbled much either. He knows – because it's a family joke – that Mannie was jealous of his arrival into the world, but by the time he was old enough to be conscious of her sisterly presence, she'd got over that. It seems so strange that now their roles have reversed and he's the one trying to look after her.

He says, as casually as he can, 'It'll be all right tonight, Mannie. Brian's wife'll be there, and Joyce. You needn't sit near him or anything.'

She's as pale as a ghost and he can see her hand clenching on a tissue or something. He hates what happened, but he has done what he could to sort it, with Alex's help, of course. He perseveres, slanting the conversation away from the personal. 'Typical of Tom bloody Coop to muscle in where he sniffs out the chance of some reflected glory.'

'He's got to do something,' Mannie says, her hand still clenched, 'to recapture the high ground after Mum turned down the Ministerial post.'

'She was right. It was a way of trying to stifle her outspokenness.'

'Course it was,' Alex says. 'They would have effectively pulled your mother's teeth by taking her into the Cabinet.'

'Mum said the First Minister might be coming tonight.'

'Really? Why?'

Mannie laughs, the sound a little hollow. 'Didn't you know, he picked a Celtic Rock track for Desert Island Discs. Blatant posturing, of course, aimed at winning votes, I'm not sure he's actually into Dad's kind of music at all. But,' she adds, 'I think he wants to associate himself with the Scirocco Bursary. And Maitland Forbes, of course.'

'I wouldn't mind associating myself with Maitland Forbes,' Alex grins.

Jon frowns at her, but ends up smiling. He can't help himself, just looking at Alex is enough to make him glow with love and pride and sheer, breathless happiness. 'The Bursary is a great idea of Mum's. It's her way of keeping her father's name alive.'

'And openly acknowledging him.'

'And putting horrible little Justin Thorneloe in his place.'

The laughter this time is universal. Six months ago, on Mull, their mother made a number of decisions. Through Maureen Armstrong and with the agreement of her birth mother, she placed the story of her adoption with one of the leading newspapers and coupled it with the announcement of a Bursary, which she is funding. The Scirocco Bursary for a promising young actor is to be formally launched tonight.

In addition, she persuaded Maitland Forbes to become the saviour of the Rivo Trust, which is to be wound up and reborn as the Maitland Forbes Foundation. Tonight's event which, at Susie's insistence, is to be held in the Town Hall at Hailesbank and not in some swanky Edinburgh venue, is the formal launch of both the Bursary and the Foundation and Celtic Rock, celebrating their new album, is to play.

'What a rat that journalist is,' Jonno adds when he can make his voice heard. 'Mum really took the wind out of his sails by preempting his attempts to dig what he thought might be dirt.'

'Dirt?' A voice comes from the doorway. 'What dirt? That reminds me, Jonno, have you remembered to feed the chickens?'

Jon, who has grown up with his mother's beauty and is inured to it, nevertheless feels the breath sucked out of him as he swings round and sees her. Susie's hair, catching the light from one of the spots in the ceiling, shimmers and shines and reflects its golden glory back onto her face. A brush dipped in the same colour has painted her eyes, and

324

although they glitter, they seem to promise infinite depth. High cheekbones give her face structure and a beauty that will never diminish. Recent stresses have whittled away the small, cruel bulges of middle age, so that her lustrous gold evening dress skims neatly over her breasts and stomach and hips and falls swirling to the floor.

He says breathlessly, 'Mum. You look fantastic.'

'Wow,' Alex murmurs. 'That's an amazing dress, Mrs Wallace.'

Susie sweeps into the room, her dress rustling gently on the floor. 'I wish you'd call me Susie, Alex. And thank you.'

'I feel really underdressed.' Alex pats her floral chiffon worriedly.

'Not at all, you look wonderful, terribly pretty. I have deliberately overdressed. Any wine left, Jon? And I'm ravenous, I'd better have something to eat.'

'I put out a plate of your melting nanoseconds.' Jon hands her a glass of Sancerre and reaches for the biscuits. 'Oh! There's only one left,' he says, puzzled. Surely – there had been a dozen biscuits – Mannie? He glares at his sister, but she's deep in thought, her mind clearly in another world. 'Mannie?' He says sharply.

'Hmm? What?'

'Have you eaten all the biscuits?'

'Biscuits? Have I?'

'How could you?'

'Sorry. I ... I wasn't thinking.'

'Something up?' Archie appears, every inch the rocker in denims and leather jacket and a simple tee shirt.

'Mannie's eaten all the bloody biscuits!'

Archie laughs. 'That's great,' he says, crossing the kitchen and giving his frail-looking daughter a hug. 'She must be feeling a bit better.'

Susie says, 'It's fine Mannie, I'm glad you had them. Jon, I'd rather have something savoury anyway, there's some really good olives in the fridge, and some hummus.'

As suddenly as it flared, Jon's ill temper subsides.

'Okay,' he says. 'I'll forgive you, Mannie. This time.'

His voice sounds menacing, but he smiles at Mannie as he says it so that she knows he's teasing.

Archie doesn't wait as they all have drinks and nibbles, but sets off into Hailesbank to do soundchecks with the band. It's his evening as much as Susie's, but he doesn't really think of it that way. Celtic Rock's album has already hit the charts, the tour is to start in a couple of weeks, he's already done the rounds of the television studios and radio stations and been featured in several colour supplements and magazines.

No, this is Susie's night. The family is turning out in force to support her. Joyce Henderson will be there. Archie has met her, now, on several occasions, and has (rather to his surprise) developed a kind of respect for the woman. She did what she had to do, aged eighteen, in another time and a different society. She did it for Susie as much as herself, to give her the best chance in life. And now that she has rediscovered her daughter, she's coping with real dignity with the kind of publicity she could never have anticipated.

Brian Henderson is another matter. He's undoubtedly charming and his ability as a businessman is not in question. Archie still isn't sure how culpable he was in the whole Mannie affair and he doesn't really want to know. They are working hard, all of them, to help Mannie through a devastating experience.

There's something about the man that Archie instinctively dislikes. Perhaps he's too charming. Perhaps he takes advantage of it. Whatever, Archie is happy to distance himself from 'Uncle Brian', and to help his daughter to keep well clear of him too.

To give the man his due, Brian was horrified to learn

that he was Mannie's uncle and insisted that Jonathan stay on in his job at CommX. Jon swears that Brian is really professional and that working with him is turning out not to be too difficult. Only Mannie still finds the situation hard. She hasn't been able to simply put aside her feelings, although she is containing them.

Poor Mannie.

As a family, though, they've never been closer – that's one positive outcome from this whole difficult period.

He pushes open the door to the big hall, where his band is already warming up.

'Hi Jake, hi Sandie, everything in order?'

'Cool.'

Sandie has gone Goth and is all in black. Her hair is darker than a raven's wing, her eyes heavily rimmed with kohl, the only colour a slash of scarlet on her mouth.

'You playing your new song?' Sandie asks. 'Need anything from us?'

Archie considers the offer. He's pleased with the new album. Wrenched from his soul while he was a helpless witness to the gradual meltdown of his family, it was the most difficult thing he has ever produced – and maybe because of that he feels it's the best. Just one thing defeated him: the tune that came to him months ago, at the beginning of Susie's breakdown.

He wasn't able to find the words it needed before the album was finished and launched and the niggle remained, irritating him, until now.

He started working on the song shortly after he and Susie came back from Mull. In the couple of days they snatched for themselves in the magical remoteness of the island, they reconciled their differences and rediscovered their love. The words came then, as Sandie had said they would.

'I'd like to play it on my own, Sandie,' he says in response to her question. 'That okay?'

327

'Cool.'
I'll sing it for Susie.

Susie makes her entrance, as she planned it, dramatically.

A sea of faces turns towards her and applause erupts. As she draws breath and begins the long walk to the dais, the faces begin to separate and become individual.

There's the First Minister, beside Tom Coop, the two of them pretending she never insulted them by refusing the Ministerial post. There's no room for sentiment in politics, she reminds herself, only factional advantage.

There's Hugh Porteus, no longer Chairman of Rivo, but Chairman-elect of the new Maitland Forbes Foundation. He has earned it. He worked tirelessly to help put everything right.

Mo Armstrong. Perhaps she is an instrument of the Party, but she rallied round when Susie really needed her. And Karen, unquestioningly loyal, a friend indeed.

She lifts her chin an inch, widens her smile a fraction, adds intensity to her gaze and marches on. The applause redoubles.

There's Joyce Henderson – my mother – smiling and clapping and trying to wipe a tear away surreptitiously. *This evening will tie up loose ends in both our lives.* The Bursary is an acknowledgement of who I am and where I come from, my relationship with her and with the long-dead Jimmy Scirocco – my brilliantly accomplished, pitifully wasted father.

There's Brian Henderson. My brother.

Susie looks instinctively for Mannie. She's concerned, as she has been for weeks, about how her daughter will cope with this evening.

She sees that she needn't have worried. The family has closed ranks around Mannie in a protective horseshoe. Myra and Jen, her old friends, are there. Jon and Alex are by her side – and Callum.

Callum has come! Thank God. As Susie makes her way to the seat reserved for her at the heart of her family, she holds out a hand and grips his fingers in a brief sign of appreciation. She sees him touch Mannie lightly on the shoulder, smile encouragement at her, pull her seat aside so that she can sit down. So he still cares for Mannie, despite everything. It's still early in the journey they face, but perhaps things will come right between them, in the end.

'Got your speech ready, Mum?' Jon asks. 'Nervous?'

'Yes. And no.'

She isn't nervous, she feels elated. If her life over the past months has been a rollercoaster that left her stomach lurching at times, the ride has stopped on a high and she has the strongest of feelings that it's not going to plummet to the depths any more.

I am so lucky, she thinks, looking around her. I have friends who are steadfast and a family that's come through fire and emerged strong as forged steel. I know who I am and what I value.

She turns her face upwards to scan the gallery, where batteries of cameras are ranged ready to film the speeches. The BBC is there, and Scottish Television. A crew from an arts programme in London. A team that has flown over from Los Angeles, intrigued by the involvement of their star, Maitland Forbes, in this quaint venture. Among them, a thin, pale face, dead eyes staring right at her.

It's Justin Thorneloe, his sharp little ferret's teeth truly blunted on his own ambition.

'Mum?'

Mannie's voice at her ear brings her thoughts back. She turns.

'All right, darling?'

Mannie is still pale, but she's smiling.

'Callum came,' she mouths, her eyes threatening to water.

Susie feels tearful in response.

'I know,' she says, tucking Mannie's slippery hair behind her ear and kissing her cheek warmly. 'I know. I'm so pleased.'

'Mum,' Jonathan hisses on the other side, 'It's time for your speech. Go!'

Everything she has done feels right.

Turning down the Ministerial post so that she can still speak her mind freely about the things she believes in.

Setting up the Scirocco Bursary to acknowledge her past and bring both sides of her life together.

Succeeding in persuading Maitland to come to the rescue of the Rivo Trust by setting up the Maitland Forbes Foundation.

Being here with her family.

Enjoying Archie's success.

She stands, feels her dress settle luxuriously round her ankles, makes her way to the microphone, faces the audience.

'First Minister, Ladies and Gentlemen, friends and family,' she starts, smiling around her, 'I am, as you know, a person of passionate beliefs and fierce loyalties. And tonight, I am delighted to say, I am able to bring together all the things that are important in my life. As I bring you news of the new Bursary and the charitable Foundation we are launching here, I feel prouder than I can tell you about my cherished causes and about my family.

'My happiness is complete.'

She means what she says, but after she has finished her speech, after the applause, after Maitland has spoken and been lauded and applauded and much photographed, after she has posed with Joyce Henderson and there have been more photographs and more filming and – inevitably – yet another session of photographs at which the First Minister has smoothly and graciously taken centre stage, Archie appears again.

'Thank you, folks, thank you.' He holds up a hand to dampen down the applause. 'There's one song that's missing off Celtic Rock's new album.'

Susie looks at him, puzzled. Archie is holding his oldest guitar, the one she bought him when she came back to him after 'Calgary Bay'. To her eyes, he looks as boyish as he did then. His hair might be white and his skin no longer youthful, but his eyes shine with love just as they did all those years ago.

'I couldn't find the words for it, that was the problem. You all know about the various twists and turns Susie's life has taken this year. It's been a journey of discovery and along the way there have been many thorns as well, thankfully, as roses.

'To most of you, Susie is an actress, or a lobbyist, a passionate believer in the arts, or education, or a daughter, or a mother, or a friend. To me she is, quite simply, the most wonderful person in the world and this song is an all too inadequate expression of my love for her.'

He plugs in his guitar, swings one foot onto a chair, pulls the microphone closer to his mouth and begins to sing.

Only one thing I'm good for – Loving Susie.
One thing I'd die for – Loving Susie.
Beginning to end, my friend
I'll always be – Loving Susie ...

Susie smiles, closes her eyes and lets the music fill her heart and top up her happiness to overflowing.

Archie, she thinks, you're not bad for an old rocker.

THE END

Author's note:

Thank you for taking the time to read *Loving Susie*. If you enjoyed it, please consider telling your friends or posting a short review. Word of mouth is an author's best friend, and much appreciated.

The Heartlands Series

Jenny Harper

For more information about **Jenny Harper**

and other **Accent Press** titles

please visit

www.accentpress.co.uk

http://www.jennyharperauthor.co.uk